"WHEW . . . ONE WORD—STEAMY!"*

PRAISE FOR

The Dangerous Duke

"A witty, sensual seduction! Delicious!" —Anna Campbell

"Wells sets bedrooms ablaze with more than candles in this sex-drenched tale . . . Romance and intrigue [with] sparks of genuine passion that will keep readers turning the pages."
—*Publishers Weekly*

"Wells has graced us with a historical romance overflowing with wit, charm, and passion . . . A delightful romp engaging us with a strong heroine, a flawed but very appealing hero, a mystery that keeps us guessing, and a love story sure to warm your heart."
—*Fresh Fiction*

"Lyle is one fabulous creation, tall, dark, and dangerously sexy . . . [Wells has] fashioned extremely well-done characters . . . I sincerely hope that Ms. Wells comes back with a sequel . . . Bottom line: good suspense, superb sensuality."
—*CK²S Kwips and Kritiques*

"Wells demonstrates what it takes to be a fan favorite by satisfying readers' cravings for adventurous, sexy romance."
—*Romantic Times*

"Wells expertly weaves a tale of danger, passion, and intrigue."
—*Two Lips Reviews*

Scandal's Daughter

"A touching love story."
—Mary Balogh

"Romance with the sparkle of vintage champagne. A stellar debut from a major new talent!" —Anna Campbell

"A charming romance brimming with emotion and humor. The sensual intimacy between Sebastian and Gemma mellows like a fine wine within the friendship forged long before their first kiss. Christine Wells makes the Regency as fresh and real as her characters, and I expect it won't be long before she's a favorite on every romance reader's bookshelf."
—Kathryn Smith

"Witty, emotionally intense, and romantic—Ms. Wells beguiles us in this stellar debut. Put this writer's name on your list of authors to watch."
—Sophia Nash

"Wells captures readers' interest from the very first page, and doesn't let go . . . A sweet, tender love story that's thick with sexual tension and subtle sensuality."
—*Two Lips Reviews*

Wicked Little Game

CHRISTINE WELLS

BERKLEY SENSATION, NEW YORK

THE BERKLEY PUBLISHING GROUP
Published by the Penguin Group
Penguin Group (USA) Inc.
375 Hudson Street, New York, New York 10014, USA

Penguin Group (Canada), 90 Eglinton Avenue East, Suite 700, Toronto, Ontario M4P 2Y3, Canada
(a division of Pearson Penguin Canada Inc.)
Penguin Books Ltd., 80 Strand, London WC2R 0RL, England
Penguin Group Ireland, 25 St. Stephen's Green, Dublin 2, Ireland (a division of Penguin Books Ltd.)
Penguin Group (Australia), 250 Camberwell Road, Camberwell, Victoria 3124, Australia
(a division of Pearson Australia Group Pty. Ltd.)
Penguin Books India Pvt. Ltd., 11 Community Centre, Panchsheel Park, New Delhi—110 017, India
Penguin Group (NZ), 67 Apollo Drive, Rosedale, North Shore 0632, New Zealand
(a division of Pearson New Zealand Ltd.)
Penguin Books (South Africa) (Pty.) Ltd., 24 Sturdee Avenue, Rosebank, Johannesburg 2196,
South Africa

Penguin Books Ltd., Registered Offices: 80 Strand, London WC2R 0RL, England

This is a work of fiction. Names, characters, places, and incidents either are the product of the author's
imagination or are used fictitiously, and any resemblance to actual persons, living or dead, business
establishments, events, or locales is entirely coincidental. The publisher does not have any control over
and does not assume any responsibility for author or third-party websites or their content.

WICKED LITTLE GAME

A Berkley Sensation Book / published by arrangement with the author

PRINTING HISTORY
Berkley Sensation mass-market edition / July 2009

Copyright © 2009 by Christine Diehm.
Excerpt from *Sweetest Little Sin* copyright © 2009 by Christine Diehm.
Cover art by Jim Griffin.
Cover design by George Long.
Cover hand lettering by Ron Zinn.
Interior text design by Kristin del Rosario.

ISBN: 978-0-425-22848-7

BERKLEY® SENSATION
Berkley Sensation Books are published by The Berkley Publishing Group,
a division of Penguin Group (USA) Inc.,
375 Hudson Street, New York, New York 10014.
BERKLEY® SENSATION and the "B" design are trademarks of Penguin Group (USA) Inc.

PRINTED IN THE UNITED STATES OF AMERICA

10 9 8 7 6 5 4 3 2 1

To my little heroes,
Allister and Adrian.
May your lives be filled with love

ACKNOWLEDGMENTS

We inkies are known as a solitary lot, but the staggering number of people I must thank here shows it's not such a lonely occupation, after all.

To my editor, the lovely Leis Pederson, you are a pleasure to work with; to my agent, Jessica Faust, thank you for always being there with smart advice when I need you; to my super publicist, Kathryn Tumen; and to all at Berkley who have worked hard to bring *Wicked Little Game* to the bookstore shelves—many, many thanks.

To Jim Griffin and the Berkley art department, who consistently create beautiful covers for me—my admiration and gratitude. Kim Castillo, a.k.a. KimPossible, thank you for your amazing powers of organization and savvy as my assistant, advisor, and friend.

Denise Rossetti and Anna Campbell, every writer should be so lucky as to have friends and critiquers like you—but I'm not sharing! To the Romance Bandits, who are so talented, inspirational, and loyal, I'm honored to be part of our sisterhood. There are many readers who have been kind enough to support me, and special thanks must go to all the Bandita Buddies—in particular, Carol and Joanne Lockyer, Helen Sibbritt, Louisa Cornell, PJ Ausdenmore, and Keira Soleore.

And to the Romance Writers of America and the Romance Writers of Australia—where would we be without these organizations to nurture and promote talented romance writers? Thank you to everyone involved and especially to those contest judges who gave me such confidence in this book. Thanks also to the members of the Beau Monde, who have a staggering collective knowledge of the Regency period and are always able and happy to answer the most obscure queries.

Most importantly, I'm enormously grateful to my family and friends for their understanding and for their stalwart support of my writing. Jamie, Allister, Adrian, Cheryl, Ian, Michael, Robin and George, Vikki, Ben, and Yasmin—my love and thanks.

One

London, 1816

WOULD she see him? She could hardly believe she'd found him at last.

Sick with anticipation, Lady Sarah Cole smoothed her worn gloves, gripped the strings of her reticule tighter, and made herself step down from the hackney cab.

As she emerged from the carriage, the stench of rotting fish hit her with full force. She almost lost her footing on the uneven cobblestones and stumbled again as a large rat, with its naked pink tail twitching, shot across her path. Battling rising nausea, Sarah held a lavender-scented handkerchief over her mouth and nose to filter the fetid air.

After a few moments, she'd mastered her uneasy stomach and returned her handkerchief to her reticule. Beneath the brim of her plain straw bonnet, she swept a glance up the street.

Ragged children played some sort of ball game against the crumbling wall of a dilapidated shop front. The tavern on the corner did a brisk, noisy trade, even at this hour. A hawker pushed his cart and cried his wares, adding to the general commotion. Sarah discerned from his barely intelligible bawl that he was selling cat meat.

She shuddered. It was a depressed, filthy part of London, located a stone's throw from the Billingsgate wharves. The lady she'd once been wouldn't have dreamed of visiting such a place. She shouldn't have come.

But she'd never admitted defeat when matters grew difficult and she wouldn't start now. Dismissing the cabdriver's warning about the rough neighborhood, Sarah paid him the fare and a little extra and asked him to wait.

She caught up her skirts to keep them clear of the rubbish that lined the street and picked a path to the front door of a tall, grim house. As she inquired the way of a sharp-eyed young girl, she tried not to show her dismay. She'd imagined him in circumstances far better than this.

Sarah thanked the girl and gave her a shilling. Glancing up, she saw a small face shimmer in the grime at a second-floor window, then disappear. Her pulse jumped. Was it he?

No reason why it should be. Slum lords crammed as many bodies as they could into houses such as this.

Sarah rapped with her gloved fist and the door creaked open, revealing a dim hallway with a row of doors on either side of it and a central staircase zigzagging up and up, apparently to the heavens. No one came to ask her business, though the squalls of babies and rowdy voices penetrated the thin, mildewed walls.

Hitching her skirts a little higher, Sarah crossed the entry hall and mounted the first of several flights of stairs. Not long now.

How would he look—her husband's bastard son? Would he have Brinsley's eyes, or his riot of curls? Her heart stuttered at the thought.

The boy was ten years old, conceived mere months after she and Brinsley wed. The old pain of betrayal, a pain she thought she'd buried, rose to slap her in the face.

Pausing in her ascent, Sarah absorbed the sting with a clenched jaw, her hand closing like a vise around the worm-eaten banister. She took a deep breath, held it, then slowly let it out. The tawdry circumstances of his birth were not the boy's fault. A child did not deserve to live in poverty merely because his father was a scoundrel. She had sold more perfume than ever, scrimped and saved the moderate sum she carried in her reticule. All for him. The child she would never have.

Many stairs later, Sarah found the place she sought. She knocked and waited for an eternity, it seemed. Finally, the door swung open and Sarah came face-to-face with the boy's mother.

"Maggie Day?" The name was branded on Sarah's heart. The first in a long line of "other" women she'd prefer to know nothing about.

"Aye, that's me." The woman leaned against the door-jamb, her expression wary. She shoved stray wisps of blond hair out of her face with the heel of her hand, revealing a faint echo of former prettiness in her high cheekbones and the vivid blue of her eyes. Those eyes flared when Sarah introduced herself. After a slight hesitation, Maggie shifted aside to let her uninvited guest enter.

This was not a social call. Sarah didn't attempt pleasantries. "I've come about the boy. My . . . husband's son." She couldn't yet give him a name. Brinsley hadn't told her what he was called, and the address she'd found among his unpaid bills and notes of hand named the mother, not the child.

Sarah tried not to betray her anxiety, the strange yearning that had gripped her once the hurt and anger at Brinsley's taunts had subsided. *You're barren. . . . Useless, even as a breeder. . . . I've already fathered a son.*

She forced down the image of her husband's beautiful sneer and focused on the scene before her. A straw pallet lay in one corner, made up with a coarse wool blanket. That and a crudely fashioned chair furnished the tiny room. The place stank of boiled cabbage and rat urine.

"Is he here?" Idiotic question. She saw for herself he was not.

A derisive expression flitted across Maggie's features but she answered politely enough. "Nah, m'lady. Haven't seen him since before sunup. Goes down to the fish markets early, but after that . . ." She shrugged.

Sarah stared. Didn't she know? The boy was ten years old and his mother didn't know or care where he might be all day?

Jealousy seeped like acid into Sarah's chest. If he were *hers* . . . The corrosive burn spread through her, thickening her throat and pricking behind her eyes. She blinked hard and looked away.

Her gaze snagged on a collection of empty bottles in one corner. Did the woman drink? Sarah bit her lip. It wasn't her business; none of it was. But would Maggie use Sarah's money to clothe and feed the boy, or to buy more gin?

Disappointment flooded her, drowning her one small hope. She'd thought she could soothe her conscience by making this short journey—one small gesture to clean the slate. But not only was her mission flawed—she could not possibly hand her precious coins to such a female—she'd given herself one more problem to solve.

She couldn't compel Brinsley to provide for his love child. The pittance she made selling perfume was not enough to keep her and Brinsley, much less the boy as well.

Equally impossible to leave the child in this situation. Honor and simple Christian charity demanded that she ensure his well-being if her husband, his father, would not. Something must be done. She saw her duty clearly enough, but what *right* did she have to interfere?

Sarah offered her hand to Maggie, using every ounce of self-control to remain civil and calm. "I should—I should like to come again, if I may. To see him."

"Why yes, m'lady. Of course." Disregarding the outstretched hand, Maggie dipped a curtsey, a calculating gleam in her eye that Sarah did not like.

Sarah dropped her hand. "Shall we say Wednesday, at four?"

Wariness shaded Maggie's face, and Sarah hastened to reassure her. "The boy will come to no harm from me." Impatiently, she added, "I cannot keep calling him 'boy.' What is his name, if you please?"

Maggie eyed her for a silent moment. "His name's Tom."

Thanking her, Sarah left the shabby room. When she reached the stairwell, all the turbulent emotion she'd dammed inside her spilled over. *That poor little boy.* How could Brinsley be so heartless toward his own flesh and blood?

She fought against it, but her chest heaved with a great dry sob. Sarah pinched the bridge of her nose, trying to quell the burn behind her eyes. She *refused* to weep like a ninny over a young scamp she didn't even know, one born to her husband's mistress into the bargain. She was doing her duty. Emotion didn't enter into it. The fat, hot tear that rolled down her cheek was the product of overwrought nerves, that was all.

Sarah opened her reticule to pluck out her handkerchief and stopped with a soft, strangled cry.

Every penny of the money she'd brought was gone.

All the heat of frustration and sorrow drained from her face. But how—? Sarah glanced back in the direction of Maggie's room. No, the woman hadn't approached within a foot of her unwelcome guest during that tense encounter. Unless Maggie was a conjurer, she couldn't be the culprit.

When was the last time she'd seen the money in her reticule? Of course! She'd handed a coin to the ragged child who'd given her directions. A moment's inattention while Sarah scanned the upstairs windows would have been enough for an accomplished pickpocket. What a fool she'd been!

Sarah hurried downstairs and burst out into the street. She looked right and left, but of course the girl had vanished. And what would Sarah do if she found her? She could scarcely accuse her of theft without proof, and she balked at the thought of handing a child over to the tender mercies of the law.

Despair weighted the pit of her stomach like a millstone. All her hard work, gone.

Sarah questioned the hackney driver, but he hadn't noticed the girl.

"Something amiss, ma'am?"

She hesitated. The jarvey's open, pleasant face invited trust, but he had a living to earn. If she admitted she had no money to pay him, would he take her word that she'd obtain it when they reached their destination? Or would he whip up his horse and leave her stranded in this mean, tumbledown street?

"Not at all," she replied, trying to sound confident. "Take me to Brown's Coffeehouse, please." Brinsley was a creature of habit. He was sure to be at Brown's at this hour, smoking and gossiping like an old lady with that fool Rockfort and his other dim-witted cronies.

Sarah gave the jarvey precise directions and suffered agonies while they navigated the crowded London streets. Ridiculous, but she couldn't suppress the fear that the driver would order her to turn out her empty reticule and toss her into the street.

She pictured Brinsley, sprawled in a chair with a tankard of ale at his elbow, smoking a cigarillo and relaxing with his friends. Bile burned in her throat when she thought of the life of ease he continued to pursue, though they barely scraped enough together each month for rent and food. God forbid he should work for a living. As far as she could tell, he lived largely on credit, and supplemented the small allowance his elder brother paid him with sporadic wins at the gaming tables.

Surely he wouldn't begrudge her the cab fare? Though he might relish the blow to her pride if he refused, he wouldn't wish to appear ungenerous in front of his friends.

The hackney pulled to a stop outside the coffeehouse—a rowdy, masculine establishment thick with smoke. Sarah scanned the bow windows that gave out onto the street, but failed to see Brinsley within.

There was nothing for it. She would have to look for him inside. "Wait here, please," Sarah called up to the driver. "I won't be a moment."

"Eh? Now, see here, ma'am—" But in a fair imitation of

her mother's haughty bearing, Sarah pretended not to hear and swept across the flagstones.

Inwardly, she cringed at the prospect of seeking her husband in a public coffeehouse to beg for money. She prayed he wouldn't make the task more difficult than it needed to be. She detested scenes.

A large hand gripped her elbow, stopping her. She gasped and swung around, to see the hackney driver's reddening face.

She swallowed hard. "Let go of me. I told you, I'll only be a minute."

"Where've I 'eard that before?" scoffed the driver. His hold tightened. "I'll 'ave my money first, ma'am, *if* you please."

Before Sarah could answer, there was a blur of movement and a dull crack. The driver dropped Sarah's elbow with a grunt of pain, cradling his wrist. Sarah's gaze snapped upward. Standing between them, looking down at her with those deep, dark eyes, was the Marquis of Vane.

"Did he hurt you?" He made as if to take her arm to inspect the damage for himself, but she stepped back, evading his frowning scrutiny.

She shook her head, insides clenching, heart knocking against her ribs. There didn't seem enough air in the world to breathe. "A-a misunderstanding, merely. You are very good, but please don't—"

Vane lowered the cane he'd used to break the man's hold and switched his glare to the driver. "If you don't wish to feel this stick across your back, make yourself scarce."

The jarvey was a thickset man, but Vane towered over him, all broad chest and big shoulders and pure, masculine power. The driver blenched a little, but he retained enough spirit to mount a case in his defense.

Vane didn't appear to listen, but nor did he stem the flow. In the jarvey's eagerness to explain himself, he described Sarah's excursion in unnecessary detail. He even remarked how upset madam had seemed after visiting that dirty old house off Pudding Lane.

Sarah stiffened, so humiliated she couldn't bring herself to argue. Of all the men in the world who might have come upon her in this predicament, why did it have to be Vane?

His swift glance held a gleam of curiosity. She lifted her chin with proud disdain. She mustn't reveal the slightest hint of weakness. He'd show her no mercy if he sensed how susceptible she was, how fiercely she longed for him in the night. She'd never acted on that yearning, never allowed Vane the slightest liberty, not even a chaste kiss on the cheek. But the shame of lying in her husband's bed while she ached for another man's touch was slowly corroding her soul.

The marquis gave no sign he believed the driver's story, but when Sarah said nothing to contradict it, he flicked a coin to the jarvey and dismissed him with a nod. Before she could protest, the man was gone.

Vane turned to her. "Come, I'll escort you home."

His low, resonant tone stroked down her spine in a warm, velvet caress. A shocking wave of heat rolled through her body, left her trembling from head to toe. It was an effort to stop her voice from shaking like the rest of her. "That won't be necessary, thank you," she managed. "It is but a step." She gripped her hands together. "I haven't the funds with me, I'm afraid, but my husband will reimburse you. If you'd be so good as to find him . . ."

Vane followed her gaze to the coffeehouse and his jaw tightened. "I don't want repayment," he said harshly.

No, of course he didn't. Vane's wealth surpassed most men's dreams. There was only one thing he'd ever wanted from her. He still wanted it. She knew by the suppressed violence in him, the tension that held his large frame utterly still. As if he needed to exercise restraint over every cell in his body to stop himself from touching her.

She was in no better state. Her senses feasted on him— his dominating presence, the deep as midnight voice, that unique masculine scent. His dark hair was cropped brutally short, with no attempt to soften the slightly hawkish nose and sharp cheekbones that stood out from his lean cheeks in high relief. He carried himself like a Roman general, with the grace of an athlete and a habit of command.

Even in the open, bustling street, Sarah felt crowded, oppressed, overwhelmed by him. Her pride refused to let her take a backward step. But oh, she wanted to. She wanted to run.

All she could do was conceal her fear behind that familiar mask of ice. "Thank you. I'm obliged to you," she said in a colorless tone. She'd repay him the minute she could. She dreaded being beholden to him, even for such a negligible sum.

He continued to stand there, waiting, as if he expected something from her. She wasn't sure what it was, but she knew it was more than she could possibly give. She glanced at the coffeehouse. She needed to get away.

"So cold," breathed Vane. "You are . . . quite the most unfeeling woman I've ever met."

Sarah forced her lips into a thin, cynical smile. How little he knew her. The danger had always been that she felt far, far too much. An excess of sensibility had led to the great downfall of her existence. But she'd learned a hard lesson at the tender age of seventeen. She'd never let emotion overtake her good sense again. She'd paid for her impulsive choice every day for the past ten years.

The suffering had increased a hundredfold since she'd met Vane.

They stared at one another without speaking. The everyday world rushed past in a muted blur, as if she and Vane were surrounded by smoked glass. Those compelling dark eyes bore into hers, determined to read her secret yearning, searching for a response.

Her heart gave a mighty surge, as if it would leap from her chest into his. But she'd built a stronghold around her heart from the flotsam of wrecked dreams. That irresponsible organ was in no danger.

The miracle was that she still had a heart at all.

Someone jostled her as they hurried past. The strange bubble of suspended time burst and the world flooded back, swirling around them. Sarah turned away.

And there, in the bow window of Brown's Coffeehouse, stood Brinsley, her husband.

Watching.

THE Marquis of Vane flicked a glance at Brinsley Cole across the card table, betraying no hint of the animosity he felt. Vane was—as ever—in control.

The murmur of hardened gamesters intent on play surrounded them, punctuated by rattles of dice and the clack of a ball skittering around the E.O. wheel. Occasionally, a low rumble broke out after a win or a loss, but the object of this hell was serious play, and the general mood was quiet and tense. Even the doxies attending each table knew their charms paled next to the turn of the card and delayed their lusty propositions until the hand was done.

Vane hardly knew what brought him here tonight. He didn't care the snap of his fingers for games of chance, and still less did he care to bed any of the unappealing women who graced the establishment. Whatever had prompted him to visit Crockford's, he wished he'd ignored the impulse. Then he would not have to suffer Cole's infernal smugness, nor remember with every breath that Cole possessed what Vane desired more than anything in the world.

She was fresh in his mind, a rapid, hard pulse in his body, an ache that never quite abated, which had flared to burning agony when he'd stood so close to her that afternoon.

He'd wanted to leave as soon as he saw Brinsley Cole already seated at the card tables tonight, but that might have created talk he wished to avoid. So he'd smiled, and sat and played cards with a man he'd sooner never lay eyes on again. He doubted he fooled anyone at all.

"How fares your lady wife, Brinsley?" Rockfort slid a glance at Vane as he dealt the cards.

In spite of himself, Vane tensed. Braced for the reply.

Cole lurched to his feet, spilling a buxom trollop from his lap and a dash of claret down his gold embroidered waistcoat. A sneer crossed his angelic features as he raised his glass for a toast.

"To the Lady Sarah Cole! The woman who can out scold a Billingsgate fishwife, freeze a man's balls off with her frosty green glare. My lords, gentlemen—my damned virago of a wife!"

Cole flourished a bow and drank deep.

The gaming hell faded to oblivion. Vane heard nothing above the roar in his ears. The wild beast inside him raged to lunge across the table, wrap hands around that slender throat, and choke the life out of Brinsley Cole.

Muscles bunched and aching with the effort of restraint, Vane composed his features into a disinterested mask and picked up his cards. He had no right to defend Lady Sarah against her own husband. If he spoke up, people would assume he was her lover. He glanced around the table. Perhaps they already did. He was famed for getting what he wanted, and he'd wanted Lady Sarah from the second he'd laid eyes on her seven years before.

Everyone, it seemed, waited for him to speak.

Vane raised his glass of Burgundy to his lips. He sipped, savored, then set the glass on the table in a precise, controlled movement. Without glancing at his cards, he threw them down. "Gentlemen, I've recalled a pressing engagement. I shall bid you good night."

A murmur rippled around the table as he swept up his winnings. Cole, damn his soul to hell, smirked and waved a hand. "My lord, I'll come with you."

Over the players' heads, Vane sent him a brief, scorching glare. As he turned to leave, he saw Rockfort twitch Cole's sleeve in warning. But despite its porcelain perfection, Cole's skin was thick as elephant hide. He stumbled out in Vane's wake.

The frigid air speared Vane through his greatcoat but did nothing to cool his blood. Brinsley Cole must be blind or suicidal to follow him into a dark alley. The man begged to be throttled and thrown in the gutter along with the other refuse and scum.

Drawing on his gloves, Vane halted and turned around. "What do you want?"

Brinsley swaggered toward him. "The question, my lord Marquis, is what do *you* want? I'll wager I know the answer."

Vane's sigh fogged the air. "Is this where you try to sell me another of your schemes, Brinsley? Canals in Jamaica, that sort of thing?"

His companion barely seemed to notice the veiled insult. Despite Vane's attempt to distract him, Brinsley knew he was onto something. Vane saw it in the avid light that entered the man's wide, soulful eyes. Brinsley scented a weakness, and he'd worry at Vane like a hound at a wounded stag until he worked out how to turn it to best advantage.

Finally, Brinsley spoke. "You want my wife," he said softly. "You always have."

Shock ricocheted through Vane's mind. *Brinsley knew?* He'd always known, it seemed. Had Sarah told her husband of Vane's interest? The idea sliced his chest like a finely honed blade. Suddenly, the past rushed back; events and conversations changed color and shape.

He dragged his mind to the present. He needed to remain calm, keep a cool head. He wanted Lady Sarah more than he wanted air to breathe, it was true. Her husband knew it, but what difference did that make? As long as Vane made no admissions, Brinsley could think what he liked.

"If you wish to call me out, name your friends, Cole. Otherwise, shut your filthy little mouth." With one careless finger, he flicked Brinsley's wilted shirt-point. "Go home, man. You are drunk. Worse than that, you are tedious."

"Home. Oh, yes!" Brinsley chortled, enjoying himself now. "What wouldn't you give to be in my shoes, eh? Trotting off home to my tasty little wife. And do you know what I'll do to her when I get—"

Fury ripped through Vane's blood. He slammed Brinsley against the stone wall, pinning him with one hand to his throat. Every fiber in Vane's body burned to squeeze the life out of the cur then and there.

"Mercy!" Brinsley's face was mottled red, his eyes bulging and frantic. Vane wished he'd put up some kind of resistance, but the pathetic creature made no move to defend himself, save for a feeble kick at Vane's leather-clad shin.

Damn it, he couldn't fight such a poor specimen, much as he yearned to dispatch him to the hottest fires of hell. Vane released his grip and Brinsley crumpled to the slimy cobbles, wheezing and coughing, clutching his throat.

Vane waited for him to recover, even lent him a hand to help him up. With a glance of disdain, he stripped off the glove that had made contact with Brinsley's soiled person and tossed it in the gutter. "Now, what were you saying before I so rudely interrupted?"

Brinsley dashed blood from his bit lip. "You want Sarah," he whispered, edging closer. "Badly enough to lose your famous control. That must be worth something." He smiled. "That must be worth quite a lot."

Vane remained silent. He willed himself to ignore Brinsley's jibes, turn his back, and walk away. But he couldn't pretend not to care. He must know what Brinsley planned. Though she was beyond his reach in every way, he needed to assure himself that Sarah would be safe.

Yet, even as those altruistic thoughts crossed his mind, a small echo of honesty forced him to admit—Brinsley was right. He wanted Lady Sarah Cole in a way no gentleman of honor should want another man's wife. His passion for her was like a recurring fever, rising again and again to attack him in moments of weakness. No matter how hard he trained and fought and conditioned his body, his soul was hers and always would be. For seven years, the knowledge that this worthless piece of rubbish before him possessed Lady Sarah had torn at Vane with razor-sharp claws.

Now, Brinsley offered . . . what, exactly?

"You want her," Brinsley repeated. "You can have her . . . at a price."

Vane sucked in a breath. Disgust and desire clashed inside him. Had he misheard? Brinsley couldn't possibly mean . . .

Though Vane maintained his indifferent expression, even

managed to look a trifle bored, the very air around them seemed to thicken with his need.

"Ten thousand pounds. For one night with my wife." Brinsley repeated it, stressed each word. "Ten. Thousand. Pounds."

A red haze swept over Vane's vision. He wanted to tear Brinsley apart with his bare hands. He wanted to leave without dignifying that insane, *indecent* proposal with a response. He wanted to forget Lady Sarah Cole existed, excise her from his mind and heart.

But he couldn't. He couldn't save her from Brinsley's loathsome schemes, either. He'd tried. She'd spurned him with her cold, cruel smile. But what if the villain took this offer to another man with fewer scruples than Vane? What then?

"I ought to kill you, Cole." Vane kept his voice low, aware that a party of men had left Crockford's and headed their way. "Exterminate you like the vermin you are."

Brinsley didn't even blink. "Ah, but I'm well acquainted with your sort, my lord. I know you would not kill a man without a fair fight." He fingered his bruised throat, then shrugged. "Call me out if you wish to see Sarah's name dragged through the mud. I won't meet you."

His expression darkened. "I married that little bitch, my lord marquis. Short of bloody murder, I can treat her however I damned well please. So think well before you threaten me, sir, or your sweet Lady Sarah might suffer the consequences."

Blind rage, all the more dangerous for its impotence, threatened to overwhelm every principle Vane held dear. He faced Brinsley in the darkness, panting with the effort of keeping his hands by his sides instead of wrapping them around the bastard's throat. This time, he wouldn't have the strength to let go.

He'd never killed a man before. . . .

Their misted breath clashed and roiled upward. The moonlight glinted off wet cobbles, threw Brinsley's profile into high relief. The thoughtful poet's brow that hid a conniving, low mind, the noble nose that sniffed out weakness and despair, the sculpted lips that now curled in a self-satisfied sneer.

Damn him to hell. Brinsley knew he had won.

Two

SARAH had not stopped shaking since she'd met Vane. As the evening wore on, she grew increasingly fearful of retiring to bed. If she slept, she was sure to dream of him. Dreams as vivid as memories, false promises that would torment her when she woke.

In a desperate attempt to quell the riot in her mind, Sarah let herself into the tiny attic room her landlady had allowed her to convert into a small perfume manufactory.

Donning her apron, Sarah set to work. But while her hands were busy measuring and mixing, her thoughts refused to settle. They returned again and again to that brief encounter with Vane.

The air was drenched with the scent of roses, a dizzyingly strong odor for one unaccustomed to it, but Sarah had grown used to the sickly sweet fug. Rosewater was very popular among the apothecary's clientele; after making the stuff all this time, Sarah never wished to smell a rose again.

She scanned the jars of materials that lined the shelf on the wall opposite. If she ever dragged them out of the mire of Brinsley's debt, she might have the luxury of experimenting. With floral essences, of course, but also with compounds and extracts from more exotic sources—vanilla, sandalwood and rosewood, ambergris, patchouli, even spice. Woods and spices imported from the East were expensive, far beyond her means, but perhaps one day . . .

Her mind drifted to Vane's scent—barely detectable at the distance she'd kept from him today, yet she'd know it anywhere. Sandalwood, an unusual combination of herbs, perhaps a hint of lemon. Idly, she wondered how she might reproduce it. A shaving soap, probably made from a household recipe, ought not to be difficult to simulate. . . .

Folly! How could she even consider doing such a mawkish thing? As though she could keep him with her, if only she might capture his scent.

Sarah passed a hand over her brow, half expecting to detect a fever. But her skin was cool, a little clammy from the perfume vapor that rose from the vial heating over the flame of her small distillery. One thing was certain—she needed to stop mooning over Vane and get to work.

Bracing a cone of parchment in the circle of a wire ring, Sarah tried to steady her hand as she poured in a thin stream of the rose petal decoction she'd prepared. She couldn't afford to spill any of the precious liquid extract. Her resources had been stretched as it was; now that her savings were gone, she needed the money from selling this batch of perfume to buy ingredients for the next.

She'd managed to supplement their income for some years now by selling perfume. Her sole client was an apothecary who knew nothing of her noble connections and wouldn't have cared if he did. He had little interest in the more cosmetic side of his trade, but his customers went mad over the subtleties of Sarah's perfumes, so he was pleased to keep ordering them from her. And charge his customers extra on top of whatever he paid Sarah for them, of course.

The strained syrup dripped sluggishly to collect in the glass vial beneath, as if to mark the slow, inexorable stretch of living she had left to do. Married to Brinsley. Till death do us part. Sarah closed her eyes and swallowed hard.

Vane. Was it possible to go mad with longing? She wanted him with a ferocity that terrified her. If only they'd never met. If only she could forget him, his passionate, sensual mouth, the heat in his eyes. The large body that looked as if it could shelter a woman from all of life's storms.

Those bitter words he'd spoken that afternoon. Almost as if he truly cared . . .

When the straining process was complete, Sarah set the parchment aside and wiped her hands on the baize apron she wore to protect her gown from spills and splashes.

She spread her fingers and watched her hands tremble, then turned them over. The sight always shocked her. Perhaps she'd never grow used to the damage her new profession had wrought. Her palms showed crisscrossed scars in a network of accidents—a dire contrast from their translucent softness in those far-off days when her greatest concern had been a torn fingernail or an incipient freckle on her nose. Her lips twisted. She was a working woman now.

After her ill-fated expedition that afternoon, she needed to turn a profit from her perfume more than ever. Without money, she could do nothing about Tom's situation. She tried to think of some way to raise funds quickly, but she'd sold everything she owned of value years ago.

Except . . .

Sarah took off her apron and hung it on a hook by the door. She left the attic and hurried downstairs to the set of rooms she and Brinsley rented. In their bedchamber, hidden in the bottom drawer of her bureau, was a mahogany box. She drew it out and opened it.

Her pistol, balls, a powder horn, flint, bullet mold, and small cleaning rod lay inside. The pistol was an elegant, ladylike weapon, designed to be carried inside a muff. She turned it in her hands and watched the candlelight's gleam slide along the silver barrel, glittering around the intricate scrollwork engravings that decorated the action.

Her father had given it to her when she turned seventeen. He'd taught her to use it, too. She'd loved target shooting— the precision, the deadly power contained in one small weapon. Those days spent perfecting her aim with Papa at her side were her last fond memories of her indulgent parent before Brinsley's easy charm swept her off her feet. The last time her father had figured as the most significant man in her life.

Now, she rarely saw the man she'd worshipped all those years. Despite her estrangement from her mother, she might have made more of an effort to preserve her close relationship with the earl. But she couldn't bear his disappointment, the remoteness in his eyes whenever they met. He was a man of the world. More than anyone, he must guess what her life had become as Brinsley's wife. The thought sickened and shamed her.

Yet, even after all her jewels and silks had gone, she'd kept this pistol, hidden it away from Brinsley's grasping hands.

Sarah carried the case into the parlor. She wouldn't trust Brinsley to sell this for her. She'd have to find a pawnbroker on her own, one who wouldn't rob her blind. To part with it would be a wrench—the final snap of threadbare ties with her family—but what was a fond memory beside the welfare of a small boy?

Papa would understand. The earl had always stipulated the importance of honoring one's obligations. He'd taken care of his wife's love child, hadn't he? He hadn't sired Sarah's younger sister, yet he'd acknowledged her as his own. Papa was the very best of men.

A knock on the door shattered her reverie.

She caught her breath. Who could be calling at this hour? Even Brinsley's creditors were not so persistent as to dun her this close to midnight.

Slowly, she turned and stared at the plain wooden door, willing whoever knocked to go away. If not a creditor, it must be one of Brinsley's associates. A lone female would need rocks in her head to open the door to any of those degenerates.

She waited, hoping to hear receding footsteps, but nothing came. A taut, expectant quality in the silence beyond the door intensified her unease. The person—man or woman, she could not guess—must be listening for signs of life. Just as she listened.

Sarah's heartbeat kicked up a notch. Motionless, scarcely daring to breathe, she waited.

The visitor rapped louder. She jumped, closing a hand around her pistol. Her heart pounded in her ears, underscored by the eerie, faint hum of quiet.

Fumbling with nervousness, she loaded the pistol, praying she wouldn't need it, and that if she did, the powder would still be good after months of disuse. Rising, she primed the weapon, pointed it at the door, and willed her hand to stop trembling.

Another long silence passed.

A muttered curse outside. She jumped, nearly squeezing the trigger.

Footsteps retreated down the creaking staircase.

Sarah released the hammer on her pistol, and lowered the weapon to point at the floor. Gripping the mantel to steady herself, she exhaled a shaky breath.

As the street door opened and closed, Sarah pressed her temple against her outstretched arm. She didn't look out the window to see who it was.

She had a strange, compelling feeling it was better not to know.

HALF an hour later, Sarah heard another set of heavy footsteps on the stairs. This time, they paused on the landing below.

Sarah put her ear to the door and heard voices. Brinsley's and the shrill tones of their landlady, Mrs. Higgins. Cautiously, she inched the door open.

"Ooh, go on with yer, Mr. Cole!" There was a short scuffle and a rustle of skirts and a smacking sound like a kiss. Feminine giggles bubbled up from below. "You are naughty, sir! What would your lady wife say if she knew?"

Sarah snorted. *I'd say better you than me, my dear.*

Brinsley heaved a sigh. "Indeed, it is very bad, but I cannot help myself. And my wife is so . . . very . . . cold, while you are so very mmm . . . *warm.* . . ." He gave a lascivious chuckle, then there was silence.

Sarah's lips compressed. She ought to pity the woman. Higgins believed Brinsley was sweet on her, but Sarah knew his attentions were nothing more than a clever way to avoid paying the rent. Quite apart from that, Brinsley was the sort of man who craved female attention. He needed to enslave every woman who crossed his path, whether he was interested in her or not.

After a short interval, Brinsley continued up to their floor. Sarah moved away from the door a second before he flung it open and sauntered in. When he saw her, a smile spread over his face. He'd wanted her to hear his exchange with their landlady. She would not give him the satisfaction of acknowledging it.

"My darling wife," he said softly. As was his habit, he stripped off his coat and threw it over a chair, then untied his neckcloth.

She made her face blank and swept her voice bare of inflection. "Good evening, Brinsley. I was just about to retire."

He didn't answer. With a tug, his neckcloth came away. He tossed it on the floor and flung himself down on the sofa, looking the picture of a beautiful, dissolute rake. But where his lawn shirt fell open, Sarah saw mottled bruising around his throat.

She gasped. "What happened to you?" For the first time, she noticed the cut on Brinsley's lower lip, surrounded by puffy swelling. "Have you been in a fight? Let me look at that cut."

He gazed limpidly at her as she took his chin and turned his face to the light. "Are you going to kiss it better?"

She dropped her hand and straightened, then left the room without a word.

Sarah went to their bedchamber and poured water from a pitcher into a small basin. She returned to the sitting room with the basin and a flannel and knelt beside the sofa. Wrinkling her nose at Brinsley's ripe odor, she dipped the flannel in the water, squeezed out the excess, and dabbed at his bloody lip.

She hoped it hurt like the Devil.

"Ow. Owww, stop it." Brinsley ceased playing the wounded soldier, whisked the flannel out of her grasp, and dropped it on the floor.

There could only be one reason for Brinsley's condition. *Money.* She stood and folded her arms. "How much did you lose tonight, Brin?"

Clear blue eyes gazed, unblinking, up at her—his Archangel Gabriel face. "Did I not give you my word I would not play?"

"That is not an answer to my question."

Sarah sighed, so tired of these games, this endless charade of interrogation and evasion. He must realize she knew him too well to be taken in. Sometimes, she thought he lied to her just for the practice.

She set a pot of water over the hearth to boil. Their staff consisted of a daily maid and Brinsley's valet, who refused to perform any duties outside the exceedingly narrow sphere of his expertise. Tonight was Hedge's night off, so no doubt Brinsley would expect Sarah to brush his coat and remove his boots.

How different from the house she grew up in, where one tripped over a powdered footman or a bustling housemaid every few feet. She used to think life at Penrose Hall grandiose and tiresome. What wouldn't she give to be back there now?

But in wedding the divinely handsome, unacceptable Brinsley in a fit of girlish romanticism, she'd made her choice. Her family had done nothing so dramatic as to cast her off. Such emotive histrionics were beneath the Earl and Countess of Straghan. But she hadn't the wherewithal to move in their circle and would accept none of their charity. The connection had not been severed, but rather, allowed to lapse.

Sarah busied herself making coffee, almost spilled the

hot brew down her cambric gown when Brinsley came up behind and wrapped his arms around her waist, dug his chin into her shoulder.

She stiffened. He wanted something. The poor deluded man still thought he could seduce her to his will.

His wine-fumed breath stirred in her ear. "What would you say if I told you that *you*, my lady, could make us rich?" He pinched her waist. "We could buy a house, employ servants, go to ton parties. You could have your old life back."

Brinsley's words were far more seductive than his clumsy, probing fingers, but Sarah kept a clear head.

"I would say, Brinsley, that there must be a catch." She twisted, trying to meet his eyes. "What would I have to do?"

"You know Vane?" Evading her scrutiny, he bent to kiss her collarbone.

She stifled a gasp, and he probably thought the small sound signified pleasure at his attentions. But at the mention of Vane, her mouth dried and the blood raced through her body, a reaction Brinsley's determined prodding failed to elicit.

She swallowed hard, kept her voice cool. "The Marquis of Vane? Yes, I know him." Desired him as she'd never desired any other man in her life. Not even Brinsley, before they married.

But desire led to . . . this. A lifetime of regret. She glanced around their cramped, shabby little parlor, which their landlady had long ago decorated in vile shades of brown and bilious green. Even as Sarah toiled endlessly to scrub away the grime, it never, ever seemed quite clean.

Brinsley slobbered at her neck, rubbing his growing erection against her bottom. "Vane wants you. He offered me ten thousand pounds for just one night."

"He offered . . ." Ice closed over her heart, froze her racing blood to a standstill. It *couldn't* be true. Yet, the look in Vane's eyes that afternoon . . .

The ground shifted beneath her feet, as if the rock-solid earth she'd stood on for years had crumbled, pitching her into a storm-tossed sea.

Well, she'd go down fighting. She didn't know any other way.

Sarah wrenched free from Brinsley, lanced him with her gaze.

"And you, sir. What did *you* say?"

Need she ask? Of course, he'd agreed. No doubt he'd auctioned her like a prize filly on market day. She wondered how many bidders there'd been, whether Tattersall might claim a commission.

He opened his mouth to deal her one more lie, and suddenly, she couldn't bear to hear it. She pressed her fingertips to her temple, then flicked them, dismissing him. "Never mind."

Sarah paced the floor, chewing on the pad of her thumb. Instinct told her to pack her meager bags and leave, but where would she go? Her sister Marjory lived abroad with her diplomat husband, and Sarah would rather die than return to Penrose, admit she'd been wrong, hang her head in shame. Her friendships had fallen by the wayside since her marriage. There was no one she could rely on but herself.

She glanced at her husband. She was done with him. Finished.

But something told her Brinsley was not finished with her. His eyes gleamed. There was an air of suppressed excitement about him, as if he knew beyond doubt she would give in, that the ten thousand pounds were as good as his.

Had he always been this stupid? No, Brinsley was not stupid. So there must be something else. "What?"

"My dear, I am afraid it is more serious than you know. Vane holds a large number of my vowels which I have not been at liberty to honor." The brilliant eyes pleaded. "Darling, he has threatened to throw us into debtors' prison if you do not go to him."

Brinsley caught her hand, his curls gilded by firelight, blue eyes blazing with near religious zeal. "Just one night, my love. One night with him could never destroy what you and I have."

In a long and testing marriage, Sarah had never come

so close to slapping the disingenuous smile from her husband's flawless face. But a lady never struck a gentleman, because the gentleman could not, in honor, fight back. The indisputable fact that a gentleman would not sell his wife's virtue to the highest bidder did not signify. Her pride wouldn't allow it.

So she curled her fingers hard into her palms, took a deep breath, and paused to think. Was the threat of ruin real, or fabricated by her darling spouse? Was the entire story some elaborate joke Brinsley sought to play on her? She had always considered Vane ruthless and proud. But she never would have suspected him capable of this.

Years ago, once the golden angel she'd married had stamped out the last embers of her love with his clumsy clay feet, the marquis had approached her, with that burning look in his eyes that never failed to set her pulse racing. By subtle, unmistakable language, he had indicated his desire to enter into a liaison with her.

The longing to curl into Vane's broad, hard strength had kept her awake at night, restless and aching, but Sarah had made vows before God, and she was determined to keep them.

Only weaklings gave in to temptation.

She'd said no. He'd accepted her refusal, walked away without a backward glance. She had not seen him for many months after that, perhaps a year.

This proposal—this *coercion*—seemed contrary to all she admired about Vane.

"He says you must go to him tonight," said Brinsley, giving the lie to her thoughts. "If you're not there within the hour, he'll assume you're not coming and he'll take immediate action."

Now? Tonight? It was an enormous effort to stop her legs from buckling under her. In a daze of shock and misery, Sarah reached for her pelisse, which hung on a hook by the door. "I will go to see Vane. Talk to him. This *must* be a mistake."

"Do you think so?" Brinsley fingered his damaged lip, looking hopeful. "I should be so happy to discover I misinterpreted his words. Perhaps I should come with—"

"No!" She closed her eyes against the pain. It must be true if Brinsley was prepared to let her go.

Sarah inhaled a ragged breath and moderated her tone. "No. This is between Vane and me now. I shall—I shall take a hackney." With fingers that trembled slightly, she drew the last, precious coins from her hoard inside a hole in the sofa cushion and dropped them into her reticule.

She searched her bedchamber for a veil to wear and pinned it to her bonnet. She donned her gloves, set her hand on the doorknob, and looked back. "I have always been faithful to you, you know, Brinsley," she said. "In ten years I have never had another man."

Brinsley barked a laugh. "Of course I know it. If you were not such a damned icicle where bedding was concerned, I might not have strayed myself."

She curled her lip. "If you believe that, you are more self-deluded than I thought."

His blue eyes narrowed to slits, Brinsley closed the distance between them. "The trouble with you, my dearest *wife*, is you've not one ounce of compassion in that beautiful breast of yours." He held up a pinched finger and thumb in her face. "One mistake, one slip, and you dismissed your husband like you'd dismiss one of your damned lackeys at Penrose Hall." The fingers snapped. "Just like that."

He gripped her arms to hold her still when she would have slid away, leaned in, and pressed his hot, moist lips to her ear. "Well, *Lady Sarah*, you go to Vane's house tonight, and think about all that lovely money slipping through your self-righteous fingers. All the gowns and furbelows you could have, just for one night spent on your back and no one but us the wiser. And let us see how long you hold on to your disdain."

He released her, and with a shock, she saw that for him the stake was not just money, it was personal.

He sneered. "Because something tells me, my lady, your precious pride is about to fall."

VANE burst into his Mayfair house, sent for his groom, and continued straight to the ballroom, stripping as he went. A pair of startled footmen hurried to light candles, and soon the salon blazed.

The cavernous space echoed with his footsteps as he paced, clenching his teeth against the cold. His reflection paced with him along the mirrored wall. His black superfine coat, white cravat, lawn shirt, and green-striped waistcoat lay in a puddle of fabric on the waxed wood floor.

"Will you require a fire, my lord?" Rivers, his butler, retrieved the heap of clothing and folded each garment neatly over a chair.

Vane shook his head. "I'll be warm soon enough." *Once I pound the stuffing out of that groom of mine.* "Where the hell is Gordon?"

"I sent a lad to fetch him from the mews, my lord. He will be here directly."

Vane met the butler's troubled gaze with a curt nod of dismissal. Rivers bowed and withdrew.

Vane sat on a gilt and white love seat to yank off his boots. The operation required concentrated effort. That was a good thing. As long as he did not think, all would be well. He plunked the second boot on the floor, cursed, and dropped his head in his hands.

He must be mad. Surely, he had never made such an ass of himself about a woman before. It had been years since that cold rebuff she'd dealt him. Years since he'd exchanged more than idle social chatter with her, and that had been infrequent enough. He didn't even know her, not really. Yet she seeped into his thoughts when he wasn't paying attention, curled under his skin in the darkest hours of the night.

A cheerful voice boomed from the doorway. "Ready for a pummeling, m'lud?" Six feet and three inches of solid

Yorkshire brawn strolled in, ripped off his shirt, flexed his meaty fingers, and rolled his massive shoulders.

Vane surged to his stocking feet. "Let's cut the small talk, shall we? Nothing below the waist, nothing above the neck." He raised his brows at Gordon's scornful expression. "Can't give the ladies nightmares with a black eye, now, can I?"

The burly groom chuckled deep in his barrel chest. "Nay. Wouldn't want yon pretty face of yours to tek a beatin', would we, lad? Right, then?"

Breathing deeply, Vane emptied his mind, brought himself in hand. He wanted to pound solid flesh until he dropped from exhaustion, but to fight Gordon, he must use his mind, not just his fists. He nodded.

They jabbed, blocked, clinched, circled, landed few punches at first. As his muscles warmed, as the sweat gathered on his brow and trickled down between his bare shoulder blades, as his ears filled with the smack of fist on flesh, the squeak of feet on floorboards, sporadic grunts and rhythmic, deep breathing, a strange calm settled over him. Nothing existed but his wits and his fists and this bull-necked ex-champion from Leeds. Nothing existed but the fight.

So when a voice spoke from the doorway he heard it, but on a different plane from his conscious state. A stagecoach could have thundered through that ballroom and he would not have paid any heed, his mind was so focused on seeking an opening, a gap in Gordon's guard.

Suddenly, he found it, bore in with a wrestling move and threw the big man a cross-buttock, sent him crashing to the floor.

Gordon shook his bald head and lifted himself on his elbows. His fearsome fighting glare split in a huge grin. With a hoot, Gordon leaped to his feet and bounded over to grip Vane's hand. "Don't know what has yer steamed up tonight, lad, but that were some right crackin' work." He clapped Vane on the back and turned to pick up his shirt.

Laughing for what seemed the first time in years, Vane stood for a moment, savoring his victory. Raw energy coursed through his body. He would never sleep now, but his mind felt at peace, under control. The night was still young; he thought it not much past midnight. He would have a wash and then stroll down to his club.

A cough sounded from the doorway, and his head snapped around. He saw a lady, heavily veiled, but he'd know that woman anywhere.

Only years of training kept his expression neutral. After a slight hesitation, he bowed.

Rivers hovered anxiously behind her, bleating excuses for the interruption. Vane waved the butler away, dismissed Gordon with a nod.

When they were alone, she lifted her veil and regarded him steadily across the vast space. Vane stared back at her. Drank her in.

Jade green eyes dominated her face. They tilted slightly at the corners, accented by a sweep of black lashes and strong, fine brows. Men wished to believe those eyes invited them to intimacy with the rest of her slender, full-breasted body; he'd learned they were more likely to slice him in two. Her hair was not quite ebony, but close enough as made no difference, dressed simply, without embellishment. Her skin was cream and roses, her lips too full, too lush for beauty, or so the connoisseurs said. He gazed at them, wondered how they might taste, how they might feel drifting over his skin.

"Do put a shirt on, Vane, and stop gaping at me like a zany," those lips commanded.

His brows snapped together. He had been about to do just that, but now, with the sweat rapidly chilling his back, he wondered what right she had to tell him to wear clothes if he did not wish to.

"This is my house. I'll wear what I damned well please."

Why was she here? Simply to torment him with that sensuous mouth? She muddied the waters of his mind, when he'd fought so hard—literally fought—to clear them. He needed time to think, to consider the ramifications of her presence before he faced her again.

He headed toward her, intending to brush past. "I'm going upstairs to bathe. Rivers will show you to the drawing room to wait."

She squared up to him, all five and a half feet of her, and if he hadn't already pegged Lady Sarah as a far more formidable adversary than Gordon, he might have smiled at the contrast.

"Rivers," she replied, "will do nothing of the sort. I came to speak with you, and I wish to do so now, not wait until you deign to accommodate me."

He folded his arms and saw her steady gaze flicker, follow his movement. "My lady, I am sweating like a blacksmith. I need a wash. You can go home, or wait downstairs, I don't care, but I shall have my bath."

"I'm not going anywhere." The luscious lips set in a line.

Vane snorted. "You wish to join me upstairs, do you?"

Her gaze locked with his. Between gritted teeth, she said, "Thank you, my lord. I will."

A torrent of lust swept over him, so strong it nearly knocked him sideways, a force more powerful than any of Gordon's blows. The struggle to stop himself from reaching for her then and there nearly killed him, but he managed to keep his hands fisted at his sides. Without a word, he strode past her into the corridor.

As Vane led the way to the stairs, Sarah paused and closed her eyes. Spite had fueled Brinsley's parting words about her freezing disdain, but there was enough truth in them to stab at her heart.

He was wrong about one thing, though. No amount of money was worth sacrificing her pride. Pride had seen her through ten soul-destroying years of marriage. And pride would rescue her tonight, no matter how much she wanted Vane.

With a renewed sense of purpose, she lifted her chin and marched after him.

Coming to Vane's house in defiance of all precepts of good conduct, she'd set herself a test. She had not, however, expected it would be quite so difficult to pass. Seeing the marquis half-naked, sweating, and cursing as he fought that giant northern bully had fired her blood to an alarming degree. She had always disliked big men; they made her feel powerless and fragile. She preferred fine-boned types like Brinsley. She supposed she had not seen many men without their shirts.

Vane was big and overwhelmingly male, muscular as a farm laborer. His tailor must be a talented artist to transform that brawn to Vane's customary suave elegance. She'd never noticed before how very large he was.

But nothing could have been further from his usual demeanor than the sight that met her eyes in his ballroom tonight: a wild, primitive display of masculine aggression. She ought to be disgusted. She'd never seen anything more magnificent in her life.

He mounted the stairs without looking back. Sarah followed, and watched with unwilling fascination as all those muscles worked in glorious unison. His cropped dark hair spiked damply at his nape and perspiration shone on his shoulders and back. There was not an ounce of spare flesh on him. He was all muscle and bone and sinew, all strength and power. An angry red bruise bloomed on his right side, beneath his rib cage. She had the strongest urge to touch it, to smooth away the pain.

Her gaze lowered, and the blood rose to her cheeks as she studied the shift of his buttocks under skintight grey pantaloons. Her body thrummed with awareness, anticipated what might happen if she succumbed.

But the man could be Adonis and Casanova rolled into one and she would not give in. To resist him, she need only remember that he'd sought to buy her favors as if she were a common streetwalker, a piece of merchandise, albeit an outrageously expensive one. She would show Brinsley, she would show *herself*, that she valued her honor and the marriage vows she'd made more highly than money or spurious pleasure.

This might have been a lot easier to achieve had she

agreed to await their discussion in the drawing room rather than conduct it in his bedchamber. But Vane had thrown down the gauntlet, never expecting her to pick it up.

Sarah gave a grim smile. She almost welcomed the challenge.

Vane's heart thundered in his chest, and he knew it wasn't from the fight. He barely made it to his door without ravishing her on the stairs. He was achingly aware that she studied him, painfully reminded of what he wanted—had always wanted—from her.

But she was in his house to earn Brinsley his ten thousand pounds. She was not there because she desired him. If she desired him, she could have had him any time these seven years or more.

Obviously, Brinsley had not given up on his contemptible scheme. Was she here to seduce Vane into changing his mind? The real question: Was he strong enough to resist her if it came to that? Did he even want to?

Ten thousand pounds was nothing. A lot more than he'd ever needed to pay for his pleasure before, but a drop in the vast ocean of his wealth. He had, he reminded himself, paid for pleasure in the past. He did not make a habit of consorting with certain married women of the ton who granted their favors freely. Uncomplicated relationships with practiced courtesans were more his style.

Until Lady Sarah Cole.

They passed through a small sitting room and entered his private domain. He'd never taken a woman there before.

He indicated an overstuffed armchair, displaced from its position beside the fire by the enormous, high-backed bathtub. She took off her bonnet and laid it on the table next to the chair. Then she sat, arranged her skirts, and folded her hands in her lap. She kept her gloves on, he noticed.

Her eyes grew large in her fine, oval face as she contemplated the waiting bath, but when she caught him watching her, all sign of anxiety vanished. She smiled, regarding him with that amused contempt with which she always seemed to view Brinsley.

Vane's temper flared. His gaze gripped hers as he shucked his pantaloons, peeled off his stockings, and finally, undid the string of his drawers and pushed them down.

He was aroused. He didn't try to hide the fact. God help him, he relished the momentary dip of her eyes, the slight flush that crested her cheeks as she took in his size, then cut her gaze away.

Hadn't she believed he'd carry out his threat to bathe in front of her? Of course, she was accustomed to dealing with Brinsley. Perhaps now she'd realize the man standing before her was a different beast altogether from that spineless weasel she called husband.

Vane stepped into the tub and lowered himself into the steaming water. Laying his head against the tub's high back, he gave a throaty sigh that was supposed to signify contentment.

It sounded more like a hungry growl.

Three

"WELL, this is . . . interesting." Lady Sarah's tone struck Vane's ears as inappropriately calm and cordial. "What novel notions of hospitality you have, my lord."

Lazily, he stretched his legs, laid his arms along the edge of the tub, and smiled. "Perhaps I'll start a fashion."

"Perhaps you will."

Her gaze roamed his bedchamber, looked everywhere but at him. The crackle of the fire and the faint slap of water on the sides of the tub as he moved were all that broke the silence. He narrowed his eyes, watched her appraise the rich gold and black furnishings as if she were an auctioneer itemizing them for sale.

Why had she come? And what was he going to do about it? He tried to apply reason to the problem, set his mind apart from the physical, from his body's rampant reaction to hers.

Of course, the wild beast inside him didn't care why she was there, finally, in his bedchamber, ready to lay her ravishing beauty at his feet.

The beast licked its chops, slavered to devour every

delicious, mouthwatering curve under that sturdy pelisse. Anticipated her wet heat, the pull and power of ultimate release. Raged to leap from the tub and throw her on his bed and plunge into her until she forgot everything she had ever known. Everything but him.

He sank down into the water, came up and raked his hands through his wet hair. Caught by the movement, her attention switched to him.

Her dispassionate gaze wandered over his body, direct and palpable as touch. Heat washed through him, as if the steaming water flooded his veins, simmered in his blood. His erection had relaxed slightly, but under that contemplative scrutiny it hardened to an aching throb. The beast in him howled to be unleashed.

And yet . . . he had smarted at her rejection years ago. He'd cursed himself for misreading the signs, believing she might one day be his in fact, if not in name. He'd vowed then and there he'd never let such primitive urges control him again. Never would a woman make him beg.

Especially not Lady Sarah Cole.

So, part of it was animal lust, and part of it was pride, this need for action at war with the temptation to sit back and let matters take their course. Part of it was curiosity, an itch to see how she would go about seducing him. She hadn't tried very hard thus far.

Another part of him—his intellect, perhaps—detested the idea that what had seemed such a foul, unthinkable act mere hours before had suddenly become a course he seriously considered pursuing. Paying a virtuous lady for the use of her body.

Did her acquiescence make the difference? Or was it simply that she was there? Did Brinsley know all Vane had to do was see her, smell her, taste her perhaps, to thrust his honor, his pride, and his intellect aside, and lay his money on the table?

Lady Sarah spoke. "I must say I find your methods of seduction quite . . . unusual, my lord."

His methods?

She must have seen the question in his face. "You will not take no for an answer, it seems. My husband informed me of your discussion tonight."

"Did he?" He should have realized Brinsley would not give her the truth. What poison had that little snake dripped in her ear?

He waited. A long pause ensued.

In a low voice, she said, "I always believed you were a gentleman."

He raised his brows. "If you recall, Lady Sarah, you are the one who insisted on invading my bath time. You are the one who came to this house. With very little attempt at discretion, I might add."

She gave him back stare for stare. He had to admire her pluck.

"Ten thousand pounds is a vast deal of money," she observed. "I wonder if I am worth it."

Oh, she was worth it, all right. Still uncertain where he wanted this to lead, he continued to fence. "My lady, you are a diamond of the highest quality. No doubt you are aware of the fact."

She gave a tight smile. Her gloved hands clenched in her lap. "Then Brinsley would be a fool to accept a paltry ten thousand. Wouldn't he?"

Vane scarcely believed his ears. The jade had the unmitigated gall to try to drive up that ridiculous price? Just how desperate did she think he was?

Under Vane's hard scrutiny, Sarah found it difficult to come to the point. Ordinarily, she was no coward, nor was she averse to plain speaking. She possessed a large and varied vocabulary, so why, when he stared at her with those dark, endless eyes, did her tongue roll over and play dead, refuse to assemble the words?

She'd come here for a purpose, and that was not to watch Vane soak in his bathtub, however stimulating the activity might be. She'd come to throw his insulting offer in his face. Or at least, to discover whether he really intended to consign her to debtors' prison if she did not do as he wished.

And then throw his insulting offer in his face.

She hated Brinsley for putting her in this position. Despite all their hardships, despite the humiliation of his public infidelities and his lies, she'd never felt powerless before. She'd never submitted to any man. Not Brinsley, and certainly not Vane.

Now that she was here, she couldn't bring herself to discuss any of it. She was all but convinced Brinsley had fabricated those threats Vane was supposed to have made. If not for them, she never would have darkened Vane's door.

Sarah caught her bottom lip between her teeth. But now she was here, and there was still the matter of that ten thousand pounds. Vane had bargained for her like a costermonger or some money-grubbing cit. He'd just admitted it, bold as brass.

Yes, she owed Vane for that.

"Would you mind handing me the soap, Lady Sarah?"

She started. "Soap?"

"On the counterpane, next to the towel. I forgot to bring it with me."

She eyed the soap. Then she eyed him. Perhaps there was one way she could wreak her revenge without saying anything at all.

Sarah rose and moved unhurriedly to the bed. She trailed her fingertips along the gold and black striped counterpane and pressed down her palm, as though testing the ticking for firmness. She picked up the soap, felt him watch her as she raised it to her nose, closed her eyes, and sniffed.

Ah, that was it. His scent. Clean and fresh like an ocean breeze after a summer storm. A subtle hint of lemon.

At that familiar, longed-for scent, her resolution wavered. But only for an instant. She laid the soap down and put her hands to her pelisse.

Her trembling, glove-thickened fingers stumbled a little over the small buttons that marched down the fitted wool coat, but she must not remove her gloves and let him see her hands. Then he'd know she could no longer lay claim to gentility. One might always tell a lady by the softness of her hands.

She shrugged off the pelisse. Her chartreuse gown was old and plain, but well constructed from good-quality cambric. Not the most alluring garment, but given the state of Vane's obvious arousal, a more enticing ensemble was hardly required.

She laid the pelisse on the bed, took the soap, and moved to the side of the bath. Under her lashes, she glanced from Vane to the soap and back again, a clear question in the lift of her brow.

His lips compressed. Danger sparked in his dark eyes. He held out one hand. "Thank you."

She whipped the soap higher, just out of his reach. When he dropped his hand, looking wary, she forced a smile.

"Allow me."

He stared at her and held out his hand again, implacable despite his body's contrary response. "I don't think so."

All the heat drained from her cheeks. Nonplussed, she dropped the soap in his waiting palm and turned away to hide her confusion. Hurt seared her chest, pricked behind her eyes. She'd meant to punish him, make him burn and leave him wanting. It seemed she was the one being punished.

He did not want her, after all.

But now that she'd set the course, her foolish, suggestible body yearned to follow it. Sarah dragged in a breath. She desperately needed to collect her thoughts, gather the reins again, seize control.

With her back to him, she heard water slosh, and the slap of him soaping, lathering, and sluicing himself clean. She did not turn around, though the thought of his hands on his own body, skimming over the slickness of his wet, soaped skin, made her heart pound so hard it pained her chest. Her face burned as with fever.

She heard a loud whoosh and a creak of the tub, and realized he stood now. The fever entered her brain. She couldn't think. Why had she been taunting him? What madness had brought her here?

"The towel please, Lady Sarah, if you'd be so good."

With an effort, she forced her limbs to move, to cross the

room to the bed, pick up the wide linen towel, and turn back.

Her mouth dried. She'd never fainted before, but her over-wrought senses swam at the sight of that gleaming, damp body, limned by firelight. A fat drop of water fell from his hair, hit his shoulder, and streaked a path over one flat, brown nipple. Rivulets coursed between the hard plates of his chest, skipped down his ridged stomach.

"Here." She shoved the towel at him and turned her back. She was stupid to have come. She must get away.

She snatched up her pelisse and dragged the sleeves over her arms. It seemed to take forever for her fumbling fingers to button it to the throat. When she finished, she realized she'd done it wrongly. One missed eyelet left a gaping buckle of fabric at her breast, and somehow, the prospect of unbuttoning it all to begin again was too much.

A sob gathered in her chest, threatening to rise. She forced it down, battled the shudders that heaved through her so he would not see.

One missed button. Such a small failure in a life filled with monumental ones, and yet it cracked her rigid composure, made her want to throw herself on the bed and wail.

She felt his presence behind her. A hand touched her shoulder and she flinched.

"Don't cry." His voice was deep, rough with emotion she couldn't identify. "Please, there is no need."

Vane watched Lady Sarah stiffen, lift her chin. By God, she was a fighter. He'd give his soul to have her as his wife. For the thousandth time, he cursed that bastard husband of hers for meeting her first.

She turned slowly, dry-eyed. "I'm not crying. Why should I weep?"

Because your husband has degraded and humiliated you until you were prepared to do this, he thought. *Because you believe I would sink you further.*

He pulled her close, wrapped his arms around her, despite the resistance he felt in every line of her body. "Hush," he murmured, fighting his own body's aching need. "Just let me hold you."

But the towel around his waist did not conceal his arousal. She gasped as she brushed against his rigid flesh. So did he, but he ran a soothing hand down her back.

"You have nothing to fear from me. I'll do nothing you don't wish."

Vane wasn't sure she heard him. Her body shook in a final, heart-wrenching quake, and stilled.

For one long moment, all the air left the room.

Then her lips brushed his collarbone, soft as a sigh. The shock of that light, sensuous touch held him motionless, suspended between disbelief and the most powerful surge of desire he'd ever known.

When that fleeting kiss came again, Vane knew he hadn't been mistaken. He tightened his hold, and she melted against him, and her warmth and sweetness flowed around him, seeped into the deepest recesses of his soul.

He took her face between his hands, kissed those wicked, lost eyes closed, brushed a path to her mouth. Her sensuous, sinful mouth.

He groaned as he tasted her for the first time. Her breasts crushed against his chest and her mouth moved against his, and she gasped as his teeth tugged at her full bottom lip.

He lingered in their kiss as if he could draw out her essence and keep it, as if they had all the time in the world and not just this one solitary night. He freed her hair from its pins, made short work of all those buttons that seemed to give her so much trouble, eased the pelisse from her shoulders. When he drew the garment free and looked down, he saw her nipples outlined against the dampened bodice of her gown.

"Sarah."

Her hands were on him now, running along his shoulders, down his arms, smoothing over his back. She still wore gloves, and though he'd rather feel her, the slide of butter-soft kid against his skin was strangely erotic. Her breath came in short, low-pitched pants as he lifted away her shining dark hair and kissed her neck.

She choked and shivered, one hand on the back of his head, trapping him there. Tantalized, intoxicated by the elusive scent of lilies, he nipped the soft, white skin, felt the moan vibrate in her throat like the purr of a cat.

He undressed her with ruthless efficiency, kissing and touching every new inch of skin he revealed. He needed to be inside her so desperately he thought he might splinter into pieces, but he'd be a fool to rush her. This night, this one time, was his only chance to show Sarah how perfect they could be together. If only she'd be his, if only she'd stay.

A pang of tenderness flashed to burning need as her fingers raked down his back. She freed the towel from his waist, let it drop to the floor, and molded his buttocks with her hands.

Vane's mind blanked, the beast seized control, and everything became instinct, pure and simple. He ripped away the last scraps of her clothing, baring her breasts to his gaze. "Beautiful," he whispered, reverently tracing their shape. Dropping to his knees, he fastened his lips around one taut nipple and tasted, feasted. Worshipped her as he'd never thought he'd have the chance to do in this life.

Oh, no, please! Desperate at the tumult of sensation swirling inside her, Sarah writhed under Vane's hands. But he had her trapped against the massive bedpost, giving no quarter, allowing her no escape. He suckled her with firm, relentless pressure, and the pull of his mouth was an undertow in her blood, dragging her down, drowning her with wet heat and prickling sensation. Her loins throbbed in time with the rhythm of his tongue, and when he touched her there, matched the rhythm with one firm, probing finger, she cried out, bucked against his hand.

It was too much. She tried to twist away but he surged up and captured her mouth with his, holding her steady against the bedpost. Still, he touched between her legs. Teased, conjured exquisite, unbearable pleasure, so dark and consuming it terrified her even as she wanted more.

This was *Vane*. Vane, doing these things to her. She gasped. "I can't—"

He smothered her protest with his mouth, fingers insistent, working over her tender flesh. When she was silenced, too overwhelmed with colliding sensations to say more, his lips brushed against her cheek. "Stay with me, love. Oh, God, Sarah. Stay with me."

His words struck a chord deep within her, an answering longing, a desperate need she'd fought too long. She whimpered as the pressure inside her spiraled and coiled tight, then shudders racked her body over and over, and still he wouldn't let go. Unable to bear more of that intense, agonizing pleasure, she pushed him away.

The next moment, his hands settled at her waist, lifting her. He laid her on the bed and swiftly moved over her, kneeling between her legs. A thrill of fear shot through her at this sudden change of pace, but she dismissed it. She wanted this, him, inside her so badly she thought she'd die of it. She closed her eyes as he opened her, pushed into her a little way.

The sensation of stretching almost to a breaking point jerked her body from its sensual haze. It had been many years since she'd lost her virginity, yet she remembered the shock of tissue rending, the sting. Sarah shifted and squirmed to ease the way, tamping down her slight, unreasonable panic at the sheer size of him.

He seemed to gather himself, then gripped her hips and thrust. She cried out, in fear or delight, she didn't know. After a pause, he surged deeper, far deeper than she'd thought possible, until something inside her gave way in an explosion of pleasure bordering on pain.

Vane's dark eyes were glazed with heat, his face stretched taut, lips parted, shoulders shaking as he held still, accustoming her to his thick, iron-hard length.

The sight of his struggle filled her with a sense of feminine power, making all her doubts take flight.

She arched toward him, but he restrained her, held back. "Not yet."

He withdrew, then eased into her again, until she felt every inch of him, until his body covered hers. "Relax," he whispered in her hair. "Let it happen."

Let what happen? she wondered, but the hot, slow, sliding friction felt glorious, and her bones seemed to melt away, so she let him do as he willed, ran her hands down his back, shamelessly gripped his buttocks, tasted his groans as he kissed her, relished all his hard maleness, wished she could feel the texture of his skin through her gloves.

She's still wearing those gloves, he thought vaguely, but her lush, wet heat enveloped him, tight as any glove and he didn't care. He focused all his will on holding back until she was ready. They might only have this one night, but he'd make sure it was a night she'd never forget. She would feel him in her blood until the day she died, just as he knew he would feel her.

So as he thrust steadily into her, sensed the changes in her, watched for the signs, he pondered all the least erotic subjects he could think of. Calculated the amount of money he had invested in the funds, named each winner of the Derby as far back as he could remember, recited passages from Horace and Virgil he'd learned at Eton as a boy.

But as her head thrashed from side to side and her brow puckered as if she searched for something just outside her reach, as her breathing grew labored and small sobbing sighs escaped her, he increased the pace, and she held him and stayed with him until their bodies clashed together and she convulsed and tightened and pulsed around him, strong, insistent, irresistible as the tide.

The world went black, and as she cried out, he hurled himself over the edge, fell through space and shattered on the stars, spilled himself inside her.

It was the most perfect moment of his life.

How could he sleep? Sarah lay on white silk sheets beside him, winding a lock of hair around her finger. Her body still sang with the memory of his.

Afterward, Vane had tried to speak, but she'd pressed her fingertips against his lips, not wanting to break the strange spell of contentment. He'd lain beside her and stared into her eyes for a long time in silence, perhaps waiting for her to change her mind. Eventually, he turned down the coverlet and pinched out a few candles before he clasped her hand and collapsed into slumber.

After a few minutes, she'd eased free.

She still wore her gloves, stockings, and garters. Her slippers had fallen off at some stage or she would still be wearing them, too.

The fire had died to sullen embers and the night air chilled her. But when she glanced at Vane, an unfamiliar warmth flooded her chest.

She gave a faint smile. He would probably sleep through a blizzard. She crawled to the foot of the bed, where the coverlet bunched at his feet, and pulled it over him. He remained so still, she looked closer to make sure he breathed. Even with his hard features softened in slumber, they stirred her.

Dangerously tempted, she unbuttoned her right glove. She tugged each finger loose, stripped it off, and laid it on the bedside table. She rose onto her knees, swept her hair behind her shoulder, and bent over him. Holding her breath, she reached out and traced the sleek line of an eyebrow.

When he did not rouse, or move in the slightest, she grew bolder, touched trembling fingertips to his firm, parted lips. The gesture felt more intimate than anything else they had done.

Suddenly, his hand gripped hers and pressed her palm against his mouth for a kiss. She gasped, fear and desire shooting through her in equal measure. His lids drifted open and he stared into her eyes. She tried to draw her toil-roughened hand away but he trapped it in his own, caressing her bare palm with his thumb.

Vane's straight, black brows snapped together. He raised himself on one elbow, spread her hand open, and tilted it to the dim light afforded by the lamp he'd left burning at the bedside.

His widened, shocked gaze lifted to hers, and her stomach clenched in pain, as if he'd driven his fist into it. He'd seen the ugly scarring on her hands. Now, he knew what she'd become. With that foolish, weak need to touch him, to feel him with no barrier between them, she'd destroyed everything.

Her mind lurched, pulled up short.

Destroy what? There was nothing to destroy.

Without a sound, he yanked her into his arms, and his mouth was hard on hers, demanding, and even while the heat and yearning swelled within her, she felt she was being sullied. Used.

Incredibly, she had not felt like that when he had taken her before. The experience had been so perilously close to heaven, its piercing brilliance had cast sordid reality aside.

But now, his powerful, almost desperate possession wrenched her conscience from its slumber. For the first time, she remembered. She was an adulteress and a whore.

And he had made her so.

Four

LOST. Utterly lost.

Even as guilt and shame lashed her with sharp, stinging cuts, even as she despised herself and Vane—most especially Vane, for doing this to her, for making her need him, for *making her feel*—her treacherous lips answered the passionate question on his.

A resounding, unequivocal *yes.*

He wasn't gentle, but he didn't need to be. If he'd been tender like the first time, he would have broken her. Thank God he didn't know it, or she'd never be free.

He kissed her with a force that snapped her head back, gathered her tighter in his arms, enveloping her in muscled strength. The big hands roving her body could crush her, but the knowledge did not frighten her as it should.

Against her will, against all reason, she felt protected, safe. A heady sensation for one who'd stood alone so many years.

Anguished, craving him, knowing it was wrong, she couldn't stop, couldn't resist that masculine power that was quintessentially Vane.

But she *could* make him feel some of her agony.

Like a cornered vixen, she turned on him, bore him back against the headboard, nipped and scratched and licked his wounds, then scored them again.

He groaned and shuddered, arched into her mouth as she bit his throat, threw his head back when she ripped his chest with her nails. She took one nipple between her teeth and tugged with just enough pressure to make him bunch his fist in her hair and moan.

He gripped her hair as she slid lower, grazing her teeth down the ridged stomach, aware of his erection nudging her, big and hard below. Her breast brushed the swollen shaft.

On a strangled groan, he put his hands on her waist, pulling her up for a kiss. With a buck of the hips, he rolled and pinned her, flat on her back, helpless beneath him.

Vane fought to master himself, but for once, his iron will proved too weak to cage the fierce passion, the rage and hopeless longing that twisted and strained inside.

It was as if her damaged hands, the final evidence of Brinsley's cruelty and neglect, had broken his last link with civilized behavior. She'd caught this wildness and fed it with her own, driving him to the pinnacle of torment and desire. Now, all he could do was slake his need, and trust she could handle the man that he was, the beast he could be.

He pinned her wrists above her head with one hand, nudged her legs apart and thrust into her. Only blind luck found her ready for him, slick, hot, lush, everything he desired.

A soft beat in his brain urged him to think of her, her needs, her pleasure, but the beast gave no quarter. He thrust in a strong, selfish rhythm, then gripped her hips and tilted them so he could stroke deeper.

With a long moan that was almost a sob, she wrapped her legs around his waist and moved against him. The rasp of a stockinged foot skimming his buttock nearly shot him to oblivion, but he hung on, determined to stay inside her as long as he could, as if by maintaining that intimate connection he could keep the morning, his conscience, the rest of the world at bay.

He cupped her bottom as he slid into her, ran his hand up the thigh that clamped his hip. The satin ridge of her garter beneath his fingers made him gasp and hold still, jaw clenched, a pulse throbbing in his temple as he battled the threatened rush of ecstasy.

Breathing so hard he thought his lungs might explode, he opened his eyes to look at her, at the parted lips swollen with kisses, at her soft, dark hair fanned beneath her head and spilling over milk white shoulders, at the high, firm breasts with their delicious pink nipples. He stroked into her more powerfully still and she thrashed her head and cried out, her eyes closed in a look of agonized delight.

The sight of the icy Lady Sarah writhing in pleasure beneath him, the feel of her hot, wet sheath gripping him, drawing him in, filled Vane with pure, masculine triumph. Finally, he'd breached her defenses, conquered her resistance.

With an effort at control that made his teeth clench and his whole body tremble, he slid out of her with excruciating slowness, inch by inch. With a sobbing gasp, she threw her head back, exposing her lovely neck. He bent to her and nipped the skin there with his teeth and felt her shiver and quake around him.

"Oh, yes."

The hot whisper in his ear shredded his thin veil of control. He pumped his hips fast and hard, barely registered her climax before his own ripped through his body and burst into hers. He collapsed, shuddering, and rolled to the side.

His heart still thundered in the distance.

"SARAH. Sarah, speak to me."

Fighting craven, useless tears, she shrugged his hand from her shoulder. "I don't know what you want me to say."

With her back to him and the sheet pulled over her, she glared at the window opposite, at the crack in the heavy damask curtains, thinking of what lay beyond. Brinsley. Their shabby rooms. Her family. Society.

How could she face them? How could she live with what she'd done?

Because it hadn't been just once, a few moments of madness in which real life faded to nothing. She'd repeated her offense, this time fully aware of her infidelity, that she'd sold herself like a common slut in the stews.

His deep voice sounded too close. "I want you to say you'll leave him. I want you to come to me."

"Be your mistress, you mean." Her own voice was pleasingly cold and hard.

"It wouldn't be like that."

"I am married. Brinsley is my husband. How else could it be?"

His fingers traced a curl behind her ear, feathered a path down her nape. Sarah stiffened, fighting the thrills that shivered down her spine. She couldn't let him see how he moved her.

She strangled a bitter laugh. How could he not see it? She hadn't exactly lain like an effigy beneath him when they'd made love, had she?

It would be so easy for him to persuade her to stay. Even now, with those gentle, clever fingers stroking her skin, she felt her resolution melting, slipping away.

He kissed her nape and a spear of longing shot through her. She didn't want to look at him, didn't want to see the naked desire in those dark eyes, the raw need that ravaged his face.

And know it was mirrored in her own.

Desperately, she clung to the thought of that ten thousand pounds, held herself stiff and unyielding as his lips brushed her shoulder, their heat branding her skin.

She must go. She must not stay here and suffer this delicate assault. It seemed wildly improbable that a man so tender and careful could have bought her, bargained for her with her own husband without sparing a thought for how he degraded her by doing it.

But he had. He'd told her so, and that should give her the strength for what she needed to do.

As if in answer to her prayers, suddenly she saw thin, watery light filter through the sliver between the curtains.

Morning.

HE watched her rise from the bed, walk to the window, and peer out, one hand raised to draw the curtain a little aside.

Her silky dark hair rippled halfway down her back—no modern crop for Lady Sarah. His gaze lowered to her slender waist, slim hips, and those amazing legs still sheathed in sheer white stockings tied with delectable, pink-ribboned garters. Her bottom was rounded, pert perfection. His mind slid to other positions they might try.

God, he was an animal. He needed to *think*, persuade her to stay, or there'd be no time left for them at all. Even now, dawn caressed the soft curve of her breast as she stood framed by gold damask and brocade.

He would not let her go.

Before he could speak, she left the window, rounded the bed, and bent to pick up something from the floor. It was her shift. She shook it out and threw it over her head. With an expert flick of her hips that made him swallow hard against desire, she let it fall. Without glancing at him, she tied the ribbon at her bosom.

"What are you doing?"

"Getting dressed. I am going home."

He launched out of bed as she gathered up her gown. He gripped her wrist before she could put it on.

"Stay." Reaching out with his other hand, he tilted her chin so she had to look him in the eye. "Stay with me."

She flinched, though she couldn't escape his grip on her wrist. In a clenched, gritty voice, she said, "One night is all you get for your money, I'm afraid."

For an instant, her words confused him. "All I—?"

She returned his stare with an insolent flex of her brows. "One night," she repeated. "For your ten thousand pounds."

He barely stopped himself from gaping. He'd told her the

truth about that, hadn't he? Didn't she know he'd refused Brinsley's offer? He frowned, trying to remember all the words that had tumbled from his lips in the course of the night. He'd taken her with no thought of that filthy commerce in his head.

But she . . .

A cruel little smile curled her lips, and only then did the real truth dawn on him like the pale, crisp light of day. His first surmise those few hours ago had been correct. She did know he'd refused Brinsley. Seduction had always been her aim.

He stood there, naked to the skin, chilled to the marrow, freezing from the inside out, and knew a faint inkling of gratitude that the bitter chill holding him immobile lent him the appearance of composure. Still, his mind floundered. He had no voice, no words, no defense just then. At that moment, the world was black and the dawn far away.

She slipped free of his slackened grasp and turned to put on her gown. That venom green gown. Poison, like her eyes. Like everything she was.

Through the ice seeped anger and disgust and self-recrimination. How shaming, how unutterably sordid, that his life had come to this. Abasing himself before a ruthless, heartless baggage, a woman no better than a bit of muslin selling her wares at Covent Garden, for all her airs and graces.

No, she was worse than that. At least those doxies didn't pretend to give their favors freely. At least they didn't hoodwink their clients into thinking it was love.

Well, she might have betrayed and deceived him, but she would not best him in this fight. "I'm afraid you've chosen your mark unwisely, madam," he drawled. "I made no agreement."

Her gaze flew to his. "Brinsley—"

"Your pimp, d'you mean?" He flashed a dangerous smile, noting the angry flush that rose to her cheeks. "Or perhaps you prefer the term *procurer*? Far more elegant, I agree. But I'm sure you already know what transpired between Brinsley and me. And I don't recall you insisting on payment when I had you against that bedpost."

Small, white teeth bit into her plump lower lip. The green eyes grew bright.

"Ah, now come the tears," he mocked. "The only element lacking from your earlier performance. But you were so clever, weren't you, Lady Sarah, letting my fevered imagination do your work for you? To think I actually pictured you the injured party in all this."

She threw back her head and glared down her nose at him. He'd never seen a woman more magnificent, couldn't help but admire her, even as her venom pumped through his veins, constricted his heart.

Her voice dripped disdain as she buttoned her pelisse. "If you wish to haggle like a merchant, I suggest you address yourself to Brinsley. You and I have nothing more to discuss."

He frowned. Was it his imagination, or had her voice trembled on the last words?

Gathering up the rest of her undergarments, Sarah wrapped them in a bundle. She made as if to sweep past him, but he caught her elbow. "How did you get here tonight? Is your carriage waiting?"

"I hired a hackney. I'll take one home." She stared at his hand as if it were a slug, as if it hadn't stroked every soft inch of her a short while ago, as if she hadn't reveled in that touch. Her pleasure, at least, had been real. He couldn't be mistaken about that.

Could he?

He cleared his throat. "Permit me to convey you home."

"What? Arrive at this hour in a carriage with your crest on the panel? I don't think so, my lord."

He returned her haughty glare with interest. "I don't flaunt my crest on my carriages. You'll be anonymous, and safe." When she still looked skeptical, he added gruffly, "I don't like the thought of you out alone at this hour. Indulge me in this . . . if nothing else."

She seemed to have trouble meeting his eyes. Quietly, she said, "Very well. Thank you, my lord."

The impulse to go with her, to use the short drive to

Bloomsbury to try once more to persuade her, was one he swiftly quelled. Begging would only rate her scorn. They were finished.

They had never begun.

He rang for Rivers to show her out and watched the door close behind a flash of green.

Then he turned to his empty room, where the scent of her still lingered, and a kid glove lay on the bedside table like an unfinished prayer.

Five

SEVERAL excruciating minutes passed before the carriage was brought around from the mews. Sarah spent them pacing the empty drawing room downstairs. She couldn't have lasted a second longer in that bedchamber with Vane, but the drawing room afforded slender relief. Had she chosen the wiser course and awaited Vane there instead of following him upstairs, her life might be quite different now.

Had she wanted this all along? Had she gone to his bedchamber knowing in her heart what the outcome would be? What a fool *not* to predict the result of such an intimate encounter. How willfully, wantonly stupid!

But she'd been so secure in her pride, so smug and self-righteous in her determination to honor her marriage vows, she'd thought herself immune from Vane. If only he'd set out to seduce her from the start, she would have been prepared, capable of rejecting him.

But he'd waited, with a patience that showed a true master of seduction. He'd displayed himself to her like a male peacock, strutting in all his naked glory, but he hadn't allowed her to touch him, pretended disinterest to fuel her desire. The tension had mounted to an unbearable pitch, but instead of trying to force the issue, he'd held back. Killed her with compassion and silent understanding. Offered her comfort, not humiliation. Or so she'd thought.

But now, she realized it was not only her body that he had violated, with her as a willing participant. He had touched her heart, reached into her soul, struck a massive blow to her pride. Then asked her to stay for more.

She'd been tempted—unbearably, wrenchingly tempted. She could never forgive him for that. She could never forgive herself.

Once in the carriage, Sarah closed her eyes and leaned back against the blue velvet squabs, the luxury a powerful reminder of what she left behind, what she'd refused when she rejected Vane's offer.

The smell of sex on her body nauseated her, filled her with shame. She wished she'd had the chance to wash before she left.

How would Brinsley react to her betrayal? Would he rub his hands together and await the banker's draft that must follow, despite Vane's harsh denial of an agreement? Or would his conscience finally prick him? Would he be jealous, angry even? He had loved her once, she knew. As deeply as a man like Brinsley could love anyone.

She'd often wondered whether a child might have made a difference to them, but it seemed she was barren, for she'd never conceived. Sarah spread her hand over her flat stomach. She knew the fault lay with her. Tom's existence was proof of that.

Sarah shivered. Useless to dwell on their past. She must try to carve out some reasonable future, or why go on? Somehow, she must work for peace between her and Brinsley, or a truce at least. Her former scheme to leave him seemed irrelevant now she'd become as great a sinner as him. If she'd found the strength to resist Vane, it would be another matter entirely.

But she'd be foolish to hope Brinsley would ever change.

There was little for her now except to tread her lonely path, selling her perfume to make ends meet. Perhaps one day, one of Brinsley's fund-raising schemes might succeed. She hoped he didn't think her body would make his fortune. She would rather die than pursue that course.

Her lips twisted. No. She would rather grovel to Mama.

The countess had criticized Brinsley almost from the beginning of Sarah's marriage. As a new bride still floating on dreams of love, Sarah had taken violent exception to her mother's jibes. She'd said things, hurled accusations she wished now she'd never voiced, even if they were true.

Later, when the state of Sarah's marriage had become too threadbare to mend, the countess had refused to step in unless Sarah apologized to her on bended knee. Sarah had preferred to starve rather than go cap in hand to her mother, begging for charity. The years had fled; the reasons for their estrangement no longer mattered. They were locked in a stalemate, borne of stubborn pride.

And while all this had happened, her father had stood apart, remote and untouched by it all. His indifference had hurt Sarah the most.

The carriage halted. Sarah assumed she was home, but she dared not draw the curtains in case she attracted attention. When the door opened, she darted across the pavement and up the steps like a mouse to its hole, fumbling in her reticule for the latchkey.

But she didn't need it. The street door stood slightly ajar.

Thankful for that small boon, Sarah slipped inside and trod lightly up the stairs to the second floor.

VANE galloped his horse through the watercolor dawn as if the Devil were at his heels. He shook his head. A man less inclined to excessive passions and impulsiveness might have taken his luxurious barge to his Richmond estate—a far more convenient and comfortable mode of transport. But the need for physical activity had never been stronger. Nor had the need for escape.

He slowed to a trot through awakening city streets, the clatter of hooves on cobbles echoing the throb in his brain. He wove among orange sellers, hawkers and drays, street sweepers and urchins. He rode hard at a group of young bloods staggering an erratic path home from a night of revelry, scattering them like skittles as they leaped free of trampling hooves. Anything to distract him from the pain.

When they met open fields, he let Tiros fly and they thundered away from London, away from her. The mud churned under the gelding's hooves and the countryside passed in a rush of damp wind and a blur of lush green.

But no matter how fast they went, no matter how hard he tried, he couldn't rid himself of the image of those wicked, merciless eyes the same green as the hedgerows, of her scent that still clung to him no matter how vigorously he'd scrubbed in that ice-cold bath, of the husky voice telling him he'd got what he paid for. No more.

Each new sense of her was like brandy on an open wound. He wished it had never happened, wished he'd thrown her out when he'd had the chance. It had been so much safer, that hopeless, almost idle longing, a dull kind of pain he'd learned to live with, one that flared from time to time when he saw her, or when someone mentioned her name, but one he'd never allowed to control him.

Last night, he'd thrown off his armor, shed his skin, laid himself open, raw and vulnerable. And she'd ripped his vitals out, plunged a dagger in his heart.

Did she know what she'd done? He prayed she had no idea how much, how greatly he cared for her. If he hadn't cared, he would never have allowed her to stay in his house. Strong though the temptation might have been, if lust had been all that drew him to her, he would have sent her away without a second thought. He would never have considered accepting Brinsley Cole's foul proposal only to slake his carnal appetites. He valued his honor far more than a tumble between the sheets with a beautiful woman, no matter how desirable she might be.

But he had cared. Far too much. Now, he was well served

for losing his grip on himself, for trying to banish the desolation he'd glimpsed in her eyes.

He must have imagined that look, or perhaps she was that good an actress, he didn't know. All he knew was that it was over. That brief, soaring exaltation, the conviction that he and she were connected, that she belonged to him, no matter what promises she had made in St George's, Hanover Square, evaporated like the morning mist. She had betrayed him, humiliated him, shredded his soul to pieces. Left him to doubt he would ever find happiness or even contentment again.

Damn those pitiless green eyes to hell. Damn the rest of her, too.

Most of all, damn *him* for being the worst kind of besotted fool.

PAUSING on the landing before the final flight of steps, Sarah heard voices. One, a deep rumble. Not Brinsley's. One, a piping shrill she recognized. Mrs. Higgins, her landlady. An excitable woman at the best of times, but now, her strident voice held an edge of hysteria.

The rent wasn't due for another week, and even then, Brinsley could usually charm their susceptible landlady to wait until he could pay. Good Lord, what was going on?

She hurried upstairs and opened the door.

"Brinsley!" The cry ripped from her throat, tore through the landlady's wails.

He sprawled on the sofa, his chest covered in blood. White to the lips, Brinsley lay with his eyes closed, his breath a labored, gurgling wheeze. A middle-aged man she'd never seen before held a blood-soaked pad of cloth to the wound in Brinsley's chest.

The world slowed to a heartbeat. Sarah felt as if she were floating, drowning, water cushioning her ears against sound. She swayed and gripped the arm of a nearby chair for support.

Blood everywhere. The wall, splattered crimson. God, the smell.

He must be dying. Anyone who lost that much blood must surely die. She couldn't move her feet.

Then Mrs. Higgins's screech pierced the strange bubble that cocooned her.

"Murderess! That's her. She done it. That's the one!"

"Brinsley." Breathing his name, Sarah staggered forward with her hands stretched out, almost tripping over a footstool that stood in her way.

Ignoring the stranger's mutter of disapproval, she dropped to her knees beside him and took his hand, slippery with blood.

"Brinsley, you cannot die. I forbid it, do you hear me?" She spoke in a vehement whisper. It was stupid to think she could command him in this, but he had often knuckled down when she spoke to him in that tone.

His lids fluttered open. His eyes rolled, then focused on her. "Sar—"

"Yes, I'm here." Her lips trembled. She looked up at the stranger, a fearful question in her eyes. Slowly, he shook his head.

Her vision swam in tears, but she saw Brinsley move his mouth, trying to speak. His breath had so little force. She couldn't hear what he said.

"Brin, who did this? Who shot you?"

The clasp of his hand grew stronger. "Can't . . ." He wheezed a painful breath. "Vane. Did you . . . ?"

The question stabbed her conscience, lanced it like a boil. All the foul matter spilled out, sickening her. God, the things she had done while Brinsley lay dying! Her stomach lurched but she choked down the burning bile.

She watched him straining, struggling to hold on to life. She had to lie. She could not let him depart the world with his wife's lurid confession of adultery ringing in his ears.

Biting her lip so hard she tasted blood, she shook her head. "No." Her voice broke on the word.

"Good." He took another slow, ragged breath. "Glad." His fingers clenched on hers and he swallowed painfully. "Sorry, Sare. Made a damned . . . mess of us. . . ." He turned those blue eyes to her, with that angelic expression that she had steeled herself so many years ago to resist, the one that implored her to forgive.

"Oh, *God*." She bowed her head and wept in earnest, tears pouring down her cheeks, running into her mouth. "It doesn't matter now. It doesn't matter anymore."

She hardly knew who should forgive whom. She wanted to tell him she loved him, but the words wouldn't come. Too great a hypocrisy, even for her.

He dropped her hand and with another sobbing sigh, squeezed his eyes shut. He seemed to want to block her out, as if he needed to rest, or could no longer bear her presence. She couldn't tell which.

Dashing the tears away with the back of her blood-streaked hand, she rose and spoke in an urgent, low voice to the stranger. "Are you a doctor? Is there anything we can do?"

Mrs. Higgins scoffed. "That's no doctor. He's the watch, that's what 'e is! Called him meself when I heard the shot. You leave that poor boy alone! Haven't you done enough this night?" She turned to the man, arms akimbo. "Arrest her, sirrah! What're you waiting for?"

Sarah sent her a searing glare. "Be quiet, you stupid woman! Of course I didn't murder my husband. Can't you see I'm trying to help him? He needs medical attention and you're shrieking and carrying on and doing nothing to the purpose." She started for the door. "I'm going to fetch the doctor."

The watchman put his hand on her arm and shook his head. "He's done for. The missus here is right. It's my bound duty to take you in, Mrs. Cole, on suspicion of murder."

Her eyes widened. "*What?*"

"Come with me, please."

Sarah stared at the blocky, shabbily dressed individual, and then at her landlady. Higgins was agog with macabre anticipation, like the sort of woman who'd knitted at the guillotine. This could not be happening. First Brinsley, and now they thought she'd murdered him?

She tried to remain calm, clutching at the clear proof of

her innocence. "I wasn't even here. I—" She stopped as the watchman licked the point of his pencil and began to write. She couldn't admit she'd been with another man, with Vane, when her husband was shot. Panic rose to grip her throat.

"Is this your pistol?" The watchman eyed her closely.

She caught the acrid whiff of gunpowder as he held out a small silver pistol. The one she had loaded earlier that night . . .

Her pistol had killed Brinsley? The room spun around her. She closed her eyes and gritted her teeth, willing back her self-control.

She opened her eyes. "Yes," she said. "That is mine."

"Aha!" cackled Mrs. Higgins. "Told you, didn't I?"

"But that doesn't mean I fired it!" The small world of their parlor seemed increasingly bizarre. Foreign. As if everyone were speaking a language she didn't understand. How could they accuse her of killing her own husband? It didn't make sense.

"Heard them arguing tonight, and all." Higgins peered over the watchman's shoulder, making sure he wrote down what she said. Sarah could have boxed her ears, the malevolent harpy.

Struggling to remain calm, she repeated, "I wasn't *here*."

"Strange time of night to be from home, ain't it, ma'am? Can someone vouch for your whereabouts?"

The question slammed into her like a prizefighter's fist. Her stomach churned. She dropped her gaze. She couldn't tell him about the night she'd spent with Vane. Even if she could bring herself to relate that sordid tale, the marquis would see her hang before he'd corroborate her story.

"No," she whispered. "There is no one."

"Well, then, ma'am. You'd best come along wiv me."

Sarah almost gave way to despair. She stared at Brinsley. His chest did not rise as strongly as before.

"But he's not—he hasn't even . . ." She raised her pleading gaze to the watchman's homely face. "Please. Let me stay until he's gone."

"She wants to make sure she finishes him off!" screeched

Mrs. Higgins, her pinched face mottled red, as if she'd scoured it with a scrubbing brush. "You didn't oughter let her within five paces of him. I'll report you to your superiors, I will!"

The watchman looked tired. "She's right, I'm afraid. We must go."

He made as if to take Sarah's elbow but she shook him off and hurried to stand by the sofa. Inwardly cringing, she said, "Do you know who I am? My father is the Earl of Straghan, and he will have you dismissed for such rank incompetence when he hears about this. If you don't let me stay, I shall make certain of it."

She thought she'd succeeded rather well in adopting her mother's haughty tone. But the man glanced around at the dingy parlor, then made a leisurely survey of her own genteel shabbiness and raised a skeptical eyebrow. Clearly, he doubted she had any connection, blood or otherwise, to an earl.

He crossed the room and took her arm in a firm grip. "Come along, madam, nice and quiet-like. Don't want any trouble, now, do we?" A grin flickered. "Daughter of an earl should know better than to cause a nasty scene."

A choking gurgle made her twist in the watchman's grasp and look back. With a last, violent shudder, Brinsley stilled, his mouth open, blue eyes staring.

Mrs. Higgins bent forward to close his eyes in a gentle gesture that was almost loving. She straightened and shot Sarah a look filled with malice. "I'll see you in Newgate for this, *my lady*, and I'll be glad to watch you hang."

Six

THE cell was dank and freezing, occupied by three loud, slatternly women Sarah took to be the lowest kind of whores. A fitting place for her, then.

She sat in the farthest corner of the room on a wooden bench, fighting the urge to tuck her feet under her in case rats lurked in the deep shadows along the damp, grey stone wall.

The cold numbed her body enough to quell the rank nausea she'd experienced on the journey to the watchhouse. But it did nothing to dam the images that flooded her mind.

She kept picturing Brinsley lying dead on the sofa where he'd sat taunting her only before. The bright smear of red behind him on the wall. Her pistol, gleaming wickedly in her hand, winking at her, as if she were an accomplice in its dreadful deed.

Guilt suffocated her when she thought of the night she'd spent with Vane. She closed her eyes, as if she could block out the image of Vane's powerful body moving, straining over hers, or her hair flowing around him, shrouding them as she bent to kiss his hard, uncompromising mouth; the jut of his chin as she nipped the shadowed skin of his throat; his groans, hot and heavy in her ear. The scent of him, fresh soap from his bath, and later, musky and slick with sweat.

Her hand, slick with blood.

She shuddered.

"Cold are yer, luv?" A tin flask was thrust under her nose. "Get some o' that into yer."

Sarah struggled not to recoil from the pungent fumes. She looked up to see a round, fleshy face, its shrewd brown eyes regarding her with something approaching kindness.

Strange. Twenty-four hours ago, she would have looked through this woman as if she didn't exist, swept her skirts aside in high-bred disdain to avoid touching her. Now, she said, "Thank you, but I don't drink spirits, Miss . . . er . . ."

"Ooh-er, listen to Lady Muck!" Though the tart's words were malicious, her tone was indulgent. She shrugged and walked back to her cohorts, wide hips swinging a jaunty rhythm.

Sarah inhaled deeply and repressed a shudder. The watch-house cell smelled like unwashed bodies and rising damp and other, more unpleasant odors she'd rather not think about. How long would they keep her here? If only someone with half a brain would listen to her. If only she might explain.

She remembered the grisly fate her landlady had promised. It wouldn't come to that, surely. They couldn't hang someone on the scant evidence against her. And even if they could, her father would not allow it. Estranged they might be, but the Earl of Straghan would never suffer his daughter to be had up for murder.

Yet, how could she send word to him, even were she permitted to do so? How could she tell him the sordid truth about where she'd been when Brinsley was shot?

She closed her eyes and imagined how her father would look, what he would say. He was not a man given to expressing his feelings, nor even to letting them show on his face. But she would know that behind that impassive, patrician façade, he was bitterly disappointed in her. Her mother would say it served her well for marrying Brinsley.

No, she must find her own way out of this coil. And without involving her father, a member of Liverpool's cabinet, a peer of the realm.

On her arrival, she'd reasserted her innocence, but the watchman had told her she must wait for the magistrate's verdict later in the morning. The beak would decide whether the charges against her might be proven and commit her for trial.

Sarah worked her lower lip between her teeth. She ought to retain legal counsel in such a serious matter, but sending word to the family solicitor would guarantee her father's involvement, something she must avoid. And without her family's support, she couldn't afford to hire anyone else to represent her.

Squeezing her eyes shut, she tried to think of a way, but instead of solutions, pointless recriminations ran through her mind. If only she hadn't left her pistol loaded. If only she'd been home, where she ought to have stayed, perhaps Brinsley wouldn't have been murdered. In that case, she was not only adulteress and whore, but responsible for her husband's death.

Her stomach lurched. If she'd been home, would she have been killed also? Who *could* have murdered Brinsley. Why?

Heavy footsteps approached. The cell door rattled for an unconscionably long time. Her tension rose with every moment. Finally, the door opened.

Sarah squinted against the lamplight that outlined a tall, dark figure. The light was behind him, so she could make out nothing but his shape.

"Lady Sarah?" A low-pitched, genteel voice spoke.

She could barely summon the breath to respond. "Yes?"

The figure turned back to retrieve the lamp from his attendant and advanced into the cell.

Buttery light flickered over his face, and when she made out the familiar features, she gasped. "Peter! But how—"

"Not now." Her brother-in-law darted a meaningful glance at the other occupants of the cell and Sarah fell silent. Peter Cole held out his hand. "You must come with me."

Nothing made sense, but Sarah was so grateful to leave those awful conditions, she asked no more questions, simply took Peter's hand and rose to follow him. She barely heard the catcalls and lewd jests from the other women in the cell.

Did this mean her release or was it a temporary reprieve? Whatever the case, she could have cried with joy at seeing Peter's familiar face.

As they left the prison, Sarah summoned her wits and tried to fathom this latest development in the nightmare of the past night. Brinsley and Peter had never been on the best of terms, and Sarah herself had only met Brinsley's brother on a handful of occasions.

Peter Cole was everything Brinsley wasn't—industrious, principled, and honorable. He was some kind of clerk at the Home Office, or so Brinsley had said, scoffing at his upright brother and his political aspirations. No wonder Peter wished to distance himself from Brinsley. The tawdry life of an inveterate gamester and womanizer would not reflect well on a civil servant with ambitions to rise in Parliament.

She glanced at Peter's profile—not nearly as handsome as Brinsley's, and with a gravity about his mouth and jaw that contrasted sharply with his brother's sensual lineaments. A dependable face. Peter Cole, unlike his late brother, was someone she could trust.

Outside, Sarah breathed the morning air deeply into her lungs and expelled it with a thankful sigh. Peter took her elbow and hurried her to a waiting carriage.

As soon as the door closed on them, Sarah turned to him, gripping her hands together. "Peter, I don't know how you come to be here, or where you are taking me, but you must believe me. I did not kill Brinsley. I swear I did not."

Peter shook his head. "Of course you didn't. Of course not. And what they were about, putting an earl's daughter in a common cell, I can't imagine. What would your esteemed father say if he knew?"

Sarah's gaze flew to his. "You didn't send word to the earl? Please tell me you didn't."

He shifted a little. "No. I was going to as soon as I heard. But my superior at the Home Office ordered me to bring you into his offices for questioning before informing your father."

He paused, and she wondered whether it was to quell his emotions. Surely he must feel something at his brother's passing? But he continued, "Of course, we cannot allow it to become public, at least not until we are certain of the facts. Don't want the broadsheets getting hold of a scandal like this."

"But how do you propose to stop news from getting out?" asked Sarah. "There were witnesses."

"We will take care of them," said Peter. "It won't be easy, of course, but it can be done."

Sarah swallowed hard, averting her gaze. It seemed Peter was less concerned with the fact of Brinsley's death than the manner of concealing it. For her father's sake and her own, she ought to be grateful. But she was appalled.

"Don't they mean to investigate the murder?" she said, careful to keep her tone neutral. "I imagine a trial would bring everything out into the open. How could you stop it then?"

"Even the Home Office cannot save you from a murder charge if there is evidence to support it, my lady," he said, misinterpreting the reason behind her question. "*I* don't believe you did it, of course." He paused. "My superior might be harder to convince."

"Peter, I wasn't even there! I told the watchman as much but he didn't believe me." Sarah shivered. "And while you are all wasting time with me, the real killer is still on the loose."

Quickly, Peter said, "Do you suspect someone?"

She shook her head. "I was unacquainted with most of Brinsley's associates. I am led to believe that some of them were unsavory characters, but he didn't mention them or introduce them to me. I am sorry I can't be more helpful."

"We've searched your rooms." At her startled look, he said, "It had to be done. We found nothing that might point us in the right direction, however. Is there anywhere else Brinsley might have kept important papers or correspondence? Anywhere else we might look?"

Sarah bit her lip. "Not that I'm aware. But then I expect I'd have been the last to know."

"Lady Sarah, it's imperative that we know everything if we want to catch this killer. You will tell me if you remember something, won't you?"

"Yes, of course." She blew out a breath. "I daresay I am still too shocked by his death to think clearly."

Peter paused, apparently absorbed in smoothing the wrinkles from his gloves. When he lifted his gaze to hers, she saw a shimmer in his grey eyes. "Poor Brinsley," he said. "The poor, stupid fool."

VANE arrived at Lyon House, hardly knowing how he got there. The last few miles had passed unnoticed, but somehow he must have steered Tiros in the right direction, for here he was, approaching the lodge on his Richmond estate.

Quelling a sudden urge to wheel about and keep riding straight to the Devil, he nodded to Ned, the gatekeeper, and rode Tiros through the gates.

Ordinarily, this old redbrick house with its turrets and tall chimneys and oriole windows embraced him with the comforting warmth of childhood memories. While his father lived, his parents had spent each Season in the Mayfair town house, close to Parliament. The children had always stayed here, away from the bustle and noxious air of London but still within easy reach of their doting mama. Lyon House was not Vane's principal estate, but the one most beloved of them all. Which explained why the family continued to gravitate here, rather than to the grander house at Bewley.

Today, the welcoming aspect of the house did nothing to lighten his mood. In fact, he shouldn't have come here at all. He wasn't fit for company today.

A lackey ran from the house to take Vane's sweating horse. Banbury, the butler, stood at the door and permitted himself a smile in welcome.

Vane nodded and returned the smile, though his face nearly cracked with the effort. "The family is in residence, I take it?"

"Yes, my lord." Banbury beamed. "All of them."

"*All* of them?" Frowning, Vane handed Banbury his hat and gloves. "Oh, dear God."

"Ah, Vane. Just the man!" Gregory jogged down the central staircase toward him, looking pressed and neat in clerical black, his pristine dog collar echoing the gleam of his white teeth. An open, kind face and a mop of curly brown hair made Greg the picture of the kind country vicar.

"Hello, Greg." Vane struggled to keep the resignation from his tone. He'd expected his family would still be abed at this hour, but he hadn't reckoned on his brother's healthful habits.

They shook hands and Greg clapped him on the shoulder, shepherding him to the library.

As he poured Vane a glass of wine, he said, "Bad news, I'm afraid."

Vane threw himself into a chair. "Don't tell me. Freddie's been rusticated again." At Greg's start of surprise, he added, "Banbury said everyone was here."

Lips pursed, Greg said, "Our brother saw fit to steal the dean's wig and somehow managed to hang it on the highest spire of King's Chapel. The dean sent him home with a flea in his ear and an account for ten pounds."

Vane raised his brows. "Ten pounds?"

"For the wig."

If it weren't for the evening he'd spent, Vane would have laughed. Instead, he shrugged. "No harm done, surely. A prank, that's all."

Greg handed Vane a glass and leaned forward in his chair. "That *harmless* prank could have left Freddie with a broken neck!"

Vane bit down on an acid retort. This was all he needed.

His well-meaning but misguided brother on one of his crusades. Taking a long sip of wine, Vane tried to tamp down his irritation. "Surely not."

"This sort of thing cannot be allowed to go on. You ought to discipline him, Vane."

At that, Vane raised his brows. "I? How?"

"I don't know. Give him a stern talking-to."

Irritation simmered close to the surface but Vane forced a smile. "I imagine you've already done that."

"Cut off his allowance, then!"

"That would only prompt him to ridiculous—and no doubt foolhardy—measures to raise funds. You know what he's like."

"But Vane—"

"For God's sake, Greg, give over! Freddie can go straight to the Devil for all I care."

Greg blinked. "Everything all right, old man?"

Vane swallowed another mouthful of wine. "Yes, of course."

"Frankly, you look like you've been to your own funeral, and I don't think Freddie's rustication is responsible for that. Anything you'd care to talk about?"

Stretching his legs before him, Vane stared at the mud on his boots and shook his head. He could just about see himself confessing last night's work to his holy little brother.

He laid his head back in the plush leather chair. Once more, shame and self-loathing washed over him in a hot, angry tide. How could he have compromised his principles so far? He wondered if it would ever go away, this dreadful, burning, humiliating ache.

Never. He deserved to suffer for this stupid obsession. Because if she came and offered herself to him now, he knew he would take her. Again and again, though all she could ever bring him was pain.

And call him unchristian, but he could never forgive her for this power she had over him. He hated her and wanted her with the fiercest dark passion he had ever known.

No, Greg would never understand.

SARAH wasn't certain exactly what position Mr. Faulkner held at the Home Office, and no one enlightened her. From the time he kept them waiting and the deference Peter paid the older man, she deduced he must be someone of importance. Someone with the power to extract a woman from prison as effortlessly as he might pluck a thorn from his thumb.

This was all due to her father, of course. They wouldn't bother with her if it weren't for the fact that a scandal would reflect badly on her father and, by extension, on the government. It seemed higher powers were prepared to intervene to save her from imprisonment and trial. And a good thing for her, too. She must not forget that.

But she needed to tread warily. She couldn't afford to let them know about Vane. The scandal would ruin her. And despite what he'd done, she didn't want to involve him in this.

Faulkner regarded her under lowered brows. "Sit down. Please." The last word came out rustily, as if he didn't use it very often. He indicated a chair that was pulled close to his desk for Sarah. Peter assisted her to sit and remained standing behind her.

Sarah felt an unpleasant pricking at the nape of her neck. She would prefer to see Peter's face during this interview. She still couldn't gauge whether he truly believed her innocent, or even if he cared. He certainly wasn't telling her all he knew.

Faulkner's bullish scrutiny made her long for a bath and a change of clothes. She must look a bedraggled mess, dirty from the cell, gloveless, her gown and hands streaked with dried blood. Nerves taut, she managed, "I did not kill my husband, sir. You must believe that."

He leaned back in his chair, a short wooden rule propped between two index fingers. His face looked weathered and grey, almost expressionless, but those dark eyes missed nothing under their shaggy brows. His bulldog jaw worked a little before he said, "I suppose you realize just how delicate a position you've placed your father in. The entire government, come to that."

Alarm set her pulse racing. "He doesn't—"

"No, the earl doesn't know. We are doing our best to contain news of the incident, but as you can imagine, it isn't easy." He collected papers together, shuffled them, and placed them neatly to the side. "And if you did murder your husband, there is nothing we can do to save you."

"Then why bring me here?" she asked.

"Because I'm not convinced you did kill him," said Faulkner bluntly. "And I owe your father discretion. So. I will get to the bottom of this quietly, without fuss, and perhaps we may wrap this matter in clean linen and dispose of it without anyone the wiser." He eyed her thoughtfully. "You are overwrought. There is nothing to be gained by interviewing you now." He tapped the rule on his lower lip and glanced at Peter. "You still live with your sister, Cole?"

"Yes, sir."

"Lady Sarah, you will go with your brother-in-law to his house, and you will think about the events of last evening. When you have slept on it, you will be in a better frame of mind. You will have a clearer notion of the order of things."

A stifled exclamation came from behind her, but Sarah resisted the urge to turn her head. She suspected Peter's face would reflect her own puzzled frustration. If Faulkner wanted the truth, why wouldn't he question her now?

Then it dawned on her. Perhaps the man believed her guilty and intended to give her time to fabricate a plausible case in her defense?

She met Faulkner's eyes, her own gaze steady. "I did not kill my husband," she said softly. "You are determined to hush this up. I understand that. But while you concentrate your investigation on me, you let the real murderer go free."

Faulkner leaned back in his chair. "Murderer? If, in fact, it was murder. It might be found that your husband accidentally shot himself while cleaning your pistol." He paused, lowering his gaze to his papers, speaking with studied disinterest. "As

I said, once you have had the chance to reflect, you might re-call a certain melancholy about your husband lately. I under-stand there were many debts. A heavy burden for any man to bear. Perhaps his spirits were depressed. It would not be sur-prising if . . ."

Faulkner shrugged, allowing Sarah to draw the inevita-ble conclusion.

The notion froze the blood in her veins. Faulkner wanted her to attest that Brinsley had put a period to his own life.

She trembled as cold anger gripped her. For the first time since she'd walked into that blood-drenched parlor, strength flooded back into her body. A man was dead. Her husband was dead. And his murder should not be swept under the carpet in the name of politics.

As if he sensed her rebellion, Faulkner continued. "A far more plausible story than that his aristocratic wife of—how many years?—shot him through the heart." His lips curled in the hint of a grim smile. "Wouldn't you agree?"

Sarah stilled. His meaning was so shocking, her battered senses rejected it immediately. And yet, she gazed into those dark, soulless eyes and saw the utter calculation, the ruth-less coldness within, and knew her overwrought brain hadn't imagined the veiled threat.

If she didn't support Faulkner's theory of suicide, she would be charged with Brinsley's murder. The blackmail was so subtle and insidious, it took her breath away.

She bit back the angry speech that had risen to her tongue. Instead, she answered without heat or inflection. "As you say, a period of reflection would be beneficial." For the first time, she glanced behind her. "Peter, shall we go?"

As the carriage rolled away from Whitehall, Sarah closed her eyes, miserably aware she was caught like a rat in a trap. Thank God no one had informed her father of the night's events.

That would be the final blow.

Seven

THEY'D barely set foot inside Peter Cole's house when a footman hurried to his master's side and handed him a note. As he read, Peter's brows shot up. He crushed the note in his hand.

Turning to Sarah, he said, "You must excuse me. I have to deal with urgent business." As he put on the hat he'd removed only moments earlier, his gaze switched to the footman. "Foster, have Miss Cole join us here, will you?"

Sarah was positive she didn't like the new air of excitement that fizzed around her polite jailer. What news had the messenger brought? Did it have something to do with Brinsley? Clearly, Peter wasn't going to share his secret with her.

"Ah!" Peter smiled and held out a welcoming hand to the pretty blond woman who hastened toward them. "My sister will take you to your room. Jenny, you remember Lady Sarah? She has come to stay with us for a bit."

Jenny curtseyed, smiling. "Yes, of course."

Sarah curtseyed also. She'd met Brinsley's sister only a

few times before her marriage. As far as she could recall, Jenny's health had never been strong, and it had kept her from attending Sarah and Brinsley's wedding. Jenny must have been close to Sarah's own age. She would have expected her to be married by now and have her own family. But apparently, Jenny still kept house for Peter.

As Peter prepared to go out again, he nodded to Jenny. "See that Lady Sarah has a fresh gown to put on, will you, my dear? And order a breakfast tray."

Eyes demurely lowered, Jenny answered, "Yes, brother. As you wish."

"Make yourself comfortable, Lady Sarah," Peter said, drawing on his gloves. "I shall send for you again later."

The front door closed behind Peter and Sarah turned to accompany her hostess upstairs.

The note of urgency in his voice didn't bode well for her, she was sure. Had there been some new discovery? Some information pertinent to Brinsley's death?

The bedchamber allotted to Sarah was not large, but it was pretty and comfortably furnished. Sarah gazed at the basin of hot water on the washstand and longed to dive in. She felt filthy, inside and out. What wouldn't she give for a bath . . . no.

She closed her eyes, as an image she would forever associate with bathing rose in her mind. She would not think of baths now, nor of him. She would banish him from her thoughts completely. Her only concern was to find some means of escape from this coil.

"No doubt you are wondering why I am here, Jenny," said Sarah, unpinning her hair.

"Oh, no. I mean, it is not my business to inquire into Peter's affairs. Besides, with Brinsley gone, it seems fitting you should stay with us, don't you think?"

Peter had told her the news then. Sarah looked at Jenny curiously. Her pale, round face seemed utterly placid. She didn't appear in the least distraught that Brinsley was dead. But of course, she hadn't set eyes on him for many years.

And Sarah herself was scarcely wailing with grief, was she? Outwardly, she showed no sign of the sick horror churning inside her.

Her sister-in-law found clean garments for her and rang for hot water to be brought. Jenny chattered gently of inconsequential things, perhaps unsure what to say to someone whose husband had just been brutally murdered, her dress and hands still stained with his blood.

Sarah's head pounded. "Jenny, if you've no objection, I shall rest now. It has been a difficult night."

Warmly, Jenny smiled and nodded. "I will leave you, then. Ring the bell if you need anything."

Uncertainty ate at Sarah as soon as her sister-in-law left the room. How long would Peter keep her here? And what would she do once—if—she was set free? The thought of returning to the rooms in Bloomsbury made her stomach clench with revulsion, but where else could she go? To her parents? What if they refused to see her? She didn't know if she was strong enough to put their loyalty to the test.

Shivering, Sarah stripped and washed herself all over, scrubbing at the blood that still marked her scarred hands. She wished to heaven she could scrub away the stains on her soul. Biting her lip, she dried her skin and put on the clean shift and stockings Jenny had provided.

She rang the bell to ask a maid to help her with her borrowed stays and the gown. As the maid pinned her hair, she felt a curious sense of disorientation, as if her old, pampered life and this new, bizarre world of death and betrayal had merged into a bewildering whole.

When a breakfast tray fragrant with tea and buttered eggs on toast arrived, her stomach rebelled. Famished though she was, she could not bring herself to eat more than a very few bites. She ended by scraping the eggs away and forcing down some toast with her tea.

Sarah looked around at her chintz-covered prison and wondered how on earth she could get herself out of this mess.

WITH a great effort of will, Vane restrained his need to launch from the library chair and pace. What he had just heard from Peter Cole made his blood boil with the need for action, but he must keep a cool head if he wanted more information.

Brinsley dead? *Murdered.* And Lady Sarah accused. The situation could scarcely be more fantastical, yet, in a ghastly way, it all seemed to fit with the bizarre events of the previous night.

And why had Peter, a man Vane had known since their days at Eton, come to him with this news? Why would the Home Office suspect his involvement? Unless . . . had Sarah been desperate enough to call on him to support her alibi? Knowing her stiff-necked pride, he assumed she'd do almost anything to avoid admitting where she'd been last night. But given a choice between that admission and a murder charge, what would she do?

He should exult in seeing her so humbled, but all he felt was a tearing need to rush to her side and take this burden onto his own shoulders. What an utter fool he was.

Perhaps Sarah *had* done away with her husband. Had Brinsley coerced her into that skilful seduction? Had the experience so overset her that she'd shot him out of revenge? Lord, what an almighty tangle!

He tried to think of the most logical question someone ignorant of the circumstances would ask. "Has her family been notified?"

"Not yet. Nor has the event been made public." Peter steepled his fingers and looked at Vane over them, the epitome of calm. "You do realize what a delicate situation this is?"

Vane gave a ragged laugh. "Dear God, how could I not? But . . . why come here? What do you think I can do?"

Peter took his time replying. He flicked a piece of lint from his coat sleeve, then looked up. "Your carriage was seen leaving Lady Sarah's home early this morning."

The breath rushed from his lungs but Vane did his best to suppress his reaction. He needed to remain calm. The carriage he sent Sarah home in didn't bear a crest. He had assured her of discretion. Obviously, she hadn't told Peter that Vane had conveyed her home. Otherwise, Peter would have presented her statement rather than some unknown informant's. He could not allow this evidence to stand; the slur on her reputation would be irreparable. The circumstances were already damning enough.

Softly, with a dangerous edge to his voice, he said, "Your informant is mistaken, my friend."

Peter's smile flashed steel. "Oh, I don't think so. You see, you were also heard threatening to kill Brinsley outside a popular gaming establishment last night. We have the testimony of one Mr. Rockfort to the effect that Brinsley had formed some sort of scheme involving you and his wife. Lady Sarah was seen leaving an unknown vehicle in the early hours of the morning. I assume if we question your coachman—"

"Leave my coachman out of this," growled Vane. Thankfully, he could trust his staff to say nothing to the authorities about a certain lady's visit to his house.

More calmly, he added, "As I said, your informant is mistaken." He frowned. "Good God, am *I* being accused of murdering your brother? I have any number of servants who can vouch for my whereabouts early this morning."

Cole sidestepped the question. "The lady refuses to say where she was at the time the murder occurred. One can only presume she has something to hide."

Then Lady Sarah had not told them the truth. She'd prefer to go to the gallows than admit she'd been with him. Perhaps she trusted it wouldn't come to that, but what a risk to take! They might not convict her at trial on such slim evidence, but if a magistrate decided she had a case to answer, there would be no containing the resulting scandal.

"I take it you've questioned the lady about my supposed involvement?"

"No." Peter inspected his fingernails. "She had every opportunity to tell me. She spent a couple of hours in the watchhouse, which cannot have been pleasant. As far as she knows, she is the only one under suspicion of murder."

Vane tensed, his chest tightening at the idea of Sarah, scared and alone in a prison cell. But he replied easily, "Oh, come on, man! Lady Sarah couldn't kill a flea. You don't seriously expect me to believe you have evidence to mount a credible case against her."

Peter gave him a direct look. "If she has an alibi, she can go free."

Vane stretched out his legs and crossed one booted foot over the other, giving no hint of the turmoil inside him. If he told the truth, Lady Sarah would be ruined. As it was, if her arrest became common gossip, there would be no hope for her, but add to that the scurrilous matter of her night with him and she would never hold up her head again.

A rush of conflicting emotions made him bow his own head to conceal them. He was struggling to appear a disinterested party in all of this. He *ought* to be disinterested. He shouldn't give the snap of his fingers whether she lived or perished on the scaffold, whether she bore a stainless reputation or was cast off by her family and friends to live the rest of her days in the gutter. In fact, he should feel a surge of triumph that she was in this fix. No more than she deserved for setting him dancing to her tune like a puppet on a string, letting him believe he might have her at last, only to snatch herself away.

He'd wanted her to suffer, hadn't he? He'd thought no punishment would be too horrible for the mockery she'd made of him last night. He'd burned to administer that punishment himself, despite never wanting to see her again.

But murder, social ruin, destitution—none of these had entered his plans for her. Fate had been less kind than he, it seemed. Hungry for revenge though he was, he couldn't take any satisfaction from her present distress. He could not find it within him to add the final touch to her destruction.

Damn his chivalrous instincts! He would have to help her. How could he manage to salvage her reputation now? He could not think. No one would believe her innocent if she'd been seen stepping out of his carriage at that hour.

Given time, he could concoct a believable story. He could say he had lent her the carriage, but in that case, where might she have been? He would need to find someone respectable to give her an alibi for that night. Judging from Peter's determined expression, he was not about to grant Vane the time to arrange one.

Peter leaned forward. "Perhaps I should make this easier for you, Vane. You may be assured of my discretion. Whatever you tell me will go no farther than this room."

Vane rose and went to lean on the mantel, staring unseeingly at the ornate ormolu clock that ticked away the seconds of indecision. Whatever he said, Peter would still draw the same conclusion he was drawing now. The correct conclusion. But Vane could not bring himself to blacken Lady Sarah's name, not openly. Not even in confidence to her brother-in-law.

"I need to speak with Lady Sarah. I need to know what her wishes are." He looked at Peter. "You do understand?"

Peter watched him for a long moment. He nodded. "Come with me now and you may speak with her."

In spite of himself, the prospect of seeing her again made Vane's blood surge hot and thick through his body. "Where is she?" he said hoarsely.

"In my house." At Vane's reaction, he gave a slight smile. "Chaperoned by my sister, of course."

Vane frowned. It was better than prison, but . . . "I thought she'd been taken by the watch? By what right are you keeping her there?"

"By order of Faulkner at the Home Office," said Peter, as if that answered him.

And it did. Vane knew of Faulkner. He was the head of the domestic arm of the secret service, and if he was holding Lady Sarah Vane, there must be a reason. Some political angle, some kind of power play.

Of course, it might be that Faulkner merely wanted to hush up the matter, sweep it under the carpet, since the scandal of Brinsley's murder was bound to catch Sarah's father in its claws. But it would be dangerous to trust Faulkner to protect Lady Sarah. He would act according to his own agenda and never trouble himself about questions of justice or innocence or morality.

The carriage ride passed in silence. Vane refused to give Peter further details until he knew Sarah's reaction to this new development. He couldn't seem to manufacture the enthusiasm to relive their school days. The instant Peter had imprisoned Sarah, he'd become the enemy. There was little point in pretending otherwise.

He turned the question of Brinsley's murder over in his mind. Of course, Brinsley had been up to all kinds of unpleasant little schemes; his mind worked with the low cunning of street vermin. But he'd been a small player in London's underworld, hadn't he? What could he have done to get himself killed?

With a jolt of apprehension, Vane remembered the bank draft he'd handed Brinsley before they parted ways last night. He needed to retrieve it before the authorities saw it and started asking questions.

He hadn't paid for that night with Sarah. He'd paid Brinsley to leave the country and never see her again. After Brinsley's threats, it was the only way Vane could think of to keep her safe. He'd wanted her husband out of her life for good. Well, now he was, wasn't he? Brinsley's death was a very permanent solution to Sarah's troubles.

What had Brinsley done with the draft? If Peter had found it in his brother's possession, surely he'd have mentioned it as further damning evidence against Vane? Perhaps whoever now held that sensitive piece of paper was the same man who'd killed Brinsley. In any case, once he'd seen Sarah, Vane would go to his bank and stop payment. He doubted anyone would have the gall to try to cash it but he couldn't be certain.

Vane stared out the window, watching green fields give way to cobbled streets as they entered London, moving ever closer to the house where Sarah was held. The carriage lurched over a rut in the road and apprehension skittered down his spine. What would he say to her? In his wildest dreams, he couldn't have imagined stranger circumstances under which he might meet Lady Sarah again.

He cursed himself for his weakness. He should leave her to rot after what she'd done. She could expect no more from him, after all. Considering her damnable pride, no doubt she would spurn any offer of help he might make. He'd wanted her to suffer, but he would not enjoy seeing her humbled this way. He would not stoop to the level of petty revenge.

Vane curled his lips in a smile filled with self-mockery. Little though Sarah might fill the part of lady, he would remember above all that he was a gentleman.

SARAH lay on the soft tester bed, staring at the rose silk canopy above. Knowing she needed to restore herself for whatever ordeal lay ahead, she'd tried to rest. Sleep eluded her, though the comfortable bed and the sensation of being clean were powerful inducements to succumb to her fatigue.

If only she could convince Peter and that frighteningly cold man at the Home Office that she was innocent. If only she could think of information she might give Peter to turn his thoughts elsewhere, away from her and Vane.

It might take them a long time to untangle the intricate web of lies and deceit Brinsley had woven. She had guessed some of it, though she suspected his activities went beyond seducing other men's wives and cheating inexperienced, wealthy young men at cards.

She studied her feminine surroundings, the muslin-draped vanity, the cheerful prints and portraits on the walls, then focused on the sturdy oak door that no one had bothered to lock. Even so, she was imprisoned here, as surely as if she were in that watchhouse cell.

Sarah bit her lip hard, willing away tears of nervous exhaustion. The night had brought not one, but a series of shocking events. Worst of all, she couldn't rid herself of the blood. She smelled the cloying scent, heard her own tearing scream, the hoarse lies she'd whispered before the end. Guilt washed over her anew.

Ah, but she was a hypocrite! If she had not betrayed Brinsley, if she had not found him like that, if he had died peacefully in his sleep, would she be sorry that he was gone?

She blew out a breath. What was the use in dreaming of might-have-beens? She was mired in this present situation with no conceivable way out.

Vane speared through her mind like lightning. He'd been furious with her when she'd left. She'd aimed to wound him, and she'd succeeded admirably. If the worst occurred, if she were driven to a confession of her whereabouts last night, would he make it easy and corroborate her alibi, or would he deny it, leave her to sink on her own?

A man who would all but force a gently bred woman to grant him sexual favors would not balk at lying to avenge himself. How perfect his victory would be! She squeezed her eyes shut, remembering his expression of frigid disgust when she'd demanded the ten thousand pounds.

A fingertip of doubt touched her mind. If he had proposed that bargain, why should he have been so angry when she insisted on payment? Vane was not closefisted. His friends spoke of him as generous to a fault. Even as he'd poured icy scorn on her head, she'd never doubted he would pay. So why . . .

Perhaps he'd been furious at her refusal to remain as his mistress. Yes, that had the ring of truth. A man such as Vane could not bear his will to be thwarted, even if it only concerned a woman he wanted as his whore.

The thought sent a shudder through her. She couldn't think anymore. With so many unknowns, she could not decide what to do for the best. She could only pray that no one found out what had happened last night. If anyone knew about Vane and their liaison, that she'd been had up for murder, she'd be an outcast.

With a shudder, Sarah closed her eyes and willed herself to sleep.

A knock on the door saved her from chasing slumber. Wearily, she dashed moisture from her cheek and raised herself on her elbows. "Come."

Jenny opened the door and curtseyed. "My brother wishes to see you now."

"Oh, thank you. Do you think I might tidy myself before we go down?"

Jenny gave her an understanding smile. "Of course. I'll wait. Would you like me to tend to your hair?"

"No, thank you. I can manage."

Sarah straightened her tucker and shook out the skirts of her borrowed gown. As she pinned her hair, she noticed an unnatural pallor in her face. The shadows beneath her eyes were so dark they looked like bruises. Well, she couldn't help that now. Perhaps if she looked pathetic enough, Peter might take pity on her and let her go.

She would have laughed at her own stupidity, but her throat was too dry to make a sound.

Drawing on the gloves Jenny had lent her, she said, "I am ready. Shall we?"

In the library, Cole rose at Sarah's entrance. With an encouraging smile, Jenny left them. Sarah exhaled a breath, relieved that her hostess's chaperonage only extended so far. Not that she wished to be alone with Peter, but the fewer to know exactly why she was here, the better.

"Do sit down, Lady Sarah." Cole indicated a chair, one of a cluster grouped around the fire at the far end of the room. She crossed the room as he directed, grateful for the warmth of the fire when her skin felt encrusted in ice. She rounded a high-backed armchair and nearly shrieked.

Vane.

Eight

WITH a sardonic twist to his lips, Vane rose and made a formal bow.

Her heart was beating so wildly she wondered he did not hear it. Sarah looked to Cole for an explanation, but she only caught sight of the swinging tails of his coat and a flash of Hessian-booted heel as he left the room.

Slowly, she returned her gaze to Vane, trying to regain her balance, struggling not to gasp for air like a landed trout. How had he known she was here?

He indicated the sofa at right angles to his chair. "Shall we sit down?"

Oh, ever the cool, unruffled gentleman. Well, she had learned composure in a very hard school. It would take more than this man to overset her for longer than the barest instant.

Gathering brittle dignity around her like a taffeta cloak, she inclined her head and sat. He followed suit.

He crossed his legs and she noticed the mud splashes on his boots. She wondered at that. He was usually so point-device in matters of dress. And it was not so very far from his house in Brooke Street. How had he become mud-spattered over such a short distance?

Aware that her mind chased inanities, shying away from the coming confrontation, Sarah suppressed a grimace. Now Vane was here, her humiliation was complete. She supposed she should be grateful that he had not seen her in the watch-house, that she'd had a chance to remove the blood and grime from her person and change into a fresh gown.

He scrutinized her with a thoroughness that bordered on insolence. A gleam stole into his eye. "It would appear, Lady Sarah, that you are in a predicament."

He was *laughing* at her. After all she had been through! She clenched her hands in her lap and put up her chin. "If I am, I hardly see what business it is of yours."

"Of course it is my business. Cole knows you traveled home in my carriage last night."

She narrowed her eyes. "You *told* him?"

He shrugged. "Why should I? He guessed the truth without any help from me."

"Oh, I should have known! I should have taken a hackney, but you! You insisted—"

He flicked a hand impatiently. "It wasn't the carriage that gave us away." He eyed her with patent dislike. "But now that Cole has arrived at the correct conclusion, we must consider what is to be done."

She put her hand to her throat, her gaze locking on his. "You don't actually think that *I* murdered Brinsley? I could never do such a thing."

He lifted a jet-black brow. "My dear, after last night, I'd believe you capable of anything." He paused. "But Cole thinks otherwise."

The invisible choke hold on her throat loosened. "So why is he keeping me here?"

Vane studied his hands. "For questioning. Perhaps, for your protection." He paused. "I think both of us could do with a glass of wine."

He rose and crossed to the drinks tray, which stood on a

Buhl table next to a huge globe of the heavens. As he passed behind her, the air stirred at her back.

Awareness tingled at her nape. He had kissed her there, a warm, slow, sliding caress. The tingles raced down her spine.

In the shock of seeing him again, she had not stopped to think of that raw, passionate encounter. But now, she watched his broad back and sure, precise movements as he poured for each of them, the starched white collar that contrasted starkly with his dark, cropped hair. And felt . . . hot and cold all at once. Shivery with anticipation. She was facing murder charges, for heaven's sake, yet still, he moved her.

Sarah fought to summon revulsion instead. She must not pant like a bitch in heat after a man who had so blatantly and unrepentantly used her. Was he here to see her suffer? Did he mean to threaten her? Now that she was as good as ruined, he might see her as easy pickings, willing to accept the role of his mistress with gratitude. She would rather die on the scaffold.

She took the glass he offered her, silently commanding her gloved hand not to shake. She sipped the heavy Burgundy, thinking it a good thing she had eaten earlier, or it would have gone straight to her head. She needed all her wits about her now.

He sat. "Cole will not release you until he knows where you were when the murder occurred."

"But you said he believed me innocent."

"Yes, he does, but you see, my dear, these tiresome officers of the law must have a thing called evidence to back up their beliefs. Your story must be corroborated if they are to accept your word."

"And that's why you're here? If you've already told him what happened, I don't see why—"

"I have told him nothing. In fact, I denied it."

She almost sagged with relief. There was hope for her yet.

He paused, taking a ruminative sip of wine. His gaze sharpened, seemed to pierce her thoughts. "I will tell him whatever story you wish. But if you have no witness to support you, then you are no better off than if you had been home at the time of the shooting. And it is a little late to arrange for such a witness now."

Sarah had to admit the justice of this. Better to say nothing than to be caught out in a lie. "Your presence here means Cole already believes the truth. That I was with you last night. If I say nothing, he will continue to believe it. I am ruined."

A flicker of emotion crossed his face. So quickly, she could not guess what it might signify.

All of a sudden the welling resentment, the grief and upheaval of the past few hours, every indignity she had suffered rose up within her. "My God, you have a lot to answer for, Lord Vane."

She took a hasty drink of wine and nearly choked on it. Hurriedly, she set it down and walked to the window, gripping her hands together.

Staring out at the street below, she said in a low, throbbing voice, "But if I must be ruined, then I shall ruin you, too."

She turned her head to look at him. He had risen when she did, his impassive expression giving way to one as hard and grim as granite.

"Yes!" she cried. "Do you think I won't tell Cole *why* I was in your house last night? Do you think I shall keep silent about the ten thousand pounds, the threats of eviction, imprisonment?"

The silence crackled with tension. Fists clenched, he took a step toward her, his face darkened to a murderous rage. "*What* did you say? I have never threatened a woman in my life."

"Oh, were they not threats, then?" Sarah let her fury and desperation have full rein. "Calling in Brinsley's debts of honor, saying if he did not pay with my body you would cast us into the Fleet? Those were not threats?" She gave a hollow, bitter laugh. "If I must be an outcast for this, then so shall you, Lord Vane! I will shout my shame from the rooftops, just to have the pleasure of bringing you down with me."

Her entire body coursed with rage, but at least it wasn't fear any longer, or sick apprehension. This fury was powerful and certain, a shield and a weapon. This was what she wanted. To throw off that deadly weakness that stole over her when he was near. To be strong.

But he was strong, too. He strode to her, took hold of her by the shoulders in a grip that was almost painful, and gave her a small shake.

"And you *believed* these things of me? What have I ever done to give you the impression that I would stoop to such despicable stratagems? The ten thousand pounds was hard enough to swallow, but this!" He flung away from her, running a hand through his brutally short hair. "You believed I'd . . . Oh, Christ, I can't even say it, I'm so . . ." He broke off with a wild gesture, pacing the floor like a caged animal.

Sarah's eyes widened. Not even in the extremes of lovemaking had Vane betrayed such raw emotion. She had never seen him like this. She could have sworn he was genuinely horrified at her accusations.

Oh, *God.* All the breath flew from her body, leaving her gasping for air. She backed against the wall to steady herself.

Hadn't she suspected at the time that Brinsley lied about the threats? But Vane's own confirmation that he'd offered ten thousand pounds for her favors had sent those threats flying out of her head. She certainly had not been thinking of them when he'd held her in his arms. When he'd kissed her, made her helpless, mindless with desire.

Vane stopped and leaned on the back of the sofa and bowed his head, his big shoulders heaving. He looked winded, as if he had been struck a massive blow.

When he regained command of himself, he lifted his head with a level stare. "You did not come to my house to seduce me."

She stiffened. "Was that what you thought?" The conceit of him! "No, I did *not*. I came to tell you . . ." She stopped, and closed her eyes. *I came to tell you what you could do with your offer and your intimidation.*

But if she admitted that, she'd be lost, wouldn't she? He would guess; he would feel the ultimate satisfaction of knowing that she'd craved that sensual encounter as much as he had. Perhaps more.

No, despite the pain and hunger in those dark eyes, she could never admit how he'd beguiled her. The way his tenderness and passion had swept away her resistance, obliterated any thought of coercion. Better that he believed she'd been forced.

She opened her mouth to confirm that belief, and the words wouldn't come. He looked as if she'd shot him through the heart, and suddenly, she couldn't bear to inflict another wound. Suddenly, she longed to cup his jaw in her hand and smooth the distress away. She ached to press her lips to his, make him forget all the pain she'd caused him.

Oh, what a curse to be female, a prey to these tender weaknesses! And Brinsley not yet in his grave.

Shame pressed on her, hot and stifling. "I didn't believe it of you at first, but Brinsley was so convincing." He had urged her go to Vane. What a gamble he had taken! "And *you*," she said, stabbing her index finger at him, remembering that night. "You admitted it. You said—"

"You never mentioned that I threatened you with destitution," he ground out. "What an admirable figure I must have cut!"

He was mortified to discover she'd submitted to him under duress. She couldn't blame him. "But the proposal. The ten thousand pounds. We spoke of it, I know we did! My recollection cannot be at fault there."

He was hardly listening to her. "Why didn't you tell me? If I'd known all this, nothing would have induced me to behave as I did."

Her hackles rose at that. "And if you had been so kind as to tell me you had neither made nor accepted any proposal regarding me, I would have left your house in an instant!"

His head jerked up at that; his lips compressed. He blew out a breath and ran a hand over his face. "You are right. I bear part of the blame. I made no such offer, but yes, I did play along with it when you raised it." His eyes burned into hers. He blinked rapidly and flung out a hand. "You were there, in my bedchamber! And . . . I wanted you."

He sucked in a breath. "I thought you were willing. I thought you were there to seduce me into changing my mind, into paying the money. And I persuaded myself . . ."

He turned away from her, and his voice was barely audible. "I had steeled myself to resist on principle, but your distress . . . I could not ignore it." He blew out a long breath. "You were no more to blame than I."

Yes, she was. But she would never admit that to him.

Instead, she said dully, "It was Brinsley. All of it. We were tangled in his web."

She hated admitting that her husband had used her as a pawn in his little game. She should have known better. She *had* known better, which was why she must take responsibility for the coil they were in now. Oh, she could blame Vane for perpetuating Brinsley's fraud, but she knew where the real fault lay.

Brinsley had orchestrated this disaster, but he could not have succeeded if she'd felt nothing for Vane. Had she felt nothing, she would never have gone to his house alone. She would not have followed him to his bedchamber. She would not have weakened the instant he touched her. Melted like butter in the sun.

Brinsley had thrown them together, sensing the unbearable temptation he presented. To both of them. He was feckless and ignorant in so many ways, but he'd always possessed an unerring nose for weakness, for other people's secret, shameful desires.

And he'd played on hers. How she'd jumped at the chance to confront Vane! She pictured Brinsley as he had been before she left, the veiled triumph in his innocent blue eyes, the dog-in-the-manger snarl.

Perhaps he'd suspected for some time how much she longed for the marquis. She'd tried never to show it, but she must not have been as careful as she'd thought. Brinsley had set flame to dry tinder, sat back, and waited for the sparks to fly. For the chance to collect his ten thousand pounds.

But he had suffered, too. Now she looked back, she recognized that his bitter words hid pain at her inevitable betrayal. Or perhaps he had sent her to Vane, not expecting matters to proceed as far as they had. Brinsley thought she'd developed a distaste for the bedroom in recent times, after all. But even if nothing had happened between her and Vane, she suspected Brinsley would have demanded his money anyway. Once Sarah stepped inside Vane's house, no one would believe her innocent. Vane would have been obliged to pay.

She had been a fool.

Vane was watching her, and she had a frightening sensation that he saw her clearly, as no one else ever had. She prayed he did not read her thoughts.

Finally, he said in biting tones, "Your husband was the most despicable piece of filth I have ever had the misfortune to meet. My only regret is that he died before I could thrash the living daylights out of him. My God, Sarah! How could you have stayed with him? How could you have suffered such indignities?"

Stomach churning, she passed a hand over her eyes and turned away. "He was not always like that," she whispered.

"You should have left him the minute he mentioned this scheme to you."

She knew it. He was right. But she forced a bitter laugh. "And come to you?"

He flung out a hand. "Yes. Me, your family, a friend. Surely anything would have been better than living with him."

She swallowed. Slowly, she shook her head. "We see the world very differently, my lord."

He snorted. "I never had much in common with martyrs."

"A martyr! To prefer respectability and some measure of independence over becoming a social outcast, or worse, living off my mother's charity the rest of my days! I took vows before God to honor my husband and that's what I did." She looked away. "Until last night."

The horror of Brinsley lying there drenched in blood, asking her with his last breaths if she had been faithful, rushed back. How difficult it was to be furious with him when he had died so pathetically, in such pain. After she had betrayed him with another man.

Drawing on all her strength, she stiffened her spine, blocked the gruesome scene out. "We achieve nothing with this discussion. I am deeply sorry that you have been embroiled in the investigation into Brinsley's murder. But truly, you need not concern yourself about me."

The smoldering way he looked at her made her heart beat faster, but the heated expression in his eyes was swiftly veiled. As if he were discussing nothing more vital than the weather, he said, "It seems that it's my fate to concern myself in your affairs, madam, however distasteful they might be."

She was silent. After a pause, he said gruffly, "Let us agree that neither of us is thinking particularly clearly at this moment." He glanced around him and picked up his hat and gloves. "You appear comfortable here, for the time being. I will leave you and return tomorrow morning. By then, a solution to your difficulties will have presented itself."

Warily, she dropped him a curtsey. "And you will not speak to Mr. Cole before then?"

"I'll continue to deny any involvement. He won't believe me, but it's the best I can do for the moment." He turned to go, then stopped himself. In a gentler tone, he added, "Try not to worry. I'll find a way out of this mess."

She nodded, unable to make herself believe it. Despair wrapped around her as she watched him stride away.

VANE shut the library door behind him and fought for calm, but there was a sick twist in his gut and his heart pounded in his ears. His chest felt so tight he could barely breathe.

He'd thought she'd done her worst last night. But no, that had been a mere prelude for the coup de grâce she'd dealt him today.

Innocent. Entirely innocent. Tricked into accommodating him by that blackguard husband of hers. If Cole were not already dead, Vane would have taken the utmost pleasure in ripping the bastard's throat out. What kind of man would use his own wife so? And what kind of a woman was Sarah, that she would allow him to do it? At the time, she must have believed she had no alternative.

The knowledge that he had as good as forced himself on her, albeit unwittingly, made his stomach heave. He'd never taken an unwilling woman in his life. He'd thought at the time she was not indifferent to him, that she'd responded with pleasure, that she'd thrilled at his touch.

But was that wishful thinking on his part? Had he been so bound up in his own desires he'd become incapable of assessing hers? He bowed his head and tried to remember, but their first coupling had been such a maelstrom of passion and deep satisfaction, he could no longer recall precisely how she'd behaved. Their second . . . he remembered her biting him, scratching and clawing, but kissing him, too, soothing him with her tongue. Rough play, or a small, determined show of resistance? Perhaps all she'd dared at the time.

He leaned against the wall and plunged his fingers viciously through his cropped hair. He didn't know what to believe or how to get at the truth. If he had the least notion of self-preservation, he'd stay the hell away from her. But even as he thought it, he knew he couldn't do that. He couldn't leave Sarah to face this alone.

"Ah, Vane." Peter Cole came down the hall toward him, too soon for Vane to entirely regain his composure. He inclined his head. "Will you come this way?"

Cole ushered him into a small salon, furnished richly in crimson, and closed the door behind them. "Any luck?"

Vane didn't answer. Peter did an admirable impression of someone who had not spent the past half hour with his ear pressed to the keyhole of the library door.

Well, perhaps he hadn't. Vane was under no illusions about the lengths to which His Majesty's agents would go to seek information. Spying was a dirty little game, after all. But perhaps Peter had given them privacy out of respect for Vane and their long-standing acquaintance. He hoped so. The thought of anyone else knowing what had really occurred between him and Lady Sarah made his stomach churn anew.

He was growing mawkish, and she had done that to him. Every time she opened her damned mouth, she lashed his flesh and rubbed salt into the wound. He'd told her he'd leave her and try to think of a way out, but the truth was he'd been reeling from the shock of her revelations in the library. He couldn't even begin to think in his usual logical, practical manner.

Now, choosing his words carefully, he said, "Naturally, Lady Sarah is distressed and incapable of reason at the moment. I could not prevail upon her to divulge her whereabouts last night. But I have told her you will not release her until you have the truth. I'll return tomorrow. After she has reflected on the matter, I believe she'll cooperate."

Peter nodded. "Let us hope so, indeed. I do not like to keep her here. Much less do I like the idea of the earl finding out I am holding her. But I must have the truth."

Vane remained silent for a moment. "If you decide to release her before tomorrow, send me word, will you? I should like to convey her home myself."

A look of understanding, perhaps even compassion, stole over Peter's features. That was all Vane needed. Pity!

"Yes," said Peter. "I will."

VANE took a hackney to Sarah and Brinsley's rooms in Bloomsbury. He needed to establish for himself how the land lay, who had seen what, get the timing exactly right.

Sarah's belligerent landlady eyed him with dark suspicion, as well she might. A few coins dropped in her grasping hands soon had her singing a sweeter tune. He questioned

her for some time before asking to see the scene of the murder for himself. She conducted him upstairs, almost tripping
over herself in her obsequious eagerness to please.

Mrs. Higgins took out a jangling ring of keys from her
pocket and fitted one in the lock. With a nervous, almost flir-
tatious smile at him over her shoulder, she opened the door
wide.

"Mercy!" she cried, rushing into the room.

The place had been torn apart. Shelves ripped from the
walls, furniture toppled, cushion stuffing spilling from covers. He checked the bedchamber and the small attic room
where the landlady told her Lady Sarah made perfume and
found the same. Everything had been smashed or disar-
ranged. The cloying odor of roses filled the air.

"How is it that someone wreaked this sort of damage
without your knowledge?" Vane rapped out. "Have you been
from home today?"

The landlady cowered a little. "Only to my sister's for an
hour, your honor. They must've been here then."

A quick reconnoiter of the ground floor produced an un-
latched window. "This is where he must have got in."

Vane's eyes narrowed. What had the unknown intruder
been looking for? And why be so destructive? Did that mean
he hadn't found whatever he sought?

But had they found the bank draft? He needed to make
sure there was no chance that Sarah would discover it among
Brinsley's effects. She'd be certain to leap to the wrong conclusion. She'd think he'd lied about refusing to pay Brinsley
his ten thousand pounds. And even if she accepted the truth—
that he'd paid Brinsley to leave her alone—she might not
believe his motives were altruistic. It would be altogether
less complicated if she never found out.

"Who occupies the rooms on the second floor?"

The landlady sniffed. "Young artist by the name of Tristan,"
she said. "But you won't get naught out of 'im. Off with the
fairies most of the time. Opium eater," she added in a penetrat-
ing whisper. "Still, 'e pays the rent, so I don't complain."

After a predictably fruitless interview with the young

opium addict, Vane walked back to Radford House for a wash and a change of clothes. Then he set out to pay a call on the Earl and Countess of Straghan.

He was fortunate enough to find the earl at home. The butler took his hat and gloves. "Will you step this way, my lord?"

Vane followed the butler down a corridor. As they ventured deeper into the house, the strains of a piano sonata drifted toward them, light and airy, like the distant tinkle of a fountain.

The butler threw the double doors open, but Vane's hand on his sleeve stopped him from announcing his presence. With a nod, Vane dismissed the butler and waited on the threshold, arrested by the soothing, clear simplicity of Haydn.

The earl was wholly absorbed in his music, and though Vane was no expert, he could tell that Straghan played with considerable skill and feeling. Vane had moved in the same circles as the older gentleman since he was first let loose on the town, but he had never known of the earl's musical talent. Vane shrugged. Young ladies were encouraged to display their skills in that regard; gentlemen tended to keep musical proficiency to themselves.

The earl played with intense concentration, a stray lock of iron grey hair falling over a high, unlined brow. His features were patrician, with a straight nose, prominent, rounded cheekbones, and thin lips, at this moment pressed together in an effort of concentration.

When the music wound to a close, Vane cleared his throat. The earl looked up at him over the music stand, focus instantly returning to those hooded grey eyes. Vane recalled the earl's reputation as a brilliant, even Machiavellian politician, a characteristic all the more lethal for its concealment beneath his gentle manner.

"Ah, Lord Vane! Good to see you." Smiling, the earl rose instantly and walked around the pianoforte, holding out his hand.

Vane shook it. "How do you do, sir?"

The earl indicated a chair and they both sat. Though he

was too well-bred to wonder aloud why Vane was paying this call, Straghan wore a look of inquiry that allowed Vane to get straight to the point.

"I am afraid I have bad news concerning your daughter, sir."

The earl's eyelids flickered, but his affability did not diminish. "Oh? I pray you, do not keep me in suspense, Vane. Is she ill?"

"Lady Sarah is perfectly well. But her husband died last night." Vane paused. "It was murder, I'm afraid."

The earl sat back in his chair, clasping his hands together. His expression did not change.

"You do not seem surprised, my lord."

Straghan inclined his head. "No, I cannot say that I am. My son-in-law observed certain . . . practices that made him the focus of much resentment, I understand."

The impassive face, the measured tone, the fact that the earl made no move to rush instantly to his daughter's side caused the gorge to rise in Vane's throat.

What manner of man was this, that he could take such dire news so calmly? Well, the sort of man who allowed his daughter to marry someone like Brinsley, obviously. Vane would have loved just fifteen minutes to tell the earl exactly what he thought of that piece of rank callousness. But he needed Straghan's cooperation, so he clamped down on his anger.

"Lady Sarah is being held for questioning by a member of the Home Office."

The earl's brows rose a little. "They cannot suspect Sarah had anything to do with the murder, surely?"

Vane leaned forward, fixing Straghan with his gaze. "They wish to know where she was when the murder took place. Her pistol was the murder weapon. Lady Sarah was from home when the shooting occurred. She returned at dawn, to find her husband dying. Her landlady had called the watch and the fool arrested her for murder."

Still no reaction from the earl beyond the polite concern and attention a stranger might bestow on the subject.

Struggling not to let his disgust show, Vane continued. "Obviously, it is essential that Lady Sarah provide an explanation of her whereabouts when the incident occurred. So far, she has refused to provide one."

The earl flicked a piece of lint from his coat sleeve. "Lady Sarah is my daughter. She does not have to explain herself to anyone."

"Given the circumstances, if she does not give some account of her movements, conclusions will be drawn that are not at all favorable to her. In short, my lord, your daughter might have to stand trial for murder. At the very least, she will be ruined."

"Will she, by God?" said the earl, entirely without inflection. "And what is your role in this, Lord Vane?"

Vane spread his hands. "One of disinterested benevolence, you may be sure."

The earl snorted. As Vane had known he would, the earl understood the inference well enough. "Bluntly, Lord Straghan, Lady Sarah needs an alibi. Who better to provide it than you?"

Straghan's fine brows drew together. "You expect me to perjure myself? A member of His Majesty's government?"

"I am sure it is not without precedent," said Vane dryly. "Your testimony will save your daughter from scandal, and perhaps worse. If I could see another alternative, believe me I would take it, but the more time that passes, the more likely it is that rumors will leak out. Your involvement could nip them in the bud."

The earl was adamant. "I am a man of honor, Lord Vane. I have never abused my position. Never."

"And you won't make this one exception?" Vane held on to his temper with an effort. "Not even to save your daughter? She is innocent, by the way."

A strong female voice spoke from the doorway. "What is this, pray?"

Lady Straghan swept into the room, gesturing impatiently when Vane rose. "Sit down, sit down, man! What is this about my daughter? I gather you mean Sarah, for t'other one is in Vienna and far beyond our reach if she needed saving."

She turned green eyes, so like her daughter's, on Vane and waved an imperious hand. "You may proceed. Tell me all."

With a glance at the earl, who remained maddeningly impassive, Vane repeated his story.

When he'd finished, he added, "But it seems I ask too much of Lord Straghan. While I applaud his ethics, it does put Lady Sarah in a rather awkward position."

The countess snorted. "To say the least!" She cast a contemptuous look on her husband. "Richard, you may leave us and keep your lily-white reputation intact."

It was the first time Vane had seen the earl react. His mouth tightened and his grey eyes filmed with ice.

But the countess took no notice of him. She simply waited for her husband to remove himself. The earl bowed and stalked from the room.

Alone with Vane, the countess didn't answer him straightaway. Her gaze switched to the window and the garden beyond. The green eyes lost a trifle of their ferocity, blurring a little, as Lady Straghan became lost in contemplation. "You never knew Sarah as a young girl, did you, Lord Vane?"

Surprised at the question, he replied, "No. Lady Sarah was already married when I met her." To his eternal regret.

"She was a delight. Quick-minded, intelligent, and strikingly handsome. But willful. Oh, very willful, I'm afraid. And so puffed up with pride . . . Well, no doubt you've seen how she is. I didn't handle her very well, Lord Vane. I admit that now."

Vane could do nothing but agree with her, so he remained silent.

She turned to look at him.

The countess nodded slowly. "Very well. I shall lie for her." She bent her sharpening stare on Vane. "What do you desire me to say?"

Relieved and heartened by the countess's unquestioning

cooperation, Vane found the forceful lady admirable, and utterly charming in her own decisive way. Lady Sarah might not know it, but in her mama she had a formidable champion. Together, the three of them might just bring this off.

Vane outlined his proposal, and the countess listened attentively, without interrupting him. Then she summarized. "Yes, I have that. I bought your matched bays privately for five hundred guineas last week. I can arrange the books to account for it, and my coachman has been with us forever. He will stand by us, never fear! Our town carriage is similar to yours, or as similar as could easily be mistaken at that time of morning. Sarah came to dine with us, intending to stay the night, but she and I had an argument—that will not stretch anyone's credulity, as we are always at outs—and rather than face me at breakfast, she took the town carriage home at first light. I saw her leave from my boudoir window at precisely seven o'clock. Have I that right?"

"Perfectly, ma'am." Vane smiled at her. "I shall have my nags conveyed to your stables tonight and collect Lady Sarah in the morning."

"Thank goodness I was at home with a headache yesterday evening," she said. "And Richard spent the night at his club so we need not concern ourselves with *him*." She frowned. "The story is not watertight. If they question the servants—"

Vane raised his brows. "Question the word of the Countess of Straghan, ma'am? They would not dare."

Lady Straghan chuckled. "Aye, brazen it out! That I shall. I'm good at that." She bent her shrewd gaze on Vane. "And now I'll have the truth, sirrah. What is my daughter to you?"

He'd prepared a glib answer for this question, but he had the strangest urge to tell this redoubtable woman the truth. He compromised. "Shall we just say that Lady Sarah's welfare is my paramount concern?"

Her brows climbed higher but there was a gleam in her eye. "I see. Well, when she is let go, mind you bring her to me. Between us, we should steer this business to a satisfactory end."

Vane rose to take his leave, but as he took the countess's hand to bow over it, she squeezed his fingers. "If you have so much concern for my daughter, my lord, perhaps you ought to marry her."

He smiled enigmatically, bowed, and left her, the words ringing in his ears.

Nine

SARAH did not like wearing these borrowed clothes. At first, she'd been pathetically grateful to put off her soiled, bloodied gown, but feeling beholden to a virtual stranger made her uncomfortable, amiable though her sister-in-law might be.

"Where is my green cambric?" Sarah asked the little maid who attended her.

"'Tweren't possible to get the stains out, my lady," said the maid with an apologetic grimace. "Miss Cole said you must please make use of her things while you are here."

The gown laid out on the bed was made of black bombazine. Belatedly, Sarah realized that she should be in mourning, that she ought to make funeral arrangements. That she did not even know where Brinsley's body lay.

When she thought of Brinsley, it was with the blank, echoing horror of his sordid, painful death, not the grief of a devoted wife. Wasn't that wrong? He'd been a constant in her life for ten years, and now he was gone. Shouldn't she feel something more profound about his passing?

She sought out Peter Cole, determined to do her duty by her husband in death if not in life. He answered her questions calmly. He had arranged everything, including the funeral, on her behalf.

Ordinarily, she would have objected to such a high-handed approach, but she was grateful to be spared the need to think about such details. She thanked him and reminded herself not to become too dependent on such consideration. Dangerous to treat Peter Cole as a friend.

She looked up as the butler ushered Mr. Faulkner into the room.

She'd expected Peter would take her to see Faulkner. She hadn't anticipated receiving a visit from him here. Sarah sent a sharp glance to Peter, but he seemed as surprised as she.

Once greetings were exchanged, Faulkner gazed at her intently. "I think perhaps you could do with some air, Lady Sarah. Take a drive with me."

The abrupt, commanding manner in which he spoke made Sarah bite back a sarcastic retort. She couldn't deny that she longed to be outdoors, if only for a brief reprieve from the suffocating atmosphere of her genteel prison. But of course, Faulkner hadn't suggested the drive for the sake of her health, had he?

"Let me fetch gloves and a bonnet, and I shall be with you directly," she answered.

Ten minutes later, she sat tensely in Faulkner's curricle as he drove them up South Audley Street. When they drew near Grosvenor Square, she feared he might take her home to her parents, but he turned left into Mount Street and she allowed her shoulders to relax a little.

In silence, they passed through the Grosvenor Gate of Hyde Park. Sarah sent up thanks to the heavens that it was not the fashionable hour, when all the ton would be exchanging bows and gossip there. She wondered if news of Brinsley's demise had reached the beau monde yet.

Sarah stiffened her spine, poised for battle, but Faulkner merely made polite conversation as they toured the park. An unreal sensation stole over her that this was a social occasion—she a young, unmarried miss being tooled around the park by a gentlemanly admirer. Perhaps he wanted to lull her into a false sense of security. It would take more than fresh air and conversation to achieve that.

"Peter Cole told me you received a call from the Marquis of Vane yesterday." He glanced at her. "Lord Vane takes a great interest in your case for someone who denies any involvement."

She didn't quite know what to say to that. "Lord Vane and I have some acquaintance, yes. He is a true gentleman. He would not abandon any lady in distress, I am persuaded." *Unlike some others*, she thought. But the words didn't need to be spoken.

Faulkner grunted. "Did you know Lord Vane played cards with your husband the night before he died?"

"No, I did not." Strictly speaking, that was the truth. Brinsley had not mentioned anything beyond Vane's proposal. She turned her gaze to the sheeted water of the Serpentine, squinting a little against the reflected sunlight that danced on the surface like a fall of glittering diamonds. Gathering her defenses. She could not afford to slip now.

"There was an altercation," continued Faulkner in his gruff, dispassionate tone. "A witness saw Lord Vane manhandling your husband outside a St James's gaming hell." He paused. "Another heard him threaten to kill him. It doesn't look good under the circumstances."

So that was how Brinsley came by those bruises on his throat. Vane must have tried to throttle him, incensed by the suggestion he might pay for the use of Brinsley's wife. Despite Sarah's anxiety, a strange warmth stole over her. No one had defended her against Brinsley before.

Suddenly, the implications of Faulkner's statement hit her like a bucket of iced water. *Vane* had become a suspect in the murder investigation.

Her brain flew into action. She couldn't allow this. Vane couldn't possibly have killed Brinsley. Furious though the marquis might have been at her betrayal, surely if he'd been in a murderous frame of mind, it would have been *her* body left for someone like Mrs. Higgins to find. She couldn't believe Vane would kill Brinsley in cold blood. He would have been far more likely to thrash him with his whip.

But what she knew and what she could prove were two different things. The only way she could clear Vane's name would be to admit she'd been with him that night.

Still, Sarah baulked at telling the truth. She tried to reason it out logically. "You are right, Mr. Faulkner. It does not look well. But I am persuaded Lord Vane is not stupid enough to argue with Brinsley openly and murder him later that night. He's a highly intelligent man."

Her companion eyed her. "In a crime of passion, often the cleverest of us act without forethought."

She managed a startled laugh. "Crime of passion? I do not understand you, sir."

"Balderdash, Lady Sarah," growled Faulkner. "You take my meaning well enough." He paused. "The shot was heard at about half past six in the morning. Can you tell me where Vane was at that time?"

Sarah struggled to appear indifferent. "I expect Lord Vane's servants would say he was abed. Why don't you ask them?"

"No use asking the servants. They're devoted to him. They'd say anything he told them to." One of the bays shied a little at a passing carriage, and Faulkner halted the interrogation to bring the horse under control.

Once he'd succeeded, he transferred the reins to one hand and turned to her again. "Vane is a man of strong passions and formidable strength, Lady Sarah. Everyone knows that. He took exception to a comment your husband made about you at the card table. Later, he was seen throttling your husband in an alley. The next morning, Cole was found murdered. Vane's carriage was recognized outside your rooms, and Vane has no satisfactory explanation of his whereabouts at the time of the murder."

Returning his attention to his horses, Faulkner added, "And then there is the matter of your husband's accusation."

Her gaze flew to his face. "Accusation? What accusation?"

"Surely you must know, Lady Sarah. You were there."

She shook her head in instinctive denial, but he continued. "You asked Brinsley Cole who had shot him. I believe his answer was 'Vane,' was it not? I am sure I read it in the watchman's notes. The fellow wrote it as V-A-I-N and could not make anything of it, because he didn't know Brinsley referred to a person. But *we* know to whom Brinsley referred, don't we, Lady Sarah?"

Sarah's blood froze. She couldn't remember the conversation exactly, but she knew the only mention Brinsley made of Vane had been in connection with her visit to his house. Panic fluttered in her stomach and her mind raced. She tried to place the events in correct order, tried desperately to remember what Brinsley had said.

Sarah took a deep breath. She needed to calm herself or she would never find a way out of this disaster. She could not allow Faulkner to accuse Vane of murder. Hadn't she injured him enough?

The silence grew taut. If she didn't make some answer soon, Faulkner would take it that she agreed with his theory. But how could she tell him the truth?

"You must know that Lord Vane's politics make him an unpopular figure with the government," murmured Faulkner. "There are some who would love to see him clapped up in prison for murder. And it takes the heat off you, which is also a desirable outcome, considering your father's standing in the party." Faulkner shrugged. "We've got him with or without your testimony, Lady Sarah. The circumstantial evidence is quite damning, wouldn't you agree?"

Sarah drew a breath through her teeth with a hiss. She couldn't allow this to go any further. She couldn't allow Vane to be destroyed because of her.

Choosing her words carefully, she said, "If I tell you what happened, Mr. Faulkner, will you give me an assurance it will go no further?"

Faulkner regarded her without pity and shook his head. "I can't make guarantees like that."

Could she bear it? Sarah swallowed hard, her thoughts in utter disarray. Ruin stared her in the face. Her family would disown her. She had no money, nowhere to go. But how could she let Vane suffer for her pride?

"Very well," she said quietly. "Very well." Better to get it over with. She took a deep breath. "I was with Lord Vane at the time of the shooting," she managed. "In his house. He sent me home in his carriage. I arrived at our rooms, as I said, to find my husband dying, with the landlady and watchman attending him. I have no idea what time that was, I'm afraid, but I know I didn't leave Vane's house until a quarter to seven." She said it quickly, so as not to give herself a chance to take the craven's way out.

She waited, tension cording her neck and pinching her spine, but Faulkner made no comment. His face was shuttered, but she sensed his chagrin. Had he wanted to denounce Vane so badly?

"So that's it," he breathed. "Well, well."

Faulkner said no more, but he didn't have to. What use he would make of the information she'd just handed to him, she couldn't guess. Would his desire to discredit Vane outweigh his loyalty to her father? All she knew was that she couldn't trust him to keep her secret. He'd told her as much, hadn't he? She'd no doubt he'd use the information, if it were expedient to do so.

In the ensuing silence, Sarah watched the sylvan surroundings pass in a blur of primrose and emerald green. *Ruined.* The world she had taken for granted at seventeen would now close its doors to her, once and for all. Her parents would refuse to see her. She would be left without a penny to her name and scant means of earning any more.

Perhaps she might find a position somewhere as a companion to an elderly lady. She didn't think she had the temperament to be a governess and she certainly no longer held the requisite pristine reputation. Even an elderly lady might baulk at her reputation, come to that. She would have to change her name and falsify references. A cold weight of dread settled in Sarah's stomach at the thought.

Remembering Vane's offer to make her his mistress, she shuddered. The thought of accepting his carte blanche, allowing him to use her body until he tired of her and cast her aside seemed a terrible fate. Would he even want her now? She didn't know.

As they drew up before Peter's house, Faulkner finally spoke. "I might as well tell you, Lady Sarah, that now that we have the full picture of events, our investigation is closed. We will put it about that your husband's death was an accident. He shot himself while loading your pistol." He eyed her with a gleam of contempt. "If you are wise, you will support that story."

Sickened at the relief that flooded her, Sarah nodded. Brinsley's murder would go unsolved; his killer would walk free. Her reputation would now be in tatters unless Faulkner kept his mouth shut about her confession. Regardless, she would live with the guilt of that night for the rest of her life.

But at least, she had saved Vane.

"You did *what*?" Vane locked the door of Peter Cole's library and took her elbow, hustling her toward the sofa. He looked like thunder.

Her heart beating wildly, Sarah snatched herself away. She swung to face him, refusing to be cowed. "I told Faulkner the truth. I had no choice."

Vane gritted his teeth. "You had a choice. I told you yesterday I'd come up with a solution, and I have, but now it's too late." He stared at her. "What's the matter with you? Have you taken leave of your senses? Do you know what this means?"

I did it to save you, you rotten swine! But she didn't say it. She said nothing, but listened as he outlined the plan he'd made to provide her with a false alibi.

She frowned, incredulous. "My mother agreed to this?"

"Yes."

"Good God!" Mama would have lied to the authorities to save her? She couldn't credit it. Her father, perhaps, but Mama?

Hope flickered inside her, but ruthlessly, she tamped it down. "I suppose any scandal involving me was bound to reflect on the family." Yes, that was a better explanation than the one that first leaped eagerly to her mind.

Vane breathed out through his nostrils, raked a hand through his hair. "You don't seem to grasp the seriousness of the situation."

"There is no need to explain the consequences to me, my lord. I am ruined."

He paced about the room. After a few moments, he paused. "Not necessarily."

She raised a skeptical eyebrow, but said nothing.

Vane drummed his fingers on the back of the sofa, gazing at her steadily. "You have three choices, as I see it. You can return to your family and hope their influence will be enough to help you weather the storm."

She almost shuddered at the thought. "And if my family casts me off?"

"I doubt they'll do that. But if they do, you might retire to the country, or go abroad, perhaps."

"And live off the fresh air? My lord, I am entirely destitute." She gestured down at herself. "I don't even own the clothes I stand up in. They're borrowed from my sister-in-law. And I don't doubt by now that my landlady has sold the rest of my possessions and pocketed the proceeds."

He cleared his throat, not looking at her. "You are mistaken. I believe you'll find your husband left you considerably well-to-pass."

She blinked at that. Was it possible that Brinsley had secreted a nest egg somewhere? But how could Vane know anything about Brinsley's finances?

Then the truth dawned on her. "No. Not the ten thousand pounds."

He spoke with absolute indifference. "It need not be that sum. I can make it appear that the funds came from legitimate sources. An inheritance from a distant relative, perhaps."

Shame threatened to stifle her. In a low voice, she said, "Are you determined to make a whore of me, after all? You're no better than Brinsley, to say such a thing."

"I meant it more as reparation than payment," he said stiffly. "But if you think the distinction is too nice, then there is only one other way." He watched her without a vestige of emotion showing on his face. "You must marry me."

For one dizzying instant, she felt as if she were falling from a great height. She closed her eyes and gripped the chair back next to her. Faintly, she said, "What?"

"I think you heard what I said."

She opened her eyes to stare at him. Was he made of stone, to utter that proposal so calmly? She'd never dreamed of this consequence emerging from that awful, awful night. After the cruel way she'd treated him, his generosity made her feel very small and low.

"You know I cannot do that," she whispered.

"I know nothing of the sort." He straightened his shoulders, as if to face an unpleasant task. "Sarah, I believe you're aware that I have always . . ."

She cut her gaze away. It was impossible to bear the intensity of feeling she saw in his eyes. He shouldn't look at her that way. What had she ever brought him but pain and sordid scandal?

His voice deepened. "I'd be honored if you'd be my wife."

Honored? By an alliance with an adulterous, barren, weak-willed woman, whose name would be tainted forevermore with death and betrayal? Sharply, she said, "You are mad."

He took a step toward her, and she retreated from him, hugging herself. If he touched her, she might burst into ugly sobs. And then he'd take her in his arms, and she might say yes, condemning them both to a lifetime of regret. He'd always feel she'd manipulated him into this declaration. He'd come to resent her, and she couldn't bear that.

When finally she could speak, she said, "You are kind,

Vane. But I don't think anything, even marriage, could save me now. People will whisper. You cannot prevent it."

His mouth tightened. "My reputation is hardly that of a complaisant man. No one would dare cast a slur on your name if you were my wife."

He looked grim, and the image of him throttling Brinsley in a noisome alley sprang to mind. She narrowed her eyes. "You need not think I should let you go around killing people on my account, Vane."

"That is none of your concern." Impatiently, he said, "I know how to protect what's mine." His heated gaze caught and held hers, and a yearning to be possessed by him in truth swelled in her breast.

Yes, she wanted him, had always wanted him in some secret corner of her heart. To have such a man as Vane to husband . . . she repressed a shiver at the thought.

But she could give him nothing in return. Her capacity for throwing her whole heart into love had died within a year of her marriage. Since then, she'd grown hard, so hard. Sometimes, she did not recognize herself, or understand where the biting things she said came from. Married to Brinsley, she'd soon learned the best form of defense was attack. And he was, in all, a weak man. Not like Vane, whose strength of character seemed a thing almost palpable.

No, Vane wouldn't be satisfied until he'd conquered her defenses, mastered her in every way a man can master a woman. Even in the short hours she'd been with him that night, she'd felt her control slipping, felt herself yield to him in a way that terrified her to contemplate.

This man was dangerous. She couldn't allow him dominion over her. And she certainly wouldn't accept an offer of marriage made from charity or an entirely misplaced consideration of honor.

She gripped her hands together and took a deep breath. "Lord Vane, I am deeply grateful for your chivalrous offer. There are so many reasons why I must refuse, but let me name one: I cannot have children."

His black brows snapped together. Despite her resolution

to refuse him, her heart plummeted to the pit of her stomach. It mattered to him. Of course it did.

"Forgive me, but are you certain? Perhaps your husband—"

She shook her head, unable to keep the bitterness from her voice. "No. I assure you. Brinsley is—was—well able to father children."

He searched her face, but she couldn't bring herself to say more, to tell Vane about Brinsley's bastard. That would be the final humiliation. Of course, he would guess, but it need not be laid open between them.

"I don't see that it makes any difference," he said at last. "I have four brothers, one of whom has fathered sons. I wouldn't begrudge the title to any of them."

Shocked, she gripped her hands together. "Every man wants his own son to succeed him. It is only natural." Even Brinsley, who had nothing but debt and bad blood to pass on to future generations, had often lamented their childless state. Her fault, of course. And she had borne the blame in silence.

She was a wicked woman, she knew. Upon their marriage, she and Brinsley had derived exuberant enjoyment from each other's bodies. Even after she realized what sort of man he was, she had still craved the act of making love. She'd given in many times to Brinsley's carnal demands, despite the fact that her love for him had withered and died. And the reason? Like a man, she'd had an itch; unlike most men, her morals prevented her turning elsewhere to scratch it. She'd used her husband as most men use their whores. Without affection, without even a glimmer of respect. Deep down, she'd believed that her barrenness was punishment for this lusty nature she couldn't deny.

For all his low cunning, Brinsley had not detected that particular weakness. No doubt, in his conceit, he'd thought himself irresistible.

But Vane was another matter. Despite her insistence that she'd been compelled to lie with him that night, she knew the truth. Her response to him had been passionate and free.

He'd made her feel things that neither her heart nor her body had ever experienced before.

But how soon would he use her weakness against her? Succumb to him, and she'd lose her will and her independence. She'd almost lost them, irretrievably, to Brinsley. She couldn't afford to make the mistake of giving a man that power a second time.

"Think of your father," pressed Vane. "You're not the only one who'll be tainted by this scandal."

Sarah's throat closed over at the reminder of the damage her wanton stupidity was about to wreak. She acknowledged the force of this argument, saw the way he dismantled her defenses, one by one.

"Perhaps Faulkner will keep our . . . circumstances confidential," she said desperately. "Out of respect for my father—"

Vane's frown deepened. "We can't afford to take the risk. We can't afford to have a man like Faulkner holding this over our heads for the rest of our lives, either. I wouldn't put it past him to resort to blackmail in the right circumstances. And he's not the only one who knows, is he? Peter Cole suspects the truth. Rockfort was in your husband's confidence to some extent and he has no motive to keep his mouth shut." Vane shook his head. "Too many people are privy to this secret. It's going to leak out sooner or later, and then where will your father be?"

"My father is a brilliant politician," she said, aware how specious her argument sounded. "If anyone knows how to brush through something like this unscathed, he does."

Vane's eyes narrowed in disbelief. "You would put that to the test when the perfect solution stares you in the face?"

Good God, what an impossible choice! How could she accept such a sacrifice from Vane? Yet, how could she refuse him when the resulting scandal would ruin her family? Marry him and she'd rob him of the future he deserved: his freedom, his chance at fatherhood, the prospect of a happy marriage with a lady of unblemished heart.

But he'd chosen her. He wanted this, however misguided his desire might be. And for the sake of the family, for her own reputation, for Vane's good name, she would have to agree to this marriage.

"You are right," she said dully. "There is no other way."

His dark eyes blazed—whether in anger or satisfaction, she wasn't certain. Perhaps she sounded ungracious, but she couldn't evince any delight at accepting such a glittering prize, one she didn't remotely deserve. She pressed her fist to her breastbone, as if to dislodge the great block of guilt and shame that wedged there. Vane thought he knew her. He had no idea what she was.

"My lord." She flattened her hand and slid it to her midriff as nausea rose inside her. How difficult it was to say this! "Vane. I think you harbor hopes of me that I can never fulfill."

He started to answer but she held up her hand. "Please. Listen to me. I can't be the woman you want. I'm not in a position to make any man happy, least of all you. I ask you—I *beg* you—to believe that."

Seeing the anxious strain about Sarah's mouth, Vane almost told her the truth. That he would take her to wife on *any* terms. But it was far too soon for an admission like that. He doubted she'd believe him. He didn't want to believe it himself.

He'd intended to return her to her family untarnished by scandal. He'd planned to court her in form, marry her after she'd observed a decent mourning period for Cole.

Now, by telling Faulkner the truth, she'd forced both their hands. It wasn't what he'd wanted for her sake, but for his own, he could only be glad. It would have been torture to wait all those months to claim her.

He didn't fool himself that she cared for him. She'd made it plain that the prospect of marrying him didn't entice her, despite the fact that his rank and fortune made him one of the greatest catches on the matrimonial mart. Despite facing a choice between him and social and financial ruin. Could she humble him any further?

But for all that, he couldn't shake the belief that the immense animal attraction between them must stem from a deeper source. Even if she had been coerced into bedding him that night—and how that idea clawed at his pride!—she wasn't a talented enough actress to feign her own pleasure, or the spasms that had clutched him when she came.

His loins tightened at the memory, and he moved instinctively toward her. By God, he would have her, whether she wanted him or not.

She stood quite still, her gaze never wavering from his, as if she dared him to come closer. He smiled grimly, advancing until they stood inches apart.

He brought up one hand and tilted her chin with his finger. She didn't resist, but continued to stare at him, implacable. He let the moment lengthen, saw the slide of her throat as she swallowed, the slight widening of her deep green eyes. Heard the soft huff of breath as he slid an arm around her waist, drew her against him and lowered his mouth to hers.

Hot blood surged through his veins the instant their lips met, rousing the wildness inside him, making him hunger for more. It was a few seconds before he realized she didn't react. Her mouth remained stubbornly closed under his assault.

Despite the flaring need to take her, he made himself slow. Cradling her head in his hands, he ran the tip of his tongue along the seam of her lips again and again, nibbling at them, coaxing them open, then plunging in to tangle his tongue with hers.

Her whole body jerked in response. She gave a muted cry of protest and wrenched her head to the side, her pulse fluttering beneath his fingers, her breath coming in shallow gasps. Undeterred, he skimmed his lips to her earlobe, down her throat. "You are mine," he whispered against the dark tendrils of her hair. "You were always mine."

"No!" She choked out the word. Her elegant form stood rigid, unyielding. Though she didn't raise a hand against him or struggle in the slightest, she fought him with all of her will. He loosed his hold on her and she turned away from him, gripping the back of the sofa with both hands until her knuckles turned white.

He didn't understand her. He offered her everything: his name, his loyalty, himself, and yet she spurned him as if he held a poisoned chalice to her lips.

Blinded by hurt and need, he covered her hands with his, trapping her between his body and the sofa back. "You want me," he said roughly. "Say it!"

"*No.*"

Her shoulders were set, her head proudly erect, but he heard the tremor in her voice. He slid his hands up her arms to her shoulders and felt tremors in her body, too.

Still, she didn't surrender. He stepped closer. Gently, he traced her shape with his hands, brushing the sides of her breasts with his fingertips. Heard her breath catch.

There was no question of money or threats or coercion now. Just the insistent, powerful pull of attraction between them. He knew she felt it. Sensed she wouldn't withstand him if only he could be patient, not an easy thing when his body recalled hers so vividly, raged to plunge into her soft, dark heat.

He would marry her, regardless, because he was a man of honor who had compromised her. But now, at this moment, he needed to know where he stood. That he wasn't merely serving his own desires by laying siege to her body and heart. That this marriage of theirs was not going to be bloodless and cold, whatever she claimed.

With both hands at her waist, he bent his head and kissed the graceful junction between her neck and collarbone. A shiver ran through her, not one of revulsion, he thought. He took the sensitive skin gently between his teeth, and was rewarded with a gasp.

She must feel him by now; his cock was hard against her. But he used all his experience and training to control his body, played with her gently, caressing her with his mouth and his hands.

He sensed her softening, growing malleable, though she didn't betray herself by more than those few, quiet gasps. When he finally gave in to desire and filled his hands with her breasts, she flung her head back against his chest.

She was full and lush and weighty in his hands. Even restrained by stays and covered with layers of clothing, he felt her nipples harden. She shuddered as he played with them, rubbing and tweaking, teasing them as he teased her. As he tortured himself. He ached to taste them, to take them in his mouth and pleasure them slowly, one by one. But there wasn't time.

"You want this," he said, his voice harsh and low. "Don't deny it."

Sarah swallowed convulsively, but she didn't answer. Her brain screamed for her to break free, to tell him no and mean what she said. He'd stop if she did that, she knew he would.

But swirls of pleasure obliterated that inner warning until she was nothing but heat and light that coalesced where he touched her and spread like wildfire to her loins. Despite their roughness, his words touched her soul as surely as his large, skilled hands caressed her body. What she felt for him was raw and deep and primitive and had nothing to do with poetry or sweet murmured gallantry. Nothing to do with love.

But it was equally dangerous. She mustn't allow this.

He bunched up her skirts with one hand, skimmed beneath them with the lightest touch. The heat of his breath brushed her ear. "Husband and wife, Sarah. We could be like this every night. I could come inside you, deep inside, where you want me."

She shuddered, inner muscles clenching at the thought of taking his thick length into her once more. *Dangerous, fatal.* She couldn't let him weaken her this way. "No. Stop!"

Her voice rang with conviction. He froze. Then his hand left her thigh and he spun her in his arms and kissed her. His lips were earnest and seeking and scorching hot.

Sarah didn't want him to find what he sought. She put her palms to her chest and pushed, but it was like trying to move the side of a building. He didn't let her go, but he groaned softly, brushed a final kiss on her cheek, then bent to rest his forehead against hers. Their breaths mingled, both of them panting as if they'd run for their lives.

His body was like sun-warmed stone against her, so solid and strong, she might easily persuade herself to cleave to him, to forget the past.

With a sickening sense of déjà vu, Sarah passed a shaking hand over her lips. Gently, she disengaged from Vane's embrace.

She stood there, growing cold without him, and faced the truth. Once more, she'd given in to passion. Once more, she'd allowed a man to overcome her reason with bold caresses. Hadn't she learned her lesson with Brinsley? Hadn't she learned it again that night with Vane?

She looked far into the future and saw where she would end. A slave to her own passion, long after Vane's desire for her burned out. A captive of her own ungovernable lust.

No, she could never love again. She was in no danger of falling into that trap. But wasn't this helpless infatuation of the flesh equally damaging? Vane could do with her whatever he willed; she was too weak to stand firm against him. Those hot words he'd whispered in her ear had shocked her, but they'd excited her, too.

What would become of her now? In her own defense, she'd made herself hard and unyielding against Brinsley. But Vane was so much more powerful than her dead husband. She already disliked the woman Brinsley had made her; she was terrified of the kind of woman she would have to become to succeed in withstanding Vane.

And she might destroy him in the process.

She glanced at him but there was no triumph or satisfaction in his face. His eyes were dark and watchful, as if he knew she sought a means of escape.

Sarah took a deep, shaky breath. "I need to go home. Peter said I was free to go."

"Yes. Your mother is expecting you."

She bit her lip. "I mean I wish to go home. To our—to the rooms in Bloomsbury."

There was a pause. "Sarah, there's nothing there."

"What?"

"I went there yesterday afternoon. The place had been

ransacked. They've even smashed your perfume stills to pieces."

Her hand flew to her breast. All that work, destroyed. But that, of course, was the least of her problems now.

Vane went on. "I've ordered what's left to be packed up and sent to your parents' house until you decide what should be done with it. Your landlady has already re-let your rooms. You cannot go back."

She sank into the nearest chair. What would she do now?

If there'd been a palatable alternative, she'd be glad she couldn't return. Her stomach revolted at the thought of re-visiting that blood-spattered parlor, but she had no money to take rooms elsewhere, no friends who would harbor her.

She looked up at Vane. "You mean to take me to my parents' house?"

He nodded. "I believe we'll have your mother to thank if we brush through this without gossip."

Oh, yes. The countess was a master of discretion, of sweeping peccadilloes under the carpet like dust.

Vane cleared his throat. "We have a lot to discuss, about the wedding and so forth, but I daresay you don't wish to go into that now. I'll take you home and call on you in the morning."

"Brinsley's funeral is on Tuesday," she murmured.

He gave a brief nod. "Of course. I'll be there."

An unpleasant task in the extreme, but he was not a man who shirked his duty. He looked so resolute and strong, she had to fight the urge to lean into him, to twine around him like a parasitic vine.

She must give him a chance to disentangle himself from this mess. "Vane, I have said I will marry you, and I will, but I want you to reconsider. Think carefully before you commit yourself."

His eyebrows slammed together. "I've asked you to marry me. I'm not about to change my mind. What the hell do you take me for?"

"And when you think about this offer you've made me,"

she continued huskily, as if he had not spoken, "remember what I am. Remind yourself that I dishonored my husband while he lay drowning in his own blood and then lied to him that I had not. That I was cruel to you—that was but a taste of how cruel I can be, Vane. You have no idea. That I am barren." The last drop of warmth seeped away from her body, leaving her bleak as a winter's night.

"That I do not love you. And never shall."

Ten

V ANE drove Sarah the short distance to her parents' house in his phaeton and escorted her to the door.

"Don't come in," she said, staring past him. She felt remote from her body, as if nothing could touch her now.

It is done. He will marry you. You were weak. You said yes.

Sarah gave him her hand and told herself that her flesh was numb to the warm pressure of his touch. She turned to go inside. She didn't look back at him, or flinch when the heavy door closed behind her, shutting him out. She didn't need the door to cut him off from her. The process had started when he had forced her consent to their marriage.

Because the very thing she had feared had happened in that room at Peter Cole's house. She'd surrendered control. Or rather, he'd taken it from her.

She looked around, blinking, suddenly bewildered by the soaring ceiling of the entrance hall, the pillars and marble statues of gods and heroes and senators ranged around the walls.

Fatigue, she thought. She had not slept for two nights. She needed rest and then she would face everything squarely. But she could not seem to summon the will to move her feet.

The butler was speaking to her but she hadn't caught a word. She put a hand to her temple. "I beg your pardon, Greville?"

"Will your ladyship make an extended stay?"

"I don't know. I expect so." She drew a deep breath and tried to collect herself. "Yes, Greville, prepare a bedchamber, will you? My . . . baggage will follow directly. Where is my father?"

"The earl is from home, my lady, but Lady Straghan is in the drawing room."

"Thank you. I'll go to her." She managed to smile at him. "It is good to see you."

The butler beamed back. "And you, too, my lady."

When Sarah walked into the drawing room she was surprised and relieved to see none of her mother's friends in attendance. Perhaps the hour for tea and gossip had not arrived yet, or perhaps it was her mother's day for paying calls.

The countess looked up and immediately put her embroidery aside. "Come in, Sarah. Where's Vane?"

Straight to the point as always. "I told him not to stay." She braced herself. "You know the story, then?"

"I know the one I'm supposed to give that brother-in-law of yours. Sit down, girl. Staring up at you like this is giving me a crick in my neck."

Obediently, Sarah seated herself opposite her mother. So Vane had not given her the truth. She wondered how he had convinced the astute countess to lie without knowing the real circumstances. "You were to support my alibi?"

"That's right. Vane asked your papa but he—" The countess lowered her gaze and plucked at the arm of her chair. "We thought it better if I did it." She shrugged. "I am the more facile liar, for all that he is a politician."

Vaguely, Sarah wondered that her mother should trouble to explain herself, but she shrugged off the thought. "I thank you, ma'am, but that is no longer necessary. I have told Faulkner the truth of where I was that night."

"You did, did you?" Her mama regarded her shrewdly. "Thought to catch yourself a new husband, eh? Quick work, my gel, but risky. It doesn't do to try to manipulate men like Vane. They have a way of making one regret it."

Many would speculate on the reason for this marriage, but only the countess would dare voice those doubts to her daughter's face. Sarah's spine stiffened until her neck felt like a steel rod. "I certainly did not do it for that reason. Credit me with some integrity, I beg you." She bit her lip. "They told me Vane was a suspect. He had a public altercation with Brinsley that evening. The theory was that he had come back to Bloomsbury to finish Brinsley off."

"Hmph! Seems unlikely to me."

"I know, but they gave me to understand that unless Vane could prove his whereabouts he'd be arrested. I was obliged to tell the truth."

A smile flitted over the countess's features. "Were you, indeed?" she murmured. "Yet you were not prepared to tell the truth to save yourself, I gather."

Sarah didn't know what to say to that. Her mother was right; she had sacrificed her honor for Vane.

And he'd been furious.

If she'd considered the matter logically and waited, if she'd hesitated to rush to his defense, everything would be different now. She would have her reputation, and she would not have had Vane's proposal.

"I'll . . . I'll go up and change, shall I?" said Sarah after an uncomfortable silence. She rose to go. Then she remembered she'd brought no other clothes.

Faltering on the threshold, it took all her courage to turn and voice her request. "Mama, I don't seem to own any gowns appropriate to mourning." She looked down at herself. "This one is borrowed from Miss Cole. Do you have something I might wear?"

Without pause, the countess rose and moved toward her. There was no triumph or satisfaction in her eyes. "You and I are still much the same in build, though perhaps I have the advantage in height. It should not be too difficult. Come to my bedchamber and we shall see."

Inordinately grateful to have been spared one more humiliation—her mother's pity—Sarah followed the countess upstairs to her domain.

The paneled door swung open, and Sarah tumbled back in time.

Perhaps the cobalt blue curtains were new, and the chairs had not always been upholstered in precisely that pattern of cream and gold, but essentially, everything was as it had been when Sarah left at the age of seventeen.

She remembered, vividly, watching her mother dress for a ball or the opera. The way the rich satins and silks shimmered and swirled over the countess's elegant figure, the priceless jewels that glittered like stars in the candlelight. The teasing, exotic scents that Sarah burned to reproduce herself one day.

The memories of shared smiles in that mirror blurred, tainted by the knowledge Sarah later acquired: The countess did not dress to please her husband.

After Sarah discovered what went on in the countess's boudoir during the earl's frequent absences, she couldn't bear to watch her mother dress again.

Oh, her mother had been thoroughly discreet in her affaires. If Sarah had not been sent home early from a country holiday with a friend due to an outbreak of measles in the household, she would never have stumbled upon the gentleman leaving Lady Straghan's boudoir, kissing his fingers to her as he turned to go down the stairs.

Idolizing her father, Sarah had suffered her mother's infidelity as a personal betrayal. She'd told no one what she'd seen. She'd never returned to her mother's boudoir if she could help it.

And she'd never forgiven her.

The countess dismissed her dresser, which Sarah knew boded ill. Her mother wished to be private, which meant she was not done probing into Sarah's affairs. Well, she couldn't blame her for being curious. The past two days seemed fantastical to Sarah; they must be doubly so to anyone who knew her. She'd flouted the very principles that had been the mainstay of her life for more years than she cared to count, with disastrous consequences. And now, she didn't know where to turn.

Suddenly, all Sarah wanted was to crawl into her mother's lap and sob, as she had often done as a little girl all those years ago. Before adult awareness of what her mother was had been thrust upon her by a stupid twist of fate.

Lady Straghan rummaged through her clothespress and threw a number of gowns onto her large, cream coverlet on the tester bed. The yards of unrelieved black deepened Sarah's somber mood.

"Black can be elegant. You need not look like a crow, you know," her mother was saying. "And it suits you, with your coloring. You are more fortunate than some."

Sarah didn't reply, just stood staring down at a black silk evening gown, fingering the jet beading. She hadn't worn anything that fine in years.

"Why so glum, my dear? Do *not* tell me you sincerely grieve for that blackguard!"

No, she didn't. Wasn't that an awful thing to admit? Sarah drew a long breath. "It was a horrible way to die."

The countess gave a small shudder. "Pray, spare me the details." Throwing one final garment on the bed with a rush and rustle of silk, she shut the clothespress. "What do you mean to do now?"

"I don't know." Vane's proposal rushed to the forefront of Sarah's mind. Another man might think better of his offer upon reflection. She was a bad bargain all around. But Vane was determined, perhaps even obsessed. He wouldn't let her go.

The countess went on. "Of course, you may make your home here as long as you choose. That goes without saying, I hope."

Did it? She hadn't felt welcome in her parents' house in many years. How violently she wished she'd never opened her lips on the subject of her mother's licentious behavior, especially when she'd done it in defense of Brinsley. A vicious irony that now she stood squarely in her mother's place.

She deeply regretted the years they had lost. Pride had become a vast chasm between them, one that only the Marquis of Vane's intervention had managed to bridge. Perhaps the countess had learned her lesson, for she made no mention of Sarah's disgrace. For her own part, she would never presume to judge someone else for their peccadilloes again.

"Thank you, ma'am," Sarah said stiffly, gesturing at all the finery before her. "You are kinder than I deserve." She raised her gaze to her mother's. "I am sorry for everything, all of it. I—"

Her mother held up a hand to silence her. "Yes, yes, never mind that now. Of course you must stay here. We are family, are we not? Besides, you won't be here long if Lord Vane has his way."

Sarah frowned. Her mother had always been annoyingly acute, especially in matters of the heart. Then again . . . "What has he told you?"

"Nothing at all. But with men you must always look at what they do, not what they say. He has stood by you. He would have moved heaven and earth to save your reputation if you'd let him. And now you've made such a mull of it, he will marry you, I daresay."

Mortified, Sarah wrapped her arms around herself, staring down at the gowns her mother had laid out for her. "He did offer for me," she admitted. "I accepted. But I asked him to think on it carefully before he committed himself."

"Sarah, once Vane has asked you, he will consider himself bound." She felt her mother move closer, try to look into her face. "Don't you want this marriage?"

If she were a young debutante, stainless, with a whole heart to give, she wouldn't hesitate. But she'd learned how susceptible she was. How a man could break her down, piece by piece, until there was nothing left of her but a stark core of pride. And in the end, between them, Brinsley and Vane had struck at her pride as well.

"No," she said in a hollow voice. "I do not wish to marry the marquis."

The countess stared. "Then you are a fool, my dear."

SARAH stood on the threshold of her father's music room, listening to the notes of the pianoforte tinkle and ripple like a fast-flowing brook. The earl had arrived from the country a bare hour earlier, but she hadn't yet seen him. He had immediately immersed himself in music upon his return.

She ought not to disturb him. She ought to wait until he sent for her, she supposed, but she hated putting off their inevitable meeting. Papa would be the most disappointed in her for the tangle she'd made of her life. Of all people, his was the opinion that mattered most.

In the days that followed her incarceration, the sorrow and shame ebbed and flowed. Sometimes, for five minutes, perhaps ten, she'd forget and find small pleasure in something. A piece of music, the single, perfect bloom of a daffodil, or an elusive scent that teased at her mind and sent her hurrying down to the stillroom to see how she might capture it.

But all too soon, awareness flooded back, swirling over her like a wave. In those moments, her heart rolled over and died a little more. She would never feel clean again. She could not bear to think of what she'd done, yet she could scarcely think of anything else.

She thought often of Tom. She'd said she'd return to see him when she'd visited Maggie Day, but the ensuing disaster had driven the scheme out of her head. She'd meant to make plans for him. She'd meant to do something to relieve his dreadful situation. But all she'd done was embroil herself in this awful mess.

Her pistol, the last valuable item she owned in the world, had been used to murder Brinsley and was now in possession of the Home Office as evidence. She had no money and no means of getting it until she married Vane. Then she'd have every material thing she could possibly desire, and more.

But how could she use her new husband's money to support her dead husband's love child? What a ridiculous proposition! How could she possibly approach the issue? What might she say?

With a flourish, the light cascade of notes ceased. The earl looked up, his eyes distant.

Sarah swallowed and bent her gaze to her hands. She'd dreaded this moment, the disgust he must feel when she told him all that had occurred. Best to get it over with, before she turned tail and ran. She cleared her throat, and the earl's head jerked toward her.

The old tenderness broke over his face but a deep sorrow clung to its edges. He rose from the pianoforte and held out his hand.

She moved forward and he took both her hands in his. "Ah, Sarah, my dear. Come. Sit down."

He drew her to sit beside him on a comfortable sofa. In the morning light he seemed a great deal older than when she'd seen him last. The character lines in his aristocratic face were more pronounced, his hair almost uniformly grey. His eyes seemed as weary and cynical as time. "A bad business, this."

"Yes, sir." Sarah perched on the edge of the sofa. "I would have given much to have spared you this unpleasantness." She bit her lip, then blurted, "I don't know what you must think—"

"Never mind that now," said the earl, patting her hand. "You have had a terrible, anxious time. I'm so sorry."

A hard lump formed in her throat. She willed herself not to burst into tears of self-pity. His understanding and kindness were so much more difficult to bear than her mother's brisk support.

He paused. "I am told the authorities are calling your husband's death an accident."

So, Faulkner had been as good as his word. Relief spread through her, softening her limbs, releasing tension she hadn't realized was there. "I don't know what to think about that," she said. "I am relieved, of course, that I'm not a sus-

pect in Brinsley's murder, but if it means the authorities are
not looking for the real killer—"

The earl raised his brows. "Do you know for a certainty
that your husband *didn't* shoot himself?"

Sarah shook her head. "No, but it seems unlikely that
he—"

"Then I suggest we voice no more doubts on the subject,"
he finished smoothly.

He studied their joined hands for a few moments. "Sarah,
I believe—" A sound made him look up, and Sarah turned
her head to see the butler at the door. "Yes?"

"The Marquis of Vane to see you, my lord."

Sarah's stomach somersaulted. Heat flamed in her cheeks.
There could be one reason for Vane to call on her father—to
ask permission to pay his addresses. He'd come to claim her
and she wasn't ready—not remotely ready—to face this next
step.

Vane stood on the threshold, his gaze fixed on her. His
dark eyes held a gleam of anticipation. If his mission hadn't
been so obvious, his startling elegance would have confirmed
it. He wore a severe black coat, exquisitely cut to mould his
shoulders, a pearl waistcoat, and grey pantaloons. His shirt-
points and neckcloth were so dazzlingly white, it made his
skin look slightly tanned.

Sarah stood and curtseyed, a little overwhelmed by this
display. She wondered why he'd bothered. Surely, this marriage was a foregone conclusion.

"Ah, Vane." The earl rose and moved forward to shake
hands. "Thank you for coming."

"Sir." Vane bowed to Sarah and held the door open.
"Will you excuse us, my lady?"

Sarah narrowed her eyes at his polite command. She didn't
like this autocratic means of getting rid of her. She had half a
mind to tell him so, to insist on remaining, to have a say in her
future. But a glance at the earl told her he'd order her to go if
she demurred, and that would be mortifying.

One side of Vane's mouth twitched, as if he sensed her
frustration and found it amusing.

She shot a dagger-glance at him and swept from the room.

As the butler had directed, Vane found Sarah in the still-room, of all places, wrapping twine around bunches of some leafy twigs or other—herbs, from the smell of them—and hanging them up to dry. A sprigged dimity apron covered her gown, a pale splash of color over her somber widow's weeds.

Vane suppressed an oath of frustration. She must have surmised the purpose of his visit to her parents' house, yet she hadn't awaited him in the drawing room as almost any other lady might await a suitor she intended to accept. Nor had she troubled to make herself presentable. It was a clear message she didn't care the snap of her fingers for him or his proposal.

Even when she must have sensed he stood on the threshold, she didn't interrupt her work. The maid, who had been busy laying out tea things on a tray—presumably in honor of his visit—took one look at him, bobbed a curtsey, and scampered from the room.

Sarah barely paused in her task, her slender fingers working nimbly with twigs and twine. If he hadn't known better, he might have thought she wanted to show her contempt for his offer. Yet, only days earlier, she'd expressed her sense of obligation to him.

He should have guessed that even his proposal, which he'd assumed was a mere formality at this stage, would be anything but plain sailing. She made him fight her every step of the way.

A sense of injustice formed a hard, burning knot in his chest. The last thing he expected or wanted was her gratitude. But would willingness be too much to ask? Common courtesy, even?

She continued to snip and bundle that damned greenery while he stood there, silently watching, and all the fury and frustration of the past days seemed to build and build within him, until he wanted nothing so much as to turn her over his knee and give her a damned good spanking.

The idea made his groin tighten.

Hell and the Devil confound it! Couldn't he be in a room with her without his cock taking over from his brain?

She glanced at him. "Did you wish to speak with me now? Are you quite finished discussing my future?"

He ignored the petty jibe. "The wedding is set for Thursday next."

Her gaze flew to his, her fingers moving to touch her throat in a defensive gesture. "So soon? But . . . it's indecent! Why, Brinsley's funeral is on Tuesday. I-I could not possibly—"

The stark horror in her eyes made him ill-inclined to placate her. "Nevertheless, we will marry on Thursday." He paused. "There's been a development."

Apprehension marred her features. "Oh, no."

Grimly, he nodded. "Rockfort has seen your father. Traveled all the way to Hertfordshire to see him, in fact."

"Rockfort? Brinsley's friend?" Sarah's brow furrowed. "What can he have to say to anything?"

"It turns out that Rockfort recognized my horses that night. He was the one who alerted Peter Cole to my connection to this whole business of Brinsley's death. He's guessed about us, Sarah. Tried to make your father pay him to keep quiet."

Her eyes flashed. "I hope Papa sent him straight to the Devil."

"He didn't. The earl stalled him, playing for time. He sent for me."

Sarah hissed a breath through her teeth. "So, now—"

"Now, it becomes imperative that we marry as soon as possible. Your father commands it, and I can only applaud his good sense. He will keep Rockfort dangling, waiting for an answer, until the knot is tied."

Why hadn't Papa told her? Sarah's hands twisted together. "Oh, but it's so soon! You know people will talk if I marry bare days after Brinsley's death."

"There will be talk, yes. We can't avoid it. But we have a few advantages on our side. Brinsley was almost universally despised. Most will say you're well rid of him." In fact, they were already saying it, but he wouldn't tell Sarah that. "They'll hardly expect you to remain constant to that scoundrel's memory. Besides, our families are well-respected. Your mother and mine have more combined social influence than just about anyone in England. With their help, we'll brush through."

She pressed her fingertips to her temples. "I don't know. I don't know what's best to be done."

"Sarah, there's no choice. If we don't nip this in the bud, the scandal of that night we spent together will break and there'll be hell to pay. A little talk about your hasty remarriage would be nothing to the furor that would cause. Once we're wed, you'll be safe. Rockfort values his skin far too much to make any nasty insinuations once you're my wife."

When she didn't speak he added, "You know as well as I do we can't wait. After the wedding, we'll live quietly for a few months to throw a sop to the conventions, if that's what you wish."

"But—"

"Did you ever consider you might be with child?" he said harshly, making her flinch. Her reaction showed how little she wished for the circumstance.

Stonily, she replied, "I told you: I am barren." Her restless hands moved among small pots ranged along the wooden table, all neatly labeled. "Vane, I trust you are not harboring ill-founded hopes in that regard." She glanced at him, then lowered her lashes, veiling those green eyes. "In fact, I . . . I ought to make it plain that I wish there to be no physical relations between us at all."

Was she out of her mind? "You can't be serious."

"I cannot have children, so there is really no point—"

"No point? *No point?*" He swung away from her, running a hand through his hair. A chaste marriage with Lady Sarah Cole? That was just about his idea of hell on earth. Worse than not having her at all.

He breathed out heavily through his nostrils. She had to be doing this out of some twisted need to torture him, surely. Though he'd no idea what unforgivable crimes he'd committed to deserve such treatment.

That cool voice with its clipped diction continued. "I wanted to tell you now, before you commit yourself. Of course, I would have no objection if you wish to have"—she took a breath—"*liaisons* outside marriage. That would only be fair."

He snorted. "Magnanimous of you."

"As long as you're discreet, of course."

"Oh, of *course*." He turned quickly and caught her staring at him with such desolation in her eyes, he wanted to shake her and kiss her and claim her then and there.

But he held himself in check. Oh, she was frightened, all right. She was terrified he'd accept her offer and betray her with other women the way Cole had.

He moved closer and heard her breath catch. His voice came out a little hoarse. "There is only one problem."

"Yes?"

"*You* are the only woman I want. I don't plan to have affairs. And I'll be damned if I'll live like a monk for the rest of my days, either."

She faced him. "Then don't marry me."

"And where would either of us be if I didn't?" A pulse beat in his temple. He sensed the fear beneath her bravado, yet he couldn't possibly enter this marriage on the understanding that it would be a chaste one. He couldn't begin to imagine such an existence. He'd go mad.

And what about Sarah? How could she spend the rest of her life without passion? Despite that cool as ice exterior, she'd flamed with wildness and desire all through that memorable night. Did she mean to shut herself off from those emotions forever?

The notion that she might also wish for liaisons outside of marriage tugged at him. He was almost sure she didn't have the taste for such things, but perhaps that one night of illicit passion had opened the door. . . . God, he couldn't think about that now.

There was only one promise he could sensibly make. "I don't force women," he said at last. "I won't bed you unless you wish it." He'd make damned sure she pleaded for his touch before their wedding night was over.

She looked up at him, full of doubt and suspicion. Was she lying to herself as well as to him? Did she really think the only way he could have her was by force? Or was she well aware of how brittle her resolve was and counting on him being kind enough not to push her?

Kind? He'd need to be a saint to follow that course.

He took her hand, stained green and pungent with the scent of herbs. He turned it over, examining the delicate bones of her wrist, the soft skin her manual labor had not altered, the faint blue lines underneath. He raised her hand and pressed a kiss where her pulse beat strongly, then looked up, directly into her eyes.

"Lady Sarah, will you marry me?"

She remained silent for a long, troubled moment. Then she gave a helpless, fatalistic shrug, as if to say she'd done all she could to prevent this catastrophe.

"Yes, my lord. I will marry you."

Eleven

TIME slowed as Vane watched his gloved fist connect with the bruiser's unguarded temple, sending his head ricocheting back, sweat spraying off his shining skin as he crashed to the floor.

Victory surged in Vane's blood. The pain in his knuckles, the burn in his muscles, the sharp ache in his side—all forgotten. He glared around the club. "Who's next?"

The room was silent but for a faint groan from the pugilist at his feet.

A small, wiry man with a face like a monkey and a cauliflower ear swarmed over to him, brandishing a towel. "Fink that's enough now, sir, don't you? You'll 'ave all me best boys laid up for weeks if you keep mowing 'em down like that."

Vane sent his trainer a searing glare. "Don't handle me, Finch. I'm not finished." The fighting fury was upon him, sinking its demonic claws into his gut. He wouldn't stop until he'd exorcised it. If he stopped, he'd start to think, and thinking brought fresh memories of that last conversation with Sarah, the nightmare prospect of a chaste marriage looming before him.

At a nod from Finch, the rest of the inhabitants left the training saloon. "You can't go on like this, sir."

"You are mistaken. This is my club, damn it. If I want to spar till Doomsday, I'll do it."

"No, sir." The pugnacious face turned up to him, uncompromising. "I'm not saying this as your employee but as your trainer, my lord. You're lashing out wild. Your form's off-kilter and your technique is worse. You'll do yourself an injury." Impatiently, Vane shook his head, but Finch stuck to his guns. "You've already upset the regime we put in place. Months of work, that was, and now we're back to square one."

Vane hissed out a breath. Much as he hated to admit it, the little trainer was right. This reckless afternoon had disrupted his carefully planned schedule. Aye, it was his club, and a damned poor example he'd set his bruisers today.

He was proud of this place. He looked around him, at the rows of boxing gloves hanging by their strings, rack upon rack of swords, foils, and rapiers. Sporting prints and fencing diagrams covered the walls. The man-sized scale in the corner where the boxers weighed in, the black counterweights piled high on the other side. The small table in the corner that held the betting book and another businesslike ledger to record members' vital statistics.

He'd founded the club ostensibly as an academy for professional pugilists, but his personal involvement meant that many of the ton followed his lead. Not the showy nobs who sparred for exercise at Jackson's Boxing Saloon, but serious athletes, men who wanted to hone their bodies and pursue the classical ideal of manly grace to its zenith.

He owned this place. But while he trained with Finch, this low-born Cockney owned the marquis, body and soul.

Finch dictated his diet, his exercise regime, the sweats and purges and putrid elixirs he poured down his throat. Vane's body was a finely tuned instrument thanks to Finch's meticulous prescription. And he owed it to the man as well as to himself not to tear down what they'd so painstakingly built.

Finch must have taken his relaxed pose as assent, for he clapped Vane on the shoulder. "C'mon, sir. You need a goodly rubdown or you'll take a chill. Strip and I'll be with you in a trice."

Vane rolled his shoulders as he moved into a small adjoining room, where a long, uncomfortable wooden bench awaited. Shelves with various unguents and remedies lined one wall and a large, high window let sunlight stream in, warming the floorboards beneath his feet.

He stripped and sat while Finch toweled the sweat off his body, then Vane lay on his stomach on the hard wooden planks, his head turned to the side. As Finch rubbed liniment into Vane's sore muscles and worked and pummeled his flesh, Vane watched the dancing dust motes caught in a shaft of sunlight.

And tried not to think about her.

Small, strong hands dug into the tendons around his neck. "Tight as a fish's bum you are, sir, even after that warm-up."

Vane grunted. He didn't doubt it. He hadn't felt so tense, so lacking in control over himself since . . . well, since his father died, he supposed. This tangle with Sarah was slowly driving him mad.

Every encounter with her felt like the next round in a years-long prizefight. He sparred like a raw schoolboy against a professional heavyweight. She kept him perpetually off balance; he hadn't finished reeling from one blow when she followed it up with another lightning strike.

But he would have her. Inside that fortress of steel and ice dwelled a passionate woman who yearned to break free. He'd glimpsed that woman on occasion, most compellingly on the evening she'd come to his bedchamber. His mind slid toward fantasy, remembering that night. He wrenched it back into focus.

For seven years, he'd tried to breach her defenses by stealth, by charm, by strategy. Come their wedding night, he would storm her walls and sweep that imprisoned damsel away. The slow hum of arousal ever-present in his blood since that fateful night swelled powerfully at the prospect.

"You're tensing up again, sir."

"Hmph. Sorry."

"Try to think calm thoughts."

Vane's mouth twisted in a wry grimace. Impossible. With Sarah as his wife, he doubted he'd ever reach an acceptable level of calm again.

After half an hour of pummeling, Finch admitted defeat. "It's not the body we 'ave to work on, sir." He tapped his head. "It's up 'ere." He glanced at Vane shrewdly. Those little black eyes never missed a thing. "Take a few days to rest. Sort out whatever your problem is. Then come back and we'll begin again."

Vane scowled as he sat up and put on his shirt. "There's no problem. Can we just get on with the next stage—"

Finch nodded, as if Vane had confirmed rather than denied the accusation. "Aye, it's a woman and don't I know it. Like poison, they are. You can't get fit again till you've worked 'em outer your system."

The little man wiped his hands on a towel as Vane bade him good afternoon. "You'd better give her a good poke afore you come back, sir, or ye'll be no use to me at all."

When Vane finally arrived home that evening, he found his brothers waiting for him.

All of them.

Vane frowned, irritated at the intrusion. He knew why they'd come—to interfere in matters that didn't concern them. Greg, he'd expected, but not this convocation. Given that Finch's parting recommendation was clearly ineligible, Vane hadn't shaken the edginess or the tension or the burgeoning need to hit someone. He eyed Nick, the biggest and most infuriating of the four siblings who lounged around his library, and thought, *You'll do.*

Nick's blue eyes held brilliant lights that danced wickedly as he pushed away from the wall he'd been leaning on. "The king is dead," he murmured. "Long live the king."

The lazy words made Vane's hackles rise but he resisted the bait. His gaze flickered over the assemblage. "Ah. I take it you had my note."

"Old King Cole was a merry old soul—"

"For God's sake, Nick," Vane said. He glanced around at his brothers. "Come to wish me happy, have you?"

"It's true, then?" Greg's brows knitted together. "You are marrying Lady Sarah Cole? But—"

Vane cut off his indiscreet protest. "Wish me happy, Greg," he repeated, his voice soft with menace.

Greg didn't heed the note of warning. "But such haste! Couldn't you have waited? It's so sudden, and the connection with Brinsley Cole is one I cannot like—"

Vane's fists clenched, his bruised knuckles protesting the movement. Pity. He'd hoped it would be Nick. He stepped toward Greg but Nick's hand gripped his shoulder. That firm, restraining pressure reminded Vane that he never, ever lost his temper, particularly not with his brothers.

"Be damned to that," Nick was saying. "Vane should do as he pleases. He's earned the right."

"Yes, do curb your lamentable tendency to speak your mind, Greg," said Christian. He crossed to the drinks tray and took out the stopper from the brandy decanter. "Cole shot himself, I hear." He poured a glass and handed it to Vane. He was quite as tall as Vane, but leaner and more streamlined, his features more refined.

Vane took the glass, ignoring his brother's presumption in acting the host.

"Rather a difficult thing to do, accidentally shooting yourself, isn't it?" said Christian.

Nick snorted. "I heard a rumor that someone walked right into his parlor, offed him, and got clean away. Now, that wouldn't surprise me. I could list half a dozen people who would have done the deed and an even greater number who would have lined up to shake the murderer's hand."

Greg said, "I didn't know you ran with that crowd."

"I don't. But one hears things."

Vane studied Nick. Not for the first time, he wondered

what his brother had been up to since he'd sold out of the army. Vane usually kept a close eye on all of his family, but Nick eluded his attempts at reining him in. He remained somewhat of an enigma, despite his free and easy manner. He accepted an allowance from the estate, but yielded not the slightest control over his life in return.

With all of Vane's responsibilities, he should have been glad not to have to manage his brother. Yet, something about Nick these days disturbed him. A sort of cold recklessness underlying the carefree demeanor that had not been present before Waterloo. As if Nick cared nothing at all whether he lived or died and was determined to tempt Fate at every opportunity. It was unsettling when one remembered Nick's joie de vivre as a youth.

"So." Vane traced the rim of his brandy balloon with his finger. "You have come, en masse, to dissuade me from this match? You expect me to withdraw my suit even though Lady Sarah has accepted me?"

"No, damn you," said Christian. "We've come en masse to see whether you've taken leave of your senses."

"I haven't," said Freddie, the youngest of them, raising his glass. "I came because Greg said I had to. I don't want to be here."

"Shut up, Freddie." Christian's nostrils flared as he turned to Vane. "Are you entangled with the woman? Is this marriage your wish or has it been thrust upon you?"

Vane regarded Christian evenly. This was no more than what everyone would say. In a controlled voice, he replied, "I have never wanted anything more in my life. Take care, brother. I'm likely to resent any more aspersions cast on my future wife."

Light broke over Nick's face. He gave a short bark of a laugh. "By God, you're in love with her!"

Vane said nothing. The truth was that after all that had occurred, he didn't know whether he loved Sarah, or even if he ever had.

"She has certainly bewitched him if he's prepared to be embroiled in that mess," said Christian coolly.

"If he loves her, he should marry her, shouldn't he?" put in Freddie. "Stands to reason."

Nick sent him a pitying glance, tinged with easy affection. "You'll soon learn differently, cub."

"Lady Sarah's blood's as good as anyone's. It's the connection with Cole I'm concerned about."

"Since when did you become guardian of the family honor, Christian?" Vane's tone was filmed with ice.

"Since *you* started thinking with your cock! Damn it, Vane, you've always been the steady one. There are dozens of innocent, lovely, eligible girls lining up for your favor and you've ignored 'em for years. Now, you're suddenly getting shackled to the recent widow—the *very* recent widow—of a man who was probably murdered in cold blood. And in a hole-in-the-corner fashion that doesn't do you or your bride any credit. What are we supposed to think?"

Vane and Christian stood toe-to-toe now. Vane spoke through his teeth. "You still haven't given me a good reason why I should give a damn *what* you think, Christian."

For a fraught moment, Christian stared into Vane's face, searching for answers to this unexpected conundrum their dependable eldest brother had dropped in their laps. Then his shoulders relaxed a little. "We're your brothers, Vane," he said quietly. "Don't you think you owe us an explanation?"

"No."

"I see." Christian's eyes glittered, hard as diamonds in the candlelight. "I'd like to be private with Vane, you lot. Out."

When the other men had filed out, Christian turned to Vane. "You do know this unseemly haste creates problems for the succession."

A strange pain stabbed Vane's chest. "It doesn't."

"Yes, of course it does! If there's a babe within the next nine or ten months, who's to say it isn't Cole's? Good God, think of the speculation that would cause. How could any of us stand by and let a brat with Cole's blood succeed you?"

As Sarah had said, a child from either marriage was highly unlikely, but Vane refused to discuss the matter with his brother. If Christian knew Sarah was barren, that would make him even more opposed to the marriage.

Vane exhaled through his nostrils, struggling to keep a rein on his temper. "Listen to me, Christian. This wedding will go ahead next Thursday, no matter what you say. Do you really wish to continue this conversation? Because more in this vein will almost certainly create a breach between us."

Christian's fury hardened his features, but shock flared in his eyes. Vane hadn't meant it to come down to a choice between his family and Sarah. If he'd had time to think— but they'd ambushed him and now he'd uttered hasty words that could never be unspoken.

"As long as we know where your loyalty lies."

"It must be with my wife. You know it must." Vane ran a hand through his hair. "Of course, you're right. There will be talk. But the alternative . . . I have wronged her and I *must* make it right." He held up a hand to arrest Christian's argument. "I know you're thinking it was entrapment but believe me, that couldn't be farther from the truth." He paused, setting his jaw. "I want her, Christian. I always have."

"Then you do love her."

Vane simply bowed his head.

There was a silence. Then Christian spoke. "In that case, there's no more to be said. I trust you'll accept my apologies for misreading the situation, Vane. I suppose I must wish you happy." He paused at the door. "I just wish to God I thought you would be."

When the door closed behind Christian, Vane threw himself into a chair and laid his head back against the leather upholstery. He stared at the plasterwork on the ceiling and wondered if he'd misled his brother about his feelings for Sarah.

Did he love her?

The truth was, he didn't know anymore. All these years, he'd never named this hopeless passion *love*, though if pressed he might have called it that. His desire for her was stronger than ever, that much was certain.

But love . . . Could you love someone without knowing

them at all? The Sarah he'd seen in the past week was not the same woman he'd worshipped all those years. He'd thought there was some softness in her, joy and passion and kindness. He thought he'd glimpsed it again when she came to him that night.

Had he fooled himself? Sarah's subsequent demand for payment, and later, her accusations of coercion and lies had tainted his memory until he couldn't be sure whether his perceptions of that night had been the product of wishful thinking rather than reality. Her insistence that their marriage be chaste seemed unnecessarily, almost deliberately cruel. He hadn't seen that side of her before. He didn't like it.

He wouldn't tolerate it when they were wed.

Twelve

VANE stood at the rapidly filling grave of his rival and wished they could bury all of the trouble the bastard had caused with him. But there was the matter of that ten thousand pounds, the needless guilt that stood like a bulwark between him and Sarah, and doubtless, there were others whose lives Cole had ruined in his relentless quest for easy money.

One of those people had been desperate enough to kill.

Vane didn't know yet whether that ought to concern him, whether Sarah might also be in danger from this unknown assassin. It seemed unlikely, but one could never be too careful. If she was in danger, the sooner she entered his protection the better.

Not many had attended the funeral. The graveside service had been perfunctory; the eulogy mercifully short. He suspected Peter Cole had written the latter. There was a true civil servant's knack of discreet gaps and smoothing over the ugliness that pervaded his deceased brother's existence.

Rot in hell, Vane said silently to the spirit of Brinsley Cole, and turned away.

As he did, he realized he was the last of the mourners left
standing there, looking for all the world as if he was incon-
solable at the scoundrel's passing. Vane's lips twisted. The
universe had a sharp sense of irony sometimes.

As he walked toward the yard where his carriage waited,
he passed by a high, dense yew hedge and heard voices raised
a little as if in argument. As he came out the other side, he
glimpsed a gentleman and a slatternly looking woman, whose
cheap bonnet imperfectly concealed a mass of dirty blond
hair.

A moment passed before he realized he knew the man. It
was Peter Cole.

The woman laughed. A low, hoarse laugh that held no
mirth at all. Vane left before either of them sensed his presence and headed for his carriage.

SARAH didn't attend the funeral. The ladies of her family
never went to funerals other than occasions of state. In this
instance, she was content to follow the convention.

She didn't relish all the curious looks and pointed questions, although she'd be certain to receive her fair share of
those in the course of the lavish wake her mother had arranged. Sarah knew what her mother intended by this: to
announce to all that Sarah was free and thereby prepare the
way for her remarriage.

Truly, the gathering seemed more in the nature of a
celebration than a measure of respect for the departed. The
countess had sent out black-edged cards to her acquaintances,
announcing her son-in-law's demise. A steady procession of
carriages brought the sympathetic and the curious to feast
on a lavish spread of delicacies, to gossip, and almost as an
afterthought, to pay their respects. Sarah steeled herself to
meet them all with her usual cool calm.

Underneath, her pulse fluttered wildly and a feverish horror burned low in her stomach, though her cheeks remained
pale as befitted a recently bereaved widow. Her hands, en-
cased in black gloves, were as cold as ice.

The Home Office had done a sterling job of concealing the manner of Brinsley's death. He had shot himself by accident while cleaning a pistol. It seemed such an improbable story that she expected the truth to be exposed at any moment. The image of Mrs. Higgins pointing an accusing finger rose before her.

She might not be guilty of the crime of murder but she was guilty, nonetheless.

Guilty as sin.

Vane was present at the wake, half a head taller than the crowd, but he wisely kept his distance from her rather than occasion any talk. Still, she could not be easy, and hoped no one noticed how often her eyes sought him in the teeming salon, how often their gazes met while silent strength passed from him to her.

She ought not to lean on him this way. Yet she couldn't stop. She was not herself today.

Her heart squeezed as Brinsley's sister greeted her with a sad, sympathetic smile. "Poor Brinsley," she whispered. "Though I know what he was, I shall mourn him."

Sarah looked at her sister-in-law curiously. Did she really know Brinsley's true character? It seemed unlikely that this soft, innocent woman would be acquainted with the depths to which her brother had sunk.

Sarah murmured, "I, too, find it difficult to believe he is gone."

Jenny opened her reticule and took out a gold chain with something attached. "I brought you this." She turned and stood shoulder to shoulder with Sarah, holding the object in her palm for her to see.

It was an oval locket with a miniature of Brinsley painted on its surface. The likeness had obviously been taken before she and Brinsley met. He appeared as a young man of eighteen or nineteen, and his expression . . . The look in his eyes was innocent. Not that false mask of virtue he sometimes wore to wriggle out of trouble in later years, but true, shining purity. It was an artist's trick, no doubt, to imbue such angelic features with a soulful air. Sarah stared at it for some time, conscious of a sweeping feeling of anger and regret for the man he might have been.

"Thank you," she whispered.

"There is a lock of his hair inside," said Jenny, moving to show her.

Sarah closed her hand over the locket, gently obstructing her sister-in-law's access. She swallowed hard. She couldn't bear to see that small part of him still fresh and new as the day it was snipped from his head. Not now.

"Thank you," she said again. "Are you certain you won't keep it yourself?"

"Oh, no," said Jenny. "No, that wouldn't be right. I'm sure he'd want me to give it to you." She hesitated, darting a glance to where her brother stood conversing with Sarah's mother a short distance away. "There are other items, some valuable ones, that my mother wished our brother to have. Peter forbade me to give them to Brinsley. He didn't think Brinsley would value them as he ought—"

"I daresay what Peter meant was that Brinsley would pawn them and gamble away the proceeds," agreed Sarah coolly.

Jenny blushed, which told Sarah she'd hit on the truth. Her first impulse was to refuse the items, but then the thought of Tom flashed in her mind. She wouldn't accept them for herself, but for Tom's sake she couldn't refuse. She hadn't reconciled herself to using Vane's money to keep Brinsley's love child. Generous though Vane might be, he would understandably draw the line at that and it would be heinous of her to go behind his back.

"Thank you. As long as you're positive—"

Jenny gave her arm a reassuring rub. "Of course I am. I tell you, these bits and pieces were Brinsley's, and he should have had them when Mama died. If you call on me tomorrow, I will give them to you. And we can talk a little."

"I should like that." Sarah bent her head, battling shame. What would Jenny say when she discovered Sarah was to marry Vane? She sighed. That news could certainly wait until tomorrow.

Impulsively, Jenny kissed Sarah's cheek. "I wish . . . I wish we had known each other better all these years."

"Yes." It did seem a pity. She would have welcomed a friend in those dark times. Sarah tried to smile.

Jenny moved away, only to have her place filled by another and another, until Sarah's head spun with inane, meaningless words of condolence. She could count on one hand the people who truly mourned Brinsley's loss. Most often, there was a look of heartfelt congratulation beneath the platitudes. Mortifying to learn that so many guessed what trials her married life had brought.

Rockfort was one whose distress at Brinsley's passing seemed genuine. Her husband's former boon companion took her hand in both of his. "Please accept my condolences, Lady Sarah. It is a sad day, indeed."

With a cold glare, Sarah twisted her hand a little and tugged it free. How could he have the effrontery to address her, after he'd tried to blackmail her father? It was down to Rockfort's lack of morals and insatiable greed that she must marry Vane with such embarrassing haste.

He looked like an overgrown schoolboy, with his round, ruddy cheeks, curly hair, and big, long-lashed eyes. According to the drunken tales Brinsley had carried home about his friend, Rockfort was a man without morals, wholly preoccupied with gluttony and vice.

His small, red rosebud of a mouth puckered, and he blinked rapidly as he dug in his pocket for a handkerchief. Involuntarily, Sarah stepped back. Surely he did not mean to weep?

But no, he merely mopped his brow with the snowy white square of linen, then stuffed it in his pocket again. "I say, Lady Sarah. I'm sorry to broach the subject at a time like this, but your husband's tragic, tragic demise has come at a most inopportune time. *Most* inopportune."

Thinking back over the past week or more, Sarah could well have echoed that sentiment. It hardly seemed in good taste for Rockfort to phrase it that way, however.

His tongue darted out to lick his lips and he edged closer,

lowering his voice. "You see, your husband owed me money. Quite a substantial sum, in fact—"

"Mr. Rockfort!" she interrupted him. She'd expected him to make some kind of insinuation about her involvement with Vane, not ask for money. "This is hardly the time or the place to discuss—"

"No, no, ma'am. You're quite right. Quite right. It's just that if you were to come across some papers of your late husband's, perhaps you might be good enough to advise me?"

Suspicion snaked through her. "What sort of papers?"

"I'm not sure. But I'll know them when I see them. If you bring them to me, then of course I should be happy to forgive the debt."

These papers must be valuable, then. Sarah wondered what was in them and where on earth they could be. She had examined the strongbox where Brinsley kept some official documents, but nothing in it was of value to anyone but her.

She wouldn't show Rockfort that her interest had been piqued. Fixing him with a quelling stare, she said, "Whatever money my husband owes will be paid from his estate." Which consisted of a wardrobe of expensive tailored suits and custom-made boots, hats, and gloves and a collection of naughty snuffboxes, as far as she knew. Oh, and those items Jenny mentioned. But Brinsley's meager fortune would not grease Rockfort's chubby fist if she could help it; it would support that poor child.

"The debt must be settled at once!" His voice rose a little and his jowls quivered with outrage. "Good God, ma'am! It's a debt of honor."

Sarah raised her brows and said icily, "My dear Mr. Rockfort. Surely you, of all people, know that my husband had no honor."

He took a hasty step forward, but something he saw behind her made his face drop with almost ludicrous suddenness. He swallowed and fell back apace.

A charge shot up Sarah's spine. She knew without doubt it was Vane. First, there was that rippling frisson of excitement. Then, the warmth of his body all down her back—close, but not touching. He could have rested his chin on the top of her head if he chose. He was so near, his breath stirred her hair.

Recovering, she stepped aside and turned, to see Vane regarding Rockfort with hostile contempt from his superior height. In a bored tone, he said, "Try not to be an ass, Rockfort."

Rockfort mumbled an apology and scurried away.

"Thank you," she said. "Brinsley's valet was here yesterday, demanding his wages. I suppose they'll all descend on me now."

Vane shrugged indifferently. "Send the valet any of Brinsley's personal effects that aren't too valuable, clothes and such. He's entitled to those. I'll arrange to pay his wages and spread word that if anyone wants their bills paid, they must apply to me."

"No, I couldn't—"

"Don't argue, ma'am. I won't have my wife importuned by every loose screw and tradesman in London. Hush, now. This isn't the time to discuss it."

She bowed her head, torn between shame, stubborn pride, and gratitude. Vane should not have to pay Brinsley's debts. On the other hand, there was no possibility of her doing so, and she didn't quite know how she was to stop him if he was determined to follow that course. She trusted Vane to distinguish the legitimate claimants from men like Rockfort.

After that, Vane remained at her side, and she didn't doubt his presence shielded her from many more barbed and prying remarks. She shouldn't feel warm satisfaction spread through her when he took her arm or deftly turned aside an avid inquiry. But it was useless to deny the sense of protection that settled over her like a warm cloak when he was near.

The cynical part of her mind divined his intentions. He was staking his claim on her before any other designing gentleman could signal his interest. No man who valued his skin would dare approach Vane's lady.

An ignoble, deeply feminine part of her basked in this

show of possessiveness, while her rational mind saw clear danger in such a primitive, instinctual reaction. She, who had always prized her independence so highly, was growing needy and weak.

Perhaps by tomorrow she would regain her equilibrium. At this moment, she didn't have the strength to gainsay him.

Dimly, she understood that even as Vane championed her against the world, he proved himself the most formidable adversary she'd ever faced.

In two days, he would be her husband.

Panic rose within her at the thought.

Two days.

Thirteen

ROCKFORT nearly choked on his ale when he saw Vane looming over him, flanked by his brother Nick, who was almost as large as he was.

Vane inclined his head toward Rockfort's two companions. "Do excuse us, gentlemen." And smiled faintly as Rockfort's friends almost tripped over their feet in their haste to get away.

Nick and Vane took the vacant chairs. Nick sat back and folded his arms, relaxed, as if he were there as a mere observer. Vane leaned in. "I want a word with you about Brinsley Cole."

Rockfort shook his head so violently his jowls flapped. "I don't know anything about Cole's death."

Ignoring the interjection, Vane continued. "There were certain papers in the late Mr. Cole's possession. Papers which seem to have vanished. What do you know about them?"

"Nothing. Nothing! Why, we didn't live in each other's pockets, y'know. I have no idea—"

"You're a liar, Rockfort. I heard you ask Lady Sarah about them at the wake. You had the audacity and sheer lack of taste to mention her husband's debts of honor and importune her for payment on the very day of his funeral. But you were prepared to take payment in kind, weren't you? You mentioned papers."

"I told you, I don't know anything about papers. You must've misheard." He looked from Vane to his brother, and back.

Vane fixed Rockfort with a hard stare. "If you were prepared to take those documents in payment, you must know what's in them."

"Stands to reason," said Nick.

"Yes, it does." Vane watched Rockfort squirm. "But no one can find them. Perhaps Brinsley's killer has them, or perhaps the killer didn't find them, either. You know something about them, Rockfort. Didn't it occur to you that the killer might come for you next?"

The man's childlike eyes widened and his hand went to his chest.

"What's in those papers, man?" said Vane.

He licked his lips. "I don't know. Not specifically. I know that Brinsley ran a few rigs, said he had evidence of certain important people up to no good. He was bleeding them—"

"Blackmail?"

Rockfort nodded. "That's the impression I had, but of course he didn't say it in so many words."

"Can you guess who might have wanted to kill him?"

Rockfort shifted his shoulders uneasily. "There were people who didn't like him."

"That's hardly news. Any particular enemies?"

"Other than his wife?" Rockfort shot back.

In a flash, Vane had Rockfort by the throat. "You will not speak of that lady again." Vane couldn't let him know he was aware of Rockfort's attempt to extort money from the Earl of Straghan. He needed to maintain appearances until the knot was safely tied.

"Easy, Vane," murmured Nick. "Don't want to kill old pudding-face here. Not until he tells us all he knows, anyway."

Vane glanced around. In the general noise and haze of smoke, no one had noticed his reflexive move. Nick was right, and besides, Rockfort had mentioned Sarah with the express purpose of baiting him, just as he had on that first fateful night when all this began.

Vane flexed his fingers and let Rockfort go. "Names, Rockfort. I need names."

Rockfort fell back, gasping. "All right! Yes, all right!"

When he and Nick left Brown's, Vane had a tidy list.

"A neat afternoon's work," said Nick, "but you scarcely needed me, old fellow. You could handle Rockfort with one hand tied behind you."

"You weren't there to handle Rockfort. You were there to handle me."

Nick snorted a laugh. "He wanted to take up the blackmail where Cole left off. What a blockhead. Best way to get himself killed."

"Yes. Did you notice he showed no surprise at the fact that his crony was murdered? Even though the official story is suicide?"

"You think he could have done it?"

"It's possible." Vane considered. He raised an eyebrow at his brother. "Would you see what you can find out about the fellow, Nick? And see if you can track down his movements on the night Cole died. But be careful. His sort will fight like a cornered rat."

DESPITE the sunshine that flooded the small parlor, simply walking into the Coles' house again tightened Sarah's chest. The oppressive atmosphere had not been wholly due to her incarceration, she found. There was a pervasive sense of melancholy in this house that had nothing to do with grief over Brinsley's death.

She studied Jenny Cole as they conversed. Her flaxen

hair was dressed rather fussily around her face, frothing in tight curls out of a matronly lace cap. The black mourning gown she wore was too severe for her pale prettiness. She must be near Sarah's own age, yet she'd never married. Why hadn't she? Jenny's devotion to her elder brother was strong, but surely she longed for a husband, a family of her own.

Something tweaked the back of Sarah's mind. There'd been an illness of some kind, hadn't there? According to Brinsley, his sister had never been strong.

"Mama doted on Brinsley, you know," said Jenny, lifting her teacup to her pursed lips. "He was such an angelic little boy."

And such a devil of a man.

Sarah shook herself. She shouldn't harbor so much seething resentment toward her dead husband. He was beyond her reach if she wished to punish him, and vengeance for his sins wasn't her responsibility, after all. The better part of her knew she ought to forgive him but she couldn't manage to be quite so good. The one thought that kept swimming to the surface was that he couldn't hurt her anymore.

Why, then, did she carry this heavy foreboding like a yoke across her back?

Jenny rose and crossed to a piecrust table. "Here are the things Mama wanted Brinsley to have. They were Papa's." She brought forth a small marquetry box and handed it to Sarah.

Sarah opened the catch and peered inside.

There was a jumble of expensive trinkets: a stickpin that might be worth a considerable amount if the diamond were genuine; a large square-cut emerald ring, the kind a gentleman would have worn in the previous century; a handsome pocket watch. Sarah didn't like to examine the contents too closely while Jenny watched, but hope lightened the weight that seemed to press against her chest. These items might bring enough to secure Tom's future without her ever having recourse to Vane's massive wealth.

She must be truly without a conscience, because she had no qualms about selling the heirlooms for whatever they might bring. These items held no sentimental value for her. If Brinsley had received them on his mother's death, he would have pawned them and spent the proceeds on one of his many vices. And if Tom had not entered the equation, Sarah would have told her sister-in-law to keep it all.

As Sarah thanked Jenny and rose to take her leave, a step sounded in the hall. Jenny froze, her gaze flying to Sarah's face.

Before Sarah could react, Jenny had whisked the box out of Sarah's hands and hidden it behind a large embroidered bolster.

The next instant, booted footsteps grew louder and erupted into the parlor, carrying Peter Cole with them, an abstracted look on his face. "You know, Jenny, I—"

He halted on the threshold, taking in Sarah's presence. "Oh. My apologies. I didn't mean to interrupt." He bowed, showing all the discomfort of a man who meets a lady he recently held prisoner. "How do you do, Lady Sarah?"

She rose and curtseyed. "As well as can be expected, Peter, I thank you."

"Yes. Well. Very well, then." He gave a polite, social half smile. "I shall let you ladies get on with it." He bowed again and left.

A tiny twinge of satisfaction at his unease made Sarah bite back a grin. But when she saw the distraught look on Jenny's face, any desire to smile left her.

Sarah gestured to the cushion behind which the box of trinkets hid. "Peter doesn't know you are giving me this, does he?"

Slowly, Jenny shook her head.

There had been no legacy, Sarah was sure of that now. But Jenny knew Sarah had no money and she had decided to give her charity in such a way that would assuage Sarah's pride. That was what this "legacy" amounted to.

Sarah made a business of smoothing out her gloves to hide the shamed flush that rose to her cheeks. "I'm sorry. I thank you, but I cannot accept them."

She didn't touch the box again or even glance at where it

hid. Once more, the solution to her most pressing problem moved out of her reach. Jenny looked surprised and hurt now, but when she heard about Sarah's impending marriage, she'd be glad Sarah hadn't accepted her kind offer.

"Jenny, I came today to give you news that I'm not sure you will like. But I wanted you to know before the rest of the world." Sarah clasped her hands together and sucked in a breath. "I am to marry the Marquis of Vane."

She hardly needed to see Jenny's reaction. She almost heard her sister-in-law's jaw drop.

"The wedding is . . . imminent, for reasons which I cannot discuss." *Tomorrow. The wedding is tomorrow.* She couldn't bring herself to tell Jenny that.

"I wish you very happy," Jenny stammered helplessly, her fear of her brother and the box beneath the cushion forgotten.

Sarah accepted her stunned good wishes with a wry smile.

Happy? At this moment, happiness seemed as distant as the stars.

FEWER than twenty people attended the marriage of Lady Sarah Cole and Lucas Christopher St. John Morrow, sixth Marquis of Vane. Sarah was glad for the lack of fuss. She'd endured enough attention from the curious at Brinsley's funeral to know what a sensation this wedding would create. By the time the union became common knowledge, she and Vane would have left London for his Richmond estate.

It appeared Vane's family was in residence at Lyon House, in Richmond. She wasn't entirely certain how she felt about that. On the one hand, Vane's family must be suspicious of this hasty marriage and the circumstances surrounding it. On the other, she would do almost anything to avoid staying alone in a house with Vane.

The ceremony began. As her father led her forward, panic threatened to choke her. Vane seemed huge standing there, and so very male. He turned his head to look at her and his deep gaze made her absurdly conscious of her own body, of the flutter of her pulse, the rush of her breath, the pounding of her heart.

The earl joined her hand to Vane's, pressing it slightly just before he let go. She was grateful for the courage that small pressure gave her. She laid her hand so lightly in Vane's they almost weren't touching. Despite her care, she felt his heat, the subtle warmth of his gaze. Soon, they would be alone together, man and wife.

As the vicar began his sonorous recitation, a disorienting sense of unreality filled her. The warmth left her body and fierce cold swept over her, banishing her to some faraway place of snow and ice. She repeated the vows through frosty lips and they echoed through her heart as if it were an empty cave on a snowy peak. She tried to think about what the vows signified, to mean the words she spoke, but it all seemed so distant, as if it was happening to someone else.

With my body, I thee worship. . . .

The next thing she knew, it was over, and Vane was raising her hand to his lips. Their eyes met, and a hot current raced through her body, enlivening her senses. As he drew her close to kiss her cheek, his blatant masculinity almost overwhelmed her. His lips brushed her skin and weakness attacked her knees and a melting sensation inside turned that ice to a flood of unwelcome longing.

Again, that unique scent. Sarah closed her eyes, trying to fight the rising tide of passion and fear.

His brothers converged on them then, all gallantly vying for a chance to kiss the bride. Whatever they thought of Vane's hasty nuptials, they concealed it well. No doubt she'd discover their true sentiments soon enough.

Vane's mother glided forward, wreathed in smiles. "My *dear*! Come, let me kiss you. There! I am so looking forward to having a daughter to side with me against all these horrid *men*. You will help me, won't you?"

Sarah made some banal answer, accepting the dowager's embrace. She couldn't imagine being part of Vane's life, much less part of his family. She didn't want to grow attached to these people.

The elaborate wedding breakfast didn't tempt Sarah's appetite. Now that the ordeal of the ceremony was over, the specter of their wedding night loomed large.

Vane had said he wouldn't coerce her, and she believed him. That left the real possibility that he would do his level best to seduce her or, indeed, that she might put an end to her own suffering by throwing herself at his feet. Knowing how susceptible she was to him lent a knife edge to her fear.

But she'd known what she faced when she made her terms and agreed to marry him. She must set the rules from the beginning. If she could but hold on to her resolve tonight, if she could convince him never to try again to entice her to his bed, then she might have a chance of surviving this marriage with her heart and pride intact. Perhaps, in time, he would seek pleasure elsewhere and they could live separate, amicable lives.

Many married couples lived that way. She ought not to feel a stab of pain at the prospect, nor the sharp tang of regret at the solitary existence that stretched before her. The life of perfect happiness she'd thought her due at sixteen existed only in a fairy tale.

Sarah grimaced. She'd be a fool to hope Vane would agree to her plans with complacence. He'd scarcely be amenable to such an arrangement tonight, anyway. But in time, he might greet the suggestion that they pursue separate lives with relief. In time, he would find someone else.

Men always did.

Fourteen

VANE'S impatience to have Sarah to himself was laced with anticipation. His finer self told him not to rush her, to accept she needed time to recover from Cole's sudden death. But the beast inside him slavered to claim her without further ado.

If she appreciated how very close to the surface the beast prowled, she might think better of leaving their wedding celebrations so early. But no sign of apprehension appeared in her clear green eyes as he handed her into the awaiting carriage. Those eyes swept him a glance through thick black lashes. If he hadn't known better, he would have detected an invitation in that look. An invitation was the last thing she'd issue him now, not when she'd made it plain she wanted none of that sort of thing.

But hadn't he felt the quick rush of her breath as he'd kissed her cheek, the slight, involuntary pressure of her gloved fingers when he'd kissed her hand? Her gaze had been upon him often throughout the day. He'd caught her looking at him many times when she'd thought his attention engaged elsewhere. She ought to know he was aware of every move she made.

He ducked his head and climbed into the carriage beside her. The door shut behind him and in a moment they moved off.

He was a big man. Even if he'd wanted to—and he didn't—he couldn't have prevented his shoulder and thigh from touching hers as they sat side by side on the banquette seat. Of course, he could have sat opposite, he supposed, but then his legs might have tangled in her skirts. He'd always cursed the small dimensions of carriages and preferred to ride. Now, it seemed the vehicles did have something to recommend them, after all.

Silently, Vane laughed to himself. A newly married man ought not to be thankful for such small mercies as the license to brush his person against his wife's in a closed carriage. But as a first step in luring this difficult, contradictory, fascinating woman to his bed, he couldn't afford to let any opportunity pass. She was aware of him. He saw it in the way she carefully regulated her breathing, the stiff manner in which she held herself, the hard swallow she gave when she thought his attention elsewhere.

He let the silence stretch, let her feel him. The Devil of it was, she had quite as powerful an effect on him as he seemed to be having on her. By the time the carriage drew to a halt outside his house, he burned to haul her up to his bedchamber and begin where they'd left off a few days ago.

When the carriage halted, her gaze flew to his face. "What do we stop for so soon?"

Amused, he said, "My house is not so far from your parents'. Don't tell me you've forgotten."

A flush bloomed in her cheeks. She cut her gaze away, muttering, "I thought we were going to Richmond."

He handed her out, wondering if she'd thought to escape him in the midst of his large family. Surely, there would have been little privacy for the newly married couple with that lot in attendance. The precise reason he'd brought her here. Let everyone who mattered think they were in Richmond. He did not intend to let her dilute his presence with others until they'd sorted out her problems with the marriage bed.

Judging by her martyred demeanor as they stepped inside the Georgian mansion, they might still be there at Christmas.

Despite whatever misgivings she harbored about staying in this house alone with him, he was pleased to see Sarah's graciousness toward his staff. She behaved as if she'd never set foot in the place before, and Rivers most correctly greeted his new mistress with a reciprocal respect. Which was only what Vane expected, but he did acknowledge to himself a slight twinge of relief.

It was possible, of course, that Rivers hadn't made the connection between the new Lady Vane and the heavily veiled female who'd invaded Vane's house that night. Whatever the case, Vane was glad. He wouldn't like to dismiss his butler after so many years of faithful service.

Mrs. Brodie beamed, clearly delighted to have a mistress at last. "Come and I'll show you to your bedchamber, ma'am."

Vane watched them go, suppressing his impatience to get his wife alone. He headed to his library for a drink.

He'd barely poured himself a glass of wine when Rivers entered with a discreet cough. Vane looked up. "Yes?"

"My lord, Lady Vane wishes you to join her, if you please."

Blood surging, Vane set down his glass and obeyed the summons. He shrugged off a brief fantasy that Sarah had at last come to her senses and awaited him reclining nude on his bed. That would be altogether too much to hope for.

The door to the bedchamber was open. Another bad sign. He walked in, to find his wife fully dressed and furious.

He raised his brows. "Is something wrong?"

Her lips curled into a snarl. "Wrong? Of course something's wrong! Your housekeeper informs me that we are both to sleep in this chamber."

Ah. The battle had begun.

VANE leaned lazily against the bedpost. "Yes?"

The self-satisfied look on his face made her want to claw his eyes out. How dare he put her in this position? She hadn't even thought to insist on separate bedchambers when they'd come to an understanding about how their marriage would proceed. She'd never dreamed she'd be obliged to spend every night lying next to him. Separate bedchambers, then separate residences, and eventually, separate lives was the progression she'd planned in her head.

But sleeping in the same bed, in the selfsame room where all this began? When she'd wrung that agreement not to force her to have intimate relations with him, she'd never expected to have to fight to put even this small a distance between them.

"Well, it won't do," she said. "I require my own bed-chamber and dressing room."

He inspected his fingernails. "I'm afraid that won't be possible."

She glanced around. "Surely this house is large enough to accommodate me."

"Of course it is. But I want you in my bed." He allowed his dark gaze to flicker over her, clearly picturing her there.

Her face flamed. "You said you wouldn't coerce me. You gave me your word."

He smiled, and she wished that rare sight didn't make her body quicken and heat. "Requiring you to sleep in my bed is not forcing you to do anything more." One eyebrow flew upward. "But if you think you won't be able to keep your hands off me . . ." At her infuriated snort, he shrugged and moved to the door, as if there was no more to be said.

Her gaze dropped to the bed and a fluttering panic rose to her throat. She couldn't bear him so close, touching her, testing her response, night after night. She'd go mad.

When she lifted her gaze, she saw that he watched her from the doorway. The amusement had vanished from his face, leaving an intent look that pinned her to the spot. Softly, he said, "I trust you will make yourself comfortable. I'll be up shortly."

He left her suffering the most turbulent emotions she'd ever experienced, and that was saying a lot, given the events of the past week. She'd thought he'd be gentleman enough to allow her to hold him at arm's length. How could she have been so mistaken about his character? Only now did she see the ruthlessness beneath the compassion, the steel behind that elegant exterior.

She'd outmaneuvered herself neatly by making him promise not to insist on his rights as a husband. It was no concession on his part, she realized. He would never have forced her anyway. All she'd done was register her unwillingness, and by that, she'd set herself up as a challenge.

Men loved challenges. Any woman knew that. How could she have been so stupid! Perhaps that was all she'd ever been to him: a challenge, a worthy foe to be conquered. The thought struck a hollow note inside her.

What to do now, though?

"Oh, my lady!" Barker, the maid her mother had engaged for her, hurried in. "May I wish you happy, ma'am?"

Happy? She was furious. "Thank you, Barker," Sarah forced a smile.

She eyed the white silk peignoir the maid laid on the bed. "Where did that come from?"

"A gift from his lordship, ma'am," said Barker briskly, without embarrassment.

Sarah tried not to stare, but the lace! She'd never seen anything so fine. However, her feminine appreciation for a truly exquisite piece of bed-wear didn't cloud her thinking for more than a moment.

Vane expected her to wear that for him, did he? He was certainly turning out with all guns blazing. Grimly, she ordered Barker to unearth one of her more practical nightgowns from her trunks and to put the silk and lace confection away.

As the maid undressed her, Sarah glanced at the clock.

It was too late to order a separate bedchamber prepared without making a fuss and creating talk amongst the servants. Particularly on their wedding night, such behavior would appear exceedingly odd. Despite her anger at his high-handed tactics, Sarah didn't for one moment forget how much she owed Vane. She refused to make him look foolish in front of his servants. There would be no scenes in this household if she could avoid it.

She washed her face and hands in a china basin and dried them on the towel. Unbidden, memories emerged of this room and another towel, wrapped around male hips, dropping to the floor. . . .

Abruptly, she sat in the chair at the dressing table. Sleeping in that bed . . . Sarah squeezed her eyes shut as Barker brushed out her hair.

Barker paused. "Am I hurting you, ma'am?"

"No, no. I just have a slight headache, that's all. And how do you go on, Barker? Is the place to your liking?"

"Everything is most satisfactory, ma'am. A well-run household if I may say so."

"I'm glad," said Sarah. The housekeeper did appear to know what she was about. Yet, appearances could be deceiving. Sarah would make a thorough inspection in the morning.

Now, she just needed to get through the night.

Barker put down the brush and brought a rich silk dressing gown, a loan from the countess.

Sarah couldn't resist running her fingertips over the slippery blue silk before she put it on. It covered her night rail completely and flowed to the floor.

Dismissing the maid, she sat at the dressing table and took up her hairbrush, running it slowly through her long tresses. Had this dressing table been here on her last visit? She didn't think so.

Vane must have ordered its installation. Considerate of him. He was a considerate man.

Shame burned in her chest. Vane deserved a woman who would come to him gladly and give him joy and light and . . . children. She swallowed hard.

When he looked at her, Vane saw an object of desire, a beautiful *thing* that he dearly wished to possess. He didn't know she was like a ripe, red apple with flawless skin but riddled and worm-eaten inside.

Rotten. All but a thin core of pride that the recent past hadn't quite obliterated. From there, she would rebuild, layer by layer, until she had made something of herself. She couldn't let Vane take what he wanted from her and toss her away.

His interest in her was so intense, so baseless, so unreasonable in light of all she'd done that it could only be infatuation. An ephemeral emotion, one that wouldn't last much longer now that he had her, as he'd wanted for so long.

Sounds in Vane's dressing room caught her attention. She heard his voice. There must be another entrance, because he hadn't walked through the bedchamber to get there.

She waited, heart pounding, for the murmurs to cease. Finally, the connecting door opened and he stood there, a huge figure in a patterned silk dressing gown, crowding the doorway and then stepping into the room.

It took all of her will to sit where she was and not shrink away and cower from him like some milk-and-water miss. He couldn't force her to carnal relations; he'd given his word. All she needed to do was remain cold and aloof *and not let him touch her*, and she would retire the victor this night.

His gaze took in her voluminous dressing gown but he made no comment about her refusal to wear the garment he'd sent. "Are you hungry?" His deep voice had a husky timbre tonight. "You ate very little today." He gestured toward the adjacent sitting room. "I ordered a light supper for us if you'd care to have some."

She would rather walk on a bed of nails than force one morsel down her throat, but she grasped the opportunity to stave off bedtime and stepped into the sitting room.

It was furnished comfortably in a masculine style, decorated with sporting prints and memorabilia. There were even a few cartoons of Vane pictured with various pugilists.

One of him posed in a fighting stance, shirtless and tousled and gleaming with sweat, recalled a vivid memory of him fighting in the ballroom downstairs. Heat raced through her bloodstream. She turned away.

Seeing her interest, he said, "I'm the patron of a number of prominent sportsmen, mainly pugilists." He smiled faintly. "The wags like to jibe at my apparent taste for low company."

"And do you?" she said. "Have a taste for low company?"

"I don't ask a man's pedigree before I agree to train him, if that's what you mean. But it's true that sporting circles admit men from all classes." His eyes warmed with enthusiasm, and it seemed he was about to say more, but in a moment his gaze caught on one of the pictures. Grimacing, he reached up to remove the cartoon of him, stripped and fighting, from the wall.

"My apologies, some of these are not in good taste. I'll have them taken down." Glancing around, he added, "In fact, all of this can go. Have the room re-papered and furnish it however you wish. It's yours now."

She'd be pleased at his thoughtfulness if he hadn't also constrained her to share the adjoining bedchamber. And strangely, she liked this outrageously masculine room, which seemed so much a part of him.

Briskly, she said, "Thank you, but I have no intention of displacing you. I'm sure there's another parlor that will be suitable for my use." She hesitated. "I shall order a separate chamber made up for me in the morning, Vane. It's a common enough arrangement, and I trust you won't make things difficult. We don't wish to provide fodder for gossip below-stairs."

He watched her for a long moment, seeming to debate with himself. Finally, he shrugged. "I suppose it makes little difference where you're based. Do as you wish." He held out his hand. "Come and eat."

Little difference? Did that mean he would come to her room instead?

Stiffly, she moved to the small table and sat down, disconcerted by her easy victory, distrusting his motives. She suspected that his sudden agreement had nothing to do with her demand. He'd decided to let her alone quite independently. Or perhaps he was merely acquiescing now to lull her into a false sense of security. Perhaps he thought it would only take one night to change her mind.

He served her small portions of cheese and fruit and a slice of ham. Far too much for her uneasy stomach, but she made an effort to nibble at some apple while maintaining a flow of polite conversation.

He ate none of the supper, she noticed, but poured them both wine, a heavy, dark Burgundy, and sat back with his glass in hand, watching her as she battled on.

"The stillroom you had in the attic at Bloomsbury," he said abruptly. "You made perfume there, the landlady said."

Too late, Sarah remembered her scarred palms. Thoughtlessly, she'd removed her gloves to eat. She fought the urge to hide her hands beneath the table.

Well, he'd seen them anyway, hadn't he? Kissed them passionately, reverently, that night, as if they'd been the hands of an angel, not an adulteress.

Hoping the heat in her face didn't show, she lifted her chin. "I made perfume and sold it, yes." Her voice hardened a little. "I needed the money."

"What sort of perfume? That scent you wear . . ." He looked an inquiry, his eyes burning into hers. His familiarity with her scent seemed an intensely intimate thing.

She lowered her gaze, certain now that she blushed. "Lilies. And a few other things—tuberose, jasmine, lemon, a touch of musk. I like to experiment with different fragrances for my clients, but for myself, I only use that one scent."

"It's an unusual accomplishment for the daughter of an earl. How did you learn to make perfume?"

Sarah smiled as she remembered. "The housekeeper at Penrose Hall made me her apprentice. Her family owned a perfume manufactory in Montpellier before the Terror. They supplied scent to the French queen, among others, but of course, their fortunes fell along with their clients'. Madame Vissier took charge of our stillroom and taught me all she knew."

Thank God for Madame. Where would Sarah have been all these years without the means to earn a little extra income? "I didn't have the right equipment, or all the raw materials I'd have liked, but I did well enough. I survived."

He asked more questions, and seeing his genuine interest, she went on to describe the various techniques of extracting floral essences, of the processes of maceration and the far more time-consuming practice of enfleurage. Then the mixing, the blending of scents to create a subtle symphony, with a base note that lingers in the nasal receptors like a fine wine lingers on an appreciative palate.

Vane listened and questioned as if the subject truly fascinated him. Even as something within her blossomed at his attentiveness, she knew she played for time, staving off that moment when the silence stretched taut between them and the battle began.

Vane studied her intently. "Do you miss your work, Sarah? You make it sound like a cross between chemistry and art."

"Yes, I—" She stopped. She didn't need to make perfume anymore. She was the Marchioness of Vane; she could buy all the fragrance in Grasse if she wished. She didn't have to scramble for the best flowers at market anymore or toil in a hot, steamy room or make oceans of insipid rosewater.

She shook her head, reaching for her wineglass. "As your wife, I have quite enough to occupy me now."

VANE watched Sarah sip her wine, staining her lips deep red at the center. His groin gave a painful twinge. He'd waited all this time to have her. And yet, still she evaded his grasp.

He'd never been in this position before, he realized. He'd consorted with many women, but none who were unwilling to bed him. Not that he flattered himself that he was any great prize. Those females had been generously rewarded for their compliance, after all.

Vane couldn't recall that he'd ever seduced a lady, but women weren't so very different beneath the skin, were they? There'd been signs that he affected Sarah. A faint flush, a small gasp. The betraying tremor in her hand as she reached for her glass.

He spoke to her of perfume, watched enthusiasm for her art light her eyes, animate her in a way that almost pained him to witness. It was such a stark contrast to her usual cool remoteness.

In turn, he answered her questions about his family, about his principal seat and his other holdings, but all the while his brain ticked over the question: Why? Why wouldn't she bed him?

He refused to believe there was no passion in her. She'd burned like a brand in his arms on that fateful night. He refused to believe she had a distaste for *him*. He was experienced enough to interpret the way her body responded. He'd always been adept at reading the telltale signals the body sent; it was one way you kept ahead of your opponent in a fight.

But a contradictory message came out of her mouth. And damned if he wasn't too much of a gentleman to force the issue.

"Your brother Gregory has sons, I think you mentioned," she was saying now. "How old are they?"

He nearly growled with frustration at these inconsequential nothings when there were words of great moment that remained unspoken between them. However, he answered her, and a dozen questions like it.

Finally, she seemed to run out of talk and could no longer maintain the pretense of toying with her meal. She dabbed at her lips with a napkin and made as if to stand.

Vane was up before her and held out his hand.

He'd only meant to assist her to rise, though the excuse to touch her had motivated the gesture, it was true. But her head jerked back to look at him, and the flare of her eyes spoke her wariness more clearly than words.

Was she afraid of him?

His heart sank as he turned to pull out her chair, accepting her tacit refusal to even touch his hand. Stubborn defiance was one thing. He could sweep that away with a kiss. But what did he do with her fear?

I am not Brinsley. He wanted to shout it, to shake her. Hadn't he shown her by now what kind of man he was? How *dare* she be afraid?

He detested bullies. He'd never fought anyone who wasn't up to his weight, always acutely aware of his superior strength. The notion that Sarah saw him as a man who'd use force to get what he wanted from her wrenched his guts.

This was all wrong, and he didn't know how to make it right. Or if he ever could.

He must have moved toward her unconsciously. She put a hand up to her throat and stepped back, a defensive movement that struck him to the soul.

A sick sadness welled deep within him, overwhelming his resolve to make her his tonight. Without a word, he left her. Walked out of that sitting room with aching loins and a raging heart.

IT was late when Vane finally came to bed. The tension since he'd left her standing alone in the sitting room had wound tighter and tighter, until she was sick with it. It was almost a relief when the bedchamber door opened. Finally, they could get this confrontation over with.

She'd deliberately doused the candles and let the fire die so that the only light in the room was a golden red glow from the coals in the grate.

Enough light to discern his outline as he shrugged the banyan from his shoulders and let it drop to the floor. She didn't need to see to know he was naked beneath.

Everything inside her clenched with alarm as he slid under

the covers next to her, his heavy weight depressing the mattress so that she nearly rolled toward him. She clung to her edge of the bed as hot awareness pulsed through her, throbbed in her ears and pounded in her throat.

She could have pretended to be asleep, but that wasn't her way. "Good night, my lord," she forced out.

The words were stiff and strained, but pride gave them a tone of command. She wondered if he noticed the faintest hint of desperation. She eased farther away from him, until she was in danger of falling out the other side if she moved an inch more.

"What, my lady? No dutiful good night kiss?" His words sliced through her.

She swallowed. The note of sarcasm hadn't entered his voice since that awful dawn. "No."

"Do you think you're in danger from one small kiss? Flattering."

Coldly, she replied, "Kisses might lead to expectations I can't fulfill. I wouldn't want you to suffer the disappointment."

"My dear, I'm hard as a pikestaff just lying here next to you. There's not much you can do that will make it worse than it is already."

She sucked in a breath and fought the images his crude words brought to mind. Her body thrummed with tension and fear and something melting and hot, which she knew was pure desire.

Sarah squeezed her eyes shut and tried to regulate her breathing. The big, strong, aroused male lying next to her was the greatest temptation she'd ever faced. But this time, this one time in her life, she would be strong. If she could get through this night without succumbing to the insistent clamor in her body and heart, the next night would be easier, the next easier still, until they were both set firmly on divergent paths. Paths that would never intersect in any meaningful or troubling way again.

She gripped her hands together and remained silent.

He rolled away. "Never mind."

Vane seemed to think that was the end of it. He lay with his back to her and settled his head into the pillow and exhaled a long, relaxed breath as if he'd have no trouble falling into slumber. She knew that couldn't be so. He'd just confessed to his state of arousal, hadn't he?

Uncomfortable, she shifted a little, anxious not to attract his attention. But she couldn't escape the sheer force of his presence, lying there beside her. She felt prickly and hot and distressingly alert.

Ah, she'd never get to sleep all cramped like this. Frustrated, thwarted, ready to scream with vexation, she turned onto her back and stared at the canopy above as helpless tears leaked from her eyes.

A rustle of the sheets told her he'd rolled toward her again. She held her breath, half longing for him, half terrified. He raised himself on one elbow, then bent his head toward her and brushed her lips with his, gossamer light, then whispered against them: "If you're not going to make me a happy groom, stop flouncing and sighing and go to sleep." The faintest hint of amusement colored his voice.

That soft touch of his lips flooded her with a liquid heat that pooled in the place between her legs and flowed down to her toes. She nearly arched up to him, and clenched her hands into fists in an effort to contain the wildness he provoked with just that one soft kiss. She ached to feel him inside her, filling the empty space in her body and heart.

But he'd already turned away.

She ought to be glad that he'd accepted her refusal.

In the morning, she would be glad.

Fifteen

WHEN Sarah woke, Vane wasn't there. It was difficult to believe she'd fallen asleep after hours of wakeful anticipation, worrying that she'd remain unconscious, unguarded beside him for any part of the night.

He must have left her alone. If he'd put his hands on her at all during the night, she'd have known it.

The skies were overcast and a slight chill pervaded the air. Suddenly, it hit her. There was not an earthly thing she must get out of bed for today.

She was the Marchioness of Vane. She did not have to dress in the darkness and hurry to the market to ensure she made her purchases before all the best flowers and produce were gone. She didn't have to haggle over prices or turn away importunate tradesmen or climb to the attics to make more perfume. There would be household duties and obligations on the estate, of course, and all manner of social niceties to take care of. But for the moment, just for today, she might laze abed until noon if she liked.

Sarah rang for her maid and snuggled under the covers.

On being informed that Vane was from home, she could relax.

The luxury of breakfast in bed almost made her forget her irritation with Vane's high-handed behavior the previous evening. Steaming, fragrant hot chocolate and a freshly baked roll with butter and preserves appeared on a tray that the maid set on Sarah's knees. The silver gleamed; the china was so delicate it was almost transparent. Lost in enjoyment of this everyday extravagance, Sarah reflected that in a material sense, this marriage was everything she could wish.

And did not remotely deserve.

Guilt settled in a great weight over her chest once more. A bare week after Brinsley's death and here she was in another man's bed, enjoying this windfall of wealth and privilege.

Her newly filled stomach almost revolted. It was obscene. No one should profit so excessively from lies and adultery, wickedness and murder. All of this ought to have come at a grave cost, yet she'd suffered no retribution. The universe required no penance from her, it seemed. If she wanted, she might take Vane and all that he offered. She might live the life of a wealthy, highborn lady and never remember the soul-destroying pain and degradation of her previous existence.

She'd accepted that life as punishment for her folly in marrying Brinsley despite her mother's objections. She'd thought she was in love with him. It was only later that she recognized her devotion for infatuation, the base passion it was.

Well, she'd made that bed, and she'd lain in it for ten years. That was justice.

But then her passion had led her astray once more. This time, Fate offered her all she had ever wished in return. How could she accept it, after what she'd done?

Suddenly, Sarah remembered and cursed herself for forgetting, even for an instant. She did have a pressing task to take care of today. She rang the bell and launched out of bed, pacing until Barker arrived to help her dress.

She'd missed her appointment with Maggie and Tom on Wednesday. There was no way she could have made the journey to Billingsgate without having to explain where she was going. And besides, her mother kept her so busy with the plans for a funeral and a wedding in one week, she couldn't slip away. She hadn't trusted anyone in her mother's household with the task of taking a message. Could Maggie read? It seemed unlikely.

She wondered if Maggie knew Brinsley was dead.

From the look of her, Sarah doubted the woman was still Brinsley's mistress at the time of his death. He was much too fastidious, if what she'd heard about his other lovers was true.

But he'd kept her address. What did that mean? Sarah frowned as Barker laced her into her stays. He'd scoffed at the idea of sending Maggie money for the boy's keep, so why had he jotted down her direction?

"My lady, which gown will you wear today?"

Sarah passed her uninspiring wardrobe through her mind. "I suppose the forest green cambric will do."

She pretended not to see her maid's moue of disapproval. When she was ready, she said, "Barker, will you send one of the footmen to see me in the drawing room, please? And then I'll see Mrs. Brodie."

"Yes, my lady."

The footman appeared promptly, just as Sarah finished a short note. Will was a strapping, handsome lad with a gleam of intelligence in his eyes. She hoped he was discreet. But after all, there was nothing improper about having him take a message to another woman. If he carried tales to Vane, she'd tell Vane the truth.

She sealed the letter and handed it to the footman and gave him the direction. In case Maggie couldn't read, she added, "Will, take the carriage and tell Miss Day that I couldn't keep our appointment but if she and the boy will consent to return here in the carriage with you, I will see them."

He agreed and she nodded dismissal.

With a sense of impatience, Sarah requested the house-keeper to take her on a tour of the house. As the minutes passed, the longing to see Tom grew. She didn't know how she managed to make sense as she spoke with Mrs. Brodie about household matters.

She was so distracted, it wasn't until they reached the private apartments that she recalled her argument with Vane the previous evening.

Introducing the subject as naturally as she could, she mentioned her requirement for a bedchamber separate from her husband's, as was the prevailing fashion. "Lord Vane was planning to redecorate before he installed me in my own chamber but I assured him I don't mind taking one as it is. Perhaps when we remove to Bewley I shall leave instructions for any changes to be carried out in my absence."

To her relief, Mrs. Brodie reacted without surprise. "I'm sorry, my lady. I did venture to suggest . . . But there's not been much time, what with the wedding so quick. If you will choose a chamber that is to your liking, I'll have it ready for you in a trice."

Thankful to have leaped that hurdle without trouble, Sarah settled on the blue chamber, a light, elegantly furnished room overlooking the square. As she thanked the housekeeper and dismissed her, they heard voices in the entrance hall and Mrs. Brodie said, "Ah, that'll be his lordship, back from training." She bobbed a curtsey and left.

Training? Sarah wondered about that as she returned to Vane's bedchamber to oversee the removal of her personal belongings.

A step sounded in the corridor and he was there before her, looking well turned out, as usual, only his damp hair bearing witness to his exercise. No wonder he was such a fine figure of a man if he exercised so diligently every day. Aware-ness flashed over her body as she remembered the fight she'd witnessed in Vane's ballroom, the muscles gleaming with sweat, the intense, controlled aggression in his eyes.

Apprehension spiked within her but she managed a smile. "Good morning, my lord."

He bowed with an ironic lift of an eyebrow. "I'm glad you think so." He glanced at Barker, who was collecting Sarah's toiletries from the dressing table. He didn't comment, however, which made Sarah thankful for the maid's presence.

His dark gaze ran over Sarah, considering. "It occurred to me this morning that you might wish to buy some new gowns and such. I'm at your disposal if you'd like to go today."

Sarah couldn't mistake the implication. She flushed, heat prickling in her throat and cheeks. He thought her a dowd. Well, he was right, wasn't he?

"Thank you. That is most considerate of you. But you needn't trouble yourself to come with me."

Vane choosing gowns for her would promote exactly the kind of intimacy she wished to avoid. She was woman enough, however, to want to look her best, and she owed it to Vane to do credit to him as his wife.

New gowns. She couldn't remember the last time she'd purchased anything new for herself. The few garments she owned had been made over several times. She realized she hovered close to tears, as if she might sob her gratitude down his waistcoat at any moment. Only over a few pieces of clothing.

Her voice trembling a little, she repeated her thanks. "I'll try not to be too extravagant, but I'm afraid I'll need a complete new wardrobe." *Gloves. Lots of gloves.* She pressed her scarred palms together.

He reached out and touched her cheek with his fingertips. "Do your best to beggar me and I'll call it money well spent." His gaze softened. "I want to spoil you utterly, Sarah. I want to make up for all those lost, miserable years."

The understanding in his eyes struck her to the soul. She cursed herself for the warm, melting sensation in her belly, the flutter in her chest. Her heart was a shallow thing indeed to perform somersaults at the notion of him showering her in riches.

The overwhelming rush of tenderness she felt for him terrified her. She was walking a knife's edge, so close to throwing away caution, so close to opening herself to him. But once she did that, there would be no retreat.

"You have given me so much," she whispered, conscious that her maid had left the room for only a moment. "And now, new gowns." She made a helpless gesture. "I can give you nothing in return."

Vane's face closed like a slammed door. He dropped his hand and stepped back, saying coolly, "The pleasure of seeing you in them is all that I require." He turned to go. "Have the carriage brought around now. I don't want to see you in those rags a moment longer."

Suddenly, Sarah remembered. She couldn't go out. She must be home to see Maggie and Tom, if and when they came. "I cannot go today," she said, searching for an excuse. "Surely, it's indecent to be buying gowns so soon after Brinsley's death."

Vane swung back, his jaw tightening. "What's indecent is the style of penury he kept you in while he lavished money on his own vices." Angrily, he shook his head. "Why must everything be a battle, Sarah?"

She was saved from answering by Barker bustling back into the room. The maid crossed to the clothespress and began taking out gowns and throwing them over her crooked arm.

"Barker," said Vane evenly, never taking his gaze from Sarah's face.

"Yes, my lord?"

"Take those garments and burn them. And if there are any more where they came from, burn them, too. Undergarments, shoes, the lot."

Mistress and maid gasped as one. Barker hesitated, throwing an indecisive look at Sarah. Sarah ignored her. She was rigid with fury.

"You may go," Vane told the maid.

Barker bobbed a curtsey, her eyes brimming with excited triumph, and hurried away.

He raised his eyebrows at Sarah. "I trust I've made myself plain?"

Outrageous! How dare he make a fool of her in front of her servant? Somehow, the knowledge that his high-handed behavior was wholly to her benefit infuriated her all the more.

Tight-lipped, she gritted out, "Crystal clear. Do you want the gown off my back as well?" As soon as the sarcastic words left her mouth, she regretted them.

There was a pause. A long one, in which she could hear her own heartbeat, a strong tattoo in her ears.

His dark gaze traveled over her slowly, inch by inch. "Don't tempt me," he said softly.

Warily, she stepped back, acutely conscious of the frustrated desire that thickened the air. She could smell him, the scent of exertion and clean, honest sweat, a heady male musk. Memories of the night they'd spent flooded back, their bodies slick and glistening, moving together. . . .

Sarah swallowed hard, aware that he must have read her reaction. She put a hand to her cheek and felt it flame. Realized her hand trembled and hurriedly dropped it to her side. He noticed the movement and a frown snapped between his brows.

She forced out, "It seems you leave me no choice."

"Order the carriage when you're ready." He paused, seeming to struggle with himself. "I take it you don't wish for my company on this expedition."

"I do not." She didn't blame him for the grim look about his mouth at her rudeness. But the thought of trying on gowns and selecting intimate apparel while he watched made her stomach clench with apprehension. It smacked too much of the relationship between protector and mistress, not husband and wife.

He appeared about to say something, to argue with her, perhaps, but changed his mind. With another quick, angry shake of the head, he turned on his heel and strode to his dressing room, slamming the door behind him.

"MILADY, I'm sorry, I couldn't find her." The handsome young footman stood before Sarah, looking worried.

"Perhaps she'd stepped out for an hour or so. You should have waited."

His gaze darted to the clock and she realized it was nigh on two hours since she'd sent him. "Beg pardon but I did wait, ma'am. Then I asked about. They told me she's gone. Packed her bags and left."

Frowning, Sarah launched to her feet. "Where? Where did she go?"

"I don't know, milady. I questioned her neighbors and the caretaker but no one keeps track of each other in places like that. She'd skipped out without telling anyone or paying the rent, so I understand."

"Oh, God." Sarah put her hand to her brow and sank to the sofa. Her head was pounding viciously. She couldn't think what to do next.

Will cleared his throat, startling her. She'd forgotten he was there.

Sarah tried to collect herself. This behavior would create gossip belowstairs, and she could do without that, on top of everything else.

She thanked Will and dismissed him, then fell to pacing, biting the edge of her thumb. She couldn't possibly return to such a rough neighborhood and investigate the matter herself. She'd be sure to land herself in more serious trouble than a picked pocket. If Will had been unsuccessful, how would she discover anything more?

Her father . . . Would he understand? No, he would say the child was not her responsibility, that she ought to wash her hands of the matter. All she'd achieve by involving him would be to increase his disappointment in her and highlight the sordidness of her former life.

"*Vane*," she whispered. Could she summon the gall to enlist his aid? He had his own pride, after all. What would he say to the prospect of giving succor to Brinsley's love child?

Sarah swallowed. She'd prefer not to find out. It hardly redounded to her credit that her husband should have consorted with another woman so soon after she and Brinsley wed.

Perhaps she'd do better to ask Peter Cole for help. She didn't believe there was much of the milk of human kindness in Brinsley's brother, but surely he'd appreciate where his duty lay.

She looked up as the butler entered the parlor. "Your carriage is at the door, my lady."

Oh, no. She closed her eyes. Shopping was the last thing she wanted to do now. But if she didn't go, she wouldn't have a stitch to wear, would she? Vane had not been making idle threats about her clothing. They hadn't been burned, though. He'd changed his mind and given them to the poor. The fact that Barker made no protest at this showed exactly how far Sarah had sunk. The situation must be dire if even her maid disdained to take her castoffs.

She hoped her newfound status would move the modistes she patronized to work quickly. No doubt the Marchioness of Vane could command instant service as the genteel but impoverished Lady Sarah Cole could not.

With an exasperated sigh, she gathered her reticule and bonnet and went down to the awaiting carriage.

SARAH screwed emerald drops into her earlobes and allowed her maid to drape a fine Norwich silk shawl over her elbows. Vane had ordered her to beggar him. She hadn't quite achieved that—she doubted she'd made a dent in his vast wealth—but she certainly hadn't counted the cost of the extensive wardrobe she'd ordered today. She hadn't spent a penny of her pin money—all the bills were to be sent directly to Vane.

This deep emerald green silk hugged her curves wickedly and revealed a larger amount of bosom than she usually showed. She suspected it had been intended for another, more daring female, but the modiste had insisted Sarah take it because it looked so ravishing on her.

Sarah scrutinized herself in the mirror. She was pale and she'd lost weight but she still had a decent bosom and her hip bones didn't stick out, so that was something. Her maid had taken extra care over dressing her hair—as well she might after conspiring with Vane to get rid of all her clothes, the traitor.

There was nothing for it but to put a good face on things. She must admit, if only to herself, that Vane had been right. Amazing how dressing well could lift the spirits.

But spending all that money on finery while Tom suffered such poor conditions ate at her. She needed to find him, to take care of him. She'd called on Jenny and Peter Cole that afternoon, but Peter had refused to discuss the subject with her. She'd found an excuse to be rid of Jenny for a few minutes and quickly asked Peter to help her find the boy.

He'd flushed scarlet when she'd broached the subject and roughly snapped that Brinsley's by-blows were none of her concern, nor his, either, come to that. She was furious at his callousness, but it was no more than she'd expected. She'd have to enlist Vane's help to find the boy. There was no other way.

Absently, Sarah slid a gold bracelet up her arm as she went down to wait for him in the drawing room. She might use her pin money to mount an investigation and never say a word to Vane about it, but that would be wrong and deceitful. She owed him honesty, at least.

What if he refused her? Surely, he must see that a child's welfare, perhaps his very life, was at stake. That was more important than any considerations of propriety or pride. He was a good man. He would help her. He must.

There was only one way to find out.

When she heard Vane's step on the threshold, she whirled to face him. At the sight of her, he stopped short. A sharp inhale of breath, a clenched fist. Surprise registered on his face before he swiftly shuttered his expression and moved toward her.

"Good evening, Sarah." His voice was deep but slightly strained.

"Good evening. Won't you sit down?" Her own voice trembled a little as she groped for a way to phrase her extraordinary request.

His brows rose, but he said nothing and chose a chair at a right angle to hers.

"Vane, I need to speak with you about a very serious matter." She licked her lips, a sign of nervousness he observed with interest. She gripped her hands together. "Perhaps you recall a conversation you and I had at Peter Cole's house about"—she took a deep breath, then expelled it—"about the fact that I cannot have children." She barely glanced at him, but sensed that he nodded. "Well, a number of years ago, Brinsley fathered a son."

She looked up. There was an arrested expression in Vane's eyes and a hardening about his mouth. "Go on."

Without waiting for her to continue, he stood and walked to gaze out of the window at the street below. Without his gaze upon her, it was easier to finish her request. She wondered if he'd turned his back to conceal his own feelings or out of consideration for her.

She cleared her throat. "Now that Brinsley is dead, I am concerned that the child be cared for. I had made plans for his care myself, but . . ." She told him of her visit to Maggie and the theft of her money.

As soon as she'd finished, he said curtly, "I'll see to it."

Relief and gratitude flooded her. "Oh, but Vane—"

He turned back to her then, his expression a mask of fury. "What the *Devil* was Cole about, even mentioning the brat to you? Why should *you* have been scraping to support *his* love child?"

"It was either that or leave him in the most degrading conditions," Sarah said quietly, neglecting to answer the first question. "The circumstances of his birth hardly mattered. I couldn't allow the boy to suffer when something might be done for him."

She saw Vane cock his head, watching her, as if he'd discovered something new, something that both puzzled and interested him. She stumbled on. "I-I realize it is beyond the pale to ask it of you, but I don't know where else to turn."

Vane stood very still for a moment. Carefully, he said, "I

am glad you came to me. Undoubtedly, something must be done for the boy. Where is he now?"

"That's the problem. He's gone." Sarah told him of her failure to meet with Maggie and her disappearance.

His brow lowered farther and it was moments before he spoke. Finally, he said, "Leave it in my hands. I'll find him and see that right is done by the child."

Sarah exhaled her first easy breath since the conversation began. She had no doubt in his ability to do as he said. Vane was the most competent man she knew. Competent and good. What a sorry shame that he should be tied to a woman like her.

There was silence between them, while she struggled for the courage to voice the longing in her heart. "Please. I would like to see him, if I may. If you do find him."

Slowly, he nodded. "If that is your wish."

"Thank you." Impulsively, she rose and moved to take Vane's hand in both of hers. "It was outrageous of me to ask you this. I do thank you, from the bottom of my heart, for your generosity to an innocent boy."

He looked down at their clasped hands and a stark expression swept over his face. He lifted his eyes to hers. "Don't imagine I'm some kind of plaster saint," he said. "I'm only doing this for you."

Color flamed to her cheeks and she slid her hand free, stepping back. "Thank you. Whatever the reason. You have no idea how much this means to me."

Rivers opened the doors into the dining room and announced dinner.

"Ah," she said. "Let's go in." As he held out his hand to assist her to rise, she couldn't keep the glow from her eyes. "Thank you," she whispered again, and placed her hand in his.

VANE grimaced and brushed the rain off his hat. Mere days after his wedding a man ought to be rolling between the sheets with his new wife, not searching for an urchin through the pitiful, damp streets of east London.

Spring rain was supposed to freshen the landscape, but in this area of town all it seemed to freshen was the ghastly odor of fish. He'd visited Maggie Day's room and found a new family ensconced there with no trace of the woman left behind, not even a memory in the minds of her neighbors. Many who lived in that building were transient, the rest apathetic, disinterested. Or perhaps they did know something but weren't about to spill their guts to a gent like him.

The caretaker of that tumbling wreck claimed not to know where Maggie had gone. Owed him rent, too, he insisted with a scowl. He didn't know anything about a boy, but she'd probably kept him quiet, not wanting to pay for an extra body. Vane left with nothing more than disgust at Brinsley's improvidence and anger that Sarah should have been obliged to visit such a place.

Not for the first time, Vane wondered what the hell Sarah had been about, getting herself shackled to Brinsley Cole. She was an intelligent woman. How could she have failed to see the rot that lurked beneath the handsome façade?

He was furious with her for showing such poor judgment, he realized, had been furious with her for years. That she'd submitted to Brinsley's foul treatment all that time without seeking a formal separation was inconceivable. Intolerable. And yet, had she found someone steady and kind to marry in those years before Vane met her, he wouldn't have her now.

But he would almost have forgone this chance with her if he'd never had to see the pain in her eyes that evening when she told him about Brinsley's love child. He didn't doubt the boy had been conceived while they were married, nor that Brinsley had maliciously flung the affair in her face, knowing how his betrayal must hurt her.

Perhaps she'd longed for a child of her own. Hearing of her husband's creating a babe with someone else—what a cruel blow that must have been. He devoutly hoped Brinsley was roasting in the hottest fires of hell for that piece of arrant cruelty.

How had her parents accepted this match? *They* should have seen what the young, impressionable Sarah had not. Straghan was a man of the world and a powerful one. Why had he given his daughter to such a blackguard? The countess was no fool, and it was clear she detested her late son-in-law. Why hadn't they put a stop to it?

Vane sighed. He could do little more himself to find the boy. He wasn't familiar with the rookeries and doss-houses where a woman and a small boy might hide themselves, but he knew someone who was.

Vane visited Finch at the fight club and gave him directions to take up the search. Finch had friends in every stratum of society. If anyone could find the boy, Finch could.

The signs didn't look auspicious, though. In a place like London, it was far too easy for a woman like Maggie to disappear.

Sixteen

SARAH sat at her dressing table clad in her night rail and wrapper, rubbing a cream she'd prepared from goose grease and beeswax and rose oil into her damaged palms. She tended to her hands every morning and night in a ritual that was both restorative and a poignant reminder of her former existence. She didn't know if the cream would ever erase the scars of the past, but at least it made her skin softer, smoothed the rough patches away.

She glanced at the clock as she drew cotton gloves over her hands to protect the bed linen from the lotion on her hands. It was late and Vane still hadn't come home. She'd asked to accompany him on his search for Tom, but he'd refused to take her, saying she'd only get in the way. Given her previous experience, she didn't doubt that was true, so she'd agreed to remain behind. He'd promised to send for her if his search bore fruit.

But he'd been a very long time and it had been raining in sheets all afternoon. He would be cold and wet and hungry. Besides ordering her staff to be ready with a meal and a hot bath upon his return, Sarah had no means of easing his discomfort. Shame flooded her at the task she'd set him, all the trouble she'd given.

Judge a man by his actions, her mother had told her. All that Vane had done in recent weeks showed him to be an honorable man. Even that first night she'd come to his house, he'd tried to conduct their interview in less charged surroundings. He hadn't touched her until she broke down. And when she'd treated him cruelly, he'd still insisted on protecting her. His behavior since had been exemplary.

Her mind turned over his conduct, then contrasted it with her own. Her cruelty, the lies she'd dealt him. The pain she'd caused.

He'd given her everything, in spite of it. All he wanted in return, all he'd ever asked, was that she share his bed. How could she continue to refuse him? Regardless of what it cost her, how could she fail to repay him for the bounty he'd given her?

Pure, cold terror squeezed her heart.

Images of herself in Vane's bed that fateful evening returned, images that would be forever entwined with visions of Brinsley on that couch, covered in blood.

She had betrayed Brinsley, and in that betrayal, she'd shown herself to be no better than he was. A weak, lustful individual with neither restraint nor self-respect. Looking back, she couldn't believe that she'd forsaken her principles, the rules she'd lived by for ten years, in exchange for one night of passion. Believing Vane had paid for her to service him like a whore.

She'd given herself to him anyway, body and soul. But in the morning, she'd reclaimed them both. Or thought she had. She hadn't counted on leaving a little piece of her heart behind.

Vane had been right; she'd shown the worst possible taste and lack of judgment in marrying Brinsley Cole. She'd seen that soon enough, but far too late to do anything but endure. And she'd taken perverse pride in her endurance, hadn't she? Anything he'd thrown at her, she'd deflected with cool derision. Until at last he found a vital weakness and exploited it to the fullest.

She burned with anger at that final twist of the knife. Yet guilt and shame left her no choice but to refuse the happiness Vane offered her. How could she rebuild her pride if she weakened before Vane?

Her thoughts were tangled with violent emotion. All she knew was that if she let Vane become her lover in truth as well as her husband, she'd no longer call her soul her own. He would own her as surely as if he'd bought and paid for her all those nights ago.

Could she possibly keep the two separate? Could she give him her body and withhold her heart, keep her pride, shoulder the guilt, hold everything in a delicate balance?

Impossible, perhaps. But for his sake, she would have to take the risk.

Her movements slow and painstaking, Sarah pulled at each fingertip of her cotton gloves before sliding them off her hands. She set the gloves aside and reached for the Olympian dew. Carefully, deliberately, she cleaned the greasy concoction from her hands.

FINALLY calling a halt to his search for Tom, Vane looked in at White's and stepped into a world wholly different from the slums of Billingsgate. Redolent of beeswax and old leather, the quiet, rarefied atmosphere of the gentleman's club seemed almost obscene in contrast to the filth and poverty farther east.

Vane didn't often visit his club, preferring the earthier company of sporting enthusiasts at Cribb's, but the porter greeted him by name as he handed him his hat, coat, and walking stick.

He nodded to the man. "Is Lord Jardine in this evening?"

"Yes, my lord. Upstairs reading the paper, I think you'll find."

He thanked the porter and found his friend lazing in a

dark leather chair, staring out at nothing over his copy of the *Morning Post*.

Vane threw himself in the chair opposite and waited.

One eyebrow flew upward. "Vane."

"You were in a brown study when I walked in. Plotting more diabolical deeds?" To most, Lord Jardine was your typical debauched aristocrat with too much money and too much time on his hands. Only a very few knew he worked secretly for the Home Office.

"Why should you think that?" Jardine leaned forward and tossed the paper onto the low table before him. "Now, tell me. Do I hear correctly? Must I wish you happy?"

So Jardine had heard the news already. Vane wasn't surprised. He accepted his friend's well wishes, adding, "Sorry you weren't invited to the wedding. Strictly a family affair."

Jardine's saturnine look deepened. "That's quite all right. I can't stomach weddings at the best of times, though I'd have suppressed my natural revulsion for you." His dark eyes flickered. "But you're not here to discuss marital bliss, are you, Vane?"

When he didn't immediately reply, Jardine added, "The dear departed has left you with a damnable mess to sort out, has he? Yes, I thought so."

Vane met his gaze. "I thought if anyone could tell me what was behind this murder, it would be you. It *was* murder. And not with a damned muff pistol, either."

"You want to know who killed Brinsley Cole?" Jardine's eyebrows flexed with surprise. "I'd have thought that the least interesting part of the whole affair."

"Who did?"

"Word among the fellows is it was you, old man, and they're lining up to shake your hand. Oh, I know it wasn't, and so would they, if they'd use their brains." He paused. "Faulkner was ready to stitch you up, did you know? Your valiant bride came riding to your rescue. She must be quite a woman."

Shock held Vane speechless. She'd told them the truth

for his sake? She'd admitted where she was, braved the ruin that awaited her, all for *him*? And he'd berated her for it, he remembered. He'd been furious at her, and yet she'd kept silent about her reasons for disclosing her whereabouts to Faulkner that night.

A cynical man might suspect she'd done it to force his offer of marriage, but he didn't think so. No, recalling her extreme reluctance, the many times she'd exhorted him to forsake her, he didn't believe she'd come to his rescue for so self-interested a reason. The knowledge shed new light on her character, perhaps even on her feelings for him. It would be altogether too much to hope . . .

"Cole's demise was damned convenient for you, wasn't it?" said Jardine.

Vane's brows snapped together. He didn't like the trend of this conversation. "Just what are you implying?"

"You have her at last," said Jardine softly. "I envy you, Vane."

By now, he ought not to be taken aback at Jardine's perceptiveness. Vane changed the subject. "Who *did* kill him?"

Jardine spread his hands. "The powers that be have quashed any hopes of an investigation. One particular power, in fact: the Earl of Straghan."

"Understandable that he wouldn't want his daughter's name bandied about."

"Ye-es." Jardine watched Vane with a peculiar, sharp intensity that told Vane his own suspicions were shared. "Or perhaps he doesn't want anyone delving into Cole's other nefarious activities. Perhaps . . ."

Perhaps the Earl of Straghan had killed his son-in-law. Or paid someone else to do it.

Jardine continued smoothly, "The list of suspects is large. The late unlamented set up quite a racket in blackmail and extortion if my sources are correct. Did you happen to find any papers when you searched?"

Vane shook his head. "By the time I arrived, it was too late."

"Someone was before you."

"The place had been turned upside down. It wasn't pure vandalism but a thorough search. Someone was looking for something and they weren't too careful about advertising the fact. Possibly, they sought those papers you mentioned."

Vane neglected to add that he'd been intent on finding a certain document on his own account. Somewhere, someone held Vane's bank draft for an obscenely large sum. He'd already informed his bankers that the draft had gone astray and stopped payment on it. But he needed it back before it found its way into Sarah's hands, or the hands of the authorities.

Regardless, he had sought out Jardine to find the answer to one question. "What reason might someone have to blackmail the Earl of Straghan?"

A quick shake of the head. "Sorry, old fellow. He's a government minister. Even if I knew, I couldn't tell you."

There must be something there, thought Vane. If he'd been barking up the wrong tree, Jardine would have told him so, straight out.

Jardine was silent a moment. Then he said, "Blackmail usually feeds on one of two sources—sex or money. If Brinsley Cole knew something damaging about the earl, how did he come by the knowledge? What is the history of their association? How did Brinsley meet Lady Sarah? How did he snap her up before her mama had the chance to throw her to the tender mercies of the Marriage Mart? Follow those lines of reasoning and I believe you will end with the truth."

Those lines of reasoning had been tugging at the edges of Vane's mind for some time.

Was Jardine hinting at something or merely assisting, in his usual detached way, greasing the wheels of Vane's mind?

Whatever the case, it seemed that the earl's involvement in Brinsley's death bore further investigation. Vane wasn't at all sure he'd like what he'd find.

IT was almost midnight when Vane arrived home. He found Sarah curled up on a chaise longue in the library, a volume of poetry open on the floor below her outstretched hand, as if she'd dropped it there. Wearing a patterned silk dressing gown and a lacy white cap and dainty slippers, she was asleep and dreaming, her features softened and relaxed, one hand curled beneath her cheek.

Something tugged sharply at Vane's heart. She looked . . . vulnerable. Innocent and trusting, as he imagined she must have been when she married Brinsley all those years ago.

He couldn't help but remember Jardine's words—she'd ridden to his rescue when she thought they'd charge him with Brinsley's murder. A warm glow spread in his chest. He couldn't recall a single incident in his life when anyone had seen the need to save him.

After dining with Jardine, Vane had looked in at Cribb's Parlor, ruefully admitting to himself that he lingered away from home rather than return to an empty bed.

How had he and Sarah arrived at this state of affairs? That first night, he'd concluded she was frightened of him, but was that really the problem? She hadn't been afraid of him later, when she'd come to him for help. She'd trusted him enough to reveal her most painful secrets. True, she was desperate to find the boy, but she might well have turned to her father for help instead.

After their first night together, she must know in her heart he would never force her to accommodate him. Until now, he'd been too tired and wound up to think clearly, but he ought to have known it wasn't his physical strength that made her so jittery and defensive.

She *was* afraid. But perhaps what scared her wasn't him. Perhaps she was frightened of her own passion, the intensity of what they shared. He understood that fear because in some moments that first night he'd been afraid of it, too.

If that were the case . . . Hope stirred inside him and the blood quickened in his veins.

She looked so soft and sweet. He studied her with growing hunger. If she rejected him tonight, he might as well take a pistol and shoot himself.

His mouth quirked upward at the melodramatic trend of his thoughts. At the very least, he could put her to bed.

Sliding one arm beneath her shoulders and the other under her hips, he lifted her easily and held her against his chest. Her head shifted a little to rest on his shoulder and she snuggled into him and sighed. For a few moments, he stood very still, his eyes squeezed shut.

Holding her.

And she was warm in his arms, so scented and pliant. A need built within him, to bury himself in that softness, to make her sigh again with pleasure, to turn into him, fully aware that there was no going back, no repudiating their passion this time.

Heart racing, Vane carried her out and strode up the stairs and through the sitting room, into his bedchamber. He laid her carefully on the bed and stepped back.

He closed the door and locked it. Then he turned back and looked at her, still sleeping deeply, lying on her side with the flaring line of her hip outlined against the semi-darkness and the swell of her bottom just visible beneath her dressing gown.

A dim voice inside him said he shouldn't try to seduce his wife when she was asleep and vulnerable like this. She might well respond with pleasure now; she wouldn't thank him in the morning.

But while his conscience voiced objections in his head, his hands stripped the clothes off his body. Long before he'd shucked his trousers, that voice had been drowned out by the insistent tattoo of blood drumming through his veins, the clarion call of desire.

He climbed into the other side of the bed, careful not to disturb her. She lay on her side, facing him, and he remembered another time, when their positions were reversed, when she'd feathered her fingertips over his mouth as he drowsed.

The surge of desire that met that recollection made him freeze, fighting to bring himself under control. And in that moment, her eyelids drifted open and her eyes focused on him. She gasped and struggled up on her elbow, but he pressed a fingertip to her lips, then replaced it with his mouth.

One hand cradling her head, he kissed her gently, trying not to threaten her or frighten her into retreat. With a small moan, she slid her arms around him and sank into the pillows, pulling him down with her, into her warmth and scented softness, where he longed to be.

HE was so damned thankful for this change of heart he didn't stop to consider what it might mean. He simply kissed her with everything he had, all the tenderness and yearning that he'd kept in reserve for so long. Her hands smoothed over his shoulders, molding him, driving him mad with their featherlight touch. Her low sigh tickled his ear as he kissed a path across her cheek to her throat.

He breathed in the smell of her—lilies and a hint of spicy something that infused his brain and drove his body wild. He undid the strings of her fussy little cap and flung it aside, combed his fingers through her long braid to loosen it. Spreading her hair over the pillow, he drank in the sight.

"Sarah, I—"

"Shh." She laid a trembling finger on his lips and said, "Now. Please. I want you now."

As if to illustrate her words, she reached for his shaft and closed her fingers around it, drawing it toward her.

He gave a shuddering gasp and held on to his sanity with everything he had. Gently, he clasped her hand and removed it from his flesh. "Not yet. You're not ready. Let me—"

"I am ready. I'm ready," she whispered. "Don't stop."

He hesitated, torn between consideration for her and a truly awe-inspiring desire to accede to her wishes.

She swallowed and said thickly, "Now, Vane. Now or not at all."

Confusion pulled at his mind but he was too far gone to pay it much heed. He bunched layers of linen and silk in his hands and slid them up her thighs. Kissing her deeply, he spread her legs and positioned himself.

He nudged into her a little way. She was moist and hot but not nearly wet enough. He knew from experience that a woman needed more preparation than this to take him. He rubbed the head of his cock against her, coating it in her moisture, then rubbed it repeatedly over the small, sensitive knot of flesh above, resisting her efforts to make him stop, ignoring her murmured encouragement to dispense with preliminaries and plunge inside.

By the time he judged her ready, he was almost crazed with need. Who would have thought that after insisting on separate bedchambers, separate lives, she'd turn into this demanding wanton who couldn't have him inside her fast enough?

More than anything, he didn't want to hurt her, so he made himself slow, press into her gradually, one inch at a time. She shifted to accommodate him and the slick slide of flesh and the heat and softness drew him in.

God, that feels sublime. Instinct, as well as the woman beneath him, urged him to drive into her, but he knew that if he was too fast or rough he'd hurt her. He took a few deep, unsteady breaths and mastered his trembling body, forcing it to settle for measured, shallow strokes instead. He kept that pace despite her urging, felt the tension and frustration in her and beat back his own answering need.

Her hands slid down his back to his hips, caressing as he moved inside her, slowly, so slowly. Without warning, she gripped his buttocks, thrusting downward as she arched up toward him. Before he could stop himself, he surged home, ramming the entrance of her womb.

The shock of it made him lose his tenuous grasp on control. His climax broke over him in a torrent of fire. But he heard her cry of pain, too. Filled with remorse and anger, he broke her hold and wrenched himself away from her, spilling his seed onto the sheets.

SITTING with his head in his hands, Vane shuddered in the last throes of his orgasm. "God. I'm sorry."

"Don't," she said softly. She'd wanted to give him this,

but she'd wanted it over with quickly. She'd wanted to remain aloof while he took his pleasure. That's why she'd urged him to penetrate her so deeply and fast. She hadn't expected that sharp stab of pain inside, nor the slight queasiness that followed. It hadn't happened that way before.

"I hurt you."

"No, no." She sat up and moved over to kneel behind him. Couldn't resist placing a kiss on his shoulder blade.

His skin burned. "It was my fault," she whispered, her lips drifting over taut muscle. "I . . . I was impatient."

She'd barely managed to contain the ripples of pleasure that coursed through her when he moved inside. She'd fought her passion, fought the melting sensation in her heart when he'd kissed her so tenderly, fought with every ounce of strength against the compelling need to give him all she had, all she was and could ever be.

Her crisis had been almost upon her when she'd taken the initiative from him. She didn't want it, would avoid that ultimate explosion of bliss, that loss of self, at all costs. She'd risked that loss when she'd taken him inside her body. But she hadn't guessed it would be so difficult to lure him to take his pleasure without thought for her. She ought to have known he'd never be so selfish as to comply.

Unable to stop herself, she pressed her cheek to his back and slid her arms around his waist. "I don't deserve you," she breathed. "You have been so good to me."

His body stiffened. Then he swiveled in her embrace and caught her upper arms, his fingers digging into her flesh.

His dark eyes drilled into her. "Was that all this was? *Gratitude?* I agree to find the boy, so you thank me by letting me share your bed, is that it?"

For a moment, she was stunned. Instinct told her to deny it, but if gratitude had not motivated this decision to let him have her tonight, then what?

She stared at him, her thoughts, emotions, and reasons so tangled, she didn't know what response to give. She didn't even know the truth, much less what lie she should offer him. How did she protect herself without hurting Vane?

She forced the words out. "Not gratitude, no."

"Then why?" he demanded. "To what do I owe this sudden change of"—he blew out a breath—"I was going to say 'heart.' But sometimes, my lady, I doubt you even have one."

His words struck like a blow to the stomach, winding her. She bowed her head, willing the hot prickle behind her eyes to go away. He would truly despise her if she wept now.

He let her go and launched off the bed, then turned to face her with his hands on his hips. He was gloriously naked and completely unself-conscious. She resented the sharp tug low in her abdomen, the pure animal creature that was *woman*, which bloomed within her at the sight.

"Well?" he said coldly.

"I don't know."

"Not good enough, Sarah."

His tone stung but she deserved it. She deserved everything he dealt her.

He ran a hand through his hair. "That first night, we shared uncommon passion. You must know, you must realize how rare that is, how precious. I don't understand why we can't have that again."

All the reasons she could never be happy with him flooded back and filled her, choking her. "Do not speak to me of that night. The guilt . . . Oh, I can't bear it! I can't believe you would refer to it again."

"Guilt? Listen, Sarah, he *sold* you to me! Or tried his damnedest to do so. He betrayed you as soon as the wedding vows were out of his mouth. You thought we'd made a bargain, he and I. You thought I was going to throw you into debtors' prison, for Christ's sake! You don't have *anything* to feel guilty about."

"It doesn't matter what he did," she said, hugging herself. "His conduct was never a reflection on me, just as it is no excuse for my behavior. I let myself . . ."

She closed her eyes, squeezed them shut. Perhaps if Vane knew the truth about her desire for him it would not be so very bad, the least of all evils. Surely any woman with a pulse desired him. She was only flesh and blood, after all.

She drew a deep breath. "When we made love that night, I did not feel coerced. Not in any way. As soon as you touched me, as soon as you held me in your arms, I forgot everything else. *Everything*."

His eyes glittered in the candlelight. His body remained poised and still, as if he didn't want to move in case he halted her confession.

She choked back a cry. "But I keep seeing Brinsley lying there, covered in blood. I keep hearing myself deny that anything happened between us. I lied to him, Vane. He lay there, drowning in his own blood, and I lied and said we had not . . ."

She swallowed hard and tipped her head back a little, willing away the tears. "Don't you see? I behaved despicably throughout. I violated my own code of honor. I'd been punishing Brinsley for years for his infidelities, so secure in my self-righteousness, so smug in my determination never to stray despite the most blatant provocation. What a hypocrite! And where have my sins brought me? Not to poverty and ruin, but to this!" She flung out her arm, the gesture encompassing both Vane and the expensive elegance around them. "You have given me so much. How can I live with myself if I don't try to atone for what I've done?"

There was a long silence. His shoulders heaved as he sucked in a breath. "Atonement. So that was it. My *God*." When she raised her gaze to his, she saw the fury in the taut lines of his face, the blaze of anger in his eyes.

She'd never been frightened of him before, but now . . .

Involuntarily, she edged backward, deeper into the bed.

The grim smile on his face didn't give her ease. Silkily, he murmured, "You wish to do penance for your sins. Well, I believe I know how to achieve that. Take off your clothes."

"Vane, no."

"Do it."

She swallowed. With shaking fingers, she began unbuttoning her dressing gown. Her insides heated and trembled with something that was mostly excitement yet partly fear.

He watched her with a searing, hungry gaze as she

shrugged out of her gown. Her nipples hardened under the night rail she wore. She pulled the thin ribbon at her bosom until the bodice loosened, then grasped the hem and drew the garment over her head.

"Lie down on your back. Stretch your arms above your head."

She complied, feeling vulnerable and exposed and shamefully aroused.

Vane approached the bed and reached behind her. She angled her head to see what he was doing. In an instant, he'd unfastened the sash that tied the bed curtain back and was wrapping it around her wrists.

"Vane, I don't think—"

"Did I ask for your opinion? This is your punishment, not a debate."

He secured the end of the sash around the bedpost and stood back to survey his work.

Punishment, penance, yes, that's what she wanted, what she needed him to give. Now, he would do what she'd intended at the beginning. He'd take her without tenderness or mercy, and she could set her mind and her heart and soul apart. She could let him do what he wanted without feeling pleasure herself. And in that way she would prove to herself he was not so different from other men, after all. He was not so different from Brinsley.

He'd arranged her so she lay diagonally across the bed, and now he climbed between her parted legs, kneeling over her. His erection nudged her belly but with her hands tied, she couldn't do anything about it except lift her hips in response.

"So eager," murmured Vane. "But I'm not going to punish you like that."

Confused, she said, "What are you going to do?"

"You'll see." And he bent his head to her breast, swiping the nipple with his tongue, making her gasp. "Forty lashes," he murmured, and gave the hardened peak another hard lick that made her body jolt with unwelcome pleasure. "That's two. Yes, I think forty should do it."

Her protest lengthened to a dull moan as he took his time administering her punishment. She gasped and squirmed, even pleaded, but he ignored her, or said she'd made him lose count. And then he'd start again.

When he'd finally finished with her breasts, he moved slowly over her body, kissing and licking every inch of exposed skin, until there was little left of her he hadn't intimately explored.

Her body hummed and throbbed, and where the air hit the moisture from his tongue, her skin tingled deliciously. He built her desire with excruciating patience, and when he finally touched her between her legs, she fell apart, shaking and convulsing as pleasure exploded and radiated up to her bound hands and down to her toes.

"That's right," Vane said, nuzzling against her breast, working her with his fingers. "Come for me, Sarah."

She hated the smug certainty in his voice. Hated it, hated what he did to her, hated ceding control of her emotions to him even as ecstasy stormed through her body time and again.

The pleasure grew too intense and she tried in vain to squirm away, but he held her down and plunged two long fingers inside her and stroked inside and out until she couldn't stand it anymore.

"No, stop!" she begged, but he just smiled wolfishly and ducked his head to replace his hand with his mouth.

Sarah nearly shot off the bed. She wanted to push him away but she was helpless to stop this intimate assault. She'd never experienced this before, the decadence of it, the pure wicked delight. Seeing his big hands holding her thighs wide apart as he worshipped her flesh with his mouth, she felt like a goddess being serviced by a slave. His tongue burrowed into the knot of sensitive flesh, kneading and swirling and flicking until Sarah gave a hoarse scream of pleasure.

She gritted her teeth to cut off the sound that ripped from her throat, squeezing her eyes shut. She'd never realized she would relish being punished so much.

Sarah lost count of the times he brought her to climax,

finally gave up begging him to stop because the more she begged, the more exquisitely he tormented her.

Somewhere during that virtuoso performance, she stopped fighting what he did to her and how it made her feel. She tried concentrating on the physical sensations, but the urge to submit, to surrender, to let him breach that stronghold around her heart grew and grew.

The need to take him into her became a sharp craving, heightened by the knowledge she was helpless to do anything about it, completely at his mercy. She thought of his hardness and his size and her mouth watered and her insides clenched, desperate to feel him there. She couldn't use her hands to bring him to her, so she would have to ask instead.

"Vane." She bucked her hips a little as he moved up her body, nipping her flesh lightly with his teeth.

"Mmm?" He laved one nipple with his tongue, then drew it into his mouth and sucked until she writhed. He released it with a small popping sound and said, "What is it, my precious?"

"I-I want you."

"I didn't ask what you want. This is your punishment, Sarah." He nipped her throat and as she shuddered, his erection brushed her sex. "Or had you forgotten?"

She was almost crying with frustration, and yet he remembered how this had all started; he held firm to his purpose when she'd surrendered completely. She wanted to weep in earnest.

"Yes," she breathed. "Yes, I had forgotten."

He stilled at that and lifted his head. She tried to look into his eyes, but he kept them lowered, his expression veiled.

Vane raised himself and sat back on his heels. His erection jutted out from between his powerful thighs, and she stared at it, hungered for it in spite of herself. She had the most curious and shocking urge to lick the slitted head, to take it into her mouth. She knew about such practices, but she'd never felt the least inclination to indulge before, despite Brinsley's coaxing.

"You want this?" Vane closed his fist around his erection.

Lost to shame, she nodded.

Dragging her gaze from his member, Sarah looked into his face. Fury still masked his features, and suddenly, she realized her mistake. "No. Not that," she said quietly. "I want you. Make love to me, Vane. I need *you*."

He was silent for a few moments and the harshness of his expression didn't abate. She wondered if he would untie her and tell her to get out.

Finally, he reached forward to release her wrists from their binding, only to capture her hands in his. Deliberately, slowly, he made a meal of each one, starting at her fingertips, kissing and suckling them, then licking, tracing his tongue over her palms, where the scarring made nerve endings raw and sensitive.

She squirmed with panic and delight, knowing relief and disappointment and anticipation in equal measures when he finally set her free. As he moved down her body, she sighed and stretched and wrapped her arms around him. She cried out as he entered her with a single, powerful thrust.

And then he loved her deeply and long, and made her scream once more.

Seventeen

THE bed was empty, save for Sarah, and she was naked and cold. The coverlet had slipped off some time in the night. She pulled it over her shoulder and tried to allow the warmth to comfort her, to ward off the chill of apprehension in her heart.

There was no going back now. Her plan to hold Vane at bay had been predicated on his civilized behavior. There'd been nothing remotely civilized about the way he'd tied her up and pleasured her until she was nothing but slack muscles and raw nerve endings and naked need.

Now, she would have to face this intimacy, this stripping to bare self. She would have no excuse, nowhere to hide from his passion, or her own.

Fear gripped her lungs so tightly she could scarcely breathe. How could she have let this happen? But she hadn't allowed it; she'd been overwhelmed by a will even greater than her own. Could she have stopped him from tying her to that bedpost? Yes, certainly. Yet, she hadn't even voiced a protest. She'd wanted it, wanted to surrender her will to him, for this one night.

But her capitulation had consequences as actions always did. And now she would have to live with them. She would have to concede to Vane her body and her passion.

That did not mean she must surrender her heart.

It was still dark. She must not have slept long. Sarah sat up, shivering a little as goose bumps swept over her exposed skin. A glow of candlelight in the sitting room drew her to her feet.

She couldn't find her garments in the gloom, so she hauled the coverlet off the bed and swung it over her shoulders, pinning it in place with one hand at her breast. Modesty was probably superfluous, but she felt it nonetheless. And besides, the night was chill.

She moved to the threshold and stood there, arrested by the sight of Vane, in a chair by the fire, head bowed, his elbows on his knees and a glass of brandy cradled in his hands.

Despair. She felt it emanate from him in powerful waves, thickening the air between them. And when he raised his head to drain his glass, she saw it in his face.

His strong throat moved as he swallowed. Then he dropped the glass. The empty brandy balloon fell to the thick carpet with a soft thud and rolled a little way. He shoved his hands through his hair, then rubbed them over his face, as if trying to erase something awful from his brain.

"What is it?" She scarcely breathed the question.

Slowly, he turned his head and raised his eyes to hers. Dark eyes, full of pain. "You're awake." For once, he didn't stand when she entered the room. Something was very wrong.

"Yes. I was cold." She pulled the coverlet closer around her shoulders. More urgently, she said, "Tell me. What is it?" What *could* be wrong after the passion they'd shared? Wasn't that what he'd wanted? Fear clutched at her. She didn't know what he was about to say but she braced herself for a mortal wound. Cursed herself for lowering her guard.

"I've been trying to justify my behavior." His voice was low and graveled. "But I cannot."

He took a deep, long breath. "My actions toward a defenseless woman, one, moreover, who is my wife, was inexcusable. Please accept my deepest apologies."

"But Vane—"

"I should have acceded to your wishes. A gentleman would have done as you asked and left you alone. It seems I am not the gentleman I thought I was—the man I thought I was—after all."

Sarah watched him force out the words. And relief would not come.

She ought to thank heaven for her deliverance. She ought to agree with his assessment of the situation, allow him to wallow in this ridiculous, unfounded guilt. Use his shame as insurance. *Yes,* she could say. *You frightened me. You hurt me. Don't ever touch me again.* A month ago, two weeks ago, she would have said that without mercy or hesitation, to protect herself.

It was nothing less than she'd done before. Hadn't she let him think she'd been coerced into his bed that first night? Hadn't she let him carry that burden for far too long? She'd wanted a white marriage; well, here it was, handed to her on a silver platter with a noble crest etched into its surface. With a little judicious fanning of the flames of his guilt, she could get everything she'd wanted, go her own road, keep her life separate from his.

But instead of applying bellows to the fire, she heard herself say, "Vane, don't. Not another word."

She moved toward him, dragging the rest of the coverlet behind her like the train of a ceremonial robe. Lifting her free hand to his face, she brushed his lips with her fingertips, as she had done that first night. This time, without more than a passing thought to her scars.

He closed his eyes at her touch, as if in pain. "I was angry. I should be horsewhipped for treating you like that."

She opened her eyes wide. "I don't remember complaining."

There was the faintest hint of laughter in her voice but he missed it. He sucked in a breath and turned from her to stare into the empty fireplace. "I detest bullies. Men who bully women are the worst kind of scum. I can't believe I've just joined their ranks."

Sarah cocked her head to the side, studying him. He really had no idea what went on inside a woman, nor how utterly irresistible he was. The notion filled her with a strange satisfaction, tinged with fond amusement. And a faint, warm glow that felt something like hope.

"Yes, it was very bad of you to pleasure me until I was nothing but a quivering jelly," she agreed. "But then, you know, I could have refused to do as you asked, couldn't I? I'm not entirely without a backbone, Vane, though I suppose it must seem so to you, of late."

His gaze snapped to hers and his eyes burned like hot coals. "Is this more of your penance?" he said harshly. "Or do you need a man to mistreat you in order to give yourself to him? Was that the way it was with Brinsley?"

She flinched, stunned at this vision of herself. Had she *enjoyed* being mistreated at Brinsley's hands? The doubt crept into her mind and made her pause. Perhaps she had relished torturing him as much as he tormented her, but that was quite different from taking pleasure in the torment in the first place.

She'd received a devastating shock when Brinsley had shown his true colors. She didn't recall that she'd ever viewed his misbehavior with anything other than disgust. She'd never conceded mastery over her body to him, couldn't imagine reveling in his physical power over her, the way she'd done with Vane.

"No," she said, her tone strong and confident. "It wasn't that way with Brinsley. Not at all."

This conversation wasn't leading them anywhere she wanted to go. And now she'd made her decision to let Vane in and face the consequences, the prospect of reneging seemed less and less enticing. She deserved the punishment of living alone, without the warmth of a lover's touch. But Vane didn't deserve that existence, and she couldn't continue to pretend that he didn't need her. She couldn't go on hurting him.

So instead of punishing herself, she'd give herself to him freely. And take the risk to her own heart as penance for her sins.

Holding his gaze, she simply shrugged.

The coverlet fell away, leaving her naked, exposed. She stood without covering herself and let him look.

For long, breathless moments, he sat there motionless, while his gaze traveled slowly over her. His lips parted, but no sound came out. She realized she would have to move first.

She placed her hand on the arm of his chair and bent to him. Her hair swung forward in a dark, tangled curtain as she kissed his lips gently, then ran her tongue over them in a teasing swipe.

He was like warm granite, very hard and still. She longed to touch him, to explore the hot skin and strong, muscled contours of his body, to worship his flesh with her mouth. She took his head between her hands and touched her lips to his, then opened her mouth and kissed him with all the passion inside her.

With a groan, he responded, letting his hands caress her curves from ribs to hip and up again, his thumbs brushing her nipples on each pass. She straddled him, knees hugging his thighs and fumbled through his dressing gown to find warm, hard flesh. His mouth opened beneath hers as she stroked him. He moaned into her and a surge of triumph and excitement shot straight to her loins.

She took as much as she gave, words of need and desire and passion tumbling from her lips as he kissed her ear and bit down on the tender skin of her throat. She eased herself over him until they were joined, shuddering at the perfect way they fit together. And she stared into his deep, dark eyes as she moved with him, filled with tenderness and awe.

SARAH woke to find herself still in Vane's embrace, their heads on the same pillow, limbs entwined. He'd kept her up most of the night, wrung the last drop of pleasure from both their bodies, until they couldn't move anymore.

If she were a different woman, if she were not barren, she might wonder if the beginnings of new life might grow in her womb at this very moment. She might dream of a boy with Vane's stark male beauty or a girl with green eyes. Of a love so perfect and pure and strong that nothing, no mistake or loss or betrayal, could ever shake it.

Not for her. Not to be.

She pushed that thought aside, unwilling to mar the beauty of this moment, lying with him in sated contentment. Her limbs felt heavy, her throat parched, her insides raw. She gazed at his face and experienced such an overwhelming rush of tenderness, her eyes moistened. Could she bear to go on this way? The more she gave, the more he demanded, and the more he demanded, the more she wanted to give.

That was the Devil of it. She didn't know how or when her emotions had become so inextricably linked with the cravings and pleasures of the flesh, but last night she'd had no more will to guard her heart than she'd possessed to deny him her body. This was a dangerous state of affairs.

He stirred and slowly opened his eyes. She blushed, then smiled faintly at the absurdity of her shyness. His eyes crinkled in response. Wordlessly, gently, he stroked her bare shoulder, watching his hand wander over her skin.

"No training this morning?" she murmured.

"Mmm, the best kind. Good morning, Lady Vane." Inhaling deeply through his nose, he plunged a hand through her hair to hold her nape and closed in for a kiss. The kiss flared into something passionate and profound, and Sarah became afraid at what her kiss told him and what his seemed to be asking of her.

I love you, I love you, say you love me.

If she never had to speak the words, she might be safe, she thought dazedly, as he rolled with her, nuzzling and touching and sending her into a wild spin of delight. In this moment, she wanted to give him everything. More, she wanted to *be* all that he desired, all that he deserved.

She gasped when he entered her, pressing deeper and deeper until they were fully joined. Vane's big body covered hers, a heavy weight, but so welcome, so utterly perfect. She wanted him to crush her until their flesh melded, so they'd never be apart. Her inner muscles clamped around him as he pulsed inside her, as if to hold him there. He moaned as she gripped him, his breathing hot and harsh in her ear. She never wanted this time to end.

Dangerous, these fulsome emotions, yet she couldn't block them out. They warmed her and lit her within, like the morning sunshine that poured through the windows and glistened over Vane's sweat-damped skin.

A low thrum of intense pleasure tightened every nerve ending in her body. Gathering himself, Vane broke the rhythm with one deep, decisive thrust, then her climax rushed over her in a thousand sparkling champagne bubbles of joy.

As he moved faster inside her, Sarah skated her hands—those naked, damaged hands—up his arms and over his powerful shoulders. Vane thrust and thrust, building rapture upon rapture until she thought she'd die of such extravagant bliss.

Whispering his name, she dug her fingers through his hair and pulled his head down to her. And she kissed him with all the passion inside her naked, damaged heart.

VANE stood at the window in his library and watched as a carriage drew up outside his house. He'd never passed so much idle time staring out windows as he had since this whole business began.

She'd been perfectly accommodating, his complicated wife. Her passion was real, he didn't doubt it, but . . . He frowned, turning it over in his mind. Something was missing. Something vital. Intangible. He couldn't quite put his finger on it.

It wasn't even the words of love that had never been spoken between them. It was something else. Some part of her that she withheld from him, even at the height of passion. He wanted to reach inside her and touch that shadowy, mysterious place. Not just touch it. He wanted to explore, to discover, to know.

He smiled a little and shook his head. Two months ago, he would never have dreamed he'd have Sarah in his bed every night. He'd never imagined a passion so terrifying, so all-consuming. He had everything he'd never dared to hope for. He shouldn't tempt Fate. He shouldn't ask for more.

Outside, one of the footmen hurried out with an umbrella to shield the passenger of the carriage from the downpour, so Vane didn't get a look at the man's face.

In moments, the door opened and the visitor was announced.

Rockfort. Now, there was an interesting development.

Brinsley's former crony was puffing with exertion, his schoolboy cheeks burning twin spots of pink. "Vane!" he said, lowering his bulk into a deep leather chair. "I've come on that matter of yours. Utmost importance."

The documents. Thank God.

Vane forced himself not to pounce. "What matter was that?"

"Those papers you asked about." Rockfort took out a large handkerchief and mopped his brow, matting damp brown curls to his forehead. "I've found 'em."

"Have you, indeed?" Vane wondered in that case why Rockfort would admit as much. Surely, he'd wanted them for himself, presumably to carry on the blackmail where Brinsley had left off. "Do you have them with you?"

"No! No, no, no, that's the thing! Y'see, it's Hedge, Cole's valet. He has the papers. Threatened me with blackmail. *Me!* Well, I don't know where he thinks I'll get the funds from. Scarcely plump in the pocket, am I?"

Vane had no idea. "Surely you don't expect me to frank you."

"Lord, no! Though if you could see your way clear—" At the lowering look on Vane's face, Rockfort broke off with a cough. "Never mind that. Thought I'd come to you about it, since we have a common interest. Thought you might use some manner of persuasion to see we get these papers back."

"I see." And he did see. Rockfort still thought he could put those sensitive documents to use, but he wanted Vane to be his instrument in securing their return. He wondered what sort of dirty trick Rockfort had in mind to make sure he, and not Vane, gained possession of the rest of the material.

Well, Vane would certainly negotiate with the valet but not with Rockfort in tow. "Do you have Hedge's direction?"

"I don't know where he lives. He wants to meet tomorrow at Brown's."

"I see. We will both keep the appointment." Meanwhile, Vane would pay the valet a visit. There had to have been an address where Sarah had sent Brinsley's personal effects. He supposed the papers had been among them, though he'd searched thoroughly, as had a number of others. Perhaps Brinsley had entrusted the papers to his valet before he died? Possible, but it seemed unlikely.

"Do you know how the man came to have these precious documents?"

Rockfort shook his head. "But he knew enough about my, er, circumstances to convince me he's telling the truth."

So Rockfort looked for those papers on his own account. It seemed no one had been safe from Cole's malice. "I thought Brinsley Cole was your friend."

"So did I." Rockfort snorted. "Live and learn, eh?"

Vane grunted, while his mind worked. "I'll go with you to Brown's tomorrow. By then I should have made inquiries about this Hedge."

Vane barely waited for Rockfort's carriage to pull away before he called for his own conveyance and questioned Rivers about where Sarah had sent Brinsley's effects.

Armed with the direction, he set off for Hedge's address.

The boardinghouse where Hedge lived was a respectable one with a curious, comfortable-looking landlady. Vane did his best to appear benign as he greeted the proprietor and inquired the way to his quarry.

Two flights up, he rapped a peremptory summons on the door. It opened, to reveal Hedge himself, dressed to go out. The irritated look on the valet's face faded a little when Vane stepped over the threshold toward him, forcing him to retreat.

Hedge took off his hat, but whether it was as a mark of deference or because he realized he wouldn't be going anywhere for a while, Vane couldn't tell.

Kicking the door shut behind him, Vane looked around. He ignored the short, indignant protest from his companion and passed beyond him, taking a seat in an easy chair by the grate.

The place was sparsely furnished and kept with almost military neatness. Vane glanced at Cole's former valet. He was wiry enough, with a hard look behind his unremarkable features. Perhaps he'd been a soldier at one time.

Vane smiled, stripping off his gloves, but his smile was not calculated to set the fellow at ease. "I am fortunate to find you at home, Hedge," he said. "Have you been unable to secure employment since your master's death? Or could it be that you've found alternative means of securing income?"

Not by the flicker of an eyelid did Hedge betray knowledge or fear. "Not at all, sir. I came into a small legacy shortly after Mr. Cole died, which allows me to pick and choose where I go next. I haven't found the right place yet."

"Ah."

Vane let the silence lengthen until the man shifted his stance a little. Then he said, "You must wonder why I am here. It concerns some papers you, ah . . . found? Yes, *found* is probably the right word. Papers that belonged to your late employer."

"Papers?" The valet's brow furrowed.

"Save your histrionic talents for someone who appreciates them, Hedge. I know you have them. I've just seen Mr. Rockfort. No doubt there are a dozen more unfortunates you've set dancing to your tune. I want the documents. All of them, please."

Vane disliked using his rank to intimidate, but in this case it seemed expedient. "No doubt you know who I am. If that is so, then you know my reputation. I can ruin you, Hedge. In fact, I have so little tolerance for the kind of parasite that feeds off other people's fear, I'm minded to haul you up to the nearest magistrate and damn the consequences."

He paused, noting the flare of alarm that crossed the valet's face. "But that would be irresponsible, wouldn't it, with so many peoples' reputations at stake? So I'll give you a deal. Hand over the documents and no more will be said."

In his soft, gravelly voice, the valet replied, "Don't know what papers you mean, my lord. Was there one in particular you were looking for?"

Vane restrained himself from knocking the cur's teeth down his throat. In fact, he *was* looking for one paper in particular—that damned bank draft—but he couldn't afford to let Hedge know that. Still, if the valet had the paper in question, he'd know already, wouldn't he?

A calculating gleam entered Hedge's eye at Vane's hesitation. He licked his lips. "You'll understand, that if I do have such documents in my possession, I can't just give them away. Worth thousands, they are, in the right hands."

Rising, Vane spoke softly. "You play a dangerous game, my friend. No doubt your late unlamented master thought the same. And look what happened to him."

Hedge's eyes narrowed. "Are you threatening me?"

"Oh, you're just catching on, are you? Bit slow on the uptake for a blackmailer. Looking forward to a bullet through your chest?"

Finally, he'd managed to ruffle Hedge's composure. He shook his head, edging to the door. "You *are* threatening me! You . . . *you* murdered Mr. Cole."

"Don't be more of a fool than you can help, man. If I had a motive to kill him—and I didn't—do you think I'd have done it before I'd made him tell me where those papers are?"

The valet truly had the wind up now. Vane made a quick decision and reached inside his coat for his pocketbook. "Twenty pounds for the lot. If the document I'm looking for is there, I'll give you fifty. That's my final offer. Take it, or I'll tear this room to shreds." He smiled grimly. "And then I'll start on you."

Ten minutes later and twenty pounds lighter, Vane made his way down the stairs of the boardinghouse, cursing as he went.

ALONE in his library, Vane picked up the bundle of documents with a grimace of distaste. He needed to decide what was to be done with them.

In one bundle were some fairly innocuous missives from family and friends. Vane scanned these without interest and set the pile aside. The second collection of papers had his eyebrows climbing higher as one shocking revelation followed another. Some of the letters were written in veiled terms, no names mentioned. He was sufficiently acquainted with the circumstances to recognize the Earl of Straghan as the author of one of these. What he read made him blow out an unsteady breath.

He glanced again at the date. So that was how Brinsley had forced Sarah's father into agreeing to their marriage. He saw it all now, the reason the earl hadn't interfered, had perhaps even encouraged the match. The reason the countess hadn't overridden him, though God knew, she must have wanted to.

Had the earl killed Brinsley? Vane frowned. It didn't smell right. Lord Straghan might be accounted a ruthless schemer in matters of politics but he would never have committed so obvious and gruesome a murder, nor left his daughter to survive the aftermath as best she might. *Surely* not. But if given a choice between having his secret made public and Brinsley's elimination, perhaps . . .

Vane tapped the letter against his fingertips, his gaze losing focus as he thought.

In his circle, one tended to know, or at least suspect, which gentlemen preferred their own kind. He accepted it was none of his business—he knew and held in high regard a number of gentlemen he suspected were of that persuasion. As long as there was no scandal, homosexual men might do as they pleased without repercussions or reprisal.

But if their sexual proclivities were to come out in the open, that was quite a different story. The cruelty, the sheer hypocrisy of those rules made Vane sick to his stomach, but they were frighteningly real. A man could be hanged for the crime of buggery. Even if the earl weren't prosecuted, the scandal would ruin him and his family, too.

Vane shook his head. The earl must have been mad to put his sentiments toward this other man in writing. But who was ever sane when it came to love?

Brinsley had placed the earl in an impossible position. Vane felt a deep compassion for the man who had lived with the Sword of Damocles hanging over his head for over ten years. But he couldn't forget that the earl had sacrificed his daughter to save himself. Straghan had refused to lie on his daughter's behalf to support her alibi. A true show of moral fiber? Or had he feared being drawn into the murder investigation and what it might ultimately reveal?

Did Sarah suspect the truth? He was almost certain she did not. He was equally certain it was not his place to tell her.

Vane pocketed the letter, extracted the document that had concerned Rockfort so greatly—a letter about some swindle he'd planned which had never come to fruition and interested Vane not at all—refolded the letter, and sealed it. Then he ordered a footman to deliver it to Rockfort's chambers with his compliments.

He'd solved one part of the mystery surrounding Brinsley Cole's death.

But he still hadn't found that bank draft.

SARAH walked in the park each morning, well before the fashionable hour. She went heavily veiled in case some early rising member of her acquaintance happened to be about.

Nannies were out in force, herding their broods along, helping small hands feed the ducks or fly kites, scolding for venturing too close to the water or playing in the mud.

As she sat on a bench to watch them, a bittersweet ache

filled Sarah's heart. The thought of finding Tom sustained her, but it tantalized her, too. She longed for a child with such ferocity that sometimes she didn't know what to do with herself. It was an almost physical yearning, a crying emptiness inside. Did other childless women feel this way? She didn't know.

A small girl in a cherry pelisse over a froth of petticoats tottered a few steps over the grass, holding out her arms to her nanny, gurgling with delight. Sarah laughed, too, then stopped as both nanny and child turned to stare at her.

Flushing at her mawkish intrusion into that little scene, Sarah ducked her head and hurried away.

Her eyes burned with unshed tears as she turned toward home. Wasn't she done with weeping over what couldn't be fixed? Hadn't she sobbed out her heartache years ago? But now, thinking of how much she wanted to give Vane a child, how much she wanted her own baby to love, her chest tightened until she could barely breathe. She bit her lip to stem the threatening flow of tears and quickened her pace.

Once she arrived home, she ripped her hat off and her gloves and fled blindly upstairs, through the sitting room and into the privacy of her bedchamber. Crumpling into an armchair by the window, she finally gave in to her grief.

A door clicked and her head jerked up. Vane emerged from his dressing room, the epitome of manly grace. Bewildered, she glanced about her and realized it was to his bedchamber she'd flown, not hers.

"Sarah? What is it?" He strode toward her, his hand outstretched.

She shot out of her chair, gulped and sniffed and dashed a hand across her eyes. "Oh, *oh*! I beg your pardon. I didn't mean to come here."

He said nothing, simply took her in his arms. At first, she stiffened slightly. She was an utter, sniveling mess! But he rubbed her back in gentle circles, as if he didn't mind at all that she was incoherent, red-nosed, and ugly with crying. His warmth and solid strength was so comforting, she nearly started sobbing all over again.

Vane murmured reassurances to her in a soft, soothing

tone and soon, the tension began to drain from her limbs. She sank into him, put her arms around his waist, and hugged his big body. The steady beat of his heart calmed her until the weight that had crushed her lungs seemed to lift.

"I shall ruin your beautiful coat." She sniffed and drew back a little, smoothing the damp lapel with her fingertips.

"This old thing?" The deep rumble of his voice vibrated through his chest. "I never liked it anyway."

With a soft chuckle, she let him draw her head back against him. He hadn't held her like this since that first awful night. She couldn't remember anyone else embracing her with such tenderness, not since she was a little girl.

After a few precious moments, he drew back a little. "What is it?"

She raised her head. "I want a child, Vane. So badly, I—" She stopped when she saw his slight grimace of pain. Of course, she wasn't alone in that wish. Of course, he felt the sting of their childlessness, too.

Ashamed of her outburst, she shook her head and wiped her eyes with the heel of her hand. "Forgive me. I gave in to a moment of self-pity. I don't usually do that. Really, it's all right. I accepted this a long time ago." She searched his face. "Do you wish . . . ?"

"Of course I do. But if it's not meant to be, then I'll accept that."

"It's so unfair to you."

He touched her cheek. "You gave me the choice, remember? And I chose. I would choose the same again, a thousand times over. Never think otherwise."

He raised her palms to his lips, one after the other. Instead of cringing at the thought of him touching the roughness and the scars, her heart swelled until it seemed to fill her completely. He accepted her as she was.

Barrenness, scars, and all.

VANE sorted through correspondence, hoping for news. His conversation with Sarah about their childless state seemed to make it even more imperative to find Tom. But the more time passed, the less likely it looked that he would ever find Brinsley's natural son or the woman who'd been entrusted with his care. Vane had done his best and so had Finch, but the little Cockney hadn't been able to glean hide nor hair of the boy.

"No one remembers him, or not well enough to give me a description, anyways," Finch had reported.

"What about the woman?"

"They remember *her*." Finch leered a little. "Made her living on her back, didn't she? But the boy must have made hisself scarce-like 'cos none of her customers remember him. And none knows where she went."

Where to look now, besides the mortuary, was anyone's guess. Rockfort had heard nothing of the boy. Vane had visited him again and given him every opportunity to let the information slip, but Rockfort either didn't know or he was far more discreet than Vane gave him credit for.

If Peter Cole knew where Tom could be found, he certainly wasn't telling. It was hardly surprising that Peter might not be aware of the brat's existence when one considered the brothers had been estranged for most of their adult lives.

Vane finished sorting through the post and opened a letter from Lyon House. It was from his mama, inviting him and Sarah to stay, alternately scolding him for keeping his bride from them and cajoling him to remain for the summer.

He grimaced, reluctant to share Sarah with anyone. Yet, he knew it was incumbent on him to see his new bride reestablished in Society. They ought to go, and he would like to show her Lyon House, after all.

Vane found Sarah in the sitting room, in command of the tea tray. He was still somewhat bemused by her refusal to alter the masculine tone of this enclave but he'd discovered he liked to see her there. She looked delicate and very dear, perched on the edge of a deep leather armchair, her back straight as she poured tea for him and arranged three of the cakes he liked on a plate. Had she noted his preference? He'd like to think so.

His lips twitched as he took the laden plate. "You are trying to make me fat."

Her gaze swept him from head to toe. A smile warmed her mouth and danced in her green eyes. "Yes, indeed. Soon you will need stays, just like the Prince Regent."

With a snort of laughter, he handed her the letter. "My mother wishes us to visit."

Something flickered in her eyes as she took the letter. Anxiety? Relief? He added, "She wants us to stay for the summer, but I thought not above a week."

"How kind of her," Sarah said, scanning the page before she handed it back. "We must certainly go."

"Yes, I suppose we must. Though I had hoped to have you to myself for a while longer, it is probably time you came out of hiding."

She glanced up swiftly, as if the faint challenge in his tone took her by surprise. "Perhaps you are right," she said slowly, a slight frown drawing her sleek eyebrows together. "I have been a coward, haven't I? Afraid of what people might say. And a hypocrite to boot. How paltry of me."

She looked quite indignant, and Vane's chest filled with a strange warmth. "Most women in your situation would have long since expired of the vapors. All I meant was that I'd like to see you reclaim your place in Society." He smiled. "My mother is a flighty piece, but she has a good heart and will certainly grease the wheels of your next Season if you wish."

Sarah thought of her own mother with a sharp twinge of regret. "Let's not be precipitate. Let's begin with this visit and then we'll see." While Vane's mother was a delight, Vane's brothers were a different matter. It hadn't escaped her that Christian, at least, didn't approve of Vane marrying her.

Despite Christian's coolness at her wedding, she'd sensed a deep bond between Vane and all his brothers. If she wanted to make Vane truly happy, she'd need to win their friendship.

And why she'd suddenly begun thinking in such terms, she couldn't imagine.

A slight commotion downstairs had them both lifting their heads to listen. A rough Cockney accent made Sarah stiffen in alarm but Vane's face broke into a grin.

The door opened and an ugly little man popped his head around it. "Sorry to disturb you, guv, but I thought as how you'd want to know straightaway like. I've found 'er."

Eighteen

"You've found Maggie?" Vane started forward to shake the man's hand. He gestured to Sarah.

"Lady Vane, this is Mr. Finch, my trainer. He has been making inquiries about Maggie Day on our behalf."

Finch bowed, turned his hat in his hands as if he longed to jam it on his head and be off.

Sarah smiled. "Won't you sit down, Mr. Finch?"

He started, as if she'd tried to bite him. "What, me, my lady? Bless you, no. I jest came up because I knew it was urgent like." He took a breath. "I found her and I brought her 'ere. Promised her a yellow boy if she came wiv me."

"Oh, that was well-done of you," said Sarah quickly. She could barely restrain herself from charging down the stairs. "I take it the boy wasn't with her?"

"No, my lady. She says she don't know where 'e is."

He gave a small shrug that said, see for yourself, that's all I could get out of her. Vane thanked Finch and saw him out.

When he returned, Vane and Sarah exchanged a long gaze.

"I think you'd best let me handle it," he said.

"Certainly not." She pulled on her gloves, willing her hands to stop shaking. Her gaze flickered up at him and away. "I would like you to come with me, though."

It cost her something to make that admission. He seemed to know it, because an alert look came into his eyes as he bowed and offered her his arm. They went down to the south parlor, where Rivers said Maggie waited.

With every step, Sarah's anxiety and anger burned brighter. Why didn't Maggie know where her son might be? It was callous and irresponsible, but more than that, it was stupid. Losing the boy was against Maggie's interests. Surely she'd gathered from Sarah's visit that Sarah wanted to help them financially?

When she and Vane entered the parlor, Maggie swiftly turned from contemplating a Reynolds that hung above the fireplace. A full minute passed before Sarah could equate that blowsy, sullen wretch she'd encountered in Billingsgate with the self-possessed, well-turned-out woman she saw now. Perhaps Maggie had moved up in the world. Perhaps she'd no need of Sarah's help.

But if that were the case, why was she here?

Vane's swift sideways glance told her he was thinking the same.

Sarah invited the woman to sit, and a self-satisfied smile spread slowly over Maggie's features as she spread her muslin skirts and perched on the edge of a spindle-legged chair. "Very polite for someone talking to a woman what's had your husband, ain't you? Real lady, you are."

Sarah's insides clenched around a cold, hard core. "Let us avoid that sordid subject, shall we? I want to ask you about Tom."

The scornful expression Sarah had seen before swept over Maggie's face. "That's what I came to tell you. There ain't no Tom." She looked from Vane to Sarah. "Made him up, didn't I? Thought there was money in it so I told you what you wanted to hear."

Sarah sat there, stunned. She couldn't speak.

Slowly, Vane said, "That would explain why we couldn't find hide nor hair of the lad."

"But—" Sarah knew she was grasping for words like a fish gasping for air. "Lies? Was it all lies Brinsley told me, then? You didn't bear his child?"

"Oh, there was a child, all right. All I'm sayin' is I'm not the ladybird you're after." She paused, glancing from Vane to Sarah. "If I was to tell you what I know, what's in it for me?"

Vane spoke. "That depends how much your information is worth." He drew out a coin and flipped it so that it landed in her lap. "I believe you were promised this for attending us. That should show you our good faith." He paused, narrowing his gaze. "I've seen you somewhere before."

The bold wench looked him over from the top of his head to his shining black boots. "If you saw me, I sure as eggs didn't see you, guv." She gave him a saucy smile. "You, I'd remember."

The faintest flicker at the corner of Vane's mouth told Sarah he wasn't immune to such nonsense. She cleared her throat loudly and said, "Do go on. I await this grand revelation with bated breath."

Vane's lips twitched. Most certainly, he was suppressing his delight at her jealousy. Let him have his little victory, she thought sourly. All she cared about was finding Tom.

Maggie primmed her mouth but laughed at Vane with her eyes before she turned sober again and answered. "I was the midwife who delivered the boy you're looking for, not the mother. The mother . . . well, I expect she's dead now, poor love."

"But Brinsley told me *you* were the mother." Sarah put a hand to her temple. Had he? Or had she just assumed the mother was Maggie because the timing was right? She'd supposed he had only been with one woman in that first year of their marriage but what a naïve supposition that had been! That poor pregnant woman could have been anyone.

"What happened to the child when he left your care?" she asked.

"He was taken away to the country, dunno where. My niece went as wet nurse."

"Her name?" Vane demanded.

"Polly Lawson."

That was all they gleaned from Maggie. She hadn't seen Polly since she'd left with the babe mere days after his birth. The mother's name had never been given. Maggie could tell she was from a good family, one who'd disown her if the truth of her condition became known. She'd had good reason to keep her identity secret.

As Maggie sauntered out, wide hips swaying, it struck Sarah that Brinsley had asked one mistress to deliver the baby another woman had borne him. Wearily, she acknowledged it was precisely the sort of thing Brinsley would do.

"We need to find that Polly Lawson," Vane said, moving to ring the bell. "I'll get Finch and some others onto it while we're away. If he has news, he can post down within a day. I think we're close, Sarah."

She squeezed her eyes shut. "I pray you're right."

WHEN she and Vane arrived at Lyon House, Sarah immediately perceived that this was a family home. As soon as the carriage pulled up outside, an avalanche of dogs tumbled from the open door to greet them, and a small boy brought up the rear.

Chuckling, Vane ordered the young lad to call off his hounds, which the boy did with a cheeky grin and a shrill whistle produced through a fork in his fingers. He was a strong-featured, dark-haired lad. He carried a fishing rod over one shoulder and a satchel over the other.

Turning to Sarah, Vane handed her from the carriage and introduced the boy to her. John dropped his fishing rod and snatched off his hat, making a jaunty little bow. "Pleased to

make your acquaintance, Aunt Sarah." Eagerly, he turned
to Vane. "I'm glad you're here, Uncle Vane. Coming for a
fish?"

Vane started to refuse the invitation, but Sarah put her
hand on his arm. "Oh, do you think we might? I haven't
been fishing since I was a girl."

John eyed her askance, clearly doubtful that a mere
female would be equal to the excursion, but Vane smiled.
"Why not?"

John hooted a cheer and raced off to find them more fishing rods.

Vane gave directions for their luggage to be taken into
the house and offered his arm to Sarah. As they strolled toward the lake, he said, "Young scamp. He's Greg's eldest."

Sarah tilted her head. "He's more like you."

"Heaven forbid! But yes, if you mean he's a handful, you'd
be correct. He's forever falling into mischief." Vane tilted his
head back and scanned the cloudless sky. "What a remark-
ably pretty day." He glanced down at her. "I can think of better things to do with you than fishing out here."

"Oh?" she said, not quite taking his meaning. She searched
his face, and at the gleam in his eye, she choked on a gasp.
"You mean you and me . . . out *here*? Oh, you are wicked,
sir!"

His lips tilted upward at the corners. "What a lot you
have to learn," he observed. "And how I shall enjoy teaching
you."

Her face heated. How ridiculous that after all they'd done
together, he could still make her blush. "I don't—"

"Here we are!" John came running up behind them, a
quiver of fishing rods in his hand.

Vane took them from him, and they all trooped down to
the lake. As Sarah trailed a little way behind on the well-
worn path flanked by tall grasses and wildflowers, her pores
soaked in the sunshine and the fresh country air. Suddenly,
a sense of well-being flooded her. It was a joy to see how
wonderful Vane was with the child.

The two of them shared an easy rapport, trading jests

and good-natured insults. The boy's antics clearly amused Vane, but he also reminded him of his manners when they arrived at the lake and instructed him on the art of making a lady comfortable before the fishing could begin.

"First, you must find her something on which to sit, as the grass is invariably damp." Vane removed his coat and handed it to John, ignoring Sarah's murmured protest. "Now, find a relatively dry spot and spread that out for your aunt to sit on."

"Like Sir Walter Raleigh," said John, nodding. He took his time choosing a place and then set the coat down, smoothing it carefully with his small palms. "There. Now what?"

"Now, you offer your hand to the lady and bow." Vane smiled as John followed his direction. "Then she takes your hand, and you help her sit down."

Laughing, Sarah joined in the game, perching on the coat on the slope of the bank and arranging her skirts.

"And then?"

"And then you offer her refreshment." Vane took John's satchel and rummaged but he only turned up an ancient crust of bread, which he pitched to a cluster of ducks that quacked and fluttered greedily around the morsel.

"Never mind," said Sarah. "Next time, we'll bring a picnic." She fluttered her hand. "Now, I do thank you for your amazing gallantry, but please go on and throw your line. I'll be along in a minute to try my luck."

She didn't need to urge him twice. John was off before she'd finished speaking. Vane's eyes twinkled. "He is a brat."

"He is charming. Do go and join him." She smiled at the small figure who had turned back to see what was taking his uncle so long. The sun danced on the lake behind him. "He's waiting for you."

THE gentle ease of that afternoon left Sarah invigorated and relaxed. She'd even caught a fish, a slippery, silver carp, which she hoped was a good omen for her visit. She suspected she'd need all the luck she could come by when she joined the family for the evening meal.

By the time they arrived back at the house, disheveled, wet, and cheerful, it was time to bathe and dress for dinner. Sarah took extra care with her toilette and wore a demure gown of muslin embroidered at the bodice and hem with spring flowers. She didn't doubt she figured in Vane's brothers' minds as the temptress who had bewitched their beloved eldest sibling. She did not wish to look the part.

Vane's mother waved away her apologies for not coming directly to the house to greet her hostess. "Nonsense, nonsense! We do not stand upon ceremony here, and you are family now, my dear."

The dowager smiled, patting the sofa next to her. "Do sit down. I thought we'd have a family dinner this evening, nice and cozy, to welcome Sarah, and then tomorrow we will pay calls in the neighborhood and make you known to everyone." She put her hand on Sarah's upper arm and rubbed it with easy affection. "They will love you, my dear."

The words gave Sarah comfort, as did her mother-in-law's touch. The dowager was always touching—things, people. Her delicate hands never stilled. Sarah tried to remember the last time her own mother touched her in such a casual fashion and couldn't.

Slowly, the brothers began drifting in. Freddie, with an easygoing charm that echoed his mother's, kissed Sarah on the cheek and shook hands with Vane, clapping his elder brother on the back as he made a rather warm joke about their honeymoon.

Vane took it in good part but deflected the boy's curiosity and redirected the conversation with a deliberately provocative comment about the latest prizefight in town. When Nick and Greg arrived, they were immediately drawn into the argument and Sarah breathed a small sigh of relief.

Christian sauntered in late and her tension returned. "Ah, the blushing bride," said Christian softly, bowing over her hand.

Unobtrusively, Vane withdrew from the sporting conversation and ranged himself at her side. She frowned at him. She would fight her own battles. She didn't need his protection. A man like Lord Christian Morrow would never respect her if she cowered behind her husband.

She quickly withdrew her hand. "I am very happy, sir. Thank you for asking."

The cold grey eyes flickered, as if he was surprised at her answer. Smoothly, he said, "Of course you are. Like a cat in a cream pot. Happy as a clam."

"Christian." Vane's tone was a warning.

Christian shrugged and turned away to pour himself a drink.

Sarah willed the flush to recede from her cheeks. She ought not to be surprised at Christian's opinion of her. To outsiders she must seem like a scheming, designing woman intent on hooking her claws into the most eligible bachelor in the ton. She glanced at Vane and wondered how much Christian knew of the circumstances surrounding their marriage, whether he was aware Vane had been trapped, considered himself honor-bound.

If she were in Christian's position, she'd be suspicious, too.

The relief that swept through her when dinner was announced spiked to apprehension when Christian was placed on one side of her and Gregory on the other. The vicar disapproved of her, but at least he remained civil. Christian was like a hornet, circling her and stinging until she wished she could swat him with her fan.

But she needed to make peace with Vane's brothers. That was why she was here. She took a fortifying sip of Burgundy and turned to Gregory. "I met an enchanting young scamp this afternoon," she said. "Your son, I believe. I took a great liking to him."

Gregory flushed a little. "I trust he didn't annoy you."

"No, the boot was on the other foot entirely, for I imposed upon him to take me fishing. We had a marvelous afternoon by the lake."

The vicar glanced down the table at Vane. "John sticks to his uncle's side like a burr whenever he is here."

Did she detect a note of wistfulness in Greg's voice?

Smoothly, she answered, "I'm not surprised. Uncles are so much *fun*, aren't they? They just swoop in and take one on wild adventures without a care for everyday rules of behavior. I expect when you have nephews, they'll think of you the same way."

Arrested, Gregory paused with his cutlery in midair. He turned his head to consider her, and she noticed a distinct softening of his expression. "Perhaps." He smiled. "It would be pleasant to simply enjoy children without having to worry about them all the time."

"And your wife? What does she say?"

He reached for his wine. "My wife died two years ago."

"Oh, I am sorry. I didn't know." Sarah's heart sank. What a blunder! She ought to have kept her mouth shut. Why hadn't Vane warned her?

"It's quite all right." There was a gentle dignity about Gregory, which did not invite sympathy. Sarah admired him for it. He sipped his claret, then set it down carefully. "I have two boys without a mother to raise them. I fear for them, my lady, indeed I do."

"Please, call me Sarah," she murmured, her heart aching for those little boys, and the sadness she saw in their father's eyes.

"You are. You're in love with her. I knew it." Nick's deep voice was laced with amusement. He drew on his cigarillo and shot smoke upward, coiling into the night.

Vane leaned against the balustrade behind him and finally surrendered to his fate. "Yes."

"Does she know?"

Vane grimaced and stared up at the stars that sprinkled across the heavens. "I haven't told her, if that's what you mean. I've only just discovered it myself."

It was true. Oh, he'd always loved her in some way, ever since that first evening he'd laid eyes on her at a mutual friend's ball. He'd always found her maddeningly alluring, but the tug he'd experienced had never been confined to his nether regions. He'd never wanted to possess a woman, body and soul, in quite that way before.

But what he felt for her now was so all-encompassing, so profound, it dwarfed that earlier emotion, the longing that had been more than lust but less than true, deep love.

Nick tapped ash over the side of the balcony. "I'd say the feeling's mutual."

For one brief, dazzling moment, Vane allowed himself to believe it. Then he shook his head. Sarah's love would be far too much to hope for just yet. But he was working on it. Her relationship with Brinsley had been a complicated one. He'd hurt her so deeply that she still hadn't recovered, now he was gone.

If only he could find a way to free her from that sad history. If only the past would die.

Oblivious to Vane's dark thoughts, Nick went on. "I like the way she looks at you, as if you're her savior and all her wicked dreams rolled into one. Wish some woman would look at me like that."

Vane laughed once he'd recovered from the shock of Nick's description. "They all look at you like that. At least, the wicked dream part."

Nick gave a leer that turned into a grimace. "Anyway, I like her. I like the way you are with her. I just wanted you to know."

Absurdly touched, Vane grunted and clapped Nick on the shoulder. Then they lounged in companionable silence, watching the clouds drift over the moon.

Nineteen

VANE paused in the grey dawn light, watching his young brother sleep. Freddie was absurdly sophisticated for his years, but in slumber he looked innocent as a child. Vane watched that blameless slumber with a faint smile on his face. And waited a full minute before he upended the pitcher of water he held over his brother's head.

Freddie gasped and roared upright with the shock of cold and wet. Still yelling, he shook his head like a dog, then launched himself at Vane. Laughing, Vane caught the human missile and wrestled him to the floor, with the voices of Nick and Gregory chanting and urging in the background.

"Come on, my son!" said Nick, in a fair imitation of Vane's trainer, Finch. "On your feet, lad! We're going for a run."

Freddie groaned, wiping the icy water from his eyes. Blearily, he pulled on some breeches and tucked his nightshirt into them, cursing his brothers and laughing as he did.

As they trooped downstairs, Vane outlined the course, which all of them knew like the backs of their hands anyway.

It always ended at the local King's Arms, where the men took refreshment after their exertions. Freddie groaned again and protested that no gentleman ought to hare around the place as if the Devil were at his heels.

Gregory ruffled his hair, pushing him along. "It'll be good for you, boy. Put some spring in your step, get the heart pumping."

"Papa! Papa! Uncle Vane! Where are you going?" Vane looked up as the small figure of Edward appeared at the top of the stairs, rubbing his eyes. "Can I come?"

"You're too little." John pushed past his brother and ran down, taking a flying leap at Vane's back.

Vane caught him under the knees and hoisted him onto his shoulders. He eyed Greg, who had stopped a few steps above him and cocked his head toward the small boy who was about to be left at home, too young to join in his elders' fun.

Greg turned to Edward and held out his arms. Edward gave a whoop that must have woken the household, and skittered down the stairs to launch himself into his father's embrace. Greg swung him up on his shoulders, remarking it was just as well he was knobbled, for Freddie needed all the help he could get to beat them.

They stomped outside, and the frigid air hit them like a slap in the face. With a few showy poses and stretches and catcalls, they took their marks on the gravel drive in front. Banbury, his dignity unimpaired, dropped the handkerchief, and they were off on their cross-country run.

LATER that morning, Sarah prepared to pay calls in the company of the dowager and Lord Christian. A sense of unreality filled her as she stepped into the carriage, dressed as finely as any lady of her station and with nothing to do this day but make herself agreeable to her neighbors. This was the mode of living she'd abandoned to become Brinsley's wife. Or part of it. She would be fully occupied managing Vane's numerous households once their life settled into its normal pattern.

There would be much for her to do once they retired to Bewley for the summer. She wondered whether she'd find Vane's principal seat as welcoming as Lyon Park. While it might be more fitting for the family to live at Bewley, she saw what drew them to this house. It was more than a handsome establishment. It was a home.

Sarah foresaw that she and Vane would spend a great part of the year here, too. She'd missed living amongst a large family. And a small corner of her heart rejoiced at having John and Edward to love.

She had not forgotten about Tom, of course. No, she could never forget that unfortunate child. She only hoped to God Finch would find the boy, and soon.

Sarah looked about her as their carriage entered the village. She'd only glimpsed it briefly as they traveled through it on their way to the house. Pretty shops with bow windows lined a wide street, overlooking a green that flowed up to an old Norman church.

The dowager turned to Sarah. "I have some commissions to execute in the village, my dear. Would you like to wait in the carriage or would you prefer to look at the shops? Mrs. Foster always has a wonderful selection of ribbons and lace. Or the church is quite historical, if you like that sort of thing."

Before Sarah could answer, Christian spoke. "Perhaps a walk on the green. Shall we?"

It would have been rude to refuse, much as Sarah would have preferred to be anywhere but strolling on a patch of bright green grass with Vane's insolent brother.

She felt as if she were on display. The villagers, naturally curious about their landlord's new wife, stared at her with unabashed interest as they walked past.

"Are you looking forward to living at Lyon Park, ma'am?"

Surprised, Sarah glanced at him suspiciously. It seemed an innocuous question but she rather thought that very little about Christian could be termed *innocuous*. She answered, choosing her words with care. "I had not thought we'd make

Lyon House our home. We would surely live at Bewley, wouldn't we? Isn't that Vane's principal estate?"

He sent her a sharp look. "Would you?"

"I am not sure. We haven't spoken of where we would live. But I do love it here and mean to visit often, if your mother does not object."

"Oh, well done! What a perfectly artless answer." He halted and gripped her elbow. "But you and I know you are not artless in the least, don't we, Lady Vane?" He let her go before she could protest at his manhandling. "I want you to know something. Vane might be blinded by your obvious charms, but I see you for what you are."

Warmth drained from Sarah's face. "You know nothing about me."

Between his teeth, Christian snarled. "Then let us review the history of your association with my brother, shall we?"

Her hands began to tremble, but she would not retreat from this battle. She gripped them together and faced him squarely. "No, I don't wish to do that. Whatever conclusions you have drawn, you are wrong. I never sought to trap your brother into marriage. I cannot expect you to believe that, I suppose, but it's true." She drew a deep breath. "I do not say, however, that he was right to marry me. I do not say that I am good for him."

The change of his expression to arrested interest made her stumble on. "He believes I am the woman who can make him happy, so he forced this marriage. I think . . . I think he is happy now, but I worry that it is an illusion. I cannot trust it, most especially because . . . I am very nearly happy, too." And why should she tell Christian this, of all people?

There was a long silence. Then Christian muttered something and proffered her a handkerchief. She waved it away. "I am *not* crying." But her eyes had blurred. She blinked to clear them and took a deep breath.

When she looked up, Christian was staring off into the distance, his eyes calculating. "This might very well be a performance for my benefit. But I don't think so." He glanced down at her. "No. I do not think so."

Her cheeks flamed as anger took hold. "Think what you like. I'm going back to the carriage."

With her spine very straight, she stalked across the green toward the awaiting vehicle. As she approached, sounds of an altercation carried to her from across the street and a small boy's voice rose above the rest in protest. She looked beyond the carriage and saw a familiar curly black head, apparently defending his honor and a bag of sweets from two older boys.

"Edward!"

The poor little fellow was putting up a gallant fight, apple cheeks rosy, his mouth set in a grimace of pain and determination. He was just a baby, only five, but he wanted to do everything his elder brother did. Fisticuffs were natural between boys, of course, but two against one was not fair. As Sarah started forward, she realized that one of the older boys was John.

She heard a deep shout and turned to see Vane striding down the street toward the small group, a look of thunder on his face. He was dressed only in his shirtsleeves and breeches and appeared even larger and more formidable than usual.

She switched her attention to the boys, who had stopped immediately when they saw who accosted them. Vane made a gesture that sent the third boy running, then turned to his nephews.

Sarah hurried across the street, dodging a farmer's cart and a rattling gig before she gained the pavement that ran along the row of shops.

By the time she reached them, John was in tears and his brother white-faced.

But Vane's tone never rose above a murmur and when she'd finally caught up to them he'd finished the short speech. Whatever he said, it had reduced both boys to silence, punctuated by John's sniffles.

Sarah put a gentle hand on her husband's arm. "Vane."

At the word, he turned, and his severe expression lightened a little. How glad that subtle change would have made her under normal circumstances.

"What's amiss here?" she said.

Vane looked from one brother to the other. "A matter between men." He raised his brows at John and said in a biting tone, "I trust we understand one another?"

John nodded. There was no glimmer of the bright, happy boy of the day before. "Yes, sir."

"Go. And take your brother with you. I shall see you in the library this afternoon."

The boys moved off sluggishly, heads hanging.

Vane looked down at Sarah, then at himself. "Forgive me." He rubbed a hand over his bare head.

"Training?" she said, smiling faintly.

"Uh, no. A race."

"Need I ask who won?"

His lips quirked upward and he bowed.

She went to take his arm, but he stepped back. "I am not fit company at the moment. I must stink to high heaven."

"Not at all," she answered. "Or at least, whatever scent you give off is one I like."

He grunted, clearly bemused, and she took his arm while he hesitated.

As they walked, she said, "I never told you how much I admired you that first night, did I? There's something so thrillingly primitive about seeing a man fight. I can't explain it."

She didn't look at him, but she felt his astonishment. "Little Edward gave a fair account of himself just now," she went on. "You would have been proud of the way he weighed in."

"*He* weighed in?"

"Why yes. John and that village boy were fighting over a bag of sweets, then Edward joined the fray and somehow came up trumps. Then of course, the larger boys started on him. Which wasn't right, but I've noticed even the best of men lose perspective once a melee is in progress."

She stole a look at Vane. He seemed surprised, but then his mouth thinned. "Still, it was an unfair fight. Whatever the circumstances, John should not have—"

"Of course not," she said soothingly. "No doubt his papa will punish him for it."

Vane said nothing, but she could tell she'd disconcerted him.

"Of course you'll let Gregory deal with it, won't you, Vane?" She said it as if confident he would do just that. "He is their father, after all."

She turned the conversation to other subjects, allowing her final words to sink in. Vane strolled with her to where Christian awaited them, having watched the scene from a distance.

Curtly, Vane bowed. "I'm not fit for paying calls, so I'll see you back at the house."

Sarah bade him farewell and turned to Christian.

"Mama has been delayed," he said. "She cannot decide between two shades of ribbon that look to me precisely the same. Would you care to join her?"

Sarah shook her head. "No, but I wish you will tell me something. Why was Vane so irate at that little scene?"

Christian's eyes sharpened, but he gave a small shrug. "Why don't you ask him?"

"I suppose I will," she said. "Eventually, when the time is right. But you know, don't you? And I suspect it would be less painful for him if you told me the story."

"Why do you want to know? Do you think the information will give you the upper hand?"

Sarah gasped. "You are the most cynical, detestable man! I can scarcely believe the two of you are brothers."

Christian gave a smile that wasn't wholly unpleasant. "You are right, that was uncalled for. Well, I suppose one of them will tell you, so I might as well. You have seen how my mother is, the most affectionate creature. When my father died, she was grief-stricken and lonely, and a blackguard of the first order called Horrigan wriggled his way into her good graces. She married him. And he made her life hell."

Christian's features harshened, if that were possible. "We were too young to stop it and none of the servants dared. Then one day, Vane—he was only ten years old, you know—loaded one of our father's shotguns. He said if Horrigan didn't leave Mama be, he would shoot him.

"Well, Horrigan laughed and kept laying into her, and Vane pulled the trigger. Only the powder was wet or he hadn't loaded it properly, so the gun didn't fire. Horrigan came for Vane then, took the gun, and beat him to within an inch of his life. I didn't see all this, but I heard about it. That was when Mama finally applied to one of our kinsmen for help. He ran Horrigan off the estate, and we didn't hear from him again until we received notice of his death three years later."

Sarah listened to the tale with horror and a growing understanding of all that had made Vane the man he was. "He said to me that he detests bullies. That men who bully women are the lowest kind of vermin."

"Yes. And it was the determination to grow strong, never to find himself so helpless again that led him to train and fight like his very existence depends on it. Every day. He will never forget."

Sarah swallowed past the lump that swelled her throat. "He is a fine man," she said.

"Vane has been single-handedly running the family, his own estates, and various other concerns as well." Christian jerked his head. "Yet he won't unload any of his burdens onto us. He gave the rest of us the carefree, happy childhood he should have enjoyed."

And you resent him for it, thought Sarah. Yes, you would have helped him if you could. What a strange thing, to feel a sense of kinship with Christian.

"A fine man," Sarah repeated. And she did not deserve him. Not at all.

IT was late afternoon when she saw Vane again. Enlivened by the social interaction she'd been denied for so long, Sarah unpinned her bonnet and went in search of her husband, eager to tell him how greatly she liked his neighbors and of the invitations they'd received.

She found him on the terrace, giving directions to a footman. He looked up and smiled at her, a genuine, full-bodied smile, and her heart gave a heavy thump.

She glowed at him, and when the footman bowed and left them, she placed her hand in his.

"Are you at leisure?" he inquired. "I've scarcely seen you today."

"Yes, I'm entirely at your disposal," she said. "Although, Vane, I must take care dressing for dinner tonight. Your brother seems to think I am a honey trap, so I'd like to show him exactly what I'm capable of in that direction."

Vane laughed ruefully. "No need to ask which brother." He led her down the terrace steps, drawing her close to his side so that her skirts brushed his legs and their arms were comfortably entwined. "Thank you for enduring his barbs. Christian is . . ."

"Very fond of you. And protective, too. I understand."

Vane's stride broke. He glanced down at her. "Do you?"

She nodded. "Brothers must look out for one another. You did a foolish thing, marrying me. If your father were alive, perhaps he'd have tried to forbid it, but your mother is wholly uncritical of anything you might choose to do. There is only Christian and your other brothers to look out for your interests. It would be wonderful indeed if he accepted me easily under the circumstances."

"I can look out for my own interests," Vane growled. "I've been looking out for this family since our father died."

"Yes, Christian told me about that. About Horrigan," she added gently.

"He told you?" The dark eyes searched her face. "Then you're quite wrong about him. He does like you." He blew out a breath. "I am glad. Not that his opinion would sway me, but life will be simpler for you if he does not make himself your enemy."

"You think he's accepted our marriage? He was rude and sarcastic to me."

"He is rude and sarcastic to everybody." The corner of Vane's mouth kicked up. "It's when he's coldly polite that one has reason for concern."

He went on to tell her about his brothers and their childhood exploits. She was aware that he'd subtly steered her away from the subject closest to the bone, but she didn't object.

In moments, she realized that what she'd thought was an aimless ramble had a destination. Vane led her toward a small stone cottagelike structure and paused before the door.

"When your things were destroyed after Brinsley died, I was anxious to make up for the loss. I hope you won't think me presumptuous in ordering everything without consulting you, but I wanted it to be a surprise."

He turned the handle and opened the door.

It was a stillroom. One specifically designed for making perfume.

Vane opened the shutters, and a stream of buttery sunlight illuminated the collection of cauldrons, stills, presses, glass flagons of every size and shape, skimmers and mortars, and a host of items that she'd never encountered before.

Sarah felt her jaw drop. She must look like a simpleton but she was utterly speechless. There were casks of raw materials, all neatly labeled. Sarah's sensitive nose detected and distinguished a myriad exotic fragrances she'd always longed to include in her palette. Blends of civet, amber, patchouli, and all the mysterious resins of Arabia. An impossible dream until now.

She turned amazed eyes to Vane. A faint smile curled his lips. His dark gaze held a warm glow, as if he delighted in her pleasure.

"How?" she whispered.

"I had help." He cleared his throat and made a sweeping gesture, encompassing the room. "You have a gift. You can allow it free rein here."

She couldn't stop the brilliant smile that broke over her face. She hurried to him and threw her arms around him. Hugging him tightly, she buried her face in his chest. She'd barely spoken of her unusual passion to him but he'd sensed it was important to her.

She didn't have to make and scrape for a living anymore.

In this room, she could *create*.

As she beamed up at him something hot flared in his eyes. "I haven't seen you like this in . . . years," he said, running his hands up and down her back. "I thought I'd never see that girl again, the one so full of exuberance and joy."

Suddenly shy, Sarah lowered her gaze and slipped from his embrace. She wandered around the room, touching things, sniffing scents, wondering how she could bear to tear herself away from this enchanted place. Removing the stopper from a bottle of rose essence, she inhaled deeply.

And the world tipped on its axis and shook around her. *That smell.* That ghastly smell that haunted her, mingled with the scent of blood. Sarah gasped for air as the ugly nightmare visions of Brinsley's death flooded back. Memories assaulted her, so powerful and real, she gripped the side of a bench to steady herself.

Vane took her elbow. "Sarah! Sarah, are you unwell?" His voice seemed far away.

She didn't know what to do. She had to get out of there. The suffocating smell, the cloying scent of roses, the blood.

"Oh, God, Brinsley," she whispered. With a hoarse sob, she burst from the room at a stumbling run. Falling to her knees on the grass, she retched so hard she thought her body might turn inside out.

"Sarah!"

Vane was by her side, supporting her as she heaved, deftly removing her hat and stroking her hair back from her face over and over. He murmured to her, trying to soothe her with gentle nothings, but all she could see and smell was blood.

When the retching finally abated, he wiped her mouth with his handkerchief. Urging her to sit on the grass beneath the shade of an old oak, he drew her against him. She was trembling and cold and the sour taste of bile coated her mouth. She must smell awful, but he didn't seem to care.

Vane's broad chest and the strong arms that wrapped around her were a safe haven in this storm of painful emotions. She subsided into his embrace, drew comfort from the steady beat of his heart beneath her ear while she drew fresh country air into her lungs.

His lips brushed her hair in a fleeting gesture of tenderness that brought a painful lump to her throat.

She continued to breathe deeply and felt a little better. "I'm sorry. That was such a lovely thing to do. I'm so sorry I spoiled it." He deserved an explanation. Gently, she drew away from him and sat up so she could look into his face.

It was difficult to find the right words. "I don't know why, but the rose essence brought back images of the night Brinsley died. So strongly, so vividly. I made rosewater that evening. The scent and his death seem all tangled up together in a way I can't explain."

"Madame Vissier told me that scent is the most evocative of the senses," said Vane. "Perhaps she is right."

Her brows knitted. "Madame Vissier? My parents' old housekeeper?"

"Yes, you mentioned her once. I needed an expert to tell me what to order for your stillroom. I wanted the best."

With an effort, she smiled. "Thank you. It is truly magnificent. I shall spend many happy hours there. I just need to become accustomed, I think."

Vane stroked a gentle finger down her cheek. "You loved him, Sarah. You loved Brinsley."

How absurd! Of *course* she didn't love—but when she would have argued, he held up a hand to stop her. "Ah, don't answer. I know you think you detested him, and perhaps that is true also. I loathe the necessity, but I'm broaching this painful subject because we cannot go on as we are, Sarah. Unless you admit to yourself that you cared for him, you will never move past this grief, this block to your own happiness."

"That—that *scoundrel*?" Sarah gaped at him. How could he believe she loved Brinsley after the way he'd treated her all those years? How could he hold such a poor opinion of her judgment?

"Think about it, Sarah. Think hard. You must have loved him at first. You married him, didn't you? And don't tell me you did so with your parents' blessing. Don't tell me you didn't have to fight hard to get what you wanted, because no parents with an ounce of gumption would have wished for Brinsley Cole as a son-in-law."

"Yes," she admitted. "I was prepared to fight hard. I was seventeen, for goodness' sake! Too young to see through his lies. Too caught up in the romance of it all. And my mother did counsel me against marrying so young, before I'd been presented and done the Season. But I didn't listen because, well, we were at outs at the time about other things. My father . . ." She shook her head. "No. He never said a word against Brinsley that I recall." Doubtfully, she added, "Perhaps I was not so stupid, after all, if my father was deceived in Brinsley's character, too."

Vane started to say something, then he stopped and sighed. "You think you recovered from that immature love, don't you? You truly believe you stopped loving Brinsley on the day he told you about his natural son." He shook his head, his lips twisting a little. "It doesn't work like that, Sarah. You don't stop loving someone just because you discover they have flaws. If you truly love in the first place, that is."

She swallowed, her gaze darting here and there. "No, that cannot be so. I was infatuated, blind. If I'd known what Brinsley was, do you think I'd have married him?" She paused, narrowing her eyes. "Is this jealousy at work? Do you believe I still loved him when he died, is that it?"

He had no cause to be jealous of Brinsley. The two were poles apart in character, surely he knew she could see that? But what else could have motivated him to make such an outlandish accusation?

Vane stared at her for so long, she thought he wouldn't answer. Finally, he said, "Yes, I do believe that you loved him when he died, at least after a fashion. Or you wouldn't carry this infernal, corrosive guilt with you now." He leaned toward her, and in a low, vehement voice, he added, "I would as soon be jealous of pond scum. But I do resent the barrier between us, the anger and hurt you've caged inside you."

"I stopped concerning myself with Brinsley's peccadilloes years ago! Do you think I have so little pride—"

"Oh, you've pride to spare, ma'am. You took your hurt and anger and pride and built a fortress with them. And they protected you from Brinsley, didn't they? But now he's gone and you're still trapped inside. You're too busy shoring up your defenses to even think what freedom might taste like. You don't know how to be happy. And if you can't be happy, neither can I." He took her face between his hands and his voice grated with pain. "Because no matter how much you keep hurting me, it's as I said. I can't stop loving you."

Her breath caught in her chest. He *loved* her. She'd always known it in some remote corner of her heart, yet to hear him say it was like waking from a dream.

But he shouldn't love her. How *could* he love her if he thought her the poor sort of creature who would pine for a worthless scoundrel like Brinsley?

She pulled away. "You're wrong about Brinsley." She struggled to rise, and he was on his feet immediately to assist her. She snatched her hand away and fought the sudden dizziness that threatened to send her reeling.

"I have a headache. I'm going back to the house." She flicked a hand when he moved with her. "No, don't come with me. *Don't.*"

He gripped her elbow and pulled her to him. "You can't shut me out forever, Sarah. I won't let you. What we share is no common passion, no common love. You know that's true. Stop fighting it. We all make mistakes. But the biggest one of all is to let those mistakes rule our lives."

His gaze lowered to her mouth and his lips parted and she thought he might kiss her. She stared at him stonily, fighting the way her body always responded to him whether her mind gave it permission or not.

But even as her mind said *no, no, no*, her face tilted toward his, her lips tingling faintly with anticipation.

"I'm not going to kiss you," he said roughly. "I'm not going to do that anymore. If you can't come to my bed with a free heart, I don't want you there at all."

She stared at him in silence, absorbing the sharp sting of those words. He wanted her to admit to something that simply wasn't true. She'd never loved Brinsley. She couldn't have!

Burning with fury and shame, she wrenched from his hold and left him without a backward glance.

IF he hadn't issued that foolish ultimatum, he could be with her now, Vane thought, as he pinched out the candle by his bed. For the first time in weeks, he prepared to sleep alone.

True, he could breach the physical distance that separated them. It was only a wall punctuated by a connecting door, after all. But the vast chasm of guilt and wounded pride that lay between them, that was not so easy to cross.

The bed was cold without her. Empty. He'd stayed up talking with Nick and Christian into the small hours but once they'd retired, he'd felt rather pathetic drinking on his own like the lovelorn fool he undoubtedly was. Pride wasn't solely Sarah's domain. He'd hauled himself up to bed, grimly sober despite the fearsome number of brandies he'd downed in his idiotic attempt to wipe out the pain.

Vane rolled on his back and clasped his hands behind his head. Staring at the elaborate silk canopy above, he breathed deeply, trying to calm his thoughts enough for sleep. He itched for activity, some dire punishment to which he might subject his body, physical pain to detract from the ache in his heart.

Had he been wrong to demand so much of Sarah? Yet, loving her, could he accept anything less? At least if he lost he would know that he'd fought hard for her love, that he hadn't acquiesced in that smooth, pleasant existence where the passion of the night became a thing quite apart from the everyday.

He pondered that. She gave herself to him with such sensual abandon he could have convinced himself it was enough. He could have told himself she loved him, regardless of what she might say.

Perhaps she did. But until she acknowledged it to herself and said it to him, he wouldn't know for certain. And he'd discovered that having coerced her into a liaison, persuaded her into marriage, and bullied her into embracing their passion, he didn't have it in him to force her final step. She would have to take it on her own.

In the meantime, his body burned for her like the fire from a thousand hells. But when she finally gave herself to him without that shadow of guilt in her eyes, the present torment would be worth it.

It had to be.

SARAH was alone in the carriage. Vane had decided to ride back to town and ordered their servants to follow later with their baggage. Tactful of him, since she longed to be alone with her thoughts awhile. Despite the sick churning in her stomach, she even dozed a little as the carriage rumbled along.

She hadn't slept at all last night. Her conversation with Vane kept turning over in her mind. Did she really continue to harbor some shred of that love she'd felt for Brinsley at seventeen?

She didn't want to believe it. She hated the very idea that she could be so weak, so lacking in pride.

But . . .

No. It was as she'd said that first time her mother questioned her. She didn't mourn Brinsley. She was very sorry he'd had to die such a sordid and painful death, but she didn't miss him. She was glad to be free.

What, then, had made her rebuff Vane's offer to make her his mistress that fateful night? What else but self-respect? What else but pride? But she remembered her dread of seeing Brinsley's face when he realized what she'd done. She remembered lying to him as he died. Would another wife who'd been sold by her husband like that have sought to spare his feelings? Certainly, if she'd been truly as hard as she'd tried to appear all those years, she would have thrown that affair in his face and damned him to hell while she did it.

Sitting in the carriage, staring out at nothing, cold fear gripped her anew. Had she constructed that hard, contemptuous woman so that she wouldn't have to face the truth of how much he'd hurt her with that careless betrayal? *Those* many *careless betrayals*, she corrected herself.

If she hadn't cared, she would have ignored it all, wouldn't she? She wouldn't have stayed with him, wouldn't have devised many and various means of making Brinsley pay.

For the first time in years, she searched her memory for the girl she'd been before the cruel world intruded on her sheltered existence. The days were sunnier then, she knew, filled with promise, not disappointment. She'd been secure in the love of her family.

And then she'd seen the evidence of her mother's infidelity and nothing had been quite the same. She'd discovered that people—even people one loved—didn't always show you their true faces.

But she hadn't heeded that lesson, had she? When Brinsley came along, he'd seemed so open and easy and carefree, she'd been deceived into thinking she saw the whole man. She'd been flattered at the attention he paid her. Angry with her mother over her own imperfect character, she'd dismissed the countess's warnings.

But Vane had raised an interesting question. Why hadn't Papa put a stop to it? He could have, quite easily. He'd always been a hero to her. Oh, perhaps she might have tried to twist him around her finger and there might have been tears and recriminations when he refused, but she would have bowed to his judgment in the end. And been spared an enormous amount of heartache.

Heartache.

Yes.

She'd been deceived in Brinsley's true character, but that man, the one she thought she'd married, was a man she'd been in love with. And even though he'd shown his true colors very soon after the ring was on her finger, she had not been able to stop.

Such a pity that the love hadn't vanished with the illusion of the man.

She'd told herself it was infatuation, hadn't she? The idle dreaming of a silly girl who had not yet been about much in the world. But she had never been a silly girl, not really. A little naïve, perhaps, but not silly.

She remembered Vane's furious words when he'd confronted her in Peter Cole's book room. How could she have allowed Brinsley to treat her so badly? And here, she supposed, was her answer.

She'd loved him. Not the sly, manipulative charmer he'd become in later years, but the young man who had walked with her through fields of spring flowers at Straghan, made her daisy chains, and told her his hopes and dreams. The young man who had gazed at her with worship in his eyes, or confessed a piece of mischief with a rueful grin. They had made each other laugh in those early days. Looking back with a less jaundiced eye, she saw that not all of his courtship had been false.

He had watched her with Vane outside the coffeehouse that fateful afternoon. Had she betrayed the strength of her feelings for anyone to see? Brinsley had cut at her viciously that night as he'd sent her to Vane. He'd accused her of being hard and unforgiving, of driving him to worse behavior after he'd made that first so-called mistake.

He was a hypocrite to have objected to any partiality she might have for another man, particularly one she'd never acted upon. But it didn't mean he'd been happy to see her go. It didn't mean he hadn't, in his own twisted way, been jealous, furious at her for taking his bait. She could see, looking back, that perhaps that challenge had been a test. One she'd failed.

Her heart gave an agonizing twist. Yes, she'd loved Brinsley. Vane was right.

Painful sobs rose and gathered in her throat, choking her, making her mouth ugly and her nose stream and her eyes blur and smart. She tried to be strong, to hold it in. Why couldn't this have come upon her in the night when she was private?

But there was no one but the blue sky and the birds in the hedgerows to see her now. And as the dappled light from the trees above raced over her upturned face, she let the agony and the sorrow flow out of her. She hugged herself and rocked with the coach and her grief, and mourned the girl she'd been, the man Brinsley had never become.

Twenty

SARAH put her elbows on the dressing table and rubbed her temples. She dug her fingertips into her scalp and massaged her aching head.

She'd done a lot of thinking in the past twenty-four hours. More than was good for her pride or her peace of mind.

Try as she might, she couldn't easily recall how and when she'd fallen deeply in love with the youthful Brinsley. She accepted now that she had. Vane's logic made inescapable, brutal sense. Like Vane's own mother, she'd had the infernal bad judgment to fall in love with an absolute rotter of a man.

But she'd retold the sordid tale of her downfall to herself so many times, she'd lost all sense of perspective on the events surrounding their courtship. Vane had a more clear-sighted view, but he wasn't there when it all began. She needed to discover the truth of that halcyon period before her marriage. She would have to swallow her tattered, battered pride and ask her mother how it all came about.

She wasn't looking for anyone to blame. She'd always

taken responsibility for her folly, though perhaps if she were a better person she wouldn't have resented her mother so much for being right. A better person, she realized now, would have apologized to her mother for the accusations she'd flung in her face, asked for her help when life became too difficult to bear.

Well, it was too late to ask for help, but it wasn't too late to apologize.

When Sarah arrived at her parents' house, they were, unusually, both at home. She handed her bonnet to the butler and followed him to the sunny conservatory, her mother's favorite room.

The earl looked up from his newspaper with an expression of dawning delight in his eyes that struck Sarah's heart.

"My dear." He rose and held out his arms to her. How wonderful it was to receive such a welcome. How wonderful to have someone in the world whose face lit when she walked in the door. Why had she turned her back on this?

"Papa." She smiled, blinking back tears, and kissed him.

The countess rose. "I'll leave you . . ."

"No, please don't go." Sarah slid from her father's embrace and took the countess's hands and kissed her cheek, whispering, "I'm sorry. Sorry for everything."

The countess's body, which had stiffened slightly as Sarah leaned in to kiss her, relaxed. She clung tightly to Sarah's hands, and the expression in those sharp eyes was soft and moist. "She's come back to us, Richard."

"Yes."

When they were seated, Sarah took a deep breath. "I want to talk to you about that summer when I first met Brinsley."

Her parents exchanged a glance, but Sarah couldn't tell what it signified.

Smoothing her skirts, she continued. "You know my marriage to Brinsley was not a happy one. Let's not speak of that, it's not why I've come. What I can't reconcile is why I fell in love with him, why I married him. I've told myself it was infatuation, but it wasn't, was it? It was love. That's why you let me wed him."

Her father's skin paled in an instant to a sickly grey. "You don't look well, Papa. Should I call for tea?"

He gave a quick shake of his head.

The countess said, "No, Sarah. Go on."

In a rush, Sarah said, "I don't understand why I didn't see through him. I don't understand how someone could be so rotten inside and act the part he did with me in those first few months of our acquaintance. I remember the conversations we had. I was convinced that he loved me. Later, when everything went wrong, I told myself I'd been infatuated. A silly girl beguiled by the easy charm of a personable man. But . . . I was never a silly girl, that I can recall."

"No, you weren't," murmured the countess.

A fierce burn of pleasure at the compliment flared in her chest. "How could I have been so wrong?"

The countess watched her husband for a moment. When he didn't speak, she said, "You weren't wrong. Brinsley was in love with you, and as far as I could see, you were in love with him. I didn't like it. You were too young. There was something about him. . . . Well, I should have done more to stop it, but . . ."

"But for me." The earl's low voice trembled. His eyes sought Sarah's. "But for me."

Sarah looked from her father to her mother and saw a large tear roll down the countess's face. She dashed it away with the heel of her hand and gestured for the earl to continue. "Tell her. You must tell her now."

The earl nodded. Hoarsely, he said, "Sarah, your godfather, Lord Templeton." His mouth worked but he didn't seem able to go on.

"Yes?"

"You know Brinsley was his secretary for a brief period."

"Of course. It was how we met."

"Yes. Of course," her father echoed. "Well, you perhaps know that Templeton has certain . . . inclinations."

Her brow wrinkled. "He likes men, do you mean? I remember being shocked when I found out, but you explained to me that he was still the same . . ." Her eyes widened. She heard her mother sob and watched her press the earl's hand in a gesture of comfort she'd rarely witnessed before.

Sarah felt hot and cold at once, her mind reeling with the implications of this disclosure. "Then you, Papa. And Lord Templeton—"

Her father nodded. "Yes, we have been intimate since before you were born."

She stared at them both helplessly while she struggled to absorb this information. So many things made sense now. Her mother—how could she blame her mother for seeking love outside of such a marriage? All these years she *had* blamed her, despised her even, for betraying the earl. And all that time, he'd loved someone else. Another *man*.

"Just like Templeton, I am still the man I was before, Sarah. I am the father who loves you." The cold grey eyes pleaded. "Please do not turn away from me."

Sarah was so shocked, she couldn't speak.

The countess, misinterpreting her silence, leaped to his defense. "Don't you think that if he could have helped it, he would, Sarah? Do you think he wanted to risk everything he'd worked for, live with the threat of exposure and ruin but a breath away? Do you think he chose this life?"

"No, I don't think that," said Sarah quietly. "I don't think that at all."

Sarah moved to kneel before him. She took her father's face in her hands and kissed him deliberately on the forehead. "You don't stop loving someone simply because you discover they're not quite the person you'd thought they were."

His own eyes glistening, her father folded her close, his body trembling with suppressed emotion.

She gently broke their embrace and said, "Brinsley blackmailed you, didn't he, Papa? He threatened to expose you if you didn't let me marry him."

The earl shook his head. "Not in so many words. It was never as clear-cut as an outright threat."

Lady Straghan spoke. "He found an indiscreet letter among Templeton's personal papers. He let us know that he knew. But Sarah, if I'd suspected for one moment you'd be condemned to the sort of marriage you endured all those years, I would have let Brinsley do his worst."

The earl nodded. "There were any number of ways we could have handled the situation. But it seemed that you loved one another and nothing would do for you but to wed. It wasn't the brilliant match we'd hoped for you, but Brinsley was the son of a gentleman and there was nothing to object to in his birth. We persuaded ourselves . . . God help us, we persuaded ourselves that you would be happy together. It all worked out so neatly. We kept the secret in the family that way. But then we had no notion Brinsley intended to resign from his perfectly lucrative post to pursue a life of leisure, nor that you would refuse our help. We did make Brinsley an allowance, but undoubtedly he frittered it away."

"Yes, he did. But you could do no more since my pride wouldn't let me accept what I called charity from you." Sarah shook her head. "I was so full of stupid pride."

Gripping her hand, the earl said vehemently, "You should never have been condemned to such a life."

"Mama tried to tell me I was too young to marry but I wouldn't listen," said Sarah. "Who knows? Had you forbidden the match I might well have eloped. It was my decision to marry Brinsley. I don't blame you, either of you. Never think that."

She turned to the countess. "I owe you an apology, though, Mama. I judged you harshly without knowing all the circumstances."

"Yes, you did. In your position, I probably would have done the same. For my part, I should have explained, rather than cutting you off like that. You are not the only one with a surfeit of pride. I was very wrong. But all that is done with now, Sarah. Painful though it's been, I am glad we had this talk."

Sarah stayed with her parents until late in the afternoon. There were ten years' worth of news to catch up on, after all, and many bridges to mend.

As Sarah came away from the house in Grosvenor Square, she felt a quiet certainty that she had finally made peace with the long episode of her life in which Brinsley had played a starring role.

Perhaps he'd been a superb actor, or perhaps he'd begun their courtship in perfectly good faith. Perhaps he'd loved her. Somehow, that love had soured. She couldn't think why or how that had happened. In truth, none of that mattered anymore.

That was the most significant revelation of all.

Sarah turned toward Brooke Street, conscious of need, a yearning to come home to Vane. The feeling disconcerted her. She'd learned a long time ago to rely only on herself. But she realized now that despite all they'd been through, Vane had never, not once, let her down. How rare that was. How utterly rare and precious.

As she hurried up the front steps she felt a warm, intense glow in her chest and a flutter of apprehension low in her belly.

The time had come to let go of the past. She would forge a future with Vane.

VANE arrived home bone-weary and very afraid. He'd returned to London with the determination to finish the business once and for all. He would either find that damned bank draft today or confess to Sarah and face the consequences.

But his inquiries had led him in circles, and no closer to that infernal piece of paper. That one document could destroy everything he'd striven so hard to build with Sarah.

As his valet helped him off with his boots, Vane gazed longingly at the awaiting bath. When he finally sank down into the steaming water, every muscle he possessed heaved a sigh of relief. He wanted to simply drift and rest his teeming brain.

He'd been right to challenge Sarah about Brinsley. He was convinced of it. But he shouldn't have told her he loved her. What was she to do with a declaration like that? She hadn't been overjoyed by the news, that was certain. Had she even listened?

He shouldn't have said it. He knew she wasn't ready to hear it. The sentiment would be a burden on someone like her. He'd long suspected she simply wasn't capable of returning the emotion.

No, that wasn't it. There were times when he thought she did return his love, even if she didn't know it herself. She was trying to reconcile the past and Brinsley's place in her heart, as he'd asked her to do, he knew that. But love shouldn't take so much work, should it? He'd fallen headlong for her without any effort at all.

Dismissing his valet, he laid his head back against the lip of the tub and let the heat of the steaming water soak into his flesh. He closed his eyes as his mind slid away.

Vane knew nothing more until something moved against his chest. Something soft and springy that trailed water and thrilling sensation in its wake. As awareness returned, hope unfurled in his chest, deep and warm.

Opening his eyes a crack, Vane saw that Sarah knelt by the tub, a slight frown of concentration furrowing her brow. She held the sponge that was now making forays along his shoulder and down his arm, and the intensity of her regard was such that his body reacted instantly, pleasurably, even while he tried not to appear conscious.

Dimly, he remembered vowing not to share her bed until she came to him with love. What a witless ultimatum that had been! He thought this as soapsuds flowed down his chest, over his nipples, and disappeared into the water, spreading along the glassy surface like foam upon a wave.

She was soaping his right hand now. It was an effort to keep himself from picking her up and depositing her in the tub with him, silk peignoir and all.

Strictly speaking, they wouldn't be in bed.

Repressing a groan of frustration, Vane shut his eyes and tried to simply enjoy.

Finished with his hands, the sponge trailed back to his

chest, teasing around his nipples, then swiping over them with well-judged pressure. His stomach contracted and he sucked in a breath as the sponge traveled lower, and lingered at his groin.

He couldn't repress a groan then. He opened his eyes and saw her gazing steadily into them, while her hand and the sponge pleasured him, so soft and wet and warm.

He wanted to launch out of the bath and finish what she'd started, but something in her steady regard compelled him to stay where he was and endure.

With the sponge encircling his cock, moving on him, he might burst at any moment. His buttocks clenched and his teeth gritted as he resisted that primal urge to spill into her hand.

He couldn't stand it anymore. With a hoarse moan, he removed her hand and stood quickly, water cascading from his shoulders and flanks.

He stepped out and reached for her, but she stayed where she was kneeling next to the tub, resisting his attempt to help her rise. She let the sponge fall from her fingers. His heart jumped at the sudden slap of it hitting the water.

She was on her knees before him. With not a word exchanged between them, instinct told him what she would do. His cock gave a mighty jump in anticipation. Her fingers closed around his length. Those wicked green eyes looked up at him, held his gaze while he held his breath, waiting, unable to look away from that sinful, knowing stare.

She licked her lips. Then very deliberately, she looked down at his cock as if it was the most delicious treat she'd ever seen.

Then carefully, slowly, she slicked her tongue over the head.

Christ! He gripped the lip of the tub as her mouth closed over him, his body bowed and taut. He'd never even thought to ask this of her. That she did it willingly, confidently, simply shattered his mind.

Proud Lady Vane, on her knees servicing him, and looking very much like she enjoyed the task. Vane stopped even trying to think and rode the pulsing waves of ecstasy she made with her mouth and hands.

Sarah reveled in this act in a way she'd never contemplated until now. Vane was a powerful man, but even as she went on her knees to perform a function men usually only asked of their whores, she was the one in control.

She was the one who made him tense and quiver like a stallion scenting his mare. Her touch made him groan and whisper husky pleas and move his hips in jerky thrusts to help set the rhythm. It was she who'd made him forget that he hadn't wanted her to share his bed.

And the feel of him, so smooth and warm and strong and hard, made her insides soften and rush with heat. She'd wanted to give him the gift of her complete surrender. Yet, in the pleasure she gave him she felt more powerful than ever before. And when he quickened and pulled away from her with a hoarse groan of completion, she felt victorious, exultant.

As his shudders subsided, she pressed her face into his taut belly and ran her hands over his buttocks. The skin there was soft and damp and burning hot. She placed a kiss on his hip bone as he continued to tremble, panting as if he'd run many miles.

Finally, his hand touched her shoulder. "You didn't have to do that."

She looked up. "I wanted to." A hard knot in her chest held her silent when she ought to have said more.

This time, when he raised her, she made no demur. He folded her in his arms and kissed her as if it were the last time, as if the world had fallen away and it was just the two of them, standing on a precipice, ready to throw themselves into the void.

She was scared of that unknown future. Terrified. But if he was with her, somehow, she would find the courage to face it.

She took the first step and flung herself into space. "I love you, Vane." She whispered it against his lips. "So much that it frightens me."

He tensed and held utterly still. She stopped nuzzling his jaw and looked up. "What is it?" *Please don't say you've reconsidered. Please say you love me, too.*

She almost begged him out loud. She wasn't altogether sure she wouldn't beg, if it came to that.

"I've waited so long for you to say that," he breathed, smoothing her hair from her forehead, searching her face. "It makes it that much harder, that much more imperative to confess I haven't been honest with you."

No! She didn't believe it. Sarah almost swayed, the sensation of falling was so acute. His hands steadied her. His dark gaze entreated her to listen, to understand.

Disappointment and terror and a familiar, anticipatory rage swirled low in her stomach. "Tell me. Tell me now. What is it? What have you done?"

Gently, he disengaged from her. "Let me get something on first."

Cold and shivering, Sarah clutched the damp folds of her silk peignoir closer. She'd come to him naked underneath, ready to surrender her body as well as her heart to him, ready to give him everything he wanted to take.

Now, he would confess his betrayal. That he *had* betrayed her, she didn't doubt from the look on his face. Why had she gone onto her knees to him?

As Vane walked back from his dressing room, pulling on his dressing gown, ice enveloped Sarah like a shroud. Her heart was breaking into tiny pieces, but that didn't mean she'd let him see it. She would hold her head up high and take this blow on the chin.

And then never, ever lay herself open to him like that again.

This is Vane, a voice inside her said. *Not Brinsley.* Vane was good, decent, honest. This revelation could not be so very bad. She couldn't make such an error in judgment again, not after paying so dearly for her first mistake.

But he looked grave as death and she couldn't afford to weaken. She'd abased herself before him, she'd given him her trust, spoken the words she'd vowed never to say. And now he would tell her how unworthy he was to receive these gifts. She wanted to be strong, to gather her pride around her, but her pride seemed a threadbare cloak this night.

"Will you sit down?"

Sarah shook her head. She wanted to get this over with quickly, and standing made her feel stronger. She would need to be strong for this. Her hands gripped together so tightly, she thought her bones might crack but she couldn't help herself. She couldn't seem to make them relax.

"All right." Vane cleared his throat a little, and ran a hand through his damp hair. He stared into space, as if bringing the past into his mind's eye. "On the night Brinsley died, he offered me a bargain: one night with you in exchange for ten thousand pounds. As you know, I did not accept it." He paused. "I did, however, offer Brinsley an alternative."

Sarah couldn't restrain a surprised gasp.

Vane's eyes flickered, held hers. Then he looked away again, his jaw set. "I said I would pay him five thousand pounds immediately and make him a yearly allowance on top of that on the proviso that he left England and never saw you or contacted you again."

All of the blood left Sarah's head in a sickening rush. Sheer will kept her upright, though she had to steady herself with one hand on the chair beside her. "You would have paid my husband to desert me?"

He threw out a hand in a frustrated gesture. "Believe me, if I'd seen any other alternative, I would have taken it. But he threatened you, threatened to hurt you if I didn't agree to his scheme. I didn't doubt he meant to make your life intolerable, more so than it already was. I gave him a bank draft for five thousand pounds, but the draft went missing that night. As soon as I'd seen you, I searched your rooms but it was gone. It wasn't on Brinsley's person. It's my guess that whoever killed Brinsley has the draft."

"What made you decide to tell me now?" Sarah was amazed at how calmly she spoke. "Is it because you haven't been able to recover the incriminating document, is that it?"

Vane sighed. "I won't lie to you. I thought—hoped—I

wouldn't be obliged to tell you. But once I'd demanded that you confront your feelings for Brinsley honestly, it seemed unfair of me to keep the truth from you."

Sarah tried to think rationally, calmly, over the faint buzz in her ears. Her throat felt sore, her chest tight. She'd never in her life longed so much for a quiet corner in which she might burst into tears. A fine time to give her honesty— after she'd gone on her knees to him, after she'd told him of her love. Irrevocably committed herself to him, body and soul.

Could she believe him? Deliberately, calmly, she said, "A cynical person might accuse you of fabricating this story to explain the existence of the bank draft. You are worried that whoever has it will come to me with this evidence of conspiracy between you and Brinsley and that I would think the worst: that you did pay for my services that night. Isn't that so?"

"Yes. I'll admit, I was afraid you'd leap to the wrong conclusion. But I'm telling the truth, damn it." He threw up a hand in a frustrated gesture. "After all we've been to each other, how can you doubt me?"

When she didn't answer, he muttered a curse beneath his breath. "If you refuse to trust this so-called love you have for me, just think about it logically, Sarah. Why would I pay for a night with you and not come immediately to claim you? Do you think I could have waited five minutes, much less a day or more? Do you think I would have allowed Brinsley to poison your mind first? Do you think, if I had paid for you, I would have insisted you await me in my drawing room when you came to my house? None of that makes sense. If you hadn't been so distraught, you might have seen that at the time."

He made it so easy to believe. A hard voice inside her whispered that they always sounded so reasonable when they lied and used your love to make you doubt your instincts and your intellect. "I don't see that paying my husband to run out on me was in my interests, either. Did you think to step into his shoes when he was gone?"

He sucked in a breath, as if she'd winded him. "My one thought was to protect you. It was the only way I could see to stop him. If I'd considered beyond that, I would have expected you'd return to your family."

Everything was awry. She couldn't trust him; she couldn't trust her own judgment. Her head pounded viciously and she felt bone-weary, sick to her stomach. Too raw to do battle with him over this.

She touched her fingertips to her temple and whispered, "I can't talk about it. I need to think." She hugged herself against the insidious cold. "I-I can't think with you near."

He turned away from her and braced his hands on the writing table at the window, his head bowed in a gesture of forbearance, or perhaps it signaled defeat.

The temptation to go to him tugged at her. She truly hated to see him like this and know that she was the cause, yet she simply could not bring herself to weaken. There'd been too many times in the past when she'd accepted excuses and made them on Brinsley's behalf, all for the love she bore him. He'd wielded her love like a weapon against her, finally forging it into hate.

Yes, she'd loved Brinsley. Hated him, too. And that hate had turned her into a hateful woman. A hard woman, who didn't know how to love someone as good and noble as Vane.

The truth was, she believed Vane about the bank draft. It was just the kind of forceful, protective, interfering thing the man she'd grown to love would do. She believed he loved her as much as any man could. She knew she loved him. Why, then, was it so hard, so very hard, to let down her defenses, to let him in?

"Sarah." His low voice made a chord of longing vibrate inside her. "I would have given my life to spare you pain. What would you have done in my place? He was going to hurt you."

"He wouldn't have hurt me. Not physically." *There were so many other ways. . . .*

"How was I to know that, Sarah? How could I take the

chance? God knows I never expected him to be greedy enough to take the money I offered him and still try to coerce you into spending the night with me. He must have reconsidered leaving."

"Perhaps he never meant to leave. He loved me, Vane. In a perverted, selfish way, he loved me. I realize now that's why he wanted so much to hurt me that night. He'd seen us together, sensed what we felt for one another."

Her throat was parched and aching. Her voice rasped. "He said he'd made a mess of things. We both did, I suppose."

Vane simply looked at her and held out his hand. "Are you willing to try again with me, Sarah?"

Well, here was the choice. She could take Vane at his word, trust him, and step out into the void. Trust was like that. You risked everything you had, everything you were for love. She imagined herself with Vane, loving him with a whole, trusting heart, and shuddered with fear and longing.

But mostly fear.

Her head told her Vane would never betray her the way Brinsley had. He was too good, too honorable. Even knowing he'd hidden the truth about the bank draft from her, she believed that. She believed he'd acted in her best interests all along.

Yet, her heart could not make that final leap. She'd thought it could. She'd thought all was resolved. But one small reversal, one setback, and her heart was doubting again.

WHEN Vane went down to breakfast the following morning, the butler handed him a letter. "The messenger said it was urgent, my lord."

Vane ripped open the letter and despite himself, his heart sank. "He's found him. He's found the boy."

He didn't hesitate, but immediately ran up the stairs to Sarah's bedchamber. With a crooked finger, he tapped one knuckle on the door and walked in.

She sat on the window seat looking out at a fine new day.

Her hair rippled down over her shoulders, the way he loved. She was wearing a prosaic linen nightgown, not one of the sheer silk and lace garments he'd bought her. That, as much as the slight stiffening of her body when she heard him enter, told him she didn't want his touch.

He cleared his throat. "Apologies for disturbing you, but I thought you'd want to know. Word has come from Finch. He's found Tom."

Her head snapped around, surprise and relief and pleasure breaking over the pallor of her face like sunlight on snow. Her eyes seemed very deep and green.

She started up and rushed toward him, snatching the letter he handed her and smoothing the edges. Vane watched the flicker of her thick dark lashes as she scanned the note. "He says Tom is in good health and spirits." A hand went to her breast. "Oh, that is wonderful news! Finch has more information and asks if he might call on us at ten. Well, of course he might! What was he about, to delay? Vane, tell him to come at once."

Pain sliced through his chest at her glowing looks for a boy she hadn't even met.

"You will eat first," he said. "The boy will not evaporate if you delay to break your fast."

She looked at him closely then and a shadow fell over her face, perhaps as she recalled the previous night. "Yes, of course. You are right." She glanced at the door. Clearly, she couldn't wait to be rid of him. She wouldn't invite him to assist her to dress in place of her abigail. He was not forgiven.

She crossed to the bellpull and rang for her maid, then stood by her dressing table and fiddled with the little silver-topped pots there.

"Are we going to speak of last night?" he said eventually.

A rush of breath. "I-I can't think about it now."

I have more important things to do.

The words, unspoken, hung between them. Even as he knew she was pushing him out, perhaps unwittingly using the boy as a shield to protect herself, jealousy surged within him.

It made him say, "You know from Finch's letter the boy is happy and cared for. Surely that is an end to it."

She turned, wide-eyed with surprise, a glint of disappointment in those brilliant depths. "Do you think I would search for him this long without seeing for myself that he is happy? I mean to go there, of course. I mean to bring him back."

Vane's brows slammed together. "You will do no such thing." He shoved a hand through his hair. "I've gone along with your quest until now, my lady, but this is the end of it. You were concerned for the child's welfare—we both were. But he is no kin of yours. You wouldn't even know of his existence if Brinsley had done the decent thing." He rolled his eyes. "What am I saying? If Brinsley had done the decent thing, the boy wouldn't exist."

"I have more responsibility toward him than some unknown people in St. Alban's!"

"*Unknown?* He's been living with them for ten years! Sarah, if Brinsley, his father, saw fit to give the boy into the care of these people, if he is being fed and housed and treated well as Finch writes that he is, then you have nothing more to do." He set his jaw. "Let it go, ma'am. I was willing to mount a search. . . . Damn it, I was willing to provide for the boy, if necessary, much as it stuck in my gullet to do so. But it's *not* necessary. He is safe and well. Let him be."

"He belongs with his family." Folding her arms, she turned her back on him to stare out the window.

All of the pain and fury boiled inside him like lava in a volcano, ready to erupt. "You're *not* his family," he said, dangerously quiet. "He is the child of the woman your husband betrayed you with. And what if he is perfectly happy where he is? Are you going to step in and tell him the truth of his origins, take him away with you? What will that achieve? Is that something he will want or something you do purely for yourself?"

Her back stiffened, then her shoulders heaved with suppressed emotion.

Reaching out, he gripped her by the arm and jerked her around to face him. "You keep chasing after love from people who are never going to give it to you, and ignoring the ones who already do."

When she bowed her head, he took her chin and forced it up so that her eyes locked on his, hurting, defiant. "I am here, Sarah. I'm right here. But I won't be forever. Do you want us to go our separate ways now? Think carefully about your answer. Because I'm not going to wait for you while you chase after that boy." He forced out the words. "I never thought I'd say it, but I've finally had enough."

The planes of her face seemed to harden, and her lips grew white. "I'm going to find him. You will not deter me from that resolve. After all I've done, I can't give him up now. I wonder that you'd think I could. You ought to know your jealous ultimatums won't work with me. You ought to know that child's needs come first."

"His needs or yours?"

There was a shocked silence. It seemed to stretch for minutes, and Vane had the sensation of falling. Falling, without even the hope of landing on solid ground.

He waited for an eternity for her to retract the words, to tell him he was right, or at least to suggest a compromise. But nothing came. She was more afraid than he'd suspected, then. More distant than he'd known. Colder, too, if she could so easily turn her back on all they'd been to one another, all they'd become.

But he couldn't see the profit in running after her while she chased this impossible dream of love. It hurt him inexpressibly that she sought another man's child when he could not give her one. In all, there was only so much battering a heart could take before it gave up the fight. His was nearly counted out.

Finally, he said, "Very well. I'll draw up the terms of our separation. You won't find me ungenerous, I hope."

"Vane, don't—"

"I must go," he said brusquely. "I'm late for an appointment."

"*Vane!*"

He never knew how he managed to walk across that room and get himself out the door.

VANE. What had she done? Sarah was still trembling with horror and fear as she tried desperately to concentrate on the facts Finch laid before her. He'd traced one Polly Lawson all the way to York and back and finally discovered her in St. Alban's of all places, still employed as nanny to the younger children of the Martins, who'd taken in Brinsley's son all those years ago.

"I watched the family for a couple of days, my lady, going to church and playing in the garden. I picked up all the gossip I could and it seems to me they's a nice, middle-class family. Happy as larks, they are. Don't treat young Tom any different from the rest of the brood. One thing I found out from that Polly, though. It wasn't Mr. *Brinsley* Cole who placed Tom and Polly with the Martins. It were Mr. *Peter* Cole."

The shock of it snapped her out of her daze. "*Peter,*" Sarah breathed. All this time, he'd known.

Anger swirled in her chest, hot and stinging like a desert storm. She thanked Finch for his efforts and dismissed him, then made ready to set out for the Coles'. She would give Peter Cole the trimming of his life for this! How dared he lie to her, send her on a wild-goose chase? Letting her think the worst, when all the while Tom had led a perfectly respectable life in St. Alban's, of all places!

Sarah snatched up her bonnet and called for her phaeton.

Twenty-one

SARAH tried to calm herself as she drove the short distance to Peter Cole's house. She needed to see Peter alone but she had little hope of eluding Jenny. Well, perhaps Jenny might be obliged to listen to a few home truths about her brother. Sarah wouldn't spare her if she saw no other way.

"Sarah!" Jenny smiled at her as she entered the drawing room. "What a delightful surprise. We were just talking about you."

For a moment, Sarah was thrown off her stride. "Oh?" she managed.

"Yes, the Fenwicks are having a picnic by the river next week, to take advantage of this fine weather we've been having. Would you like to come?"

Sarah couldn't seem to make her frantic brain understand the simple question. "I came to speak with Peter," she blurted out. "Alone." She turned to Peter. "It's about that matter you were investigating."

Peter eyed her for a moment in silence. Without looking

at his sister, he said, "Excuse us, will you, my dear? We'll go to my library."

"Oh, don't go," said Jenny, jumping up. "I shall run upstairs and see if I can locate that embroidery pattern I was telling you about, Sarah. You know, the one with the forget-me-nots."

"Oh, er, yes," Sarah said blankly. She couldn't recall such a conversation. She was merely grateful to Jenny for taking herself off without fuss.

Once she judged Jenny was out of earshot, Sarah rounded on Peter. "You told me you had no knowledge of Brinsley's bastard son!"

Peter raised his brows. "That is correct."

"Don't lie to me! You placed the boy with a family in St. Alban's."

Peter's lips compressed until they were white. He barely opened them to speak. "Who told you this?"

"I employed an investigator," said Sarah. "You've led me a merry dance, haven't you, Peter? Letting me think you had nothing to do with the business, when in fact, *you* were the one who placed the child? Probably paid for his upkeep into the bargain, didn't you? I'm sure Brinsley did not."

His gaze darted to the door. "Keep your voice down, for God's sake! What do you want?"

Sarah stood. "I want you to take me to him. I want you to tell his people who I am and that I shall be responsible for his welfare from now on."

"You don't understand—"

"Take me there, Peter. Take me there, or I swear I'll make you regret it."

"All right, all *right*," Peter said in a low, angry tone. "I'll take you there. But don't say a word of this to Jenny. I'll come up with a story to satisfy her."

Footsteps sounded in the corridor outside.

"We'll go now?"

"If you wish."

Jenny stepped into the room then, and nodded as Peter

told her they needed to go to the city to meet with Brinsley's solicitor. "Some small concern over Brinsley's will," Peter said smoothly. His sister accepted the story without demur. Well, why shouldn't she? She had no reason to suspect any other purpose to their outing.

"Ah, here's the tea," said Jenny, as Sarah rose to leave. "You will take some refreshment before you go, Sarah? Do have one of these little cakes. They are delicious!"

Sarah declined the cakes but obligingly gulped down some tea. Her stomach churned with suppressed excitement while she tried to look interested in the embroidery patterns her friend had drawn. Her heart beat hard and fast. Finally, she was going to see Tom.

She didn't know how she managed to endure another fifteen minutes of tedium, but she was thankful when Peter stood abruptly and cut short the conversation. "We'd best be going now."

Jenny jumped up also. "Oh, no! How silly of me. I brought down the wrong pattern. You wanted the forget-me-nots, not the violets, didn't you, Sarah? You must stay a moment while I fetch the right one. I'll be back in a trice."

"We don't have time." Peter frowned, then winced as if in pain, his fingers pressing his temple. His lips barely moved as he forced words out. "Must . . . go . . ."

"Do you have the headache, Peter?" Alarmed, Sarah watched him sway. "Are you ill?" She started up, toward him, hands outstretched. "Peter, what's the matter—"

She staggered as his weight sagged against her, her arms automatically going around him. "Peter!" He was too heavy for her to hold upright. All she could do was assist him to crumple to the ground.

Unconscious. His thin mouth was slack, his eyes closed, sandy lashes brushing his cheek. His skin was pale as lilies. Sarah kneeled beside him and cocked an ear to listen at his mouth. Relieved that he still breathed, she scrambled to her feet, calling for help, and almost collided with her sister-in-law.

"Oh, Jenny! We must ring for assistance. Peter has had some sort of attack."

Jenny spared her brother a brief glance, but her attention was focused on Sarah. She gripped Sarah's upper arms, bringing their faces close together. The stark fear in Jenny's eyes made Sarah gasp.

"No," Jenny whispered, a small sob in her voice. "Leave him. You must come. There's not much time."

Jenny turned, clearly expecting Sarah to follow. She yanked on Sarah's arm when she didn't move, making her stumble along with her. Sarah glanced over her shoulder at Peter's recumbent form. "You're not just going to leave him like that?"

"Yes, of course. We need to get away before he comes after us."

"But how—?" Shock had made Sarah stupid. What was happening? What was going on?

Jenny kept tugging at her arm. "It was the tea. I drugged it. Don't worry, he'll be perfectly well in an hour or so. Oh, hurry! He'll kill me if he wakes and finds us still here."

Sarah dug in her heels. "Not until you tell me what this is about."

Blowing out an exasperated breath, Jenny said in a low, trembling voice. "You are going to visit a child today, yes? A boy. Don't deny it. I heard you. I was listening at the door."

Slowly, Sarah nodded. She could see no point in denying it if Jenny already knew.

Her friend's brown eyes focused on her, compelling in their raw grief. "You called him Brinsley's son. He's not Brinsley's son. He is *mine*."

The shock of it sent Sarah's mind reeling, and Jenny took advantage of her surprise to propel her from the room. Jenny took the key and locked the drawing room door from the outside. In the hall, Jenny moved toward the front entrance and this time Sarah moved with her. "Where are you taking me?"

"I'm not taking you. You know where the boy is. You're

taking me. Quickly, now. Before he wakes." She hustled Sarah outside and down the steps toward Sarah's phaeton. When the groom had handed Sarah and Jenny up, Jenny took the reins and gave him the office. The groom stepped away from the horses' heads, clearly startled when Jenny called out a quick dismissal.

"I want to see my child," she whispered fiercely at Sarah's protest. "I heard you say you knew where he is. You said St. Alban's. Take me there."

"But . . . you mean you didn't know where he was until now?" Some inkling of the truth was slowly dawning on Sarah. Disoriented as she was at the latest turn of events, pieces of the puzzle were clicking into place. The thickheaded shock that had gripped her as she'd watched Peter crumple was beginning to fade.

Jenny shook her head, her eyes bright. "They took my baby from me, smuggled him away. They told me he was dead, but I knew better. I knew *in here*." She pressed a fist to her chest, jerking on the reins and making the horses jib and the phaeton jolt.

Sarah stared at her in horror. The poor woman! What she must have endured, being separated from her child all these years. No wonder she'd never married. No wonder there was such a sense of melancholy in that house.

Better to have no child at all than to spend weary years wondering what on earth had become of him, whether he was safe, housed, fed. *Loved.* Sarah had experienced a mere taste of that agony over Tom, but how much worse would it have been as his mother, his flesh and blood?

The phaeton swayed wildly as Jenny took a corner too fast. Sarah clung to her seat, afraid they'd overturn. Clearly, her sister-in-law was in no state to drive.

"Shall I take the ribbons, dear?" Sarah suggested it gently, easing her hands over her friend's. "I'll take you there. I promise I will." Jenny released the reins without demur and Sarah brought the horses' reckless pace back to a steady trot.

Sarah glanced at Jenny. "I cannot imagine what that

must have been like. How could Peter have kept him from you all those years?"

"You don't know Peter very well if you can ask that. He is the most cold-blooded man I know. All these years—" Jenny tilted her chin, squeezing her eyes shut as if willing back tears. "I thought my baby was in an orphanage somewhere, or worse, left to fend for himself. I'd no notion where he was until I overheard you talking with Peter."

"I can't believe it. Surely he wouldn't deny you your own child?"

"Upon my honor, he never said a word. How did *you* find out?"

Sarah told her the history of her search for Tom. At least, she could reassure Jenny that the boy was happy and healthy and living with a family who evidently cared for him. She related all that Finch had discovered, but Jenny didn't seem to take comfort from the news.

"He never told me." She repeated it over and over with a kind of wonder in her voice. "He never told me he knew where my son was."

Grimly, Sarah thought of Brinsley and the foul lies he'd told. *That fiend!* All those years, she'd believed him the father of another woman's child. That the man she'd once loved would be cruel enough to invent such a tale made bile rise in her throat. At that precise moment, any remaining vestige of that long-ago love withered.

She felt physically sickened to finally know the truth. A surge of nausea made her slow the horses, press one hand to her stomach while the other tugged on the ribbons.

Quickly, she pulled over to the side of the road, as far as she could. She gasped. "Think I'm going to be ill."

Handing the reins to her distracted companion, Sarah leaped down from the carriage, twisting her ankle a little as she doubled over to heave up her breakfast onto the grass. Even as she retched, she was aware they had no time for this. Jenny needed her. With Peter on their heels, there was no time to waste.

When the worst had passed, she wiped her mouth with a

handkerchief and took deep, steady breaths. A stray suspicion struck her. Surely, Jenny hadn't drugged her, too? Perhaps by mistake?

She turned back to the carriage and raised her gaze to her companion's, trying to divine the truth.

"Sarah, hurry! I am sorry you were sick but please hurry. We must get there before it's too late. There's no telling what Peter will do when he finds we're gone."

Slowly, Sarah climbed back up to her seat. If their positions were reversed, she would be equally unconcerned with Jenny's suffering, she supposed. She hadn't spared Vane, had she? Nothing had mattered more than finding that child.

"You must love him very much," she said gently.

Jenny nearly bounced out of her seat. "Hurry! Oh, you're too slow. Let me drive." She yanked the reins away from Sarah and the carriage lurched forward once more. Sarah clapped a hand to her bonnet as the wind threatened to lift it from her head. She prayed Jenny wouldn't overturn them before they reached Tom's home.

"Do you think Peter will follow us?" asked Sarah. "Do you think he'll guess where we've gone?"

Jenny barely glanced at her. "Why do you suppose I'm driving like this? We need to get the boy before Peter catches up with us."

"Get him? But it might not be that simple. He has a family now. People who care for him. Do you intend to steal him away?"

Jenny bit her lip. "I don't know. I don't know what I'll do, but you can be sure Peter won't even let me see the boy if he can prevent it. A boy," she whispered. "They didn't tell me when they took him from me."

"Oh, my dear." Sadly, Sarah shook her head, aching for that young, frightened girl.

They crossed a small stream and the wheels juddered over the wooden boards of the bridge. The cottage they sought was in sight through a stand of trees. Sarah's thoughts turned to Tom. According to Finch, the boy believed he was an orphan. How would he react when his long-lost mother suddenly arrived on his doorstep?

Using the directions Finch had given her, she guided Jenny down a lane shaded by chestnut trees. Jenny was tense, almost feverish in her excitement. She seemed to have no doubt of the outcome of this visit or even to give much thought to how she'd break the news of his birth to Tom. In fact, Jenny seemed to have no thought for Tom at all. No thought beyond herself.

Sarah bit her lip. Hadn't she been similarly oblivious as she'd argued with Vane?

She touched Jenny's wrist. "Wait."

Her friend glanced at her. "What?"

"Jenny, stop. Pull up. I want to speak with you about this properly before we arrive."

Jenny shook her off and kept on. "I can't. We must get there as soon as we can, don't you see? Before Peter can stop me."

"No, Jenny," Sarah said. "I beg you, consider for a moment. Think of Tom."

As Jenny continued to ignore her, Sarah gripped her wrist hard. "Please listen to me! Jenny, he is happy here. He thinks the people who look after him are his parents. He will be confused and hurt when you tell him the truth."

No reply. Jenny didn't so much as check the horses as they swept through the gate.

"And then what?" Sarah persisted. "Where will you take him if you can't go back to Peter? Do you even have the means to support yourself? Think about the consequences."

Jenny's lips set in a grim, stubborn line, her eyes burning bright. "I have waited ten years for this." She glanced at Sarah. "You're not a mother. You wouldn't understand."

VANE leafed through a small pile of letters, all that was left of the documents Brinsley Cole's valet had stolen. Vane had spent a lot of time and effort tracking down the rightful owners of this sensitive material, counseling them to burn the evidence. He'd also made discreet inquiries about the sources of funds Brinsley had received.

There remained only the small sheaf of personal letters that were most properly Sarah's. He would give them to her. He couldn't begin to say why he hadn't handed them over before now.

Jealousy. It hardly seemed possible he could be jealous of a dead man, and one as revolting as Brinsley Cole at that. But perhaps that was the reason. He could admit it to himself, even if it meant . . .

Wait. His eye caught on a phrase "with child."

What he read in the letter made him bite out an oath and ring for his carriage to be brought around. As an afterthought, he said to Rivers, "Has Lady Vane gone out?"

"Yes, my lord. The mistress took her phaeton."

"Where? Where did she go?"

"To call on Miss Cole, I believe."

Vane cursed viciously and took the stairs at a run.

VANE arrived at Cole's house to find the place in disarray. Peter Cole stood in his entrance hall questioning servants and directing others, while Vane handed his hat to the harassed butler.

He strode forward and bunched his hands in Cole's coat, lifting him clear off his feet. "Where is she? What have you done with her?"

Cole looked like he'd seen several ghosts. "I haven't done anything with her. She is gone to find the boy," he choked out. "I'm telling the truth. Please!"

Vane scrutinized Cole's face for a moment, then decided he believed him. He set Cole on his feet.

Peter said, "Quickly! Is your curricle outside?"

Vane nodded.

"Then come on. I'll explain on the way."

As they settled into the well-sprung racing vehicle, Peter said, "I have something of yours."

"Let me guess. A bank draft for five thousand pounds." Vane grimaced. "I should have known."

Peter nodded. "Of course, I didn't cash it. I'm sorry I didn't return it to you sooner. But the circumstances—"

"Never mind that." Vane shrugged impatiently. "I've stopped payment. It's just a worthless piece of paper now. I want to know what has happened to my wife."

"Of course." Peter shifted in his seat. "No doubt you're aware of this boy your wife has been seeking."

Vane threw him a searing glance. "He's your son, you bastard! Why didn't you just tell her and be done? Why let her think the boy was Brinsley's? If you only *knew* . . ." He shook his head. All the pain they could have avoided.

"My God. How did you—" Peter's voice scraped as if Vane's hands were about his throat again. "*You?* You have the letter?"

Keeping his eye on his horses as he negotiated the busy streets, Vane nodded. "Brinsley's valet sold it to me, among others. Brinsley ordered his man to sew a packet of incriminating letters into the lining of Brinsley's favorite coat. After his death, my wife sent a trunkful of her dead husband's clothes to the valet, never suspecting what was among them." Vane's eyes narrowed and he glanced at his companion. "Brinsley blackmailed you, too, didn't he? His own brother."

Cole swallowed. "Yes. But you must believe me—the accusations in that letter are untrue. The child is not mine, I—" He gave a harsh sound like a half sob. "I never did what Jenny accused me of. An abomination. I would never, *never* do such a thing. That was why I wrote to Brinsley. He could attest that I wasn't even in London at the time Jenny claimed I'd . . ."

Vane didn't comment. He'd never come across a case of incest before, but he was past the age where he refused to believe it was possible. True, in his letter to Brinsley seeking help for his pregnant sister, Peter had vehemently denied her accusation, but he would, wouldn't he? A man might father a bastard and Society would look the other way. But to father the child on his own sister was something else entirely.

Peter's story did bear the ring of truth, however, particularly the part about begging Brinsley to support him. Well, Brinsley was dead now, but no doubt a diligent investigation would support or disprove Peter's insistence that he'd been absent at the time the child was conceived. On the whole, Vane thought he did believe Peter, but he wasn't going to commit himself either way until he had proof.

His companion blew out a frustrated breath. "Listen, Vane. No matter what you think of me, you must believe me when I tell you that my sister is unhinged. She is dangerous. My God, do you know how she stopped me coming after them? She drugged my tea. Having that child, the disgrace of it, the pain, the protracted illness afterward—I think it affected her brain. She tried to kill the babe soon after he was born. I had to take him away."

"You knew Maggie Day, then."

Peter nodded. "Brinsley found her for me. Said he'd make sure she kept her mouth shut. And she did, until he died." Peter gave a grimace of disgust. "She came to see me at Brinsley's funeral. Told me Sarah had barked up the wrong tree and thought the child was Brinsley's, and Maggie had played along. Maggie wanted me to pay her to keep her mouth shut." Bitterly, he said, "I had to pawn some family heirlooms, but I paid her."

Vane frowned. So that was it. That's where he'd seen the woman before. At the graveside with Peter.

There was a pause. "I fear Jenny is going to St. Alban's because she means to harm the boy."

Vane sucked in a breath as the truth slammed into him. "*She* killed Brinsley, not you."

Peter bowed his head and said nothing. It was admission enough.

Finally, in a low, trembling voice, he spoke. "I went there that night. I thought I knew where she'd gone. She'd found out about Brinsley blackmailing me. He'd bled me until I had nothing more to give, and then he asked me to feed him

State secrets instead." He shook his head. "I couldn't do it. I could pay him money, but I could not betray those I worked for, or my country. I was so distraught, I made the mistake of confiding in Jenny."

"And she decided to remove the threat, once and for all."

"Yes." Peter's mouth worked and he blinked rapidly as if he tasted something bitter. "I was there, you know, earlier that night. Jenny went missing and I thought I knew where she'd gone. She must have given me the slip or gone somewhere else first, I don't know. When I knocked on Brinsley's door, there was no answer. I thought I must have been mistaken. But it seems she came back later when Sarah wasn't there."

"That would explain why Brinsley didn't name his murderer," said Vane. "He must have retained that much family feeling, at least. But tell me, why are you so certain it was your sister who killed him? Do you have proof?"

Peter shook his head. "There is no proof. I made sure of that. Nothing exists that would link my sister to Brinsley's death. There is only her confession to me, which I will deny if anyone asks."

Vane looked at him sharply. "If what you say is true, your sister is deranged and a murderer as well. You must think what is to be done with her now. She cannot be allowed to go on this way, you know that."

Peter stared, unseeing at the road ahead. "She is obsessed with me. She tries to portray me to the world as her jailer, but it is more the other way around. I cannot court any woman for fear of what she'll do. I think she only took up with that unknown blackguard to spite me. Then she blamed the child that came from the liaison for my rejection of her. She still does. I think she believes that if she can eliminate the boy, she will have me."

Revulsion shivered down Vane's spine as he drove his horses at breakneck speed. He hoped Sarah would stay out of the woman's way but he knew the hope was futile. She wouldn't be herself if she didn't fight.

He prayed to God she'd win.

THE boy was outside, playing soldiers under an apple tree laden with blossom. He was fair and slightly chubby and the expression in his soft brown eyes was grave and intent. The game seemed a complicated one, and he muttered to himself as he positioned his tin soldiers around the grassy battlefield.

With an illogical shiver of anticipation, Sarah glanced about as she and Jenny approached. Surely, someone would stop them to ask their business.

But there was no one. Only birdsong and the soft rush of a nearby stream disturbed the silence.

With a growing sense of unease, Sarah glanced sideways at her companion.

And saw the pistol too late.

Terror lent Sarah unprecedented speed. She screamed a warning and tackled Jenny as the shot ripped the peaceful scene apart. Birds exploded from the boughs overhead and flapped madly into the sky, shrieking.

Sarah knocked Jenny sideways with the full force of her body, and they hit the ground, writhing and struggling for the pistol.

"Run!" she screamed at the boy. She thought Jenny's shot had gone wild but she couldn't be sure. "Get help, quickly!"

Frantic to overpower Jenny before she could attack again, Sarah didn't look to see if Tom had obeyed her. She fought tooth and nail to subdue her sister-in-law, but Jenny seemed possessed of a crazed strength and a driving sense of purpose. She didn't even seem to register pain.

They fought madly, desperately, and Sarah was tiring. She knew she couldn't win. Her one hope now was to keep Jenny focused on her until help came. The breath flew out of her when Jenny slammed her onto her back, and she whimpered in agony. Jenny struggled to stand, but Sarah dug her fingers into the folds of her gown and held on, desperate to stop her going after Tom.

Muslin ripped as Jenny tore free. She turned and fell on

Sarah again, straddling her and pinning both of Sarah's arms to the ground with her knees.

Satisfaction that her strategy had worked tempered the pain, gave her courage to face whatever came next. She tried to buck and kick but she couldn't shift her sister-in-law's weight. Above her, Jenny's sweet face contorted with rage and madness. Those brown eyes held no pity and no remorse. At that moment, Sarah didn't doubt her sister-in-law would kill her.

With a shrill, animal cry, Jenny raised the pistol to strike.

Sarah couldn't get away. All she could do was suffer the blows and hope help came before she lost consciousness, or worse. She braced herself, then jerked her head to the side as the pistol came down. The glancing blow to her temple shot pain through her skull but still she clung on. Surely, Tom must have found aid by now.

She heard a distant shout and a bloodcurdling cry. Another blow made Sarah's vision blur, sent pain ricocheting down her body. Fading fast, she tasted earth as she was rolled over, her face ground into the dirt.

Footsteps thumping over the turf. Large ones. Vane's furious roar.

Vane. Thank God.

The world spun away, fading to nothing.

Finally, she let go.

ON the second day, Sarah sat up gingerly in bed. Her headache had receded and she no longer felt dizzy and sick. She stayed in the house where Jenny's son had grown up. It had been a shock to discover that the boy she'd sought for so long wasn't named Tom at all, but David. Of course, Maggie had not only lied about the child being with her, she'd lied about his name, too.

It was a pretty cottage, neat and comfortable rather than luxurious. A rambling house, suited to a large family. Dimly, she recalled she'd displaced one of the daughters of the house from this bedchamber. That wouldn't do.

She must not importune David's people any longer. She must go home.

Home. Where was that, exactly? Had Vane drawn up that settlement he'd mentioned? She didn't want to face any of it, but she must contend with it some time. She might as well do so now.

Sarah made an effort to smile as the boy she would always think of as Tom ran into the room and thrust a ragged bunch of spring flowers beneath her nose.

"Oh! Thank you." She took them and made a show of breathing in their fresh scent.

"Mama made me pick the flowers," he told her. "She said to ask if you need anything, ma'am."

"No, please tell her I am very comfortable. And about to rise from my bed and take myself home, actually. You have all been so kind."

She would have liked to have talked with him longer, but she saw that young David thought waiting on an invalid very poor sport. She smiled. "Run along and play, now you've done your duty."

Melancholy touched her as she watched him go. She'd keep herself informed of David's progress, but she wouldn't tell him who she was, nor reveal his origins to him. He was happy here, as Vane had said. And nothing but sorrow could come from knowing the circumstances of his birth. Perhaps, one day, his adoptive parents would tell him the truth, but that wasn't for her to do.

Jenny had been taken away and confined under the strict but gentle care of a couple related to the Coles. Sarah was relieved they hadn't decided to lock the poor wretch away in one of those dreadful asylums. Perhaps if Jenny had succeeded in harming David, Sarah might have thought differently, she wasn't sure. She still couldn't comprehend that it was Jenny who had killed Brinsley.

She shivered. She wanted Vane. She wanted to go home.

"Sarah."

She looked up. "Mama!" Relief and gratitude broke over Sarah like the warmth of the sun, where once she would have been instantly on her guard. She glanced toward the doorway, couldn't help but ask. "Where is Vane?"

The countess's gaze lowered. "He's gone back to town, dear. He asked me to fetch you."

Sarah's heart plummeted like a stone. "Oh." She blinked a few times, then forced her lips to form a smile. "Well, then. Shall we go?"

TWO weeks later, Sarah returned to Vane's house at a time when she knew he'd be out, engaged in his usual training regime.

Rivers greeted her without the slightest spark of knowledge in his eye. Either the man was very discreet or Vane hadn't informed his servants their mistress would be leaving them soon.

She found herself strangely reluctant to step over the threshold. Memories, too powerful and poignant to banish, flooded back. She recalled the first time she'd entered this house, so full of righteous indignation, so certain in her fury and pride. He'd undone her with kindness. Even when she believed him guilty of trying to coerce her into his bed, she'd been powerless to resist.

Drawing an unsteady breath, Sarah moved through the entrance hall and up the stairs. On this same staircase, she'd followed him to his bedchamber. Against all sense of propriety, all sense of reason, she'd done what she'd vowed never to do.

As she passed through the masculine sitting room that had been the site of so much tension and yet so many comfortable, cozy evenings, Sarah took one last good look around. This room, more than anything, symbolized who Vane was. Intelligent, forceful, more fully male than any man she'd ever known, yet with the finest sense of honor and restraint. Careful and gentle with her.

Sarah ran her fingertip around the framed print that had embarrassed him when she first arrived. She'd never dreamed that her present situation would come to pass. That one night of folly and boundless passion would end with her married to, but separated from, the Marquis of Vane. It was everything she'd longed for at the beginning of their marriage, everything she'd worked to achieve.

Perhaps, in time, she would relish this separation as much as she'd expected she would. Life would move along at a more even keel without this constant worry and pressure to find a way through the tangle of her feelings. He had been as patient as a man of his temperament could be but she needed more time—a lifetime, perhaps—to unravel her emotions, to live down her guilt.

It was better this way. She would be useful and well cared for. She would want for nothing. She would repay Vane for his care by fulfilling her duties as his chatelaine to the best of her ability. She'd been brought up to this life. She'd no doubt she'd make a good job of it.

As Sarah directed her maid to begin packing, she thought with a pang of John and Edward, those two scamps! If she and Vane truly lived separate lives she wouldn't see them often, if at all. She would miss the rest of his family, too.

She needed to talk with Vane about more than bare legalities, set the boundaries, try to work out a compromise. That conversation would be a difficult one. Perhaps she might instead take the coward's way and write a letter suggesting terms.

Finally satisfied all was in train for her departure, Sarah called for her carriage and donned her bonnet and pelisse.

"I didn't think you'd come back."

Sarah's head jerked up. Her gaze snapped to the doorway, where Vane leaned against the jamb.

"I didn't think you'd be here," she said.

Greedily, she drank in the sight of him. Her first impression was that he didn't look as well turned out as usual, but a closer examination revealed that his clothes were precise as always. The wildness was in his eyes.

She ached to touch him, to smooth the crease between those straight, black brows.

Softly, she said, "I would come back for good if you

wished it." She tried not to sound eager. She tried not to make the words a plea.

When he didn't reply, she added, "But I had your letter. I returned merely to collect some of my possessions."

There was another silence. She waited, but when he opened his mouth to speak she forestalled him, frightened of what he might say. "I am driving down to visit David today."

She didn't know why she needed to tell him this. In less than a week, her daily movements, her thoughts and dreams would be nothing to Vane. She'd write to him, of course, but she'd confine her reports to matters concerning the estate. And when he visited, he would occupy apartments in a different wing from hers.

They'd be like strangers. That was what she'd wanted.

Yes.

"You are not still thinking of taking him," said Vane. It was a statement, not a question.

She shook her head. "But I want him to know that if ever he needs me, I will come."

He nodded, as if he confirmed what he'd thought himself. Did he know her so well, then? When last they'd spoken about the boy, he'd doubted her motives. Made her doubt them as well.

And he'd been right, hadn't he? She'd painstakingly picked apart the threads of protectiveness and self-interest and plain loneliness that wove through her determination to take David under her own wing. She'd realized her plan would benefit her more than him, and wasn't that a lowering reflection?

"When will you come down to Bewley?" she heard herself ask.

He glanced away. "I'd thought to escort you down there. Introduce you to the staff. Show you the place."

So civilized of him. She forced down the hurt. "Thank you. I'd be grateful."

"We need not be complete strangers."

Her throat constricted. She could barely speak. "No. Of course we need not."

"Well, then." He made a vague gesture encompassing the trunks and bandboxes her maid had packed. "When will you be ready to travel?"

"Tomorrow, I think." The words scraped her throat. She cleared it with a small cough. "Tomorrow, I should be ready." She would spend the night at her parents' house. No sense in enduring more torture like this, having him so close in the dark, lonely reaches of the night.

"I must go," she said. "I ought not keep the carriage waiting."

"Of course." He bowed and stepped back to allow her to pass. She walked by him, felt his heat and the pull of him, too, that magnetic force that always drew her. Compelled herself to resist it and kept on, conscious that those hot dark eyes drilled into her as she walked away.

It took all of her strength, but she didn't look back.

And then she was walking down the stairs, those same stairs she'd climbed on that first night, rising toward her destiny, where now she descended into cold and lonely hell.

Something snapped, unraveling inside her. She didn't want to leave him. She *wouldn't* go.

He'd been there, all along. Since they'd first met, he'd been there, waiting for her. And even when she'd finally done the unforgivable and made him wash his hands of her, he'd come for her once more. He had never, not once, let her down. Perhaps, one day he might, even without intending to, but that was what one risked for love, wasn't it? In this life, there were no guarantees.

What a terrifying thing love was—one risked so much. But when had she become such a coward? Hadn't she always preferred to accept a challenge, to stand and fight?

She would fight for Vane. It might be too late to win him back. Part of her still cringed away at the thought. But they were married. She had the rest of their lives to convince him to let her stay. If it took that long, she'd keep trying.

She turned on her heel and flew back, up the stairs, through the sitting room, and into his arms. Automatically, Vane closed them around her and kissed her with a passion so violent their teeth clashed. But even as her heart swelled in her breast, he tore his mouth from hers, gripped her upper arms, and set her roughly aside. He flung away from her, pacing to the other side of the room.

The shock of his rejection when she thought he'd forgiven her was like a blow to her chest. She pressed a hand to her ribs, barely able to draw breath into her lungs. Looking into his face, she saw her agony reflected there.

"I can't," Vane ground out the words, his hands fisted by his sides. "Don't come back to me now, when I've . . . Sarah, I *can't* go through all this again."

Guilt at the way she'd treated him whipped her like a lash. She wanted to argue and cajole and persuade, but she recognized all too well that he needed to protect himself. She'd done too much damage to him while she'd wrestled with her own demons.

Sarah lifted her chin, tried to summon some vestige of her former self, the pride that had brought her through so many hardships and hurts intact. But her voice, when she spoke, came out as a whisper, low and trembling with uncertainty and fear. "All I want, Vane, is for you to be happy. If . . ." She took a deep, painful breath. "If our separation will truly make you happy, then I'll go."

Vane watched her without speaking. She wished he'd say something, but he waited, let her stumble on.

"But if . . ." She swallowed painfully, more terrified than she'd ever been. "If you let me stay, I vow to you that I will love you the way you deserve to be loved. I will love you as well and as wholeheartedly as you have loved me. Without reservations or conditions, without limits . . ."

No, that was wrong. Impatiently, she shook her head. "The fact is, Vane, I *already* love you that way. No matter what you do, whether we're together or apart for the rest of our lives, I will never stop." The realization hit her hard. She'd been desperate to avoid loving him, but she hadn't saved herself from that fate. All she'd done was drive him away.

Still, he said nothing. She couldn't tell what he was thinking from his expression, but regardless, these things needed to be said. She battled on. "We were made to be together, Vane. It took me far too long to accept that, but I know it now." Her voice finally broke. "Please don't say it's too late."

She ached to put her arms around him, but using her body and her touch to try to sway him wouldn't be fair. He'd remarked on the rare passion they shared. She mustn't try to cloud his mind with desire when he had such an important decision to make.

"Come here." His voice was so low, Sarah could barely make out the words.

With a flicker of hope despite the harshness of his tone, she crossed the room. When she reached him, he grasped her chin between thumb and forefinger and looked into her eyes. "You are a remarkable woman, Sarah. I didn't think the lady who spurned me so coldly all those weeks ago had it in her to make a speech like that. Much less mean every word."

His fingertips brushed her cheek. "But I was wrong. I've watched you endure and surmount every difficulty life has dealt you and marveled at your strength and the stubborn pride of you. I've wanted you, fought for you, loved you forever, it seems. I've won you at last." His voice roughened with emotion. "And I'm *never* going to let you go."

Vane's mouth came down, hard, on hers, and she flung her arms around his neck, stretching, arching against his body as she kissed him back. Their kiss raged out of control, until they were both bruised and dazed and panting for breath. It was a fierce, fiery thing, their love.

When Sarah could speak again, she said, "Vane, I love you. Can you forgive me for fighting it for so long?"

He caught her hand and clasped it, warm and safe within his own. "The most precious things are always worth the wait."

"Oh, my love." She brought his hand to her mouth and kissed his big, bruised knuckles. "Thank you for waiting for me."

Epilogue

"I love him almost more than I can bear," said Sarah. "But I will *never* do this again."

Vane looked up from the sleeping infant in his arms and grinned. Despite her exhaustion and the exquisite pain of the last hours, Sarah smiled back. Both of them knew she would do this again, and gladly. Many times, if God willed it.

Her smile grew as she watched her enormous husband cradle their newborn so carefully.

"Look how he sleeps," she murmured. Baby Alexander had done nothing much out of the ordinary since his arrival in the world five hours ago, yet every small action amazed and delighted her. He was hers and Vane's and that made him more unique and precious than any other child in the world.

She'd been unprepared for the wild joy of discovering she was pregnant, still convinced she was barren despite the news that Brinsley hadn't fathered a child, after all. Looking back, the signs had been there. The bouts of nausea in the stillroom and again on the journey to St. Alban's with Jenny.

She transferred her gaze to Vane's face, saw his connection

to their child in his absorbed expression, felt the ties of love bind them together, all three.

Nurse bustled in at that moment, giving orders, and Vane reluctantly surrendered his child. When the door had closed behind nurse and baby, he turned to Sarah.

She looked pale and tired, but her beauty and determination shone through those green eyes, more brilliant and compelling than ever. Whatever mistakes they'd both made along the way, now they lent each other strength and purpose. Together, they were extraordinary, as he'd always known they would be.

Carefully, Vane sat on the bed next to Sarah and bent to kiss her. The familiar jolt of desire surged through his body, but he easily turned it aside. Now was not the time, of course. Even if he couldn't stop wanting her or wondering how soon he might enjoy her lush body again, he wasn't mutton-headed enough to mention it now.

He raised his head and stared into those wicked, knowing eyes.

"Soon my love," she murmured, twining her arms about him, drawing him back down for another kiss. "Oh, I hope, very soon."

He studied her as he stroked the dark hair from her brow. Her lips were pale and the roses absent from her cheeks. She looked worn to the bone, despite the resilience of her spirit.

Even at this moment, her mere presence lent him calm. He fought less often now, and less desperately. He maintained his training because he enjoyed it and it made him feel healthy and strong, but the driving need to punish his body and work out his frustration by pounding human flesh had gone.

His soul was at peace for the first time. Stirred and excited by Sarah, his wife, but secure in the knowledge and warmth of her love.

The tenderness that swept over him must have shown in his expression, for Sarah's face lit with a devastating glow. "I love you, Vane," she said in that clipped, decided tone of hers. "Never doubt it."

"No," he said and smiled. "No. I'll never doubt it again."

Turn the page for a preview of
the next historical romance
by Christine Wells

Sweetest Little Sin

Coming soon from Berkley Sensation!

London, Spring 1817

IN the early hours of a damp London morning, a glossy black barouche slowed outside a Mayfair house. The carriage's door swung open. Without stopping, the vehicle ejected a long black bundle and sped away, wheels kicking up an arcing spray of water in its wake.

The bundle hit the pavement and rolled a couple of times before coming to rest against a boot scraper at the foot of a flight of shallow steps.

As the iron instrument dug sharply into his ribs, the Marquis of Jardine gave a soft groan. His body was a mass of unidentified agonies. His head pounded with a vicious, fiery pain, as if a blacksmith had plunged it into his furnace, then set to work with an anvil.

The flagway was damp from a recent downpour. He sank his lean cheek into the blessed cold, relishing the icy shock that distracted him, if only for a second, from the pain. They'd damned near killed him this time. Hell, but he'd had enough of this game.

Buttery light waxed over him as a door opened above

and footsteps clattered down the stairs. Pride urged him to launch to his feet, but he couldn't summon quite enough will for that.

He bared his teeth in a ferocious snarl of a smile. The pain had been worth it, hadn't it? Because at last—*at last*—he'd found the missing piece of a puzzle that had eluded his grasp for years.

When his footmen hauled him up between them, his legs couldn't seem to do the job they were paid for. He was a tall man, with long, loose limbs—an awkward burden—and it was bloody ridiculous that he couldn't seem to rely on his own two feet. His footmen half dragged, half carried him up several teeth-chattering flights of stairs, then heaved him through a doorway and tumbled him onto his bed.

The exquisite pain of this process sent Jardine reeling toward unconsciousness. He longed for that relief, wished to hell they'd just kill him and be done with it.

But no, there was a reason—a damned good reason—he needed to hang on to his wits. Vital importance. The fate of nations—no *his* fate, come to that—was teetering in the balance, dangling by a thread. And he must do this thing, take care of this utterly crucial piece of business. . . .

Louisa.

His body arched off the bed, riding another wave of pain. A sweeping tidal wave of agony that swept a man up and dashed him against a cliff of jagged rock.

The fuzz of black dots at the edge of his vision swarmed and thickened. He groaned and someone nipped in with ruthless efficiency to tilt a noxious mixture down his throat.

Torpor spread through his limbs, his brain. The light dimmed, then snuffed altogether.

"No, no," he muttered. "Don't let me sleep."

Then he fell, spiraling into darkness.

LADY Louisa Brooke moved through the ballroom with a smile fixed beneath her loo mask and a tight ball of apprehension lodged in her breast. She'd waited for a sign all day, but none had come. She'd thought perhaps tonight . . . but he avoided entertainments when he knew she'd be there, just as he treated her like the scantest acquaintance when they met unavoidably, as they often did in town.

He wasn't here tonight. Despite the anonymity of the masquerade, and the crowded state of her sister-in-law's ballroom, she knew that. She'd sense his presence if he were here.

Thoughts of feigning a headache and making her excuses flitted through her mind, but she dismissed them. No one would believe the staid Lady Louisa was subject to invalidish megrims. They'd question her and fuss. That would be worse than enduring the attentions of her legion of suitors.

A small huff of exasperation escaped her lips. There were times when one simply despaired of the male population. Years ago, when she'd no dowry and no prospects, the beaux of the beau monde wouldn't touch her with a very long barge pole. Now that her brother had succeeded the distantly related Duke of Lyle, they swarmed like flies around a rotting sheep's carcass.

She grimaced. An apt simile. She was alone, abandoned and moldering into dust. A dried-up old maid.

"Don't curl your lip like that, darling." Kate, Duchess of Lyle, magnificent in a confection of emerald green and peacock feathers, handed her a glass of champagne. "You'll scare off poor Lord Radleigh."

Accepting the glass, Louisa bared her teeth. "If only." She glowered across the ballroom at the tall, fair-haired man who had chosen to dress as Sir Walter Raleigh tonight. "The gentleman is persistent."

Tilting her head, Kate surveyed her guest. She blew out a breath when she saw him paused to exchange greetings with a matron in bombazine and an enormous turban. "He's rich, they say."

"Mmm. Unique, in fact."

"Unique? How so?"

"He's the only one of my suitors who doesn't want my money." Louisa paused. "I wonder what it is he does want."

Kate gave a gurgle of laughter. "Well, could it be . . . um, don't be shocked, darling, but could it possibly be . . . *you* he wants?"

The idea made Louisa slightly nauseous. Only one man had ever wanted her. And he was . . . Impossible. Dangerous. Devastating.

Not here.

Repressing a shiver of equal parts fear and yearning, she firmly shook her head. "There must be some other reason. Radleigh's probably in the market for a pedigree. I believe he's very proud."

Kate screwed up her pretty mouth in a moue of disapproval. "Cynical, Louisa. And shockingly dismissive of your charms. I won't allow it."

Smiling a little at her friend's staunch support, Louisa said nothing.

"Lord Radleigh is not so very bad, though, is he?" Kate continued to speculate. "His bow is all it should be."

They both watched Radleigh flourish in the direction of Louisa's approving mama. Turning her up sweet, Louisa thought. It was hardly necessary. Millicent Brooke would be perfectly happy to marry off her difficult daughter to any gentleman with a pulse at this juncture. Radleigh fit the bill rather better than most of the hopefuls Millicent had thrown in Louisa's path. Influential, no known vices, good family, good breeding. Any mama would approve of him.

Dispassionately, Louisa remarked, "Lord Radleigh's figure is pleasing enough, I daresay. And his features are attractive, if you admire fair men." She didn't.

"He seems amiable and well-bred," Kate agreed. "And there is that fortune." She flicked open her fan with her characteristic restless elegance and plied it rapidly. "There is only one thing wrong with him, as far as I can see."

"What's that?"

Kate's voice was gentle, compassionate. "Well, he's not the Marquis of Jardine, is he?"

The sharp, visceral stab of pain, excitement, and terror stole Louisa's breath for a moment. What terrible power in a name! Particularly when spoken aloud, unexpectedly, as if Kate read Louisa's thoughts, sensed the anticipation that lent an added tension to her erect posture tonight.

Before she could respond, Kate's wandering gaze snagged on some point in the crowd and her fluttering fan stilled. "There's that horrible Faulkner. Look! The man dressed as Mephistopheles over there." She snorted. "An appropriate guise, indeed. Can you *believe* Max would invite him here?"

Exhaling a shaky breath, Louisa turned her head to see, glad of the distraction. "Yes, of course. Why wouldn't he?" Faulkner was the head of the secret service and her brother's former superior. Max had retired from the service upon inheriting the dukedom, but obviously, he hadn't cut the connection.

"Well! Faulkner needn't think he can lure Max back into the fold." Kate vibrated with a fury Louisa didn't fully comprehend. "Max is finished with all that cloak-and-dagger nonsense. He gave me his word."

"I'm sure it's purely a social connection," said Louisa soothingly. If her brother had given his word, he would keep it. On the other hand, Faulkner struck her as the kind of man who never did anything without a purpose, and that purpose was usually Machiavellian. Kate had good reason to be suspicious.

But was Faulkner here for Max or for Louisa? After the affair of Kate's stolen diary, Faulkner had required Louisa to sign a paper in which she gave her oath not to reveal any official secrets she'd learned in the course of her involvement. She'd discovered nothing while translating the document, save the extent of Kate's rather risqué fantasies. However, Louisa had signed rather than pass that potentially embarrassing information to Faulkner.

And then he'd asked her for one small favor. . . .

One small favor often led to other, larger ones, in Faulkner's line of business.

Apprehension skipped down Louisa's spine. Yet, mingled

with that emotion was a healthy dose of intrigue. She murmured to Kate, "Tell Max you don't want Faulkner here. He'll take care of it."

"Certainly not!" Kate declared. "I shall deal with him myself."

She would, too, thought Louisa with amused satisfaction. The last Louisa saw of her sister-in-law was the jaunty bob of a peacock plume as she made her way through the crowd. Louisa had no doubt Kate would succeed in ejecting Faulkner. She wished, however, that Kate hadn't chosen this moment to desert her. Not with her mother and Lord Radleigh heading toward her.

She glanced at the clock on the mantel behind her. An hour till midnight.

She had to get away.

WITH a quick glance over her shoulder, Louisa slipped out to the terrace overlooking the square. She needed to breathe.

The air was fresh with the scent of recent rain. She gazed out into the night, watched thick clouds part like curtains in the stiffening breeze, revealing the glint of the heavens. *Where was he?*

Lost in her thoughts, she jumped when a sound behind her pierced her reverie. Quickly, she turned to see the heavy curtain at the window swing open and the figure of a man step out of the ballroom.

"Lady Louisa." The gravelly voice was familiar. He moved toward her, and the moonlight struck his face, painted to look like the Devil. It was Faulkner. So Kate hadn't succeeded in rousting him from her ballroom, then.

Inexplicably nervous, Louisa fell back a pace and felt the wrought iron rail, cold and hard at her back.

"Good evening, Mr. Faulkner," she said, as coolly as she could manage. "I came out for a breath of air, but I should be getting back—"

He caught her by the elbow as she tried to slip past him.

"I think you'd prefer me to say what I have to say to you out here. Never fear, your reputation is safe with me."

She halted, staring pointedly at his grip on her elbow. Her reputation didn't concern her. Tonight, his manner gave her a creeping feeling of unease she couldn't explain. "What is it?"

His hold slackened and she pulled away, relief pouring through her.

Faulkner paused, glancing back at the ballroom. "You are quite the belle of the ball this evening."

Dryly, she said, "You flatter me, sir."

His gaze ran over her, not in a lascivious way, but coldly assessing. "Not at all, not at all. I noticed one gentleman in particular is very clear in his intentions. Lord Radleigh is smitten with your charms."

Smitten with her aristocratic connections, more like. But it was true. Radleigh had grown even more particular in his attentions this evening, ably assisted by Louisa's mother.

Still, she wasn't about to discuss her marital prospects with Faulkner. "Lord Radleigh has been kind. What of it?"

"I believe he has invited you to spend part of the summer at his estate. A singular honor."

How did he know that? A cold trickle of unease slipped down her spine.

Slowly, Louisa said, "He has asked me. I have not said yes." To agree to attend Radleigh's house party was tantamount to accepting his proposal. She couldn't possibly . . .

"Oh, but you will say yes," said Faulkner. "You will say, Lady Louisa, enough to encourage his hopes."

Louisa blinked at Faulkner's presumption. "And why should I do any such thing?"

Faulkner didn't answer straightaway. He leaned back on the wrought iron rail that guarded the small terrace, bracing his hands on either side of him. Intrigued, despite herself, Louisa waited, holding herself very still. Anticipation and something close to excitement hummed in her veins.

Was he about to draw her further into the dangerous, precarious world Jardine had inhabited for so long?

Why did the idea entice her?

"What do you know about Radleigh?" said Faulkner. With the moon behind him, his face lay in shadow, but she knew she'd read no expression there even if she could see his features. He was a singularly unemotional man.

Louisa searched her memory. "I don't know much about him at all," she said, surprised to find she spoke the truth, even after the many conversations she'd had with Radleigh. "He told me his people come from the north but he has settled in Gloucestershire. He has a sister, Emma, who has lived abroad until recently. I am to meet her at this party."

Faulkner smiled, a gleam of teeth in the darkness, and she could have kicked herself for speaking as if her attendance was a fait accompli.

"Radleigh is a very wealthy man. Do you know how his fortune was derived?" said Faulkner.

Her eyes widened a little. "Of course not." She paused. "Well, I suppose I assumed he inherited it. He told me his parents are dead." Her brows drew together. "Are you saying he came by his fortune dishonestly?"

Faulkner shrugged. "If I could prove anything, Radleigh wouldn't be at liberty today. But make no mistake, Lady Louisa. He's dangerous."

"And you wish me to encourage him? Won't that put me in danger, too?"

"There is a lot riding on your success. More than your safety. More than you could possibly dream."

Her breathing came a little faster. "And if I say no?"

Faulkner grunted a soft laugh. "Are you expecting me to threaten you with dire consequences? I won't do that. I will always find another way. Besides, I expect that after due consideration you will say yes." He eyed her silently for a few moments. "But if it matters to you, there are issues of national security and many lives—the lives of agents like your brother—at stake."

He pushed away from the railing and walked past her. "Think about it. If you want the assignment, send me word."

Reaching into his coat, he extracted a card case and

flipped it open. "Here is my direction." He held the neat rectangle of cream stock between his gloved fingertips. Automatically, she took it.

He moved to the window, and paused as he opened the door and swept the curtain aside. "Don't delay too long. There is much to arrange."

The brief blaze of the ballroom snuffed as the curtain swung back into place. Louisa blinked dazzled eyes and tried to calm her racing pulse. She ought to throw the card away. She dropped it into her reticule instead.

Breathless, she counted slowly to fifty before she slipped back into the ballroom.

LOUISA stared dry-eyed out the window of her bedchamber while all her hopes shattered around her like the breaking dawn.

He hadn't come.

No word, not a letter nor a token, not even a halfpenny bunch of daisies sent with a grubby messenger boy. Nothing. On her birthday, the one day of the year she'd learned to depend on Jardine, he'd failed her.

When last they'd met, she'd screamed at him, told him he was a murderer, that she never wanted to see him again.

And he'd reminded her that nothing either of them could do or say would change one thing—they were destined to be together.

For years, she'd believed that, carried the hope of him like a small, flickering candle in the shelter of her hand. She'd stayed up all night—in masquerade costume, no less— waiting for him. Despite what had passed between them those months ago, she'd been certain he would come. She hadn't given up, not even after the last stroke of midnight marked the end of her birthday.

Only the lightening sky of a new day finally convinced her. As dawn touched the square below, dancing off the windows of the houses opposite, her foolish hope fizzled and died.

It wasn't even that he hadn't come—perhaps he'd had good reason to stay away. But the pathetic creature she'd made of herself, sitting up all night waiting for him, longing for some sign he remembered her existence, proved it beyond doubt.

She was nine and twenty, and she needed to get on with her life.

She wanted a husband, not this dream figure of a man who stormed in and out of her mundane, peaceful world, leaving a trail of destruction and yearning behind him. She wanted a home and children of her own.

Yet, she'd hoped for all these things from Jardine. She'd set such store by his limited constancy. He'd never missed her birthday, not once in seven years.

But this time . . . *Why* hadn't he come? Cold fear stormed over her like a blizzard. Her hand flew to her throat. What if he . . .

If he were dead, she would know it. She would feel it. She *would*.

Louisa shot across the room to the clothespress and rummaged until she found the plain black domino and loo mask her maid had put away. She swirled the domino around her shoulders and tied the string, pulled the hood over her distinctive pale hair.

Quickly, quietly, she eased out her bedchamber door and crept along the dark hall, past the half-moon table with its ornate ormolu clock. No squeaks or creaks betrayed her as she hurried down the stairs, the tread of her soft slippers on the carpet runner the barest whisper in the grey light.

The skivvies would already be up, sweeping hearths and laying out fires. She needed to be quick. A bribe in hand, she approached the door, but she didn't need to part with her money this time. The hall boy slept curled up in the deep armchair by the heavy front door.

She let herself out, winced at the slight creak of the hinge. She whipped a glance at the hall boy, but he didn't rouse save for a childish, snuffling snore. Closing the door behind her, Louisa secured her mask, then hurried toward Russell Street.

Her heart beat a frantic tattoo in her chest, and the wet soaked through her thin slippers to chill her feet. Her breath came in sobs. She must know if he was alive and well. She'd forgive him anything, everything, if only he still lived.

Louisa blinked hard, barely seeing where she went through the blur in her eyes. She had the impression of passing traffic even at this early hour, the odd cart rumbling along with deliveries or a maid on her way to market. But Jardine's house was only around the corner. Surely, luck would favor her if she was quick.

Too distraught to think of a stealthy approach, Louisa rapped a sharp summons on the door with the brass knocker. Despite the early hour, the door opened instantly. Jardine's butler, Emerson, looked down at her without apparent surprise. As if masked incognitas visited his master at cockcrow every other day of the week.

Perhaps they did.

She forced down a spurt of unreasonable jealousy and demanded the man's master.

Emerson bowed and conducted her to a sitting room, a darkly opulent parlor filled with crimson velvet and mahogany, a rich Aubusson carpet smothering the floor. "I shall inquire."

Louisa sagged, light-headed with relief. Surely, Emerson would have told her if Jardine was dead, or ill, or injured? She drew a deep, shuddery breath. Even contemplated slipping away, now that she'd received the information she sought.

But leaving when she was so close to him would be like changing the course of the planets around the sun. Impossible.

She perched on a plushly decadent couch, then she stood and paced as she waited. Why was she always waiting for him?

After a long interval, the click of boots on wood made her head jerk up.

Jardine slouched in the doorway, looking every inch the dissolute aristocrat.

Hair black as night sprang back from the suspicion of a widow's peak at his brow. He wore it longer than when she'd seen him last, and it was tied carelessly in a short queue. His skin was dead white, his eyes like gleaming jet under those devilishly drawn brows. He had thick, long lashes, high, slashing cheekbones, and lips that turned down sulkily at the corners when he wasn't curling them into a sneer.

Such unearthly, satanic beauty. Simply looking at him made Louisa's heart stumble and kick and race.

In truth, he belonged to another age, when men dressed in satins and silks, fought duels, and damned everyone's eyes. He had all the sleek, lethal elegance of a jungle cat, the stinging sharpness of a rapier's blade.

It never ceased to awe and frighten her that she, plain Louisa Brooke, had somehow caught his interest.

The visceral thrill of seeing him again held her silent, breathless.

And then he opened his mouth.

"WHAT the Devil are you doing here?" Jardine leaned against the doorjamb, felt himself slip a bit, and jerked upright. The woman before him ripped off her mask, but he didn't need to see her face to know who it was.

That mouth. He'd know that mouth anywhere.

"Dammit, Louisa. Get out." His speech slurred only slightly. Though he tried to enunciate the words, his tongue remained damnably heavy and slow. He hoped to God the foul concoction Emerson had given him would work its magic soon so he could think.

The startlingly blue eyes blazed. "You are drunk! I don't believe it."

"Drunk," he muttered. He'd give a lot to exchange the agony of last night for an evening carousing with the brandy bottle. But it was a good explanation for the state she found him in—worse for wear, muzzy with the opiate they'd given him to numb the pain, trembling like a jelly.

Drunk? Yes, it would serve.

He forced his head to nod in agreement. "Three sheets to the wind, m'dear." Damned if the look on her face wouldn't terrify a man into sobriety, if drunkenness had been what ailed him. Curling his lips into a faint, mocking smile, he watched her beneath half-lowered lids. "To what do I owe this pleasure?"

"You . . ." The tip of her tongue touched her upper lip, before her teeth clamped on it. She threw her shoulders back. "You forgot my birthday."

"*Ah*." He held up a hand that felt like it weighed a ton. "Now that's where you're wrong. I did remember. Just before I dropped off to sleep, I *knew* there was something. . . ."

She gasped, every muscle in her body stiffening in outrage.

To an outsider, her reaction might seem out of proportion to the event. But it wasn't about the birthday. This wasn't the kind of feminine tantrum that one soothed with easy words and hot kisses. He knew that.

He knew her.

And he knew he risked losing her. Risked everything he had on this one last throw of the dice.

A searing tide of remorse and impotent fury surged through his aching body, enlivening torn muscles, clearing the fog in his brain. His gaze focused on Louisa's untouched features, her skin, pale and flawless as cream, and his hands curled into fists.

If wounding Louisa made her keep her distance, it was worth it. Even though that flare of pain in her eyes seared him like a brand.

"Jardine! Are you *listening* to what I'm saying to you?"

There was a catch in the stoical Louisa's voice that struck him to the soul. No, he hadn't been listening, but he guessed what she'd said.

The need to hold her was an ache in his gut, but instead of taking her in his arms, he gave her his best attempt at an insufferable shrug. He must enrage her, make her leave him without a backward glance, but he mustn't overdo it. She was smart as a whip, and she knew him too well. This would have to be the performance of a lifetime.

He flicked his hand carelessly. "Yes, yes, it was your birthday. I forgot. I apologize. Females set such store by things like that, don't they?"

The murderous look that fell over her features told him his offhanded apology had the desired effect. Her eyes shot lightning bolts, her cheeks flushed, the lines of her body tightened until they trembled. "They do, do they? You utter *blackguard*, Jardine!"

She launched into an impassioned diatribe, but the effect her fury had on him was the opposite of chastening. Despite his manifold aches, his body roused at the sight of her, standing there tearing strips off him like some avenging Norse goddess.

She wasn't a beauty, his Louisa. She was tall and lean and strong with small, firm breasts that fit snugly into a man's hands. Her jaw was a little too decided, her nose boldly defined, her straight, black brows an odd contrast with the cold, flaxen tone of her hair.

But one look into those fierce warrior-woman eyes and he'd been bowled over, knocked for six. As he hadn't recovered in the many years since, it didn't look like he ever would.

And that mouth. A ripple of lust eddied through him as he thought of Louisa's mouth.

In her lips, she was all woman—contours and soft, ripe sweetness. And she was talking in that low, husky tone again, saying a lot of things about the future, about commitment, about fairy tales and impossible dreams, and all he wanted to do was take her to bed, drink from those lips while he made love to her slowly, sink into the blaze of her, burn to ashes in her arms.

He'd missed the chance for such lengthy exploration last night. And now . . . well, now she would hate him for what he was going to do to her. What he must do.

At last, he cut through her emotional speech.

"Louisa, why are you here? We had an agreement."

"Why do you think I wore this stupid mask?" she flashed. "I thought something had happened to you. I thought you were injured, or . . . or dead." Her voice scraped on the last word. He struggled to ignore it.

"Well, I'm not."

At the flippant rejoinder, she visibly ground her teeth. "More's the pity," she muttered.

He knew she didn't mean it, but something in his chest gave a painful twist.

"What would you do if you were free of me? Marry one of those vultures you have buzzing around you?" It hadn't escaped him that since her brother had settled a large dowry on the girl, Louisa had become quite the matrimonial prize.

Quietly, she said, "I am nine and twenty, Jardine."

"Really?" he drawled, "I'd forgotten." He strolled toward her, tamping down the panic, choking off the urge to tell her the truth.

He knew to a minute how old she was. He thought of the night he'd planned for her birthday, the heady anticipation that had probably made him a trifle less careful than usual, an easy target for the abduction and mild form of torture that followed.

The *real* torture was knowing she waited for him last night, yet he couldn't go to her.

He reached out and took her chin in his hand, tilting her head so the weak, morning sunlight illuminated her remarkable features. Her face was all planes and angles—except for that most sensual pair of lips. So tempting to take that mouth, to lose himself in her, forget what he'd sworn to do.

"You have been a lovely . . . diversion, Louisa." Disregarding her cry of fury, he went on. "You were never anything more to me, you know. And now, I find that I've tired of our little game of cat and mouse."

Softly, he said, "The time has come for us to part."

Enter the rich world of historical romance with Berkley Books.

Lynn Kurland

Patricia Potter

Betina Krahn

Jodi Thomas

Anne Gracie

Love is timeless.
penguin.com

M9G0907